The O. Henry Prize Stories 2019

The O. Henry Prize Stories 2019

100th Anniversary Edition

Chosen and with an Introduction by
Laura Furman

With Essays by Jurors
Lynn Freed
Elizabeth Strout
Lara Vapnyar
on the Stories They Admire Most

Anchor Books
A Division of Penguin Random House LLC
New York

For Joel

Anchor Books first invited me to be series editor in 2002 and then included me in the company of the intelligent, literate, and knowledgeable people who carry out its work. My thanks to Alice Van Straalen, Lisa Weinert, Sloane Crosley, Russell Perreault, Mark Abrams, and Paige Smith. The breadth of Diana Secker Tesdell's knowledge and her kindness to me gave meaning to making the smallest detail correct.

In 2003, the Jentel Foundation began offering a month-long residency in its beautiful setting in the Lower Piney Creek Valley of Wyoming to each O. Henry winner. Such generosity affirms the long connection between Jentel's founder, Neltje, granddaughter of Frank Nelson Doubleday, whose company was the O. Henry's original publisher, and *The O. Henry Prize Stories*. Anchor Books originated as a division of Doubleday. Deep thanks for this opportunity for the O. Henry authors.

The Department of English of the University of Texas at Austin gave *The O. Henry Prize Stories* a home, and for sixteen years, talented graduate students from the Michener Center for Writers and the New Writers Project assisted me in reading the many submissions. I hope that they learned to be as demanding of their own work as I've been when choosing stories for *The O. Henry Prize Stories*, and I'm grateful for their help in understanding the stories that puzzled and intrigued us. Thanks in 2018 to Rachel Heng. For the third year in a row, Fatima Kola read countless stories for *The O. Henry Prize Stories*, finding many jewels and something to praise even in the semiprecious. She was generous with her time, brilliance, and friendship, and no thanks can ever be enough.

—*Laura Furman*

Publisher's Note

A BRIEF HISTORY OF
THE O. HENRY PRIZE STORIES

Many readers have come to love the short story through the simple characters, humor and easy narrative voice, and the compelling plotting in the work of William Sydney Porter (1862–1910), best known as O. Henry. His surprise endings entertain readers, including those back for a second, third, or fourth look. Even now one can say "Gift of the Magi" in a conversation about a love affair or marriage, and almost any literate person will know what is meant. It's hard to think of many other American writers whose work has been so incorporated into our national shorthand.

O. Henry was a newspaperman, skilled at hiding from his editors at deadline. A prolific writer, he wrote to make a living and to make sense of his life. He spent his childhood in Greensboro, North Carolina, his adolescence and young manhood in Texas, and his mature years in New York City. In between Texas and New York, he served out a prison sentence for bank fraud in Columbus, Ohio. Accounts of the origin of his pen name vary: one story dates from his days in Austin, where he was said to call the wandering family cat "Oh! Henry!"; another states that the name was inspired by the captain of the guard at the Ohio State Penitentiary, Orrin Henry.

Porter had devoted friends, and it's not hard to see why. He was charming and had an attractively gallant attitude. He drank too much and neglected his health, which caused his friends concern. He was often short of money; in a letter to a friend asking for a loan of $15 (his banker was out of town, he wrote), Porter added a postscript: "If it isn't convenient, I'll love you just the same." His banker was unavailable most of Porter's life. His sense of humor was always with him.

Reportedly, Porter's last words were from a popular song: "Turn up the light, for I don't want to go home in the dark."

Eight years after O. Henry's death, in April 1918, the Twilight Club (founded in 1883 and later known as the Society of Arts and Sciences) held a dinner in his honor at the Hotel McAlpin in New York City. His friends remembered him so enthusiastically that a group of them met at the Biltmore Hotel in December of that year to establish some kind of memorial to him. They decided to award annual prizes in his name for short story writers, and they formed a committee to read the short stories published in a year and a smaller group to pick the winners. In the words of Blanche Colton Williams (1879–1944), the first of the nine series editors, the memorial was intended to "strengthen the art of the short story and to stimulate younger authors."

Doubleday, Page & Company was chosen to publish the first volume, *O. Henry Memorial Award Prize Stories 1919*. In 1927, the society sold all rights to the annual collection to Doubleday, Doran & Company. Doubleday published *The O. Henry Prize Stories*, as it came to be known, in hardcover, and from 1984 to 1996 its subsidiary, Anchor Books, published it simultaneously in paperback. Since 1997, *The O. Henry Prize Stories* has been published as an original Anchor Books paperback.

HOW THE STORIES ARE CHOSEN

The series editor chooses the twenty O. Henry Prize Stories.

Each year, three writers distinguished for their fiction are asked to act as jurors, who read the twenty prize stories in manuscript form with no identification of either author or publication. The jurors make their choice of favorite independently of one another and the series editor, and write an appreciation of the story they most admire.

Stories published in American and Canadian magazines distributed in North America are eligible for inclusion in *The O. Henry Prize Stories*. Stories must be written originally in the English language. No translations are considered. Sections of novels are not considered. Editors are asked to send all the fiction they publish and not to nominate individual stories. Stories should not be submitted by agents or writers.

(Please see p. 438 for the submission address.)

The goal of *The O. Henry Prize Stories* remains to strengthen the art of the short story.

To Ruth Prawer Jhabvala (1927–2013)

It's no wonder that Ruth Prawer Jhabvala was superb at adapting the work of other writers for the screen. She was an exemplary writer herself, and she had the wisdom to see what was most brilliant in the work of other writers and to help it to shine. Her scripts for Merchant Ivory films of works by E. M. Forster and Henry James, and several of her own novels, step away from the written word to illuminate the author's characters, settings, and mostly thorny plots.

Ruth Prawer Jhabvala was Jewish and born in Cologne, Germany. She escaped to England with her family in 1939. She wrote, "Attending school and university in London, I received an English education that has remained as the backbone to support me throughout all subsequent encounters in very varied circumstances." She married C. S. H. Jhabvala in 1951, and they lived in India for twenty-five years. Collaborating for forty years with filmmakers Ismail Merchant and James Ivory meant living part of the year in New York, then mostly settling there.

Jhabvala wasn't a cozy writer, though she was funny. Whatever she had experienced in her life, whatever feelings she harbored about her characters or the real human beings who might have inspired them, she kept herself in the background, and perhaps for this reason her readers were free to laugh, smile, or cry, or to put the book or story aside for a moment to feel the heat and the dust of India, or shiver from the damp chill of a London winter.

Central to her work, as to the work of Anton Chekhov, V. S. Pritchett, and William Trevor, was Jhabvala's indifference to whether or not the reader might find her characters appealing. Many of her characters are frustrating, even distasteful, and those who shamelessly make use of others most often triumph in worldly terms. Meanwhile, the weak and the passive exhibit real tenacity, trapped though they are by their loyalty and love for the rotten ones; they are determined to persevere in their quiet lunacy. The weak don't care for the world or its opinion. They are free in a way that the triumphant narcissists can never be.

Jhabvala won two O. Henry Prizes, the first in 2005 for "Refuge in London," set in an English boardinghouse filled with European refugees. The narrator says that she's in many ways the same as the other girls at her boarding school: "But I wasn't, ever, quite like them, having grown up in this house of European émigrés, all of them so different from the parents of my schoolfellows and carrying a past, a country or countries—a continent—distinct from the one in which they now found themselves." Jhabvala was both like and not like her narrator and the refugees who fascinated her.

Jhabvala's second O. Henry, in 2013, was for "Aphrodisiac," set in India and about the downfall of a rather silly, lazy man who develops a passion for his sister-in-law. Jhabvala wrote about "Aphrodisiac": "The origin of this story was not an incident or a character but a situation—and one that has often fascinated me: someone's desire for another turning into an obsession that destroys all of his nobler qualities and higher striving." Her statement sums up a characteristic of her work, that behind the story is a human situation and her observation about it. Her fiction is based on the notice her keen mind took without judgment of the way some people live, even though her characters themselves are often quite concerned with morals and ethics and are quick to judge others. After describing the characters and conflicts in "Aphrodisiac," Jhabvala wrote: "I have to admit that none of this came to me consciously but evolved within the situation itself: so by the time I had finished writing (as often happens to me at the end of a story) I looked at it and wondered: 'So that's what it was all about.'" Her fiction was driven by her intellect and instinct, and her curiosity about her characters, who often seem doomed, not by fate, but by themselves as they give in time and again to their obsessions and illusions.

Toward the end of her life, Jhabvala wrote about her love of the short story form: "And after all that writing, I now write only short stories, which I love for their potential of compressing and containing whatsoever I have learnt about writing, and about everything else."

—Laura Furman
Austin, Texas

Contents

Introduction

A Century of the O. Henry Prize

A hundred years ago, when O. Henry's friends and admirers created an annual book of short stories in his honor, they surely had a different idea than we do today of what constitutes a good story. O. Henry was famous for his twist at the end of a tale, the unexpected turn or ironic revelation that made the insoluble problems and puzzles in his plot disappear in a puff of laughter or a few tears. Plots were generally more ornate in the early twentieth century, and so too was literary language. Furthermore, stories such as O. Henry's weren't expected to be ambivalent. The story's meaning, often spelled out as a lesson for the reader, was a natural part of the ending.

Today, stories come in a greater variety of voices and forms. A story can be written in any tense; in first, second, or third person; composed entirely of dialogue or with no dialogue at all; in one paragraph; in play form; with footnotes; and so on. Sometimes the past of the characters is spelled out and sometimes it is nonexistent, an effort on the writer's part to create an unending present. As for meaning, that's left up to the reader. The short story is now an open field for writers, and some of the results might be unrecognizable to an early-twentieth-century reader. Still, elements of the form persist: a certain relationship between different pieces of the story, in particular, the passionate desire of the beginning and ending for reunion.

So, too, the inner workings of the collection have changed. The earliest O. Henry Prize stories were chosen by several committees of readers who started with six hundred stories and passed them on in smaller and smaller batches until the final three judges whittled the remaining contenders down to seventeen finalists. Among those seventeen, the judges then ranked three as first-, second-, and third-prize winners.

The process is much simplified now and fairer to writer and reader. Instead of the cascading sets of readers of the early years, the series editor alone chooses the stories, and while past volumes could contain sixteen, seventeen, eighteen, or twenty-one stories, the number has settled at twenty. Starting in 1997, a jury of three writers was convened by the series editor to determine the first-, second-, and third-prize winners, but in 2003, the rankings were eliminated and all the winners are now equally honored. The three jurors now read a blind manuscript separately; each chooses a single favorite and writes about it. This avoids decisions by committee and also makes the process more fun for the jurors since they don't know who wrote the story or where it was published. Only twice in sixteen years has a story been recognized by a juror.

Looking back at the O. Henry Prize's beginning decades, other differences jump out at one. Originally, most of the stories chosen for the collection were by white, male writers, though occasionally O. Henry readers could enjoy the likes of Dorothy Parker, Eudora Welty, and Flannery O'Connor. Over the years, the O. Henry has become more welcoming of different voices. So long as a story was originally composed in English it is eligible for consideration, no matter the nationality of the author. So long as a magazine is distributed in North America, it is welcome to submit stories to the

O. Henry. As a result, the annual collection is increasingly inter-national. Readers will find that the 2019 collection offers stories from a variety of writers and set all over the world, from Maui to the American West, from New York to Laos to the east bank of the river Jordan. The magazines that published the stories in the present collection range from the venerable *New Yorker*, *Kenyon Review*, and *Sewanee Review* to small magazines such as *LitMag* (in its second year of publication), *Witness*, and *ZYZZYVA*. Not all submitting publications are print ones; for instance, there's a story this year from *Granta*'s online incarnation, Granta.com.

With all the changes the decades have brought, there is a con-sistent goal: to find exemplary stories and to celebrate the short story form. It's been my privilege to be part of the O. Henry's history since 2003, and editing the hundredth-anniversary edition has been as exciting as ever. In its hundredth year, *The O. Henry Prize Stories* is alive, well, and faithful to its original purpose—to strengthen the art of the short story.

The O. Henry Prize Stories 2019

John Edgar Wideman's "Maps and Ledgers" is a marvel of con-nection and disconnection. In the beginning section, the one most conventionally storylike, a young academic just beginning his first university teaching job is called to the chairman's office to take a personal telephone call. In a sentence that mixes careful self-control among strangers with the anguish of family tragedy, Wideman writes: "I did not slip up, say or do the wrong thing when the call that came in to the English department, through the secretary's phone to the chairman's phone, finally reached me, after the secretary had knocked and escorted me down the hall to the chair's office, where I heard my mother crying because my father in jail for killing a man and she didn't know what to do except she had to let me know." His mother knows that in calling him at the university, she's crossing a border she shouldn't. The department chair—both a "Southern gentleman" and an "ole peckerwood," as the narrator's old aunt May would say—leaves the room so that the narrator has privacy to listen to his mother's news and to speak in his home voice.

The narrator lives in both worlds—community and university, black and white. He's trained himself, and been taught by family members, to switch between the "two languages, languages never quite mutually intelligible, one kind I talked at home when nearly always only colored folks listening, another kind spoken and written by white folks talking to no one or to one another or at us if they wanted something from us." When his mother calls the English department, she blows his cover.

For the rest of the story the narrator is lost and tries to find his way by using maps of his "empire," that is, the double world he's constructed for himself. He also uses ledgers, a family and community history he constructs through letters that were composed by his grandmother Martha in her beautiful hand: "Not her flesh-and-blood hand. Her letters. Her writing. Perfect letter after letter in church ledgers and notebooks year after year." He resurrects all kinds of letters, some from his mother when he was in college. "Letters I receive today from home beyond these pages. Home we share with all our dead." Poetic, elegiac, angry, just, "Maps and Ledgers" rewards its reader with the spells that a master of language casts against sorrow. This is John Edgar Wideman's third O. Henry Prize.

Every family has its own language of jokes, customs, and memories that bind them. (For an essential memoir on the subject, read Natalia Ginzburg's *Family Sayings*.) In "No Spanish" by Moira McCavana, the clash between two languages, Spanish and Basque, thoroughly disrupts family life. One morning when the narrator is twelve, her father orders her, her brother, and their mother not to speak Spanish ever again. Spanish is the language of the dictator Franco and not of the Basque Country in northern

Spain, where they live. Franco has made it illegal to speak Basque. The Basque separatist movement inspires the father's declaration, but in his enthusiasm, he overlooks a problem: no one in the family speaks a word of Basque. True, they can learn, but how to function without language in the meantime? Being deprived of Spanish threatens the family structure: "It was like removing our field of gravity, our established mode of relating to each other. Without Spanish, it seemed entirely possible that one of us might spin out into space." Moira McCavana's clear-as-water prose gives "No Spanish" a gentle, comic atmosphere while it engages the reader in the family's particular way of loving.

Family love is startlingly absent from Tessa Hadley's "Funny Little Snake." Fate has dealt nine-year-old Robyn an inept crew to care for her; what mad examples of maturity she's been given. Robyn's father, Gil, has driven to London to pick the child up for a visit, then disappeared into his university office to work on his book, leaving Robyn with her young stepmother, Valerie. Though Valerie has never met Robyn's mother, Marise, she has an idea of her as feckless and bohemian, and possibly glamorous: "Trust Robyn's mother to have a child who couldn't do up buttons, and then put her in a fancy plaid dress with hundreds of them, and frogging and leg-of-mutton sleeves, like a Victorian orphan, instead of ordinary slacks and a T-shirt so that she could play." Robyn barely speaks, is unable to say what her favorite food is or even what she's fed at home. Once Valerie gets a glimpse of Robyn's home, this mystery is solved.

Sturdy Valerie was at first impressed by her superior husband, who's climbed to a class above her own and seems to know a lot about the world that she doesn't. They are a bad match. He'd like to live in a crumbling romantic mansion because it would project the right image of his intellectual authenticity. Valerie's grateful to live in a new house where everything works. It's part of the bargain of their marriage that she be ignorant, malleable, and useful, but Valerie's docility masks a mind that's busy figuring out just how bad her situation is. The wonder of "Funny Little Snake" is the slow and sure dawning of Valerie's will and her involuntary goodness. Hadley's story gives the reader hope that the meek might this once inherit the earth. This is Tessa Hadley's third O. Henry Prize, and our juror Lara Vapnyar chose this story as her favorite.

"Goodnight Nobody" by Sarah Hall is narrated by Jem, a child who's unusually alive to everything around her: her mostly absent father; her exhausted mother, called Mumm-Ra; her baby half brother; her gran; and the news report of a dog who's killed a baby. The fascination of "Goodnight Nobody" is in following Jem's intelligent absorption of her world. Mumm-Ra works night shifts in a hospital mortuary and Jem isn't sure what she does. Gran explains that "what Mumm-Ra did was sort of what a beautician did, but much harder." Jem knows that whatever it is that Mumm-Ra does will bring her trouble at school, so she lies to the other children. The immortal *Goodnight Moon* by Margaret Wise Brown annoys and intrigues Jem as she reads it over and over to her half brother. Why say good night to Nobody? That's a reasonable thing to wonder. So are Jem's ponderings about the dog who's going to be put down and his owner, taken away by the police, and Mumm-Ra's night shifts, which Gran says will kill her—though Jem is sure that Mumm-Ra cannot die, unlike the other dead and near-dead in "Goodnight Nobody." Jem's curiosity is powerful, pulling her, and the reader, through the story. Little by little Jem analyzes the hints and half lies grown-ups tell her, putting together the bits and pieces of stories about her and her half brother's absent fathers, about cruelty and bad luck.

Cheryl is the fifteen-year-old title character of Valerie O'Riordan's story "Bad Girl." She's labeled in her school's records as "*withdrawn/hostile/uncooperative*, but mainly, in block capitals, ABSENT." According to the school counselor, Valerie can move along on the straight and narrow by attending a "therapeutic speech and drama course." Or she could be expelled. Given the choice, Cheryl's stepfather urges her to try. The problem Cheryl has won't be cured by speech and drama, however therapeutic; her mother died eighteen months before and Cheryl is grieving. She's also funny, smart, shrewd, and unsentimental. Some of the adults and other adolescents around Cheryl are innocent and clueless; others are clueless and out for themselves. Her stepfather, school counselor, and drama teacher are in the first category. Cheryl's frenemy, Tan Malone, is richer, more rebellious, and far more ruthless than Cheryl could hope to be. Tan is in a hurry for sex, adulthood, and global fame. It's easy to guess which of the three she'll achieve first. Cheryl is helpless in the backdraft of Tan's plans and conquests and soon enmeshed in a new kind of trouble. For Cheryl, youth isn't wasted on the young, it's inflicted on them, and the reader is left deciding whether to laugh or cry.

Rachel Kondo's "Girl of Few Seasons" is set in Happy Valley on the Hawaiian island of Maui. It's the night before Ebo leaves for basic training and the Vietnam War, and he faces the task of killing his favorite pet pigeon. The bird has a more distinguished lineage than Ebo: it's "a cream barred homer from the old line of Stichelbaut. The bird was from a long strain of impressive racers, a gift from his mother when he was nine years old." Ebo must kill all his pigeons because by nature and training they will return to their coop, and when he's gone, there will be no one to care for them. Killing a favorite bird and heading for war might make Ebo sound like a violent person, or at least a young man setting out to be a warrior. On the contrary, his heart and mind are turned toward a different goal. Ebo was born and raised in Happy Valley, a place of beauty and poverty. Ebo hasn't enlisted in the army out of patriotism. He knows nothing about the war or Vietnam. "He thought Vietnam might be like Maui, a place too quiet for fear. He thought the war might be a nameless river flowing strong after a heavy rain. If he let it, the war would take him away from Happy Valley to places he'd never been." Ebo's reason for enlisting is that on his way to report for duty he'll be able to visit his little sister Momo at the Waimano Home for the Feebleminded.

His flight from Maui will be paid for by the army, and that is the only way he can make the journey. He hasn't seen Momo for nine years, not since she was five years old and suffered brain damage from a virus. All his love can't change her condition, nor can he escape from his sense of responsibility for it. Rachel Kondo's deliberate and graceful prose pulls the reader into Ebo's world and his heartbreaking dilemma. Juror Elizabeth Strout chose "Girl of Few Seasons" as her favorite story.

"Flowers for America" by Doua Thao is set in Laos. Its three generations of characters were uprooted, some even destroyed, by the Vietnam War. The story begins in the market, where the narrator encounters her old friend Houa, who calls out, "Why are you running—so quickly, Goalia's Mother?" Houa is addressed as Shengcua's Mother, and the naming signifies their most important roles in equally difficult lives. The women grew up together. Both survived the war and both have daughters. The cries of the orchid sellers in the market punctuate their conversation—*"Sweetest smelling! Softest in all of Laos! For you, the flower Asian!"* The narrator tries to persuade her old friend to accept the gift of a frogfish, one she caught during her rough job helping a fisherman. Her offer is abruptly rejected. There's a tension between the women that the reader does not at first understand but hints of its true meaning emerge throughout the story. When they discuss their daughters' lives and their own, the decisions they've had to make and what they've done to survive, the narrator offers, "Maybe it's just our luck." To which her friend, angry for reasons we don't yet understand, responds by telling the narrator how lucky she is. Other people's troubles are much easier to bear than our own. Thao's story winds through time and place, through Laos, a refugee camp in Thailand, and the lives of refugees in the United States. The beauty of Thao's prose helps us to understand what remains meaningful, fresh, and sweet after the ordeals of war, life in a refugee camp, and the loss of home and family.

Immigration comes with its own gains and losses. Alexia Arthurs's "Mermaid River" is the story of an adolescent boy whose mother leaves Jamaica when he's a child and goes to New York to work. Eventually, she will bring her son to live with her. Meanwhile the son grows up in the care of his grandmother, a repository of stability and unchanging customs. By the time his mother takes him to America, mother and son are different people, changed by the time they've been apart. Of necessity, he will change even more as he adjusts to life in Brooklyn, and when he returns on a visit, he discovers that even Jamaica has changed in his absence. What is left to discover is what remains true in his heart.

In Kenan Orhan's "Soma," the narrator's goal isn't to leave his native place but to live above its ground. Soma is a town in the Aegean region of Turkey, where the work is either down in the coal mines or high above on the giant wind turbines. İzzet, who narrates the story, wishes above all to escape the darkness and dangers of being a coal miner, seeing in his father's life the cost of that job. His father in his turn scorns his son's dream: "Four years of school just so you can wear a bigger hardhat?" İzzet's friend Mesut works in the coal mine and enjoys arguing with him about the merits of being high above the ground versus well below it. According to Mesut, "The same thing is done up there . . . the gathering of electricity. So you are in the air, or in the ocean, or underground, whatever. I want to be flatly on the ground. Safe." The story's counterpoint to the mine and turbines is water, for İzzet is training to enter an open-water race from Çanakkale across the Hellespont. It's a famous and difficult course. Lord Byron swam it and so did the American adventurer and writer Richard Halliburton. İzzet, though, isn't after glory. The prize money will pay for the training he needs to become an engineer for the turbines. The tragic event that takes place the morning of the race tests their friendship, İzzet's concept of freedom, and Mesut's of safety.

"Mr. Can'aan" by Isabella Hammad is another story with a

friendship at its core. The story takes place in the Middle East and we're told in the second sentence that it begins on the eastern bank of the Jordan River a week after the Six-Day War. The country of Jordan and the Golan Heights are on the eastern bank, and to the west is Israel and the West Bank.

Sam is a counselor at a day camp for boys. On his morning off, as he walks along the Jordan River, he discovers the bloated corpse of a middle-aged man in the water and pulls it onto land. Documents in the man's wallet show that he is a Palestinian. Sam prepares the body for burial, then goes back to camp for another counselor. Together they pray, then bury the body. It's a striking incident, and years later Sam tells his friend Jibril about it in Beirut, where they're both students at the American University. Jibril, a Palestinian from the Israeli city of Haifa, has his own stories to tell, about his relatives in Jordanian refugee camps. "Freely he discussed his opinions of the different factions, positing pros and cons, explaining the guerrilla movements and Nasser and the splits in the PFLP. In a measure, this openness was at the heart of Jibril's charm, and Sam was just as captivated as the girls were." The story of their bond takes the reader from Beirut to Switzerland, from their youth until the friends are in their sixties. Sam is a contented soul, Jibril more restless. Jibril is waiting—perhaps he will wait forever—for the last piece of research to complete his magnum opus, "Haifa, An Arab History." "Mr. Can'aan" is a full-hearted story, its outer layer considering the realities of politics and place, and its inner layer exploring the radiance of an individual act of fidelity to tradition.

In Caoilinn Hughes's "Prime," it's the end of the school year and the entire sixth class, all seven children, take the reader through the day, keeping their focus on Miss Lynch, their teacher, an eccentric who is as sharp as a tack. The children explain who is who, their expectations of one another, and their regard for their teacher. Miss Lynch's dog has died, and so has Johnnie, a student from the previous year. The class takes Johnnie's desk and chair to the beach and burn them like a funeral pyre. "Death," the children tell us, "billows out like a stone plonked in water. We knew that. But we didn't know if the safe thing was to step back out of its ripples. We surrounded Miss Lynch like a net seven souls wide." Miss Lynch has her own harsh wisdom: "You should all know by now that mercy is an artificial flower. It looks very convincing and nice. But it has no nectar." The children know what's real and what isn't, and in Hughes's delightful, songlike story they lead us to the unanticipated joy of brilliant sunshine and skittering clouds "on their way to America."

John Keeble's "Synchronicity" is a magical story set among plainspoken people in Eastern Washington during a summer when portentous forest fires and smoke cover the western United States. The central characters are two buffalo, who don't say much but whose presence pushes the story's action. Bought as calves by an overly imaginative man for his wife, left with his brother-in-law, unruly, growing bigger and more uncontrollable by the minute, the buffalo stand not only for the long history of mistakes made by Anglo immigrants to the West but also for the mistakes of neophytes unaccustomed to the unending demands of rural life. In a city, the same man might buy a baby alligator and then flush it when the novelty wears off, and so an urban myth is born of alligators living in the sewers of New York. The buffalo are a much bigger mistake with great potential for causing trouble. They are magnificent animals, failed by all the human characters except perhaps the one who is the most down-to-earth and preserves their sweetness by canning their tongues.

A rabbit would seem to be more suitable as a family pet than a buffalo. The rabbit in Alexander MacLeod's "Lagomorph" becomes part of the narrator's family, adopted as a hypoallergenic pet for his children. The rabbit, given the name Gunther by its previous owner, was initially a chaotic presence, predictably ignored by the children and cared for by the narrator and his wife. At first, Gunther was not well. His diarrheic excrement was everywhere, and "he had this thick yellow mucus matting down the fur beneath his eyes and both his tear ducts were swollen green and red." Gunther's ocular-dental problems are cured by the courageous and violent tasks the narrator must undertake to save Gunther's life. They are bonded.

Eventually, his companionable friendship with Gunther becomes the only relationship the narrator has left. It has many advantages, as everyone who's decided that life with an animal is simpler than—perhaps preferable to—life with another human will understand. But even rabbits have their limits: "If a rabbit loves you or if they think you are the scum of the earth, you will catch that right away, but there is a lot between those extremes—everything else is in between—and you can never be sure where you stand relative to a rabbit."

Some marriages and friendships thrive on mistaken identity. In Sarah Shun-lien Bynum's "Julia and Sunny," two couples seem to become one another's family and they spend an annual summer vacation together. The narrating duo has a son, and Julia and Sunny have a daughter. The children don't always get along but Sunny is "there to facilitate," and he keeps the peace. Bynum's story questions the possibility or impossibility of knowing another individual, much less a couple. When the narrators idealize Julia and Sunny, are they projecting what they want to be? One of the many likable things about "Julia and Sunny" is the easy, gossipy tone of the narrative, even when the reader becomes distrustful of it. "Julia and Sunny" isn't so much a revelation of rot at the core of both marriages as a portrait of the fear of even suspecting that a relationship is less than perfect.

The marriage and extramarital affair in Bryan Washington's "610 North, 610 West" are observed and analyzed by the young narrator and his brothers. They keep a close eye on their mother while her husband is with the other woman. She keeps the family restaurant going all by herself, cleaning up at the end of the day and preparing for the next while her four boys watch: "We'd stare at the plastic with our hands in our laps like they'd show us whoever kept Ma's man out in the world." In *Aspects of the Novel*, E. M. Forster wrote that a story was a "narrative of events arranged in their time-sequence." "610 North, 610 West" is about infidelity as witnessed and absorbed by the narrator and his brothers, but the plot of the story, what Forster called "the sense of causality," belongs to the narrator alone, as he observes his mother and understands, perhaps for the first time, that she's a woman living a life that in moments has nothing to do with either her children or her husband. His new distance is an achievement that might release him from his family's web of trouble.

Liza Ward's first O. Henry was awarded for "Snowbound" in *The O. Henry Prize Stories 2005*. "The Shrew Tree" has the fore-ordained quality of a fairy tale. Gretel's father is vice principal of the 1950s high school she attends and the boys torture her for it: "Then the boys would pinch her, shoulder her up against the lockers, drop things under her skirt to see how far they could get just a hundred feet from the vice principal's office as she walked the gauntlet, hugging the line of lockers so close, the locks clocking the metal doors." The students don't fear or respect Gretel's father because he doesn't beat them and because "he could not bring himself to act violently toward anyone." He's too gentle for his job. Her mother was a dancer and then a dance teacher, and now she's the victim of an unnamed crippling disease that's slowly killing her. Gretel's father carries her mother every morning from bed to a hot bath so that she can straighten her limbs. Along with having two cursed parents, Gretel is going through the unpredictable and embarrassing changes of adolescence. Karl Olson, a farmer's son, stirs her imagination. Earthbound, materialistic, Karl seems to be connected to a better world than the one her parents have created with their love of books and ideas, and their inability to control their lives. Karl is quick to act, snapping a wounded rabbit's neck without a thought. He has an opinion about everything that's familiar and contempt for what he doesn't know. In this way, he's as different from her parents as Gretel wishes to be. The run-down farm he's determined to save looks like a refuge to Gretel, not a trap. Gretel fails to take warning from the story he tells her about his grandfather's immuring a live shrew inside an ash tree. Gretel and Karl marry, and in time her ability to escape is thwarted by a switch from that same tree.

In "Slingshot" by Souvankham Thammavongsa, the narrator begins an affair with her neighbor, a man less than half her age. Richard is sexually self-confident and seems unboundedly curious. He tells his neighbor, who's been a widow for thirty years, "There's no such thing as love. It's a construct." Her granddaughter, who lives with her, is always in love or recovering from it. In contrast, the widow has never had sex with anyone but her husband: "As far as I was concerned, I hadn't had sex for such a long time that I could consider myself a virgin. I couldn't remember how it all happens." Richard gives frequent parties, and after a while his neighbor feels comfortable enough to attend. When they are alone after one party ends, they have sex, almost inevitably. The opposing powers of sex and love veer back and forth until the narrator is content at last.

In "Unstuck" by Stephanie Reents, Liza's house is behaving strangely. The old kitchen sink is cleaner. The front walk is swept. The bed is made, though Liza's sure she didn't make it. The recycling's been upcycled. At this point, some would suggest to Liza that she should leave well enough alone. A house that cleans itself up is a rare jewel. Liza, though she hates to clean, finds the unusual happenings unsettling. She questions her longtime boyfriend, Lloyd, who spends weekends with her. He denies having done the good deeds. Liza is a sensible, rational woman, but she begins to connect the strange occurrences in her house with her terror when she was once trapped in a slot canyon. Stephanie Reents won an O. Henry in 2006 for "Disquisition on Tears," and she's won her second O. Henry for "Unstuck," which is a disquisition on being stuck and unstuck, an examination of which condition is the more unnerving.

In "Omakase," Weike Wang's couple, called "the woman" and "the man," are out for dinner at a restaurant listed as one of central Harlem's top sushi places. It smells strongly of fish, not a good thing in a restaurant serving raw fish. The woman is dubious about eating there, but the man says, for the first but not last time, that she worries too much. Also, he says, she exaggerates. But how cautious is she really? She met the man online, they dated for a while, then she moved from Boston to New York, which she finds to be a dangerous and offensive place. The man would have been happy to move to Boston, or so he said, but found it difficult to find a job as a pottery instructor, whereas she relocated easily as a research analyst at a bank. She's Chinese-American. He's not. For their meal, they agree to order *omakase*, chef's choice. The man tries to talk to the chef, and without warning the subject of race is on the table. Who is Asian and who isn't comes to matter a great deal for this uneasy, perhaps unequally yoked, couple. "Omakase" was juror Lynn Freed's favorite story.

Patricia Engel's "Aguacero" opens in another New York setting, this one an evocatively described midtown downpour. The narrator tells us that she's left her therapist's office "without an umbrella and stopped for a pack of cigarettes in one of those midtown shops, the size of a closet and smelling of nuts and tobacco, because nothing makes me want to smoke more than a visit to the shrink." She's not sleeping, not talking much, even to the therapist; she's numbed by urban life. She loiters under a shop awning, trying and failing to summon a cab with a lit cigarette. She's joined by a man who tells her he knows she's Colombian because she has "an Andean face." "Also," he adds, "you just tried to call a taxi with a cigarette. Only Colombians do that." A welcome acquaintanceship develops between the two Colombians who are far from home, though, for her own reasons, she's distrustful and doesn't quite believe his life story until their friendship advances. Engel's calm prose moves the story and its reader from an uncomfortable New York rain into the sustained pain of a ruined life.

The hundredth-anniversary edition of *The O. Henry Prize Stories* is my last as series editor, and I wish to express my gratitude to all who've made my time so fulfilling.

It's been a privilege to work with the authors of the stories and the editors of the magazines that originally published them. There is no role more important than the writer's, of course, but a story appearing in *The O. Henry Prize Stories* is also validation of its editor's skill.

One of my few regrets is that I couldn't meet every winning writer in person as previous series editors did at the annual O. Henry dinner. Those were different times, of course, and I felt a warm digital connection with the O. Henry authors. (And a more tangible connection through the U.S. Mail with Wendell Berry, a four-time winner who does not use a computer.)

Inviting a new trio of short story writers each year to act as jurors has been a light duty. I've been amazed at their real pleasure in finding a new story to love. Given their own achievements as writers, it's been no surprise to read their clear and affectionate evaluations of their favorite story.

For a century now, numberless readers have been entertained, puzzled, moved, and sometimes perhaps infuriated by *The O. Henry Prize Stories*. Since the first volume was published in 1919, what remains consistent about the authors, readers, jurors, and series editors of *The O. Henry Prize Stories* is a fascination with the short story—an art form that's both popular and elite—and gratitude for the yearly chance to celebrate it.

—*Laura Furman*
Austin, Texas

The O. Henry Prize Stories 2019

Tessa Hadley

Funny Little Snake

THE CHILD WAS NINE YEARS OLD and couldn't fasten her own buttons. Valerie knelt in front of her on the carpet in the spare room as Robyn held out first one cuff and then the other without a word, then turned around to present the back of her dress, where a long row of spherical chocolate-brown buttons was unfastened over a grubby white petticoat edged with lace. Her tiny, bony shoulder blades flickered with repressed movement. And although every night since Robyn had arrived, a week ago, Valerie had encouraged her into a bath foamed up with bubbles, she still smelled of something furtive—musty spice from the back of a cupboard. The smell had to be in her dress, which Valerie didn't dare wash because it looked as though it had to be dry-cleaned, or in her lank, licorice-colored hair, which was pulled back from her forehead under an even grubbier stretch Alice band. Trust Robyn's mother to have a child who couldn't do up buttons, and then put her in a fancy plaid dress with hundreds of them, and frogging and leg-of-mutton sleeves, like a Victorian orphan, instead of ordinary slacks and a T-shirt so that she could play. The mother went around, apparently, in long dresses and bare feet, and had her picture painted by artists. Robyn at least had tights and plimsolls with elastic tops—though her green coat was too thin for the winter weather.

Valerie had tried to talk to her stepdaughter. It was the first time they'd met, and she'd braced herself for resentment, the child's mind poisoned against her. Robyn was miniature, a doll—with a plain, pale, wide face, her temples blue-naked where her hair was strained back, her wide-open gray eyes affronted and evasive and set too far apart. She wasn't naughty, and she wasn't actually silent—that would have been a form of stubbornness to combat, to coax and maneuver around. She was a nullity, an absence, answering yes and no obediently if she was questioned, in that languid drawl that always caught Valerie on the raw—though she knew the accent wasn't the child's fault, only what she'd learned. Robyn even said please and thank you, and she told Valerie the name of her teacher, but when Valerie asked whether she liked the teacher her eyes slipped uneasily away from her stepmother's and she shrugged, as if such an idea as liking or not liking hadn't occurred to her. The only dislikes she was definite about had to do with eating. When Valerie put fish pie on Robyn's plate the first night, she shot her a direct look of such piercing desperation that Valerie, who was a good, wholesome cook and had been going to insist, asked her kindly what she ate at home. Eggs? Cottage pie? Baked beans?

Honestly, the girl hardly seemed to know the names of things. Toast was all she could think of. Definitely not eggs: a vehement head shake. Toast, and—after long consideration, then murmuring hesitantly, tonelessly—tomato soup, cornflakes, butterscotch Instant Whip. It was lucky that Gil wasn't witness to all this compromise, because he would have thought Valerie was spoiling his daughter. He and Valerie ate together later, after Robyn was in bed. Gil might have been a left-winger in his politics, but he was old-fashioned in his values at home. He despised, for instance, the little box of a house the university had given them, and wanted to move into one of the rambling old mansions on the road behind his office. He thought they had more style, with their peeling paint and big gardens overgrown with trees.

Valerie didn't tell him how much she enjoyed all the conveniences of their modern home—the clean, light rooms, the central heating, the electric tin opener fitted onto the kitchen wall. And she was intrigued, because Gil was old-fashioned, by his having chosen for his first wife a woman who went barefoot and lived like a hippie in her big Chelsea flat. Perhaps Marise had been so beautiful once that Gil couldn't resist her. Valerie was twenty-four; she didn't think Marise could still be beautiful at forty. Now, anyway, he referred to her as the Rattrap, and the Beak, and the Bitch from Hell, and said that she would fuck anyone. When Valerie had first married him, she hadn't believed that a professor could know such words. She'd known them herself, of course, but that was different—she wasn't educated.

On the phone with his ex-wife, Gil had made a lot of fuss about having his daughter to visit, as a stubborn point of pride, and then had driven all the way down to London to fetch her. But, since getting back, he'd spent every day at his office at the university, even though it wasn't term time, saying that he needed absolute concentration to work on the book he was writing. Robyn didn't seem to miss him. She looked bemused when Valerie called him her daddy, as if she hardly recognized him by that name; she'd been only three or four when he'd moved out. Valerie didn't ask Gil what he'd talked about with his daughter on the long car journey: perhaps they'd driven the whole way in silence. Or perhaps he'd questioned Robyn about her mother, or ranted on about her, or talked about his work. Sometimes in the evenings he talked to Valerie for hours about university politics or other historians he envied or resented—or even about the Civil War or the Long Parliament or the idea of the state—without noticing that she wasn't listening, that she was thinking about new curtains or counting the stitches in her knitting. He might have found fatherhood easier, Valerie thought, if his daughter had been pretty. Moodily, after Robyn had gone to bed, Gil wondered aloud whether she was even his. "Who knows, with the Great Whore of Marylebone putting it about like there's no tomorrow? The child's half feral. She doesn't look anything like me. Is she normal? Do they even send her to school? I think she's backward. A little bit simple, stunted. No surprise, growing up in that sink of iniquity. God only knows what she's seen."

Valerie was getting to know how he used exaggerated expressions like "sink of iniquity," whose sense she didn't know but could guess at, as if he were partly making fun of his own disapproval, while at the same time he furiously meant it. He stayed one step ahead of any fixed position, so that no one could catch him out in it. But Robyn looked more like him than he realized, although she was smooth and bland with childhood and he was hoary and sagging from fifty years' experience. He had the same pale skin, and the same startled hare's eyes swimming in and out of focus behind his big black-framed glasses. Sometimes, when Gil laughed, you could see how he might have been a different man if he hadn't chosen to be this professor with his stooping bulk and crumpled, shapeless suits, his braying, brilliant talk. Without glasses, his face was naked and keen and boyish, with a boy's shame, as if the nakedness must be smothered like a secret.

Gil's widowed mother had owned a small newsagent's. He'd got himself to university and then onward into success and even fame—he'd been on television often—through his own sheer cleverness and effort. Not that he tried to hide his class origins: on the contrary, he'd honed them into a weapon to use against his colleagues and friends. But he always repeated the same few anecdotes from his childhood, well rounded and glossy from use: the brewhouse in the backyard, where the women gossiped and did their washing; the bread-and-drippings suppers; a neighbor cutting his throat in the shared toilet; his mother polishing the front step with Cardinal Red. He didn't talk about his mother in private, and when Valerie once asked him how she'd died he wouldn't tell her anything except—gruffly barking it, to frighten her off and mock her fear at the same time—that it was cancer. She guessed that he'd probably been close to his mother, and then grown up to be embarrassed by her, and hated himself for neglecting her, but couldn't admit to any of this because he was always announcing publicly how much he loathed sentimentality and guilt. Valerie had been attracted to him in the first place because he made fun of everything; nothing was sacred.

She didn't really want the child around. But Robyn was part of the price she paid for having been singled out by the professor among the girls in the faculty office at King's College London, having married him and moved with him to begin a new life in the North. There had been some quarrel or other with King's; he had enemies there.

As the week wore on, she grew sick of the sound of her own voice jollying Robyn along. The girl hadn't even brought any toys with her, to occupy her time. After a while, Valerie noticed that, when no one was looking, she played with two weird little figures, scraps of cloth tied into shapes with wool, one in each hand, doing the voices almost inaudibly. One voice was coaxing and hopeful, the other one reluctant. "Put on your special gloves," one of them said. "But I don't like the blue color," said the other. "These ones have special powers," the first voice persisted. "Try them out."

Valerie asked Robyn if these were her dollies. Shocked out of her fantasy, she hid the scraps behind her back. "Not really," she said.

"What are their names?"

"They don't have names."

"We could get out my sewing machine and make clothes for them."

Robyn shook her head, alarmed. "They don't need clothes."

Selena had made them for her, she told Valerie, who worked

out that Selena must have been their cleaner. "She doesn't come anymore," Robyn added, though not as if she minded particularly. "We sacked her. She stole things."

When Valerie tied her into an apron and stood her on a chair to make scones, Robyn's fingers went burrowing into the flour as if they were independent of her, mashing the butter into lumps in her hot palms. "Like this," Valerie said, showing her how to lift the flour as she rubbed, for lightness. Playfully, she grabbed at Robyn's fingers under the surface of the flour, but Robyn snatched them back, dismayed, and wouldn't try the scones when they were baked. Valerie ended up eating them, although she was trying to watch her weight, sticking to Ryvita and cottage cheese for lunch. She didn't want to run to fat, like her mother. She thought Gil refused to visit her mother partly because he worried about how Valerie might look one day, when she wasn't soft and fresh and blond anymore.

Robyn had hardly brought enough clothes to last the week— besides the dress with the buttons, there was only a gray skirt that looked like a school uniform, a ribbed nylon jumper, one spare pair of knickers, odd socks, and a full-length nightdress made of red wool flannel, like something out of a storybook. The night-dress smelled of wee and Valerie thought it must be itchy; she took Robyn shopping for sensible pajamas and then they had tea at the cafeteria in British Home Stores, which had been Valerie's treat when she was Robyn's age. Robyn didn't want a meringue but asked if she was allowed to hold her new pajamas, then sat with the cellophane package in her lap and an expression of conscious importance. The pajamas were white, decorated with yellow-and-blue yachts and anchors. "Can I keep them?" she asked tentatively, after a long, dull silence. Valerie had grown tired of chatting away inanely to no one.

She had been going to suggest that Robyn leave the pajamas behind, for the next time she visited, but she didn't really care. Every child ought to want something; it was only healthy. And, packed into Robyn's suitcase along with the rest of her clothes—all freshly washed, apart from the dress, and pressed, even the socks, with Valerie's steam iron—the pajamas would be like a message, a coded reproach, for that mother in Chelsea. She imagined Marise unpacking them in some room of flowery frivolity she couldn't clearly visualize and feeling a pang for the insufficiency of her own maternal care. Valerie knew, though, that her parade of competence and righteous indignation was a lie, really. Because the truth was that she couldn't wait for Robyn to go home. She longed to be free of that dogged, unresponsive little figure following her everywhere around the house.

Gil was supposed to be driving Robyn back down to London on Wednesday. On Tuesday evening, when he came home early, Valerie knew right away that something was up. He stood behind her while she was preparing meat loaf at the kitchen counter, nuzzling under her ear and stroking her breast with one hand, determinedly jiggling the ice cubes in his Scotch with the other. He always poured himself a generous Scotch as soon as he came in: she'd learned not to comment. "You're so good to me," he said pleadingly, his voice muffled in her neck. "I don't deserve it."

"Oh dear, what's Mr. Naughty's little game now?" Valerie was long-suffering, faintly amused, swiping onions from her chopping board into a bowl with the side of her knife. "What's he sniffing after? He wants something."

"He knows he's so selfish. Causes her no end of trouble."

These were two of the roles they acted out sometimes: Valerie brusquely competent and in charge, Gil wheedling and needy. There was a truth behind their performances, as well as pretense. Gil groaned apologetically. A problem had come up at work tomorrow, a special guest coming to dinner at High Table, someone he needed to meet because he had influence and the whole game was a bloody conspiracy. He'd never be able to get back from

London in time. And Thursday was no good, either—faculty meeting; Friday he was giving a talk in Manchester. They could keep Robyn until Saturday, but the She-Bitch would never let him hear the end of it. He wanted Valerie to take her home tomorrow on the train. Valerie could stay over with her mother in Acton, couldn't she? Come back the following day?

Valerie had counted on being free in the morning, getting the house back to normal, having her thoughts to herself again, catching a bus into town perhaps, shopping. She was gasping for her solitude like a lungful of clean air. Biting her lower lip to keep herself from blurting out a protest, she kneaded onions into the minced meat; the recipe came from a magazine—it was seasoned with allspice and tomato ketchup. Certainly she didn't fancy three extra days with the kid moping around. She thought, with a flush of outrage, that Gil was truly selfish, never taking her needs into consideration. On the other hand, important men had to be selfish in order to get ahead. She understood that—she wouldn't have wanted a softer man who wasn't respected. She could squeeze concessions out of him anyway, in return for this favor. Perhaps she'd ring up one of her old girlfriends, meet for coffee in Oxford Street, or even for a gin in a pub, for old times' sake. She could buy herself something new to wear; she had saved up some money that Gil didn't know about, out of the housekeeping.

Theatrically, she sighed. "It's very inconvenient. I was going to go into Jones's, to make inquiries about these curtains for the sitting room."

He didn't even correct her and tell her to call it the drawing room.

"He's sorry, he's really sorry. It isn't fair, he knows it. But it could be a little holiday for you. You could just put Robyn into a cab at the station, give the driver the address, let her mother pay. Why shouldn't she? She's got money."

Valerie was startled that he could even think she'd do that. The child could hardly get herself dressed in the mornings; she certainly wasn't fit to be knocking halfway around London by herself, quarreling with cabdrivers. And, anyway, if Valerie really was going all the way to London, she might as well have a glimpse of where her stepdaughter lived. She was afraid of Marise, but curious about her, too.

Outside the front door in Chelsea, Valerie stood holding Robyn's suitcase in one leather-gloved hand and her own overnight bag in the other. The house was grand and dilapidated, set back from the street in an overgrown garden, with a flight of stone steps rising to a scruffy pillared portico, a broad door painted black. Names in faded, rain-stained ink were drawing-pinned beside a row of bells; they'd already rung twice, and Valerie's feet were like ice. The afternoon light was thickening gloomily under the evergreens. Robyn stood uncomplaining in her thin coat, although from time to time on their journey Valerie had seen her quake with the cold as if it had probed her, bypassing her conscious mind, like a jolt of electricity. The heating had been faulty on the train. While Valerie read her magazines and Robyn worked dutifully through one page after another in her coloring book, the washed-out, numb winter landscape had borne cruelly in on them from beyond the train window: miles of bleached, tufted dun grasses, purple-black tangled labyrinths of bramble, clumps of dark reeds frozen in a ditch. Valerie had been relieved when they got into the dirty old city at last. She hadn't taken to the North, though she was trying.

Staring up at the front door, Robyn had her usual stolidly neutral look, buffered against expectation; she hardly seemed excited by the prospect of seeing her mother again. And, when the door eventually swung open, a young man about Valerie's age—with long fair hair and a flaunting angel face, dark-stubbled jaw, dead cigarette stuck to the wet of his sagging lip—looked out at them without any recognition. "Oh, hullo?" he said.

With his peering, dozy eyes, he seemed to have only just got out of bed, or to be about to slop back into it. He was bursting out of his tight clothes: a shrunken T-shirt exposed a long hollow of skinny brown belly and a slick line of dark hairs, leading down inside pink satin hipster trousers. His feet were bare and sprouted with more hair, and he smelled like a zoo animal, of something sour and choking. Realization dawned when he noticed Robyn. "Hullo!" he said, as if it were funny. "You're the little girl."

"Is Mrs. Hope at home?" Valerie asked stiffly.

He scratched his chest under the T-shirt and his smile slid back to dwell on her, making her conscious of her breasts, although he only quickly flicked his glance across them. "Yeah, somewhere."

A woman came clattering downstairs behind him and loomed across his shoulder; she was taller than he was, statuesque, her glittering eyes black with makeup, and diamonds glinting in the piled-up mass of her dark hair, in the middle of the afternoon. Though, of course, the diamonds were paste—it was all a joke, a pantomime send-up. Valerie wasn't such a fool, she got hold of that. Still, Marise was spectacular in a long, low-cut white dress and white patent-leather boots: she had an exaggerated, coarse beauty, like a film star blurred from being too much seen.

"Oh, Christ, is it today? Shit! Is that the kid?" Marise wailed, pushing past the young man, her devouring eyes snatching off an impression of Valerie in one scouring instant and dismissing it. "I forgot all about it. It can't be Wednesday already! Welcome home, honeypot. Give Mummy a million, million kisses. Give Jamie kisses. This is Jamie. Say hello. Isn't he sweet? Don't you remember him? He's in a band."

Robyn said hello, gazing at Jamie without much interest and not moving to kiss anyone. Her mother pounced in a cloud of perfume and carried her inside, calling back over her shoulder to Valerie in her husky voice, mistaking her for some kind of paid nanny, or pretending to. "Awfully kind of you. Are those her things? Do you want to drop her bags here in the hall? James can carry them up later. Do you have a cab? Or he can get you one. Oof, what a big, heavy girl you're getting to be, Robby-bobby. Can you climb up on your own?"

The hall was dim and high, lit by a feeble unshaded bulb; when determinedly Valerie followed after them, her heels echoed on black-and-white marble tiles. "Hello, Mrs. H.," she sang out in her brightest telephone voice. "I'm the new Mrs. H. How nice to meet you."

Marise looked down at her from the curve of the staircase, where she was stooping over Robyn, setting her down. "Oh, I thought you might be. I thought he might have chosen someone like you."

"I'm hoping you're going to offer us a cup of tea," Valerie went on cheerfully. Of course Marise had known that she was bringing Robyn—Gil had telephoned last night to tell her. "Only we're frozen stiff, the pair of us! The heating on the train wasn't working."

"Do you take milk?" Marise wondered. "Because I don't know if we have any milk."

"So long as it's hot!"

She submitted graciously when Jamie offered to take both bags, then was aware of his following her up the stairs, appraising her from behind, and thought that Marise was aware of it, too. A door on the first floor, with a pillared surround and a pediment, stood open. You could see how it had once opened onto the best rooms at the heart of the house: now it had its own Yale lock and was painted purple and orange. The lower panels were dented and splintered as if someone had tried to kick through them. In the enormous room beyond, there was a marble fireplace and a candelabra and floor-length windows hung with tattered yellow brocade drapes; the glass in a vast gilt mirror was so foxed that it didn't double the perspective but closed it in, like a black fog. Valerie understood that, like the diamonds in Marise's hair, this wasn't really decaying aristocratic grandeur but an arty imitation of it.

Marise led the way past a glass dome as tall as a man, filled with stuffed, faded hummingbirds and a staring, dappled fairground horse, its flaring nostrils painted crimson; Robyn flinched from the horse as if from an old enemy.

In the next room, which was smaller, a log fire burned in a blackened grate beside a leather sofa, its cushions cracked and pale with wear. Jamie dropped the bags against a wall. Robyn and Valerie, shivering in their coats, hung over the white ash in the grate as if it might be lifesaving, while Marise hunted for milk in what must have been the kitchen next door, though it sounded cavernous. Jamie crouched to put on more logs, reaching his face toward the flame to reignite his rollie. The milk was off, Marise announced. There was a tin of tomato juice; wouldn't everyone prefer Bloody Marys? Valerie said that might be just the thing, but knew she must pace herself and not let the drink put her at any disadvantage.

The Bloody Marys when they came were strong, made with lots of Tabasco and ice and lemon and a stuffed olive on a stick: Marise said they were wonderfully nourishing, she lived on them. She even brought one—made without vodka, or only the tiniest teaspoonful—for Robyn, along with a packet of salted crisps, and she kissed her, pretending to gobble her up. Robyn submitted to the assault. "You're lucky, I saved those for you specially. I know that little girls are hungry bears. Because Jamie's a hungry bear, too—he eats everything. I'll have to hide the food away, won't I, if we want to keep any of it for you? Are you still my hungry bear, Bobbin?"

Robyn went unexpectedly then into a bear performance, hunching her shoulders, crossing her eyes, snuffling and panting, scrabbling in the air with her hands curled up like paws, her face a blunt little snout, showing pointed teeth. They must have played this game before; Marise watched her daughter with distaste and pity, austerely handsome as a carved ship's figurehead. For a moment, Robyn really was a scruffy, dull-furred, small brown bear, dancing joylessly to order. Valerie wouldn't have guessed that the child had it in her, to enter so completely into a life other than her own. "Nice old bear," she said encouragingly.

"That's quite enough of that, Bobby," Marise said. "Most unsettling. Now, why don't you go and play, darling? Take your crisps away before the Jamie-bear gets them."

Robyn returned into her ordinary self, faintly pink in the face. "Shall I show Auntie Valerie my bedroom?"

Marise's expression ripened scandalously. She stared wide-eyed between Robyn and Valerie. " 'Auntie Valerie'! What's this? Valerie isn't your real auntie, you know. Didn't anyone explain to you?"

"We thought it was the best thing for her to call me, considering," Valerie said.

"Well, I'm relieved you didn't go in for 'Mummy.' Or 'Dearest Mamma,' or 'Mom.' "

Flustered, Robyn shot a guilty look at Valerie. "I do know she's my stepmother, really."

"That's better. Your *wicked* stepmother, don't forget." Marise winked broadly at Valerie. "Now, off you go. She doesn't want to see your bedroom."

They heard her trail through the kitchen, open another door on the far side, close it again behind her. The fire blazed up. Jamie began picking out something on his guitar while Marise rescued his rollie from the ashtray and fell with it onto the opposite end of the sofa. Valerie guessed that they were smoking pot—that was what the zoo smell was. And she thought that she ought to leave. There was nothing for her here—she had made her point by coming inside. "So, Valerie," Marise said musingly. "How did you get on with my dear daughter? Funny little snake, isn't she? I hope Gilbert enjoyed spending every moment with her, after all those protestations of how he's such a devoted father. Was she a good girl?"

"Awfully good. We didn't have a squeak of trouble."

"I mean, isn't she just a piece of Gilbert? Except not clever, of course. Poor little mite, with his looks and my brains."

Outside, the last of the afternoon light was being blotted out, and although wind buffeted the loose old windowpanes, no one stirred to draw the curtains or switch on the lamps. Valerie wanted to go, but the drink was stronger than she was used to, and the heat from the fire seemed to press her down in the sofa. Also, she feared returning through the next room, past the stuffed birds and that horse. She was imagining how her husband might have been impressed and excited once by this careless, shameless, disordered household. If you owned so much, you could afford to trample it underfoot in a grand gesture, turning everything into a game.

"I do adore clever men," Marise went on. "I was so in love with Gilbert's intelligence, absolutely crazy about him at first. I could sit listening to him for hours on end, telling me all about history and ideas and art. Because, you know, I'm just an absolute idiot. I was kicked out of school when I was fourteen—the nuns hated me. Valerie, truly, I can hardly read and write. Whereas I expect you can do typing and shorthand, you clever girl. So I'd just kneel there at Gilbert's feet, gazing up at him while he talked. You know, just talking, talking, droning on and on. So pleased with himself. Don't men just love that?"

"Do they? I wouldn't know."

"But they do, they love it when we're kneeling at their feet. Jamie thinks that's hilarious, don't you, Jamie? Because now I'm worshipping him instead, he thinks. Worshipping his guitar."

"My talent," Jamie chastely suggested. Marise shuffled down in the sofa to poke her white boot at him, prodding at his hands and blocking the strings so that he couldn't play until he ducked the neck of his guitar out of her way. His exasperated look slid past her teasing and onto Valerie, where it rested. Marise subsided with a sigh.

"So Gilbert's sitting there steering along in the little cockpit of his own cleverness, believing himself so shining, such a wonder! And then suddenly one day I couldn't stand it! I thought, But the whole *world*, the whole of real life, is spread out underneath him. And he's up there all alone in his own clever head. Don't you know what I mean?"

"I've never taken much interest in Gil's work," Valerie said primly. "Though I'm aware how highly it's regarded. I've got my own interests."

"Oh, have you? Good for you! Because I've never really had any interests to speak of. I've counted on the men in my life to supply those. Gilbert was certainly interesting. Did you know that he beat me? Yes, really. To a pulp, my dear."

What melodrama! Valerie laughed out loud. She didn't believe it. Or perhaps she did. When Marise, mocking, blew out a veil of smoke, she had a glimpse for a moment of Gil's malevolent Bitch from Hell, the strong-jawed dark sorceress who might incite a man to violence. Poor Gilbert. And it was true that his rages had been a revelation when they were first married. In the university office, all the women had petted him and were in awe of his mystique: he had seemed thoughtful, forgetful, bumbling, dryly humorous, and high-minded. She stood up, trying to shake off the influence of the Bloody Mary. Her mother would be expecting her, she said. "And I don't know what your plans are for Robyn's tea. But I made us cheese sandwiches for the train, so she's had a decent lunch, at least, and an apple and a Mars bar."

Marise was amused. "I don't have any plans for Robyn's tea. I've never really made those kinds of plans."

She stretched out, luxuriating into the extra space on the sofa, putting her boots up. Valerie meant to go looking for Robyn then, to say good-bye, but the sight of chaos in the kitchen brought her up short: dishes piled in an old sink, gas cooker filthy with grease, torn slices of bread and stained tea towels and orange peels lying on the linoleum floor where they'd been dropped. The table was still laid with plates on which some dark meat stew or sauce was congealing. She went to pick up her bag instead. "Give her my love," she said.

No one offered to show Valerie out. Heroically, like a girl in a film, she made her way alone through the next-door room, where the pale horse gleamed sinisterly; she jumped when something moved, thinking it was a flutter of stuffed birds, but it was only her own reflection in the foxed mirror. On the stairs, she remembered that she shouldn't have called it "tea." Gil was always reminding her to say "dinner" or "supper." And once she was outside, on the path in the wind, Valerie looked back, searching along the first-floor windows of the house for any sign of the child looking out. But it was impossible to see—the glass was reflecting a last smoldering streak of sunset, dark as a livid coal smashed open.

That night it snowed. Valerie woke up in the morning in her old bedroom at her mother's and knew it before she even looked outside: a purer, weightless light bloomed on the wallpaper, and the crowded muddle of gloomy furniture inherited from her grandmother seemed washed clean and self-explanatory. She opened the curtains and lay looking out at the snow falling, exhilarated as if she were back in her childhood. Her mother had the wireless on downstairs.

"Trains aren't running," she said gloatingly when Valerie came down. She was sitting smoking at the table in her housecoat, in the heat of the gas fire. "So I suppose you'll have to stay over another night."

"Oh, I don't know, Mum. I've got things to do at home."

The snow made her restless; she didn't want to be shut up with her mother all day with nothing to talk about. She found a pair of zip-up sheepskin boots at the back of a cupboard and ventured out to the phone box. Snow was blowing across the narrow street in wafting veils, and the quiet was like a sudden deafness; breaking into the crusted surface, her boots creaked. No one had come out to shovel yet, so nothing was spoiled. Every horizontal ledge and edge and rim was delicately capped; the phone box was smothered in snow, the light blue-gray inside it. She called Gil and pushed her money in, told him she was going to go to the station, find out what was happening. He said that there was snow in the North, too. He wouldn't go to the faculty meeting today; he'd work on his book at home. "Please try to get here any way you can," he said in a low, urgent voice. "He misses you."

"I have to go," she said. "There's quite a queue outside."

But there wasn't; there was only silence and the shifting vacancy. The footprints she'd made on her way there were filling up already.

"I don't know why you're so eager to get back to him," her mother grumbled. But Valerie wasn't really thinking about Gil: it was the strangeness of the snow she liked, and the disruption it caused. It took her almost an hour and a half to get to King's Cross—the Underground was working, but it was slow. When she surfaced, it had stopped snowing, at least for the moment, but there still weren't any trains. A porter said she should try again later that afternoon; it was his guess that if the weather held they might be able to reopen some of the major routes. Valerie didn't want to linger in King's Cross. She put her bag in left luggage, then thought of going shopping—they'd surely have cleared Oxford Street. But she took the Piccadilly line instead, as far as South Ken. By the time she arrived at the Chelsea house, it was gone two o'clock.

The house was almost unrecognizable at first, transformed in the snow. It seemed exposed and taller and more formidable, more mysteriously separated from its neighbors, standing apart in dense shrubbery, which was half obliterated under its burden of white. Valerie didn't even know why she'd come back. Perhaps she'd had some idea that if she saw Marise today she'd be able to behave with more sophistication, say what she really thought. As she arrived at the corner, she glanced up at the side windows on the first floor. And there was Robyn looking out—in the wrong direction at first, so that she didn't see Valerie. She seemed to be crouched on the windowsill, slumped against the glass. It was unmistakably her, because although it was past lunchtime she was still dressed in the new white pajamas.

Valerie stopped short in her tramping. Her boots were wet through. Had she seriously entertained the idea of ringing the doorbell and being invited inside again, without any reasonable pretext, into that place where she most definitely wasn't wanted? The next moment it was too late: Robyn had seen her. The child's whole body responded in a violent spasm of astonishment, almost as if she'd been looking out for Valerie, yet not actually expecting her to appear. In the whole week of her visit, she hadn't reacted so forcefully to anything. She leaped up on the windowsill, waving frantically, so that she was pressed full length against the glass. Remembering how those windows had rattled the night before, Valerie signaled to her to get down, motioning with her gloved hand and mouthing. Robyn couldn't hear her but gazed in an intensity of effort at comprehension. Valerie signaled again: Get down, be careful. Robyn shrugged, then gestured eagerly down to the front door, miming opening something. Valerie saw that she didn't have a choice. Nodding and pointing, she agreed that she was on her way around to the front. No one had trodden yet in the snow along the path, but she was lucky, the front entrance had been left open—deliberately, perhaps, because, as she stepped into the hall, a man called down, low voiced and urgent, from the top landing, "John, is that you?"

Apologizing into the dimness for not being John, Valerie hurried upstairs to where Robyn was fumbling with the latches on the other side of the purple-and-orange door. Then she heard Jamie. "Hullo! Now what are you up to? Is someone out there?"

When the door swung back, Valerie saw that—alarmingly—

Jamie was in his underpants. He was bemused rather than hostile. "What are you doing here?"

She invented hastily, hot faced, avoiding looking at his near-nakedness. "Robyn forgot something. I came to give it to her."

"I want to show her my toys," Robyn said.

He hesitated. "Her mother's lying down—she's got a headache. But you might as well come in. There's no one else for her to play with."

Robyn pulled Valerie by the hand through a door that led straight into the kitchen; someone had cleared up the plates of stew, but without scraping them—they were stacked beside the sink. The only sign of breakfast was an open packet of cornflakes on the table, and a bowl and spoon. In Robyn's bedroom, across a short passageway, there really were nice toys, better than anything Valerie had ever possessed: a doll's house, a doll's cradle with white muslin drapes, a wooden Noah's ark whose roof lifted off. The room was cold and cheerless, though, and there were no sheets on the bare mattress, only a dirty yellow nylon sleeping bag. No one had unpacked Robyn's suitcase—everything was still folded inside; she must have opened it herself to get out her pajamas. There was a chest with its drawers hanging open, and most of Robyn's clothes seemed to be overflowing from supermarket carrier bags piled against the walls.

"I knew you'd come back," Robyn said earnestly, not letting go of Valerie's hand.

Valerie opened her mouth to explain that it was only because she'd missed her train in all this weather, then she changed her mind. "We weren't expecting snow, were we?" she said brightly.

"Have you come to get me? Are you taking me to your house again?"

She explained that she'd only come to say good-bye.

"No, please don't say good-bye! Auntie Valerie, don't go."

"I'm sure you'll be coming to stay with us again soon."

The child flung herself convulsively at Valerie, punishing her passionately, butting with her head. "Not soon! Now! I want to come now!"

Valerie liked Robyn better with her face screwed into an ugly fury, kicking out with her feet, the placid brushstrokes of her brows distorted to exclamation marks. Holding her off by her shoulders, she felt the aftertremor of the child's violence.

"Do you really want to come home with me?"

"Really, really," Robyn pleaded.

"But what about your mummy?"

"She won't mind! We can get out without her noticing."

"Oh, I think we'll need to talk to her. But let's pack first. And you have to get dressed—if you're really sure, that is. We need to go back to the station to see if the trains are running." Valerie looked around with a new purposefulness, assessing quickly. "Where's your coat? Do you need the bathroom?"

Robyn sat abruptly on the floor to take off her pajamas, and Valerie tipped out the contents of the suitcase, began repacking it with a few things that looked useful—underwear and wool jumpers and shoes. The toothbrush was still in its sponge bag. Then they heard voices, and a chair knocked over in the kitchen, and, before Valerie could prepare what she ought to say, Marise came stalking into the bedroom, with Jamie behind her. At least he'd put on trousers. "How remarkable!" Marise exclaimed. "What do you think you're doing, Valerie? Are you kidnapping my child?" Wrapped in a gold silk kimono embroidered with dragons, the sooty remnants of yesterday's makeup under her eyes, she looked as formidable as a tragic character in a play.

"Don't be ridiculous," Valerie coolly said. "I'm not kidnapping her. I was about to come and find you, to ask whether she could come back with us for another week or so. And I've got a perfect right, anyway. She says that she'd prefer to be at her father's."

"I'm calling the police."

"I wouldn't if I were you. You haven't got a leg to stand on. It's criminal neglect. Look at this room! There aren't even sheets on her bed."

"She prefers a sleeping bag. Ask her!"

Frozen in the act of undressing, Robyn turned her face, blank with dismay, back and forth between the two women.

"And I'd like to know what she's eaten since she came home. There isn't any milk in the house, is there? It's two thirty in the afternoon and all the child has had since lunchtime yesterday is dry cornflakes."

"You know nothing about motherhood, nothing!" Marise shrieked. "Robyn won't touch milk—she hates it. She's been fussy from the day she was born. And she's a spy, she's a little spy! Telling tales about me. How dare she? She's a vicious, ungrateful little snake and you've encouraged her in it. I knew this would happen. I should never have let Gilbert take her in the first place. I knew he'd only be stirring her up against me. Where's he been all these years, with his so-called feelings for his daughter, I'd like to know? Jamie, get this cheap kidnapping whore out of here, won't you? No, I like whores. She's much worse, she's a *typist*."

Valerie said that she didn't need Jamie to take her anywhere, and that, if they were slinging names about, she knew what Marise was. Minutes later, she was standing outside in the garden, stopping to catch her breath beside the gate, where the dustbins were set back from the path behind a screen of pines. She was smitten with the cold and trembling, penitent and ashamed. She shouldn't have interfered; she was out of her depth. It was true that she didn't know anything about motherhood. Hadn't she encouraged Robyn, just as Marise said, trying to make the child like her? And without genuinely liking in return. Now she had abandoned her to her mother's revenge, which might be awful. Then the front door opened and Jamie was coming down the path, with a curious gloating look on his face: under his arms, against his bare chest, he was carrying the dirty yellow sleeping bag that had been on Robyn's bed. Hustling Valerie back among the pines, out of sight of the windows, he dumped the bag at her feet. "Off you go," he said significantly, as if he and Valerie were caught up in some game together. "Her mother's lying down again. Take it and get out of here."

It took her a moment or two to understand. In the meantime, he'd returned inside the house and closed the door. There was a mewing from the bag, she fumbled to unroll it, and Robyn struggled out from inside and wrapped her arms, with a fierce sigh of submission, around Valerie's knees. But she was in her white pajamas, barefoot, in the snow! How could they make their way through the streets with Robyn dressed like that? A window opened above them and Jamie lobbed out something, which landed with a soft thud on the path: one of the carrier bags from Robyn's room, packed with a miscellany of clothes—and he'd thought to add the pair of plimsolls. Then he closed the window and disappeared. There was no coat in the bag, but never mind. In panicking haste, Valerie helped Robyn put on layers of clothes over her pajamas: socks, cord trousers, plimsolls, jumper.

"I thought he was going to eat me," Robyn said.

"Don't be silly," Valerie said firmly. She kicked the sleeping bag away out of sight, among the hedge roots.

"Are we escaping?"

"We're having an adventure."

And they set out, ducking into the street, hurrying along beside the hedge. By a lucky chance, as soon as they got to the main road there was a taxi nosing through the slush. "How much to King's Cross?" Valerie asked. She had all the money she'd been saving up to spend on a new dress. She'd have to buy Robyn a train ticket, too. Then she asked the taxi to stop at a post office, where she went inside to send a telegram. She couldn't telephone Gil; she knew he'd forbid her to bring the child back again. But she couldn't arrive with Robyn without warning him. "Returning

with daughter," she wrote out on the form. "No fit home for her."
She counted out the shillings from her purse.

Back in the taxi, making conversation, she asked Robyn where
her dollies were. Robyn was stricken—she'd left them behind,
under her pillow. It was dusk in the streets already: as they drove
on, the colored lights from the shops wheeled slowly across their
faces, revealing them as strangers to each other. Valerie was thinking that she might need to summon all this effort of ingenuity
one day for some escape of her own, dimly imagined, and that
taking on the child made her less free. Robyn sat forward on the
seat, tensed with her loss. Awkwardly, Valerie put an arm around
her, to reassure her. She said not to worry, they would make new
dolls, and better ones. Just for the moment, though, the child was
inconsolable.

John Keeble

Synchronicity

WHEN I CAME INTO THE KITCHEN, Ward was using a knife to help his wife, Irene, peel the skin from two buffalo tongues. The skin was discarded in a small heap along with the glutinous veins cut from the undersides, then Ward left it to Irene to cut the meat into cubes. He pulled out a chair opposite me at the table in the dining area and opened up a John Deere repair manual, which was my reason for being there, and began thumbing through it. Meanwhile, Irene put the cubes into a cast-iron Dutch oven and seared them. She added butter, garlic, onion, white wine, and spices, causing me to grow alert to aromas. Besides garlic and onion, I picked out the scents of rosemary, oregano, and something else I couldn't identify. A pressure cooker slowly heated up on a back burner, and on the counter beside Irene stood ranks of quart mason jars.

Irene turned down the heat under the Dutch oven, placed a lid on it, moved out of the cooking area to a niche in the wall, and sat on a stool. She wiped her hands on her apron and reached up to the back of her head, adjusting the clip on her bun.

"Buffalo," she said. "So this is what it comes to. All for my sister."

"I'm sorry," Ward said. His voice sounded dismayed, which was not typical of him, though he'd been showing more of it lately: dismay, even distress, with the world.

I surmised that it wasn't canning buffalo tongues that made him sorry. Under the circumstances, he was probably glad Irene was doing that. Rather, he was sorry that the meat had come to be available at all, that these tongues had been selected from the two formerly angry buffalo that now lay in neatly stacked white packages in the cold of their freezers. He was also sorry that the three-month saga with Irene's sister and brother-in-law, Jenna and Leland, had come to a head the way it had.

And that wasn't all. Ward, like most everybody else in these parts, was on edge over the drought and the wildfires that had been ravaging our state that summer. Though we had so far been spared the burning, the winds carried the smoke into our valley. The ridgeline of the canyon below our house was barely visible, and Irene and Ward's place, set under a hill just to the north, often vanished in a sullen pool of smoke and dust.

"I guess you'll have to show more discretion about helping Leland out, generous and competent as you are. Or stay out of trouble by keeping completely clear of misanthropes like him," Irene said. The dimples in her cheeks deepened when she glanced at me and smiled. "I don't mean you. You're no trouble."

"Leland exaggerates," Ward said. "That's all I can say."

"He's got a screw loose."

"Hmm," Ward murmured.

"It's my sister," Irene went on. "It's her I'm worried about. She's the only one I care about in this thing. But what does she mean that God is in the trees and rocks of the world, in every animal and plant? Or when she says he's not called God anymore, but Goddess? She's certainly taken on some wild ideas since she and Leland moved to Montana."

Ward sighed. "Honey, she had to be working on those ideas before they moved."

There was an edginess to this exchange, and despite Irene's exempting me from the misanthropes of the world, I began to wonder if I should leave. I had come up to ask Ward about a mundane thing, the steering-fluid leak in my tractor, a late-fifties John Deere 720. That was all. Ward had a tractor like it. Irene might have doubted his competence when it came to assessing certain types of people, but when it came to animals, machinery, the farm implements that I regularly borrowed, nobody questioned Ward's judgment. Earlier in his life, he had been a mechanic for Union Pacific, then for the Air National Guard. I'd never come across anyone who could diagnose a machine's problems as he did, often by listening to it run, sometimes by clambering up on the engine with a stethoscope and listening to the innards turn on themselves.

Most of his equipment was thirty years old. In other ways too, Ward and Irene seemed content to inhabit a time warp. They didn't have an answering machine on their landline and had no cell phone. They avoided computers. They lived close to the way they'd been raised, both of them having emerged from hardscrabble farm families whose grandparents had journeyed west during the Dust Bowl. Every Saturday, Irene did her shopping at the air force commissary, and every Sunday she went off to the Methodist church in a town nearby. She had her routines of baking, cooking, washing, and cleaning, and her life and Ward's, too, had a deep-seated sobriety and intactness. No wonder she felt that her sister, who was now living in an underground compound among celestially oriented Blackfoot rock piles, had slipped off the deep end.

Ward looked down at the service manual. "My guess is you'll have to pull the pump," he said. "Replace the hoses. As long as you've got the pump out, you might as well replace the bearings too. And there are the O-rings on the water lines."

"To get at the pump, I'll have to take the grille off too, right?" I said. "And the cowling? Do I have to take the radiator out?"

"You'll have to drain it and slide it out of the way." He pushed the manual across the table and pointed to a picture that showed the pump and the radiator levered all the way to the front of the tractor. He put his finger on another picture. "You'll have to pull the steering wheel and steering shaft too, and take down the worm-gear housing."

Ten miles to the south is the air base where Ward plied his mechanical skills for more than two decades. Twenty miles east is the city of Spokane, Washington, and just beyond it, the Idaho Panhandle, and then Montana. Fifty miles to the north are the Kettle mountains, and nestled against them is the town of Cusick, which had freshly emerged in our consciousness because of the broken-loose Kalispel buffalo—not the frozen bodies formerly linked by integument to Irene's tongues but nine or ten others. To the west, the land sinks slowly through a desolate high desert that ends at the Columbia River. There we find Russian thistle, skeletonweed, leafy spurge, and Dalmatian toadflax, among other noxious European transplants, and also the ubiquitous native sagebrush, and fescue, or bunchgrass, and in late June the exquisite yellow flowers of the northernmost cactus on the continent, *Opuntia fragilis*. It's true that much of that land is now irrigated from the Columbia River project and grows fodder mainly for livestock—lentils, alfalfa, timothy, field corn—but north of it, then arcing back eastward in our direction, is the coulee country where the fires yet burned.

Ward and Irene are dryland farmers. So are my wife and I—after a fashion, since we own what some disdainfully call a "hobby farm." We usually get between eighteen and twenty-one inches of annual precipitation, just enough to sustain our alfalfa fields and the ponderosa pines that grow on slopes leading down to the canyon.

But now we're in the second year of high temperatures and drought. The pine engraver beetle has moved up from its native habitat in California and Oregon. Pine trees are dying, and in places our woods are a quilt-work of green and brown: more tinder. At runoffs we have Douglas fir, willow, hawthorn, aspen, and some alder, and then the elderberry, serviceberry, red currant, and plum. A few of these wild fruit bearers grow near the house, where my wife has nurtured them, making sure there's space between the plants to give them room to grow. This year, the fruit came early and was desiccated. The bushes changed color prematurely. Birds that feed on the fruit moved on early.

Of necessity, we abide by what is called "farmer's time," which some also call "Indian time," depending on who's using the term and what their intent is. What it means is that one performs a certain duty or arrives at an agreed-on place when obligations permit. Though some city dwellers extol the "simplicity" of life here, tasks can grow complicated even for hobby farmers when something, such as my tractor, needs repair. Or when our cows, restless for green pasture, break out of their fence in the springtime. Or when one of them has a countermanded birth, like the heifer we discovered earlier this spring walking in circles in our corral, one of its calf's legs poking out of its hindquarters.

Ward came to help us, bringing down chains, a calf jack, and a ratchet. Once we had the heifer in the squeeze chute and Ward had stuffed the calf's leg back in, repositioning it, he hooked the chains around the legs and ratcheted the calf slowly out, timing it according to the heifer's contractions. The calf discharged and fell, thudding against the ground, and Ward bent over it and cleared the afterbirth from around its nostrils.

The calf didn't make it. Turned loose, the bereaved heifer went for Ward, but he leaped away, ending up next to my wife and me behind a panel. For a moment, the heifer glared at Ward, then resumed licking her dead calf. Such was the inauspicious beginning to the growing season—the first thing that happened. I came to believe the calf had the power of omens and that its mother, the heifer, put a curse on the summer that was to follow. My wife and

I began calling the heifer Lady Macbeth. "Out, damned spot!" we would exclaim at her. "Out, I say!"

Back in May, before the weather changed, before the drought, before the fires, and just a couple of weeks after we lost the calf, Ward acquired two buffalo. I happened to be up at his place returning a harrow I'd borrowed to knock down the gopher mounds in my fields. He was pulling out with the heaviest of his stock trailers and he asked if I could come along. He was taking the trailer, he said, to help out Irene's brother-in-law, Leland, with a pair of buffalo bulls he'd bought. "I'm glad you turned up. I could use another hand."

"Certainly," I said. I called my wife to tell her what I was doing and climbed into Ward's truck. This was before Leland and Jenna moved. I'd met them only a few times. Jenna bore a resemblance to Irene, though she was younger. Leland seemed a nice enough fellow, if a little lost, his shining eyes peering out of his face as if out of a jail cell.

"I think he's got himself into a pickle." Ward turned out of his driveway onto a gravel road. "He says he had the buffalo delivered and released into a circle of panels he'd set up in his front yard. But then he discovered the two buffalo crossing the road. They put their heads down and just walked off, panels and all." Ward chuckled. "Seems he didn't think about securing the panels to the ground. Then later he called again and said that a bunch from the Kalispel herd happened by and got his two excited. Have you heard about the loose bunch of Kalispel buffalo?"

Indeed I had. They'd been in the news. "I haven't heard anything about their coming down this way, though I guess they could have."

"Right," Ward said. "He says the Kalispel buffalo made off and his two followed them as far as a neighbor's field."

The Kalispel are an entrepreneurial tribe, and among their

projects is a buffalo herd. I had admired their fences, which I remembered as impressive five-wire affairs pulled tight with wooden posts set every eight feet. The buffalo must have broken out, or a gate had been left open. Soon after, it was reported that the buffalo wreaked havoc everywhere they went. Ordinary fences meant nothing to them. The sight of riders on horseback or on ATVs enraged them, and they lowered their heads to charge fence after fence, barbed wire, split rail, treated posts, even steel posts buried in concrete. It didn't matter. They'd gotten inside a barn and, when come upon by the farmer, crashed right through a wall.

Though we didn't know it yet, the loose Kalispel herd was the second thing that happened that season. The third thing was their running wild.

We drove north to Leland's place and found him standing out front, looking down the road at the two young bulls that had stopped in the alfalfa field. They were buffalo all right, and by now had dragged the twelve-by-five panels, which were still connected by chains, into a long rectangle with themselves at its head. They seemed content, pulling up the plants. Leland wore a bright yellow shirt, Wrangler jeans, and a pair of new Western-style boots. Behind him was the doorway to his house, where Jenna stood in a long, frilly white dress, her eyes like distant smudges, staring out at nothing I could discern.

"Is she all right?" I said.

Ward looked at her and muttered, "Jenna? Don't know if she's all right. We never know."

He pulled up and Leland came over to the truck, picking up his conversation where it had been left off. "I wondered if maybe they're from the same herd. It's like the Kalispel buffalo were lost and came to find two more of their own. But I've got a bill of sale that says otherwise."

I slid over to make room for Leland, and Ward headed for the bulls, driving into the field. Leland and I got out when he stopped. I walked toward the panels and gave hand signals for

Ward to back in, all the time warily eyeing the buffalo, which were the color of smoke. Ward stopped when the trailer came near the panels. He set the brake, walked to the rear of the trailer, and opened the door. The buffalo backed up. Ward undid the chains that held two panels together and slid one panel toward me, keeping both of them close against the trailer, making a rudimentary chute.

"Hold it," he told me. "Don't let them out. Don't give them time to think about it. But if they come through, get out of the way." He grinned, propped his panel in place, and circled around behind the bulls.

The two buffalo surprised us by looking around almost mischievously, first back at Ward, then up at Leland, who had moved to the side of the truck cab, and finally at me. Then, without any warning, they stormed into the trailer, crashing against the walls as they went. Ward shoved a panel aside, jumped in after them, and slammed the middle gate shut, so that the buffalo were secure in the front of the trailer, then he piled out. I closed the rear door, and he jerked down the latch and secured it. One buffalo grew furious, having discovered, I figured, that the trailer was not the tunnel to freedom that it was expecting. It turned and began ferociously kicking the side of the trailer. Up front I glimpsed Leland edging closer to the truck door while Ward scrutinized the buffalo through a slat. The buffalo kicked the side again.

Wham!

Ward pulled away. "Spike bulls," he said. "Maybe a little over a year old. They're full of vinegar, but I'd have to say that was a lot easier than I was afraid it might be."

Leland stayed where he was. "I guess they're safe in there."

"Safe?" Ward said.

"I guess I mean us. We're safe." Leland lifted a hand. "I just wanted the two. Then I heard about those others out of the Kalispel herd. They've gone over the state line. They're making their way up the Idaho Panhandle, clean over the line toward Priest

Lake. It's like . . ." As if he found himself suddenly exhausted, his voice trailed off and his hand floated down to his side.

"Synchronicity," I interjected.

"That's it," Leland said, his voice rising. "Way too much of it."

Ward squinted at me as if to say, I doubt Leland knows what that word means. When I considered it, I wasn't entirely sure what it meant, either: something to do with the paranormal. And thinking that, I realized I'd had a rush of adrenaline when the buffalo went into the trailer. Now I felt short of breath and my hands were trembling. I thought further that synchronicity brought the paranormal within the bounds of intelligibility. It was a question of things falling together in time, a kind of simultaneity, like Leland's two buffalo and the Kalispel herd. That was it. Two things connected by meaning, not by cause and effect.

Ward spoke to Leland. "I thought you were planning to move."

"We are," Leland said. "We were planning to rent a trailer and take the two buffalo with us." Then, affecting savoir faire, he said, "Maybe breed them."

When Ward squinted again, more fiercely than before and turning his gaze on Leland now, Leland's eyes began to shine and dance about furtively. "They're more unruly than I thought," he said. "Maybe it'd be best if you took them for now." He bent over to dust off his boots with a red handkerchief, but stood bolt upright in alarm when a buffalo kicked the side of the trailer again.

Wham!

Leland gripped the door handle. "You'll have to watch out for that other bunch in case they come looking again."

"Hmm," Ward murmured. "They came from where?"

"From up there." Leland gestured to the north.

"Nine or ten of them, you say? There's no sign."

Leland's look grew ghostly. "They were here all right, believe me, jumbling up on each other."

Wham!

Ward and I drove Leland back to the house. Jenna was absent

from the doorway, though it was still open. To one side, the corner of a curtain dropped over a window. I had to slide out to let Leland climb down from the cab, and I spied something I hadn't noticed before. He wore a silver belt buckle in the shape of a buffalo's head, with two bits of glass for eyes. It was like a token, an amulet.

On the drive back to his place, Ward said he didn't believe Leland for a minute about the Kalispel herd. "And he's scared to death of the two."

"Well, yes." I said nothing about seeing Leland stand aside during the loading, not lending a hand, or about the rush of adrenaline he must have shared with me, or about his fancy boots and silver belt buckle. I left those things where they were. I let Ward's comment about not believing Leland alone too, though I was inclined to agree with him while also wondering why he indulged Leland so. It seemed a tangle, a family thing well beyond my ken. I did say I was glad that Ward hadn't given me any more chance to think than he gave the two bulls.

Ward chuckled. "Yeah, we were lucky."

We unloaded the buffalo into the corral where Ward kept his Charolais bull during the winter. It had just been moved to summer pasture along with the cows. Built from extra-heavy planks, the corral opened up to a feeder, also built from heavy planks and reinforced with steel diagonals. Ward's bull, and now the buffalo bulls, had to turn their heads to get at the feed, a stratagem designed to minimize the amount of hay that fell to the ground. So began the three and a half months of Ward's possession of the two young buffalo, which became the fourth dire thing that happened that summer. It was followed by a fifth, the drought that brought us failed crops, and then we had the sixth thing, the fires that began as singular conflagrations but soon mushroomed into hundred-square-mile complexes, fires joining fires, tearing through the central and northern parts of the state. They were of their own energy and created their own weather—windstorms, fireballs bursting like bombs in midair, flames ripping up slopes—all of it seeming like some massive preparation for the death of oxygen-breathing creatures and the next great age of plants.

The corral's feeder faced a passageway along the edge of Ward's equipment barn. I checked on the buffalo every now and again when I came by to pick up or return an implement. It goes without saying that I kept my distance. The increasingly menacing demeanor of the pair discouraged me from getting too close, even while outside the corral, and from standing directly in front of them. Every time, they would move to the back of the corral, as if they knew I was going to watch them. Sometimes, if he was there, Ward came out and we would stand off to the side and discuss how much they had grown: Their knee joints were now more proportionate to the rest of their bodies. Their hair was luxurious and had begun to change to the straw color I remembered seeing on adults.

After three months had passed, I was returning a disc I'd borrowed. I parked and unhooked it from my tractor, then walked over to the corral. Ward joined me. He was just back from Montana, as I would learn. We came up the alleyway that fronted the corral and surprised the buffalo as they ate out of the feeder. They turned their heads and pulled free, banging against the steel diagonals. The bigger one backed clear up to the rear of the corral, not taking its eyes off us. The other looped around and ended up standing next to the first one, facing us in the same posture and attitude. In this manner they may have granted us our position of dominance, but suddenly the bigger one whipped its head back and forth, giving notice that it could break away in a flash, trampling whatever stood in its way. The other was sure to follow. Instinctively, Ward and I moved to the side, increasing the angulation between us and them.

A few weeks before, Ward had put a medicine ball in the corral. "To give them something to do," he had said. At first, still mischievous on occasion, they would lapse into a playful mode, kicking or butting the ball, but soon they stopped doing that. Now the ball lay flattened in a corner.

Irene, meanwhile, had come to fear the very sight of the buffalo. I heard her telling Ward that they darkened the whole yard, that their ominous presence overshadowed everything: the arena, the birthing corral, the haystacks, the fenced-off portion where the cows were to be kept when they returned, the repair shed, even where she parked the car at the back of the house.

"The truth is," Ward told me, "I've grown kind of fond of those buffalo. I wish I could keep them, but I'd have to build a fence that would hold them. If they broke loose, they'd probably run into a car, or vanish into the fires. Somebody could get hurt. And I'd be liable for any damage they caused. Like the Kalispels. I figure they ended up paying for all the destroyed fences and that barn."

I didn't say anything, wondering whether Ward might be edging toward the same thrall that had sucked Leland in.

The fires were rapaciously feeding on one another: the Okanogan Complex, the Chelan Complex, the Stevens County Complex, the Clark Fork Complex. There were more fires in Oregon, and it appeared that California was in the throes of suffocation, about to be wiped out. The Kalispel buffalo had run free for a month or so, but just as the media began to pay less attention to them, somebody reported that they'd been sighted way up north, vanishing into the smoke of the Okanogan Complex. Ten days later, four buffalo carcasses were found. Their feet had been burned clean off to the ankles and the bodies charred. The rest of the herd was never found, but it was hoped that they had made it to the border and tricked their way through the fancy gates and underpasses for elk, moose, sheep, and deer that the Canadians had constructed along their highways.

Ward took out a pocketknife and began whittling a stick. He leaned forward and contemplated the buffalo. The bigger one lifted its head, though otherwise they both stood frozen in their spots, eyes filled with abject distrust.

"Just look at the black pelage on their underbellies and the insides of their thighs. And the tail tufts," Ward mused. "And the thighs themselves, how big they've become. The humps beginning to fill out, the spikes starting to curve inward."

He said he had traveled to Montana for Irene's sake, to check on Jenna for her, to see whether Jenna and Leland needed bailing out yet. He said he guessed they didn't. Leland still wanted the buffalo, but hadn't done anything about getting a place ready to keep them. "I don't understand it," Ward said. "Does he really want them? He'll have to feed them too, you know, and watch after them."

There were other people living there, what Ward said Leland called a coven. They all inhabited a large underground complex dug into a hill. "It seems to me that they are plain old survivalists," he said, "but Jenna insists they have a new faith. She calls it Natural New Paganism. She showed me an altar with candles, a statue, and a set of buffalo horns." Ward shrugged. "I don't know."

He described the underground complex that was meant to protect them from fallout, from anything but a direct nuclear hit. The entryways were built around ninety-degree corners with two scallop-shaped constructions engineered to deflect blast concussions. "I have to admit it's impressive," he said. "They're pretty carefully installed."

He hunkered down and used his stick to draw a picture in the dust. "First you have a passage coming face-to-face with a large scallop, like an abalone shell placed on a smaller abalone shell. Then *that* one is placed on a smaller one yet, and on and on." Ward drew it in the dust. "They're beautiful in a way, made from cast steel coated with ceramic." He stood up beside me and gazed down at his drawing.

I saw that Ward was confused. He wasn't sure how to pit his old-school perceptions against a meticulous installation that was to serve as a last line of defense against the end of the world.

Ward gave a detailed account of how the group fed themselves. They hunted deer, antelope, elk, and chukar. But they had underground nurseries too, and grow lights powered by generators, which in turn were powered by a methane well, the whole business run by a computer system. Leland told him they were developing retractable antiaircraft guns, modifying them to shoot down the drones they believed were sure to come.

"It's their new thing," Ward said. "The hill they built the compound on had piles of stones—they call them petroforms. Jenna says they align with celestial plotting. She was talkative for once, walking me around, showing me how the petroforms line up with constellations and stars: Beta Orionis, Alpha Orionis, the North Star, Ursa Minor. There are also circles of stones that the Blackfeet used in the old days to weigh down the skirts of their tepees. The Blackfoot people were chosen. They knew. That's what Jenna says. She believes in what she calls the Rule of Three, or some such nonsense. The energy one puts into the world will be returned threefold. Whatever."

Ward gave me his characteristic squint. "I don't know what it means. Then she says, 'One can only hope.' Hope! Can you believe it?"

This is the seventh thing. I did not witness it, but was informed of it by Ward when I met him in his farmyard.

A couple of weeks after his return from Montana, he got up one morning and went out to discover the two buffalo outside the pen, right there in the turnaround in his driveway. He saw the gate to the corral open behind them: not broken, he said, just jimmied open. He made an effort to shy them that way, shifting his weight and lifting his arms, but the two kept advancing toward him, and the one lowered its head again.

He backed away and headed cautiously for the open bay door of his repair shed, where he kept his .30-06 rifle. The buffalo held their ground and turned with Ward as if he were a gudgeon and they the pins, or like a large fan, they the blades and he the nubbin. He remembered marveling at how smoothly they moved, supplely, as if they were lubricated. He slipped through the doorway, took up his gun, and saw the two had followed him to the doorway and stood in the opening. They were silent.

Again, he made a last attempt to shy them in the direction of the corral, but they wouldn't budge. "I saw I had no choice," he said. "First I shot the biggest one, the more aggressive. It went down, and the second turned tail up the driveway and toward the road. It reached the turnaround, right up there," he said, gesturing. "It stopped to look back, and I shot it. It went down, too. I got my tractor with the loader, moved them next to each other, field-dressed them, then loaded them in my truck and took them to the butcher."

I looked up the driveway. A monolithic cloud of black smoke roiled in the sky and blotted out the sun beyond the trees. Dark, suddenly it was dark as twilight, although it was only three o'clock in the afternoon. Ward's breath shuddered and I could have sworn that his eyes filled with tears. "I hated to do it. What other alternative did I have? I called Leland and Jenna to let them know." He paused, then looked up at the smoke and laughed grimly. "Leland said he wishes I'd of checked with him first."

That was nearly a month ago, and here I sat at Ward and Irene's kitchen table. Irene had got up to spoon the chunks and sauce from the buffalo tongues into jars, carefully place the jars inside the pressure cooker, and put the lid and the weight on. The cooker began to hiss. I imagined the pieces of buffalo tongue talking inside there, as if the chunks had recomposed to tell their version of the story.

Irene spooned the last of the meat into the remaining jars. She would have to do two processes to finish. I finally came to recognize the ingredient I hadn't been able to place: anise. It gave the meat an almost metallic scent. "Anise," I said. "You put that in too."

Ward had pulled the manual back to him and was studying it. He said, "You'll probably have to check the play in the spindle. Like most everything else, they didn't think too hard about taking things apart when they first put them together. It seems to be the way of the world, organized just fine so long as it keeps on running." He evinced a faint smile, as if he were being preyed on. "When something breaks and you have to stop and fix it, I guess you're in all kinds of trouble anymore."

"Sure," I said, "but fixing things is what you're best at. I can tell it gives you pleasure."

Irene turned to me, running one hand across her apron.

"Yes," she said. "Anise. We'll keep a few jars and give the rest to Jenna if she wants to come visit. Leland be damned, he can take what's frozen if he wants. But buffalo tongues are a great delicacy, you know. Maybe that will make Jenna happy."

Moira McCavana

No Spanish

I

WHEN I WAS TWELVE, when we still lived in that small, moldering farmhouse in the hills behind Guernica, my father outlawed Spanish from our household. Like a dictator, he stood at the head of our family table and yelled, "*No* Spanish, *NO SPANISH*!" waving his arms as though he were helming his own national uprising. "We will all forget about that language, is that clear?"

These demands, of course, he had delivered in Spanish, though not one of us had rushed to correct him. It was evidence that he, like us, spoke nothing else. To abandon Spanish would be to abandon the language in which all of our well-intentioned but still tenuous relationships had been built. It was like removing our field of gravity, our established mode of relating to each other. Without Spanish, it seemed entirely possible that one of us might spin out into space. How were we supposed to tell each other practical things? *Keep out of that corner; I've just spilled water and it's slippery. Hold the door; I have too many things in my arms. Please, just leave me alone. Please, don't even touch me.*

It's obvious to me now that for my father, this impulsive vow to speak only in Basque functioned as a sort of double agent: a radical act of political defiance masquerading as farce. When his lips split in a wily smile and his eyes flickered, I felt as though he were signing us up for a ridiculous play. On that first evening I was already calculating how soon I might be able to drop out.

Several days into our experiment, when he banished my brother to sleep outside for speaking Spanish offhandedly, we still didn't really believe him. My mother and I watched in silence as he pulled my brother's bedding from his mattress, and then we all followed him around to the back of the house. Until he set my brother's comforter down on the grass, his pillow at the head of it, I had been sure that he'd been joking.

Julen's makeshift bed that night had been placed right beneath my window, and I remember sticking my head out over him when we had all gone off to bed. Because my parents' bedroom was next to mine, we couldn't risk speaking, so instead we exchanged a series of faces, beginning with *Our father has gone crazy.* Later, after we ran out of faces to make, and after a long period of just staring at each other, he fell asleep. At some point, the moon came across his face, and I watched for a while as all the lines of approaching adulthood became more pronounced. My brother was older than me by seven years and three months. Sometimes I wished that he were my father.

My brother was allowed to sleep in the house the next night, but his slipup had signaled to my father that we would need to actually learn our new language if we were ever to abandon Spanish successfully. On Monday, he drove us all into Guernica to go to the market, and there he led us straight to a booth in the back where a pair of homely older women stood behind a table piled high with antique electronics. We were all embarrassed by the way my father, in his fledgling Basque, bartered with the women over the price of various old radios that he held up before them.

"Three!" he proclaimed, with a rusted radio in hand, and one of the women responded with a sentence that sounded like pure static.

My father deflated a little. "Four?" he asked, innocently.

Eventually one of the women said to him, "Thank you, sir, for your efforts, but maybe we should stick to Spanish for the moment." She gestured to the radio and the few coins I held in my hand to pay for it. "For doing this."

"*Me cago en Dios*," my father had hissed without thinking about it, and immediately he brought his hands up to his mouth in embarrassment—not for the swear ("I shit on God"), but for his instinctive deference to our banned language. The light in his eyes sputtered out and he fled, walking hurriedly around all of the vendors, picking his feet up high to avoid crates of string beans and stacks of folded used clothing. We had to pay for the radio for him, choosing the most modern-looking one, and letting the woman pick through our change, until she had collected what she determined it cost.

I think even my mother must have felt like an orphan standing before those women, disturbed as we were by the momentary loss of my father and what looked like the permanent loss of a language that we had never realized we might have loved.

I should be clear about this: to speak Basque was against the law. Of course, in some towns it was flaunted freely, even in the street. There was a certain social capital attached to speaking Basque, and an additional bonus, which I'm sure would translate into any language, if you could do so without giving a fuck. But it was still, in the eyes of our ruthless leader, illegal. And how strictly the ban was reinforced varied with the ferocity of the local Civil Guard. In some towns, it was a hand to the throat. Elsewhere, your head into water. Across the river, near where my mother used to take us swimming, you stopped going to school, or work, then church, then disappeared. But I didn't know much about that when we were back in the farmhouse. On the day of his big announcement, and in one of our last conversations together in Spanish, my father explained to me only the simple overarching facts: our ruthless leader was General Franco. Our Spain—and we—were his.

"Franco doesn't want us to speak our own language because he says that in Spain, everyone should speak Spanish," my father had explained.

"Well, that makes a little bit of sense," I said. He recoiled. "Doesn't it?"

"Ana, we are our own people."

"Okay."

"A lot of people think that we should be our own country."

"Okay." At this point he was no longer waving his arms. He was sitting down at his place at the head of the table and was crumpling and uncrumpling the napkin in front of him.

"We can't give our language over to them," he said. He was bent over the table, all the earlier bravado drained from his body. My brother and my mother stayed, petrified, in their seats, but I went to my father and put my arms around him.

After a while I said, "It's just that it's hard to feel like it's my language since I've never spoken it, Papi."

My father kissed the crown of my head and thumbed his clumsy fingers through my hair. I watched my mother and Julen fidget nervously across the table, and in that moment I felt a little like a victor for the rest of us. Then my father brought his hand to the back of my neck and squeezed it, a sign of affection that I always pretended to hate. We had our routine: each time he did it I would bob my head furiously, attempting to free myself, while he would let out a series of squawks, transforming me into some kind of theatrical bird. If I was feeling generous, I would thrash around a bit more for his entertainment.

This time the charade ended like it normally did, with my surrendering to him in a torrent of giggles, and everyone else joining in too, though my father quit before the rest of us. Without moving, or raising his voice, he brought his eyes up to mine and said calmly, "*Aita*. That's what you will call me now." In his face, any sign of apology was drowned in newfound resolve.

If we had been more prudent, maybe we would have been nervous about teaching ourselves a banned language, but it was not as if we could speak enough to ever set the Civil Guard after us. It was not as if we could even have a full conversation. For the first week or so, our pathetic vocabularies barely overlapped. I think we all assumed that at some point we would speak a word that someone else knew, and so it became a game, a test of our faith, to continue an exchange without revealing the meaning of whatever words we had spoken to the other person.

On the second or third day of our exile from Spanish, while I was eating breakfast, my mother came into the kitchen and spoke a string of sounds that I didn't understand. When I stared at her blankly, she bobbed her head around a bit as though to say, *You know these words, don't think too hard about it*. I raised my eyebrows, waiting for her to surrender to pantomiming whatever it was that she had meant, but instead she pulled her arms into her sides as though bound in a body bag, shot raised eyebrows right back at me, and then slunk slowly out of the room.

It became our silent joke, our laughless gag. Julen adopted it too, pinning his arms to his sides in defense when our blank reactions clued him in to the fact that he had spoken a sentence we didn't know. Imagine the stupid words we taunted ourselves with: *beans, bottom, salt, ear, fingernail, onion, sock.*

At that point, Julen had finished high school and I was in the middle of my summer break, and so during the endless stretch of those first wordless days, our hours became bent around breaking each other's resolve. Even when my mother pretended to be busy frying peppers or tending to our languishing garden, she would at any moment be ready to sprint after us and pry our hands from our sides if someone came up behind her and whispered *belarritik*.

From the moment we returned from the market, my father had planted himself at the kitchen table, and there, he took to repairing the radio. If we had been using Spanish, he probably would have declared something like, "*Esas malditas mujeres . . .* can you believe them? Selling me junk that doesn't even work," but after his slipup, he was careful to uphold his own rules. Instead he suffered silently, and upon this initial bed of frustration piled up layers of small annoyances as he struggled to make any headway with the repair. Each time he thought that he had made some mistake he plunged into a hysterical cough and slapped his hand against the table, as though he had crossed some wires in his own body instead. During lulls in the game, we watched his strange behavior from our various perches: the top landing of the stairs, or outside, crouched beneath a window. When he tested it, and finally a tiny sound curled from the radio's speaker, he pounded the table so violently that he left a spiderweb of cracks in the wood.

Reluctantly, we emerged from the shadows and hidden corners of the house to join him, and as I neared the radio, distinct voices separated out from the static. They hung there in our kitchen as though they were our own familial ghosts. Even after years—my whole life—living in the Basque Country, I still pinpoint that night as the first time I really heard our language. I still remember how my father's eyes blazed wildly in the settling darkness. My mother put a kind hand to his back, but she looked pained. It was clear that it was the end of our game.

We all stayed around the radio for so long that night that I actually fell asleep right there, lying beneath the table, with my head upon my father's feet. I woke up some time later, alone in the empty kitchen, my body splayed upon the floor.

Over the course of the next week, we gathered for three to four hours each day to listen, hoping to absorb whatever we could. My father perched himself over a blank sheet of paper and armed with a pen, he scrambled to copy down phrases as they spilled from the speaker, but they came out rapidly, and he was always left clawing after the end of the previous sentence while a new one dawned. And then there was the problem of no one's knowing if whatever combination of letters he put to the page existed at all.

When it became clear that the radio was a failure—that it would never teach us any real Basque—my mother took to mimicking the woman that we always heard on the Basque news station. Like the announcer, she would say *arratsalde on*, in a delicate female newscaster voice, poised with clasped hands upon the table, and then she would continue her fake broadcast, beginning with the random words that we all had learned when we finally pooled our vocabularies, and then devolving into a series of ugly, made-up sounds. She once contorted her throat so extremely that she sent herself into a choking fit. Julen had rushed up and smacked her on the back until she regained control. Spit had dribbled down her chin.

My father never applauded at the end of these performances.

I have not shared any more about that early period of my childhood or the hours spent chasing my brother around the grounds of the farmhouse, because it does not belong here. But if it's important to know anything else about that time, know this: every night, the sun set behind us (it seemed like it was right behind us), and though it's simple, it's the truth: we were happy.

That period ended abruptly with my father's announcement that we would be moving into the nearby tavern, where he had found a job as the bookkeeper and general manager of the downstairs restaurant, my mother a job as a hostess, and guest rooms on the third floor of the upstairs hotel for all of us. "And better yet," he went on, "the man who has hired me speaks perfect Basque, and so does the entire staff. We're offered complimentary lessons every Sunday afternoon between the lunch and dinner shifts, which means that this," he said, his whole face aflame, "will be the last time you'll ever hear me speak Spanish."

Would you believe me if I said that I hadn't even realized it? That the initial shock of his announcing that he had quit his job at the shipyard had distracted me completely from the language? I hadn't even recognized that of course he was speaking in Spanish until he mentioned it himself, but by then he had finished his announcement—at the end, I think he even bowed—and he was already silent, sitting down.

My mother and I found each other on the staircase later, when my father was asleep, and though I suppose we could have spoken Spanish, we didn't. Julen discovered us when he got up in the middle of the night to go to the bathroom, and stayed with us until we all departed in the early morning.

II

The walls of the Ibarra Tavern were plastered with purple wallpaper that slouched away from the molding in some places, like the last dying petals of a flower. When we arrived, a week after my father had made his announcement, we were greeted by the tavern owner in the foyer, and he paraded us through the whole ground floor with our suitcases still in hand. On the tour, he spoke to us in rapid Basque, but he gestured enthusiastically enough so that I was fairly sure I understood what he was pointing out: the range of wines on tap at the bar, the lacquered wood paneling that reached midway up the wall of the dining room, the corner of the room that could be closed off for private events, and the curtains, egg-yolk orange, that made the whole room glow as though it were the inner core of the sun when, toward the end of the day, the afternoon bent its longest beams of light to the tavern floor. In the kitchen, the new industrial-strength dishwasher, the steel countertops for food preparation, the pots and pans and cooking utensils that dangled from the ceiling, and the profusion of eggs, milk, and meat stacked in the fridge.

Upstairs in our rooms, my father repeated one of the few phrases in Basque we had all learned from the radio, *oso ondo*, which translated literally as "very good." "*Oso ondo?*" he posed to us all, and then he repeated it over again to himself as he climbed into a bed that my mother had made a moment before. He whacked the mattress with both hands, grinning as they rebounded with each effort. "Very good," he squealed. "Very, *very* good!"

The next afternoon, Julen and I padded around the upstairs floors, exploring what we hadn't been shown on Mr. Ibarra's tour. From down in the lobby, there was the distant chatter of a new group checking in. Julen pushed lightly on the nearest door and it opened to reveal a room identical to ours, with two twin beds sticking out from the wall. We both had the idea at the same time to swipe the pillows from the head of the mattress, place them at the foot, and then turn back the covers accordingly so that it looked like all the beds had been set up for guests' heads to rest where their feet should have been; to loll about exposed and defenseless in the center of the room.

When we entered the rest of the rooms on the floor to switch around the beds, we found them all unoccupied, except for the one at the end of the hall, where we found the tavern owner's wife, naked, her drooping body framed perfectly in the outline of the door.

To make up for our misconduct, we were given our first jobs at the tavern.

Julen worked the bar, and I worked clearing tables. The rest of the waitstaff were girls aged sixteen, maybe seventeen or eighteen, who were all friends of Mr. Ibarra's daughter, Maite, and who spoke to each other urgently in fluent Basque. They were nice enough when Mr. Ibarra introduced me; each of the five of them said *aupa*, in a scattered chorus, and afterward Maite herself had shown me the technique for clearing customers' plates and balancing them down the length of both arms.

When a cascade of teacups slid from my arm at the end of my first shift, one of Maite's friends volunteered to sweep it up. She didn't complain, even as she stretched the broom into the far corners of the kitchen, collecting the shards that had escaped her. Even before that, when the teacups were just beginning to shatter, she had stayed calm; she hadn't even looked at me.

In the first of our Sunday grammar lessons with Mr. Ibarra, we began, somewhat randomly, with expressions of want: "I want, you want, he/she/it wants." At first, we only had access to our very small vocabularies, and so were stuck making sentences like, "I want an onion," or "I want a shoe," but after that we learned how to pair the *want* with other verbs, and then we became able to really sound our own thoughts in the language: "I want to eat." "I want to sleep." "I want to use the bathroom." "I want to do *(blank)*." "I want to say *(blank)*." "I want to forget *(blank)*."

But as it turned out, *want* was not necessarily a logical place to start. I suspect that we began there only by my father's request. I understood—it felt liberating to air our wants. We felt like we were real Basque speakers; people who could express not just their needs, but their superfluous desires. It was a luxurious point of entry, but after that Mr. Ibarra sent us right back to the very beginning, where we belonged. The next week, all that we were given to couple with *want* was *I am, it is, my name*, and *this, that, there*, along with a small bank of bland adjectives: *pretty, short, long, small, sad, exciting, skinny*.

After our first lesson I had foolishly believed that I was on the cusp of being able to speak my own thoughts as they rose in my mind, but no matter how I toyed with that second collection of words, they never brought me any closer to sounding like myself.

And they were difficult for me, still. That was the tragedy. Even after the hour lesson with Mr. Ibarra and after another spent on my own in the confinement of my room, I couldn't even figure out how *I am* changes to *you are*. I felt the limitations of the language all over again, fumbling through those conjugations, and I lost my desire to voice even my wants.

Mr. Ibarra had us working three shifts a week, seven to midnight. Initially, my mother had stood up for me. Fifteen hours was too much, she said; I was only twelve. I had never had a curfew of any sort at the farmhouse—there was no need—but if I had, it would have been well before midnight, or one in the morning, when I really got off work, having finally pawed through a sink of dirty dishes while two of Maite's friends would lazily dry the plates and return them to their places. But when my mother brought it up, my father responded in some combination of ill-conjugated words that we were still indebted to the Ibarras, that there was nothing he could do. Mr. Ibarra was a reasonable man. He even had children himself.

It was not until my fifth shift that I learned that Maite, Mr. Ibarra's daughter, was in fact one of four Maites in the kitchen. I had called her name—I needed to know what to do with the steak knives that I had just cleared—but before I even finished speaking, three other girls turned around and stared at me with dull, probing eyes. Seconds later, the real Maite emerged from a corner of the kitchen with a potato skinner and a half-bare potato in hand. I held up the steak knives and the real Maite pointed to a soaking bin behind me. The other girls turned back to their work. I could never remember, later, who was Maite and who was not.

But the Maites loved Julen. That was true of all of them. After the night shift, they emptied into the stone alley behind the tavern and settled on the sloping bricks. They made use of the angle of the alley to recline comfortably in provocative poses. Someone was always lounging on her side with her head propped coquettishly upon a hand; others lay on their backs, and kept their bent legs open wide enough to make a tent with the skirts of their dresses. From above, the alley would have looked an oddity: a narrow chamber of stone dotted all over with soft, heaping mounds of flesh.

The first time that I was invited to join, I sat a length away, on the back steps of the tavern kitchen. A blanket of smoke hung above us in the air. After ten minutes of the Maites talking around me, I got up to leave.

"Wait, Ana," someone called out after me. I stopped and swung around on the stairs. I had been holding on to the metal railing with one hand, and I let my weight fall away from it so that my body dangled before them.

"Yeah?" I said.

"What's your brother's name?"

Every night after that all the Maites cawed after Julen until he wandered to the alley and joined me on the back steps. He accepted one of their cigarettes the first time that he sat out back with us, but each time after that he declined. Some of the Maites tried to engage him in conversation, but his answers, by necessity and, I liked to think, by preference, were short. I still can't remember feeling closer to my brother than when we sat together on the back stoop of the tavern kitchen. What had begun as a private silence, confined to our own house, turned public in front of the kitchen girls; it felt like an honest, unpretentious show of love for each other.

At this same time, in Mr. Ibarra's lessons, I was discovering all the ways in which Basque differed utterly from Spanish. Even the order of words in a sentence was different, at times nearly opposite. I had known that from the beginning, but as we continued to add new elements to our basic sentences, I began to lose my hold on even the most basic sentence formulations. When we started out, I could handle *onion-the*, and then *onion-the-pretty-is*, but soon that turned into *give-onion-the-pretty-to-me*, which, when I wasn't paying attention, became *give-onion-the-pretty-to-me-otherwise-leave-will-I-and-ever-no-return*.

The lessons revealed in painful increments the full extent to which my father's whim had restructured our lives. I began to question the order of every sentence that I spoke. There was a period when I lost track of the order of modifiers entirely, both because I was confused, and because I really didn't care, and so every sentence that I tried came out scrambled, leaving poor Mr. Ibarra stunned and embarrassed when he listened to me speak.

At some point during this period, I was filling in for one of Maite's friends on an afternoon shift. A group of men lingered at one of my tables, doling out liquor in small doses until the rest of the dining room emptied and they remained there alone, exceptionally drunk. I watched them from behind the bar with the boy who worked when Julen and Mr. Ibarra were not around. When one of the men raised a wobbly hand for the check I started toward them, but just before I reached them, he pulled the table-cloth out from under their collection of glasses and all four drunk men charged together toward the door.

As I chased after them, I yelled, "TABLECLOTH-ME-IT-GIVE," then "ME-IT-TABLECLOTH," then "GIVE," and then, as my legs gave out beneath me and the men disappeared down the street, the ruined white fabric rippling out behind them, "Tablecloth tablecloth tablecloth tablecloth."

We canceled our Basque lesson on the Sunday of my thirteenth birthday, and instead the four of us sat at a table in the corner of the dining room. My father was disappointed to miss the lesson—we were becoming relatively advanced, already moving on to the past tense of *to have*—and he sat there, poring over his notes, until my mother came in from the kitchen with a lopsided cake, and set it down on top of them.

He scowled at her, but then he pulled my head in toward his and kissed my hair. "Today, you have a birthday," he said to me.

Then, growing excited, he said, "Tomorrow, you *had* a birthday *yesterday*." His eyes darted around the room. "Today, we have cake—"

"Be quiet," my mother said, cutting into it. On the top was written "*Ana 13 urte*," which just meant "Ana, 13 years." I wondered if maybe she hadn't known the word for *birthday* until my father spoke it just then. We were all eating in relative peace when Julen came into the dining room, carrying a birdcage with a napkin haphazardly draped over it.

He shoved it at me and said, "For you."

My mother and I spent the rest of the afternoon sliding our fingers between the metal bars of the cage, attempting to pat the bird's head without getting nipped by its beak. The bird was petite and covered in ragged feathers that it seemed to shed indiscriminately. There could have been something wrong with it, but we didn't care; for a brief period of time, my mother and I directed toward that bird all of our love.

In the hour that remained before the dinner shift, we insisted on parading it around town, and on the walk we shared the cage between us, each of us nervously holding it by the tips of our fingers. And though it was obvious, by appearance alone, that the bird was no relation to a parrot, when my mother set its cage down on my bed that night she attempted to teach it phrases, as though the bird were capable of repeating them back to her. "I have to go to the bathroom," she said. The bird stared out at both of us. "I have to go to the bathroom," she repeated again, forcefully. The bird was silent.

I yelled, "I really, really, really have to go to the bathroom!"

I had been planning to name the bird the next morning, but I woke up to find that it had escaped from its cage and was lying in a wreath of its own feathers on the floor.

Julen and I were the ones to bury the bird, because my mother had to stay at the tavern for work. We wandered the town for a little, looking for the right place to perform a burial, but in the end we decided not to bury it at all, and instead to leave it in the dumpster behind the cobbler's shop. Julen swaddled the bird in discarded leather clippings.

We felt silly for having brought the bird over in its birdcage when afterward we were left carrying the empty cage back across town.

My brother left us, six months into our time at the tavern, for an apprenticeship at a tailor's shop in downtown Bilbao. He had been looking for a full-time job for weeks, and while he could have easily picked one up at the tavern, he didn't.

We all mourned his absence in different ways. The bottom fell out of my mother's jokes; she could never be properly funny after that. My father took to doubling up on Basque lessons with Mr. Ibarra. I started hanging around with the Maites until two or three in the morning, thinking of them, increasingly, as my own siblings. Maybe it was true that we had all spun out of orbit. Or maybe Julen had, and we, in the aftermath, each used it as an excuse to drift a little farther out.

A little after Julen left, I started going to the clandestine Basque-language school that Maite and her friends attended. Mr. Ibarra had signed me up, and he was the one who drove me there on my first day. The school was housed inside an old textile factory off of a road just outside of town. Its sheet-metal sides had rusted to the shade of dirt, and on the outside it bore no markings.

Inside, Mr. Ibarra led me through a hall of makeshift class-rooms to a class of students who looked at least two years younger than me. I left the building during our break for lunch and stood out on the barren grass behind the school; I had thought I would need the time to cry, but I waited for a while, and it turned out that I didn't. At one point a rush of birds burst across the sky and I watched them near each other, then separate in turns. I only remembered my own dead bird once they had all passed, and though I had never seen it fly, I imagined it dipping drunkenly around them, and the thought became hysterical to me. I actually stood out there and began to laugh.

Later, when I returned to the building, I saw a flash of Maite going up the stairs between class sessions, and I realized that she hadn't been in the car that morning, when Mr. Ibarra had driven me to school.

Initially I was furious with Mr. Ibarra for having placed me in a class of fifth graders, but within a few months, without my even realizing it, my Basque flowered. At some point I understood the majority of what the Maites fired back and forth between each other, and I began to chime in in little ways: "You're right, he's a turd!" or, "Pass me a cigarette," or even just, "Yes, yes, yes. Yes. Yes—totally."

I don't even remember when I finally moved from the back steps to the alley with the rest of them; it happened seamlessly. I didn't try any seductive poses, but I did note my own pooling flesh upon the cobblestones and the growing downhill tow on different parts of my body over the course of the nights that we spent there.

The other barman at the tavern took over Julen's old shifts, and he always joined us outside when we all got off work. His name was Gabriel, and he was immensely skinny, almost a ghost of a boy. If you didn't know him, you could honestly confuse him and his chaste shyness for a sort of specter, haunting a place.

But he was also nice to me. Out in the alley, we spoke to each other in slow sentences. The Maites lounged all around us and we carved a void in the flood of their ceaseless chatter. When he talked, I could see through his skin to each muscle in his face at work. When he listened, the dormant muscles sometimes spasmed at random, revealing the places where they lay temporarily hidden.

No one had warned me that we were going to leave the alley on the night that we did. I was the last one cleaning up in the kitchen, and when I finally came out back I found a pool of a people milling in front of the stoop. As my eyes adjusted to the darkness, I saw that the full assortment of Maites was there—girls who had worked only one or two other shifts with me, whose faces still stood out as foreign.

The real Maite and one of her friends hovered at the top of the hill, detached from the group, and when they saw me shut the door to the kitchen, they began walking, and the rest of us followed them up and out of the alley. We turned left onto the broad central avenue, the closed storefronts appearing somehow naked and indecent, and then at the end of the avenue, where the street forked, Maite took us down the narrower of the two branches until it went all the way out of town. Somewhere, in one of those early chasms that stretched between the buildings, where the stone façades buckled into sky and weeds, Gabriel found his way to my side. I had already asked the girl nearest to me where we were going but I hadn't understood her answer.

"The quarry," Gabriel said. I shook my head. "The quarry—like the place where they dig for rocks."

"Oh."

He told me about the strange rock they had discovered when they first began digging outside of our town. He described it like the inside of a raw piece of meat: blood red, roped with streaks of white.

"Ew," I said.

"No," Gabriel continued, "it's beautiful. Everyone thinks so. It was so popular that they over-drilled the quarry. They went down too deep one day and hit a water supply. Within hours the whole thing had filled up." He pantomimed water rising. The outline of his hands stood barely apart from the slate-colored clouds passing over us.

At some point after that, I drifted from Gabriel. The road declined, and we sank down the mountain. Somehow I emerged at the helm. I still remember the view from below, as the Maites descended the road behind me, the whole group of them dispersed up the hill. I still remember the drone of the car engine approaching the sharp bend ahead, and its swinging headlights as it came upon us, and even after the real Maite yelled *move*, back to her friends, I remember the light striking their white summer clothes and their clearing the street idly while the car sat there, stranded. Still, I can't decide if, caught in the sweep of the beams, the girls appeared as criminals unmasked or if the swing of their skirts as they left the road made them look instead like a suite of doves disbanding.

At the quarry, everyone stripped down to their underclothes, and our shirts and pants and dresses lay heaped in piles upon the lip of sand. At the far end of the swimming hole, a wall of stone stretched high up into the sky. It was impossible, in the dark, to tell whether or not it was red.

I went into the water with everyone else, but it was cold, and it dropped off quickly. When I saw the point of someone's cigarette light up somewhere along the sand, I swam back to join them. One of Maite's friends nodded to me and exhaled as I settled down beside her. We lounged alongside each other for a while, then she asked, "How deep do you think it is?"

"I don't know," I said. "It drops off fast." She was silent. "Have you been in?"

Out in the swimming hole, orphaned heads skimmed the water's surface. I'm sure that they were talking to each other, or else they were probably laughing about something, but in my memory the menace of the stone wall above them canceled all their sound.

"Twenty-five meters," she said. She tapped the tip of her cigarette against a rock. "That's how far down they drilled before they hit the water." When she brought the cigarette back to her mouth she looked at me for a brief moment, and she said, "No. I never go in."

Eventually other bodies surfaced and joined us up on the lip.

"Hey," Maite's friend whispered. She nudged me, then motioned toward Gabriel splayed out upon the sand in his boxers. "Are you guys going to kiss or fuck or what?"

I fake-slapped her like we were real friends.

"Okay, I'm just joking," she said. "You're too young to fuck, but what are you going to do? You like him, right?"

I shrugged. Stretched out and bent at odd angles, Gabriel's spidery legs glowed.

"You like him." She was talking louder now. "So go do something, don't waste your chance. There are some trees over there." She gestured somewhere behind us. Gabriel had obviously heard her, and he looked over.

"Look." She grabbed one of my shoulders and pointed to him. "He wants to go off with you, too." Gabriel had already gotten up and started loping over when she called out to him, "You want to, don't you?" In response, sweet, spindly Gabriel said nothing. He just continued nearing, the whole time smiling at both of us.

He led me into the trees, and we stumbled through branches for a couple of minutes until we could barely make out the edge of the quarry. When I strained my eyes I could just see the tip of the girl's cigarette flying about in the air. Gabriel put his back to a tree and stared at me affectionately. I realized how little I really knew him.

"Come closer." He grasped my arms. He whispered, "What do you want me to do?"

I don't know how else to explain it: the question struck some sort of dormant reflex. I answered instinctively, as though I had always planned to say to him, "I want you to speak Spanish to me."

He was silent. In the dark, I watched the familiar tremor of his muscles. Eventually he tried, "*Así?*" Like this? I nodded, and signaled for him to keep going.

"What do I say?" he asked, in Basque. I shrugged. Tears were already welling in my eyes. I waved my arms, to say *continue*.

It's not important what he said in the forest behind the quarry, whatever stories he told with poise and animation almost embarrassing to witness. I couldn't tell you what he said because I didn't even register the words as he spoke them. When he was several sentences in, I dropped to my knees, and listened to him like a child. I may have started crying when I heard the word *cucharilla*, unless it was instead *caserío* that began the flood. At one point, I may even have laid myself totally and completely upon the ground.

When we emerged from the trees, the Maites were all collecting their clothes and getting ready to leave. On part of the walk home, Gabriel's clammy hand held the tips of my fingers, but at some point he let go. When we reached the tavern, I slid inside without saying good night to him, and I felt no remorse for allowing him to walk alone to the far reaches of town. Upstairs, I tried to recover the words he had spoken, and that was when I realized I had never really heard them. I had listened only for their rhythm, for the shallow aesthetics of them, and alone in my room I had nothing to hold on to except for the fading memory of their sound.

After our visit to the quarry, Gabriel began leaving me little presents around the tavern. I wasn't purposely avoiding him, but I wasn't spending my nights out in the alleyway either. When I heard him go down to the basement to restock the liquor cabinet at the end of our shift, I would dart past the bar and up the stairs to my room.

First, he left me a bag of almond cookies that his mother had made, my name written in careful, feminine handwriting across the front. I discovered them sitting on one of the empty tables in the dining room on my way to the stairs. Sometime later I found a silver bracelet on the corner of the counter where I normally helped with prep work in the kitchen. There was no note, but I was fairly sure that I knew who had left it; a bracelet had been found on the floor of the dining room the day before. The next week I received a random assortment of glass beads, then a collection of tea bags, a patterned matchbook, a pile of loose stamps.

One Sunday afternoon, when my parents were downstairs in their usual lesson with Mr. Ibarra, Gabriel knocked on the door to my room.

"Ana," he called. "I know that I'm annoying you, but please let me give you one last thing."

I hadn't expected to feel nervous around him, but when he stood there before me I saw him again in his boxers, me again, in my underwear, on the ground. He apologized for his other gifts, and I told him not to be stupid, that they were very nice. He said no, they weren't right. What he should have given me from the beginning was this: he produced a small, used radio from his bag.

"So that we can listen together," he said. "In Spanish."

The radio wasn't the same model as my father's. In fact, it looked totally different, but it prompted my first thought of that original radio in more than a year. I got caught up in assessing how each of its individual features compared to the original, whose body, I only realized then, I had committed to memory. When I didn't respond, Gabriel said, "Spanish, remember?" His face thawed into that same, timid smile. "It's sort of . . . our thing."

I knew that I was being mean when I took the radio from Gabriel, thanked him, and told him that I couldn't listen that afternoon. I was sorry for a moment, when I closed the door on his sinking face, but there was nothing else I could do. When I set the radio on my bed, the hefty mechanical weight of it sank into the mattress and sprouted a crown of pleats in the covers. The whole time, I thought, that was how easy it could have been: I could have nudged the needle past the covert station that broadcast in Basque, and I could have found Spanish waiting there on any channel.

I thought then that if time were as flexible as it was in my mind, I would have done it all over again. I would have pulled a pair of my father's shoes from my parents' closet, while they remained in the dining room downstairs, cycling through their slow-growing vocabulary and diligently practicing the construction of conditional clauses. I would have put the radio on the bed, put my head on those shoes, and listened for hours. And if I really arranged it all right, maybe the year would have bent back on itself, and delivered me back to the kitchen in our old farmhouse, and maybe my father would be there, waving around his arms, saying, "We will all forget about Basque, is that clear?"

Maybe my brother would be there too, coming in through the back door, his arms wound around a tangle of sheets and a comforter. Maybe they came straight from the clothesline, clean from my mother's scrubbing, dry from a night suspended in the mid-August air.

Rachel Kondo

Girl of Few Seasons

T HE NIGHT BEFORE he left for basic training, Ebo had one
last pigeon to kill—a cream barred homer from the old line of
Stichelbaut. The bird was from a long strain of impressive racers,
a gift from his mother when he was nine years old. Ebo had put
off killing this bird, his favorite, by killing all the others first: one,
sometimes two, a day. It had to be done. The birds would not stay
away from their coop and his leaving home meant there would be
no one to care for them. Not his mother; not Daddy, who wasn't
his father; and especially not his younger sister, Momoyo, who
was a ward of the state. Momo would have if she could.

Ebo lay awake on his futon with his ankles crossed and one
arm crooked behind his head, so still he could see the moonlight
shifting about him. Even the water stain on the ceiling felt like
something new to see, as if the old blight was now a bloom. In a
matter of hours, Ebo would be a soldier, though he hadn't much
considered it. He was thinking of Momo, her absence his constant
companion.

As children, on a night like this, they'd creep through the house
and out the door. The Buddhist temple wasn't far, just down the
street. There, a half circle of taiko drummers practiced their

beats. They were bare-chested men with strips of braided cloth tied around their heads. They struck the drum skins with such force sweat leaped from their bodies in an upward rain. Momo's delight always found expression. She would throw her arms wide and bend her knees, the rhythm moving through her like a small-lipped wave. Her eyes would close, her mouth rounded to a little plum seed. Her face would cant to the moon as if its meager light was warm like the sun—something Ebo could see, but not feel himself.

Now what he could feel, he could not see—these memories of his sister, each a smooth river stone set to his naked chest. Ebo shifted on his futon and tried to bring his hand to the heaviness, but the arm behind his head was numb. He waited for life to return to it as the darkness began to lift. It was no longer late, but early.

For some, the Vietnam War was about moral duty. For others, it was a son grown too fast and gone. But for Ebo, the war was not about anything, not even killing or dying. He thought Vietnam might be like Maui, a place too quiet for fear. He thought the war might be a nameless river flowing strong after a heavy rain. If he let it, the war would take him away from Happy Valley to places he'd never been.

The United States Army had deemed him private E-1, a ranking so low it didn't even warrant insignia. Those people who knew Ebo thought his graduating from high school a minor miracle; that he'd languished for ten months without a job was no surprise. When word of his enlistment got around, they figured the army would give him a haircut, a uniform, something decent to do.

But Ebo had his plans. He understood enlisting meant a free trip to the induction center at Fort DeRussy on O'ahu, an island over. From there, he would travel to basic training on the mainland, to a place he'd never even seen on a map. But that didn't matter. It was enough to first be sent to O'ahu, to where he could see Momo at the Waimano Home for the Feebleminded. He'd waited nine years to visit; there hadn't been money for it sooner. What happened to Ebo afterward in Vietnam, he did not have the time to consider. Momo would be fourteen by now.

The newly hatched squabs were the easiest to practice on. Ebo had taken a hammer to the yellow fuzz on their heads. The first squab, he'd struck too hard; the second, not hard enough. With a few other birds, Ebo had tried a sharp knife, but couldn't get the pressure right, nearly cut them in two. In the end, with the older birds that had been with him some time, Ebo took each one tenderly in his hands, lifted them high above his head, and drove their skulls to pieces against the cement.

This was the way Ebo would kill his last bird too. Better to do it now in the dull gray light of early morning than the less forgiving blare of later. He moved soundlessly through the bedroom and into the darkened hallway. He sidled past his mother's room, timing each footstep with the click of the Westinghouse fan. In the living room, he saw Daddy sleeping on the couch with an arm draped over his head and one leg bent to the carpeted floor. Though he didn't need to—Daddy was hard of hearing—Ebo eased the screen door against its latch.

The low-slung moon was a chalky thumbprint in the sky. Ebo crossed his arms against the cool and turned by degrees to all that its sheer light touched around him. Happy Valley, he knew, was nothing more than the skin between the knuckled ridges of the West Maui Mountains. Only a smattering of houses crawled up its slopes, none of them much to look at. His feet found those few patches of grass to step on as he moved through the back-yard. He dipped his head beneath the boughs of plumeria, heavy with flower, and knew where crab spiders predictably spun their webs. He could guess the size and heft of the gecko that clicked its tongue into the darkness. *Big buggah*, he thought.

The coop was a mishmash of materials, built piecemeal with tin and scrap metal, spare plywood and chicken wire. It sat at the back of the yard on cinder blocks two feet off the ground with mounds of pigeon kaka beneath it. The landing jutted out from the roof to make the coop appear as if it leaned. The door itself was just two pieces of discarded mesh screen that Ebo had sewn together by hand.

Next to the coop was a shallow sandbox that had been Momo's playpen. Now it was where fifteen dead pigeons were buried. To ward off critters and stench, Ebo had placed a plank of plywood over its opening with a hollow tile brick on top for good measure. There was just the business of the final bird and then it would be a grave.

He sat on his heels and plugged his fingers through the chicken wire of the coop, looking for that bird now. In earlier years, it had roosted on a high post with its head tucked into its plumped body, its eyes slivered in half sleep. But recently, with age, the bird had lost the battle for a perch and lived with the weakest as puffed dots about the wire floor. And there the bird was now, still responding to pecking order, though the others were dead.

Ebo unlatched the eye hook and dipped through the door, startling the bird into winging itself backward, making little wafts of wind. Ebo called to it softly—*pssssh, pssssh, pssssh*—before swiping at it with trained hands, as was routine. He held the bird to his midsection, felt its heart like a tiny machine. He fanned the bird's wings, one after the other, to check its feathers for lice. He then held the bird up to one side and peered into its ball-bearing eye flitting in its stitch of a socket, remembering only then that his purpose was to extinguish its tiny light.

As he exited the coop, the screen door slapped against its frame as if to call Ebo awake to the yard, already flushed with sunshine.

His dawdling had cost him the gray curtain of early morning that, now lifted, revealed a world vivid with color. The killing of his bird would need to be done in clear view, without ceremony or sentiment.

Ebo stationed himself at the slab of concrete between the house and carport, widening his stance to be sure of his footing. He knew from practice to not hold back, to put his whole body into the effort. Allowing himself any fear or pity would result in pain for the bird, a dragging out of its death. The bird was just a steady heartbeat in his hands, bred for calmness, known for being trusting. With both hands, Ebo raised it high above him. He tightened his grip, working his fingers into the bird's soft give, and still, it did not struggle. He then raised himself to his toes and hesitated by telling himself not to hesitate. He reached higher, the highest he could go, and one by one, loosened his fingers as if to release the bird to the immense sky it belonged to, the sky it now climbed.

Long before any birds, it was just Ebo and his mother on their own. People had clucked their tongues in disapproval, but Ebo never minded. He had no father, but he had everything in a mother. Her hips were fuller then, more inviting, and little Ebo, wanting to be close, always had a fistful of her dress. He had seen how others watched her mouth as she spoke, her lipstick perfectly applied. He had seen this in the man his mother brought home when he was five, the man who flicked a Primo beer bottle cap at him and he happened to catch it. The man had winked, smiling so big his cheeks rounded into two mountain apples. By the time Ebo learned to call this man Daddy, there was another child, a girl they called Momo, and buckets full of bottle caps.

All these years, they lived quietly across the street from Tasty Crust, the diner Ebo had been frequenting since small-kid time. This morning, he would go for his usual breakfast. But unlike most mornings, he would need to say good-bye. He breathed in the cool morning air with the heat just beneath it. Seeing no cars, he still skipped to a jog when crossing Mill Street, his rubber slippers slap-slapping like fat rain against the pavement. When he got to the other side, he turned to look at his house against the West Maui Mountains, the mountains against the blue-gray morning. It was unremarkable, his house. Walls of thin plywood held up a corrugated tin roof that had rust in the dips of its grooves. The carport sheltered a dead Ford on cinder blocks. Clothes hung on a sagging line and brushed against the Ford's dusty hood so that the hems of Daddy's work shirts were never entirely clean. This is what Ebo would leave behind and what he would take with him like a picture in his pocket.

He walked into the sticky warmth of Tasty Crust, where the old-timers were at their usual stools, living out the best part of their day, the part that was spent in the company of others. They'd each brought their copy of *The Maui News*, though they'd read it through at home. This morning, they wore Aloha shirts and their veteran caps and pins. They'd done this, marked their calendars even, for Ebo, who had enlisted as they did for their wars.

"Howzit, young man!" said Flora, the waitress who spoke for everyone.

Ebo smiled, sat on a stool at the counter. Flora set down a mug of coffee, pivoted her body like a sprinkler as she wiped the counter. Her hair, a manapua bun sitting plump on the curve of her head, had never been let down, the coif of her fringe sprayed stiff for years. She had never been anything else, which was a comfort.

"Big day today," she said, as much to the counter as to Ebo. "We is proud of you, young man, I can tell you dat. You go get'm and say you is born and raised Happy Valley. We make'm *good* in Happy Valley."

An old-timer slapped a hand to a thigh. "I remembah when you was one small buggah, legs danglin from duh chair," he said. "*Hooooo-eeee!* You was one *cute* buggah. But some rascal, you!" Small laughter then; the others remembered young Ebo too. To this, Ebo dipped his head low, nodding, shielding himself from the gleam of attention.

"Time fo kau kau!" said Flora, setting before Ebo a plate of hotcakes with an ice cream scoop's worth of butter on top. It had been some time since Ebo's mother had been there to stab at the butter with her fork and paint circles on his stack, then her own. Back then, she'd drizzle syrup too, when Ebo would say, at whatever age, "Ma, I get'm." After Momo came along, his mother didn't have time for Tasty Crust, for their early-morning breakfasts. After Momo, she stopped being just his.

But Ebo understood. Even as a baby, Momo had been generous, smiling wide when spoken to, as if she had been born to give. Neighbors would wiggle a finger at her and she'd take it, holding their gaze. *So smaht,* they'd say, noting her dark irises, how they shone especially large and nearly covered the whites of her eyes. Her fine blue-black hair swirled into a single giri giri atop her head, a sign she would never be cause for trouble. But mostly she was a mirror for their mother, who looked at her baby girl to see her joy.

No one noticed young Ebo alone. By the time he was nine and Momo nearly five, he preferred the mountains of 'Iao Valley to the tedium of school, passing his days by the river skipping rocks, catching guppies, doing nothing. He quickly learned the word *truancy.* His mother's rice paddle had no effect and Daddy had said, *Not my kid.* When Ebo was held back a year, people just shook their heads, thinking him a good-for-nothing kolohe. But he'd proved himself good for enlisting—something to do, a way to be gone.

After clearing his plate, Ebo dipped his hand into his shorts pocket to pay. Flora, ever watchful, said, "Dis one on me, soljah boy." Her inflections and movements were a conductor's wand to a stand, orchestrating the old-timers so they knew to rise with Ebo and to salute him. To this, Ebo extended his hand to each of them as the other diners watched in silence. The cooks turned down the radio in the kitchen and peered through their cutout window fringed with open tickets. All the while, Flora kept to her work, wiping the counter where Ebo had just been.

Happy Valley by then was pulsing with moderate activity. The morning sun had risen to a low perch in a cloudless sky, emanating its white light as a softness on Ebo's skin. He stood at the edge of Mill Street again, scanning the blue brightness for his bird beneath the visor of his hands.

A Buick sounded its horn in two successive beeps, sending Ebo back a step. As the Buick coasted by, the driver threw Ebo a left-handed shaka out the window. "A hui hou!" said the driver, to say *Until we meet again.* Ebo's head tilted back with a smile to acknowledge the driver, a smile that was gone by the time he crossed the street. Soon Ebo would not be so known, something he had wanted for years.

Back at the house, his mother stood at the stove working a pan. Eggshells were halved, two Vienna sausage cans curled open, everything crackling with oil and heat. Daddy was still on the couch with a pillow pressed to his face. Ebo stood there watching the house as it would be without him in it.

One hand to hip, his mother was in her usual meal-making stance: her weight shifted left and her right foot touching down to the linoleum by just a toe. Her National Dollar dress hung on her too-thin frame like drapery, as if there might not be anything behind it. To Ebo, she was the size of a child, but she was not new like a child. Her hair had lost its luster and could no longer hold color, had given in to a blank and lifeless gray. Her gaze avoided most living things and was too often fixed to the floor. She was a woman afraid of loss so that she was first afraid of life.

Even when they were a family of four, and then three, there were only ever two chairs. As she plunked down on one now, his mother's movements quickened. Not a minute passed before she turned to Ebo with a plate of food in hand and set it before him at the two-person table.

"You hungry?" she asked.

"Nah," said Ebo, "I pau eat."

"No, you—eat."

She darted back and forth, bringing him a pair of chopsticks, a glass of milk, as though he were just a boy and not a young man of nineteen, all lean muscle and strength. But because he was her son, he was a boy still. And because he was leaving home that day, she stopped fussing about the kitchen and sat down opposite him. The only other time he could remember his mother sitting like this was the day she made that call about his first pigeon.

That afternoon, she'd sat Ebo down and told him to sit still, which made him squirm. He had wanted to go play, but she shushed him, said to listen. She picked up the receiver of the rotary phone, as gleaming black as her hair was then. The dial turned and stuttered, turned and stuttered, and by the time she spoke, two warm hands had suctioned to Ebo's eyes. He loosed himself free to face Momo, whose smile was shy one tooth. He flicked her forehead and called her *puka mout* to make fun, but she only smiled wider, which made them both laugh. Snapping her fingers to quiet them, their mother spoke a final few words into the phone. "Yes. Can." She hung up smiling, something she didn't hide then. She said, "What you tink, Ebo, you like birds?" Ebo had never been asked what he thought and looked to Momo for how he should feel. Momo beamed as if giving to Ebo was giving to her. She flitted across the kitchen floor on her toes and flapped her arms like wings. Over and over she said, "Happy Ebo! Happy Ebo!" and he knew then he'd been given a gift.

Ebo washed the dishes for his mother, the only thing he could think to do for her. At the sink, he watched his coop through the screen window, waiting for his bird, always the last to finish circling. When it finally descended, Ebo turned off the water to see it skitter back and forth along the length of the landing. He knew the bird needed food—it was long past the hour when it was usually fed. But Ebo knew he shouldn't feed what he would soon kill, something he'd allowed himself to be distracted from doing.

He reasoned with himself. Better to give the bird a little more time in the sun while he packed, was his thinking. He calculated the hours he had left before his ride to the airport arrived and went about gathering his few toiletries in the bathroom. There really wasn't much he needed where he was going, all of it amounting to the knapsack he'd had since grade school, the one with the busted zipper. He went to retrieve it from his bedroom closet and found it laid out on his futon instead. Even more startling was a shirt folded neatly and, next to it, a pair of shoes. Ebo kneeled down to these things, astonished they were there and that they were his. He pressed a finger to one milky-white button in a long line of them. He lifted a shoe to his nose to breathe in the leather, put the tip of his tongue to the heel. He'd never had anything new before, let alone anything with buttons or laces. How his mother had fixed the zipper on his knapsack, he didn't know. How she'd found the money for these things was even more of a mystery. All he knew was that this was his mother's way: to give all she could, and when there was nothing left, to give her very will.

Once she had secured Ebo's first pigeon with the breeder, the bird soon posed another problem for his mother—it needed a loft. For two weeks, she had pressed Daddy to build one, but he'd only shaken his head at the expense, though it was the effort he wouldn't give. When she made up her mind to build one herself, she made her way on foot to the junkyard, with Ebo and Momo trailing. There she selected wood panels either discarded as excess or abandoned as trash. Ebo found a large piece of chicken wire curled around a tire, which he worked hard to unfurl. All the while, Momo picked through the dirt for nails, examining each one closely, speaking aloud what she discovered. "You good for

Ebo," or, "You no good. Not for my Ebo." The usable few she clenched in one hand, as if Ebo's happiness was something she could hold and keep safe.

That his mother and sister did this on his behalf was almost enough for Ebo. All of the fuss was just for him—he didn't need more. The small makeshift coop they built, however shoddy, was entirely his. With the little coop, he started to believe. He believed in the promise of this pigeon and he believed Daddy might be pleased, maybe even impressed, with their handiwork.

When Daddy's ride dropped him home from work that evening, Ebo and Momo hurried to the jalousie window in the bathroom to watch him discover what they'd built. He nearly missed it, but then he didn't. Setting down his lunch pail and water jug, he crouched low to examine the structure. When he began to circle it, sizing it up, Momo pressed her head to Ebo's shoulder. Ebo felt her flinch when Daddy kicked the heel of his foot into the coop so that the sorry thing folded into itself and fell. Daddy used both his feet to further trample what they'd built, until there was no trace of their efforts in the tangle that remained.

Chest heaving, Daddy snapped open a folded lawn chair and set it down facing the pile of wood and wire. Ebo stared hard at Daddy sitting there, one knee bouncing wildly. By that evening hour, with everything on its way to darkness, Daddy appeared a darker shadow. But then movement caught Ebo's eye. Momo was no longer next to him—she was in the carport. She walked toward Daddy so slowly her dress barely moved at her knees. Her hands were cupped protectively in front of her, as if in prayer. When she stood before Daddy, she splayed open her hands from prayer to sacrifice. Daddy glanced at her offering, which Ebo knew was a Lucky Strike. Daddy looked at his child, who was every inch his, and scooped her onto his lap. They stayed that way awhile, long enough for Ebo's mother to flick on the overhead light and see what had happened, long enough for Momo to begin picking through the dirt again for nails and for Daddy to help.

. . .

Now, whenever Ebo looked for Daddy, Ebo knew to look there, in the carport, where Daddy smoked on the bench seat of the dead Ford. Daddy had had the bench seat removed from the car years ago, after Momo was sent away, after he'd injured his back at work and could no longer sit down in a lawn chair.

Ebo elbowed the screen door open to its usual high-pitched wheeze. At the bottom of the steps, he plugged his feet into rubber slippers and shuffled over to Daddy, who was exactly where Ebo knew he'd be. With his new pair of shoes waiting for him, Ebo now needed socks, something only Daddy owned. Ebo sat down on the bench seat next to Daddy, but Daddy stood, though there was room enough for two. Daddy relaxed against the frame of the Ford and lit another Lucky Strike. Speaking through pinched lips, he said, "You ready to go?"

Digging a knuckle into his eye, Ebo said, "I bettah be."

Daddy pulled on his cigarette and nodded. Two steady streams of smoke issued from his nostrils. He used to work for Maui County in road maintenance, but it had been some time since he'd paved a pothole or disposed of a dead mongoose. It had been even longer since Daddy served with the 442nd in the Second World War, making Daddy the closest person to Ebo who had not only left the island, but returned. In the silence, the two men were careful to avoid each other's eye, an intimacy they did not know how to share. Any other day and one of them would've walked away by now. But the moment for that had passed and Ebo was still there, needing socks.

"Gotta ask you someting," said Ebo as he stood to ask Daddy squarely. Daddy pivoted back down onto the bench seat, set his elbows to his knees, and hung his head between his shoulders. Ebo, in turn, leaned against the Ford so that like two reluctant dance partners, they'd traded places.

"I know what you like ask," said Daddy. "Some kine advice. I know. Soljah to soljah. But only get one ting fo say . . ." Daddy looked up and settled his gaze seriously into the middle distance. Ebo hadn't anticipated this. He gently pushed off from the Ford, stood tall and waited.

"Duh ting you gotta do," said Daddy, "is . . . no die."

A brief moment passed with Ebo thinking Daddy sincere. It stretched long enough for Ebo to open his dry mouth and try to match the sentiment. But Daddy threw up his arms in amazement at his own humor, amazed Ebo hadn't yet agreed. "You see? Das it! Jus *no die*. Easy." Daddy spun out laughing so hard he began to cough until he choked. Ebo could only look out at the pavement of the driveway, staring into the sunlight until his eyes began to water. Once recovered, Daddy flicked the butt of his cigarette and it rolled, still burning, into Ebo's line of sight. "Ay," muttered Daddy, groaning as he stood, as if standing would be the hardest task of his day. Before disappearing into the house, Daddy called out to Ebo, "Eh, maybe go Paukukalo. One last time. Jus fo Daddy, eh?"

Ebo slunk into the sun and faithfully toed the butt dead. He pinched its mess between two fingers and dropped it into a gallon bucket filled with sand, figuring the bucket had another week or so to go. Since he was a boy, it had been his job to empty the ashy filth into Tasty Crust's dumpster when no one was looking and to go to Paukukalo Beach for a clean bucket of sand.

Mindlessly, Ebo tapped his toe against the heft of the bucket, as if he couldn't muster the will to kick. But the will existed and manifested itself in sudden movement. Ebo tore down the driveway and hung a right onto Mill Street, jogging a ways until turning to face oncoming cars in a backward shuffle. Everything siphoned to the power of his hitchhiker's thumb, now asking for someone, anyone, to stop. He didn't have the time to walk the two miles, but he had his thumb and his suddenly supreme need to go to Paukukalo—not for sand or for Daddy, but for his own sake.

A truck slowed mercifully and Ebo swung himself into its bed, rode the distance as if it was something to endure and not a necessary means to his end. The truck puttered along the back roads down toward the ocean, which, from Ebo's position, could not be seen until he was there. Then, the ocean was everywhere, something he couldn't *not* see if he tried. Two pats against the truck's side and the truck rolled to a stop. Ebo alighted, gave another grateful tap to the truck as it drove away, and waited. He waited until he needed breath, so that when he breathed, he did so as deeply as he could.

Without anyone there, the beach before him was a lonely stretch of beige with an unfurling wave for company. In a trance-like state, Ebo trudged through the sand toward the water. In a tremor of heightened awareness, he understood this place as it might've been uninhabited, before the insistent road lined its coast, before anything so much as a human foot dimpled its surface. Like the sea-salted wind in his hair, the dimensions of time could be felt, tasted, moved through. Whatever it was that every person through all of history might've felt as they looked upon what he was seeing now, all of this Ebo experienced as a tiny pinprick in his chest.

He sat down cross-legged. The grainy warmth beneath his legs brought him back into his own skin, his own memory. As they had for so many years, his hands routinely combed the sand for opihi shells, which Momo had loved for the purple swirl of their underside. He would do this while Momo chased waves as they pulled away, the same waves that would, in turn, push back toward her and send her squealing. She was happiest here, Ebo knew. Though she would never learn to swim, the sun and water and sand were enough to animate her, like music does dancing. Now, as he remembered her, an opihi shell appeared in Ebo's fingers like a tiny sand-swept miracle. He brushed off its back and belly, blew on it for good measure. He studied its purple swirl and the thought came to him that it wasn't just its color Momo had loved, but the fact that he, Ebo, had searched for her, would not stop searching for her, until he found one.

Momo wasn't dead, which might've been easier. She was nine years gone. She had been taken from life as Ebo knew it, meaning life as Ebo lived it was arranged around what had been and what should have been—two points on an axis that would never curve toward what actually was. Staring into this regret was for Ebo the same thing as having his eyes open at all.

In the end, it had taken Daddy three full weekends to build Ebo his loft. By that time, Ebo's mother had decided on a second pigeon, a common blue bar, which she didn't say, but Ebo knew, was for Momo. What Ebo didn't say was that he resented this.

The first week they had their birds, the birds did not readily know their new home and flew back to their previous coop. Through their mother, the breeder had instructed Ebo and Momo to gather twigs and leaves and place their findings in the corner of the loft. A morning or two later, a nest was built. Three days more and Momo's blue bar sat in her nest, pressing herself into her first egg. Another speckled egg followed. It took a few more weeks for the squabs to hatch themselves through perfect circles carved at the tops of the eggs, another few for their yellow fuzz to be replaced by feathers.

With their squabs in the loft, Ebo became convinced the birds would no longer stray. He decided to test his bird, the cream barred homer, by taking it into 'Iao Valley, a mile or so up the mountain. He'd wanted to do this alone, but Momo had followed. Even though she'd had a sinus infection that week, she would not be left behind.

The basin was dark, dank, teeming with life both seen and unseen. Banyan trees laced their fingers overhead and the fragrance of white ginger was silk on their skin. Ebo carried his wicker basket in hand as his bird stamped its feet for balance. He walked at a steady pace, knowing he couldn't exactly lose Momo, but he'd wanted her to struggle in some way. And she did—she struggled to keep up when everything in her wanted to take her time. When too much distance stretched between them, Ebo turned angrily to Momo, only to see her head back, mouth open, as if the immense lushness of sight and sound might tip her over. In seeing this, Ebo saw what was beautiful. But because he had wanted it all to be his to see, and not Momo to see it through, he became mean.

"You! Some stupid, you! Hurry up!" he snapped.

Between two peaks was a riverbed of boulders rounded smooth by icy water that flowed from the mountains. Ebo's mother's mother had washed clothes there, singing her songs from home. It was where families picnicked, babies were baptized, kids passed their summers atop the rocks—every good and perfect thing.

The boulder on the other side of the river was large and flat, like a platter tipped to a lean. Because it was the only space exposed to the widest spread of open sky, it was where Ebo determined he would release his bird. But the way to it was through a thick part of the river, heavy with deep waters gone stagnant from stillness. Cresting the glassy surface was a line of rocks, like beading on a necklace laid out. Having told Momo to watch from the edge, Ebo toed his way across, alternating hands with his basket. But she followed him, put her feet wherever his had been.

On the other side, she couldn't keep still for her excitement and it angered Ebo further. He lifted the lid to his basket but when the bird didn't move, he kicked a toe into the wicker. The bird still did not move, as if it didn't know to look up, so Ebo pulled it from the basket and tossed it upward like a handful of confetti. The bird teetered and lifted, teetered and lifted higher. It made its way up and out of sight, all of it over without ever having been what Ebo imagined the afternoon would be.

For a boy of nine, his disappointment registered as injustice— what Ebo should have had, he'd been denied. And on that day, it was Momo who had denied him his freedom to be something other than what he felt he was: second in everything. Because of this, Ebo quickly maneuvered his way back over the rocks and disappeared behind a tree. He'd wanted Momo to feel abandoned and scared, just for a little while. She called after him, confused. Even when she cried, Ebo stayed hidden.

The sun, it seemed, would set on his bitterness. It was darkest first in nature. As the daylight dimmed, Ebo saw his hand become a featureless shadow and knew his game was over. But he revealed himself just as Momo was halfway across the river. When he called to her, she looked for him and slipped. He heard her go under and bob right up, pulling for air. By the time he'd crawled over the rocks to her, water had already aspirated through her nose, flowed past her already swollen sinuses, and settled its bacterial filth wherever it could.

They were late and Momo was soaking wet, a double offense. Ebo tried to hurry her along. But Momo's bare feet pinched with pain and she moved slowly, made heavy by her wet clothing. Gone was her wonder of the place.

By the time they neared home, it was dark. Their mother scoured the street with frantic eyes. When she finally saw them, she started running. Ebo put his arms up, but his mother peeled them down to slap him upside the head.

"What's duh mattah wit you? You make me sick!"

Momo was ushered straight into the bathroom. Ebo flung himself down to the kitchen table, where Daddy was sitting. Daddy said, "Look at me, boy." Ebo slowly raised his eyes to Daddy, who chose this one moment to look Ebo unflinchingly in the eye. Ebo hung his head low until the tears came and he could take no more shaming. He scurried from the kitchen to his bedroom, pausing at the bathroom door to see his mother pouring hot water over Momo's bowed head. It would be his last opportunity to see Momo as he knew her, but her hair obscured her face.

Without dinner and with the trouble he was in, it was difficult for Ebo to sleep. At some distance, he heard the taiko drumming pulsating like a gigantic heart fearful of stopping. In his mind, the drummers were slick with sweat, moving in synchronicity like streamers of light. He could see their spectral dance, arms flailing faster, harder, just short of breaking. In his dream state, Ebo believed he was the drum and the wooden sticks that pelted his body painful, but necessary.

By morning, he woke up spent. He turned over on the futon to see Momo with her back to him, as she often was. But this morning she was arched in an unnatural way, as if she, too, was in pain. Ebo poked a finger into her, then again. When she didn't respond, he pulled on her shoulder and lost his grip on her too-hot and slippery skin. He tugged harder, with two hands. When her body finally tipped toward him, it came heavily and without grace. He saw then what he would never unsee. Momo's face had rearranged itself in the night. Her eyes fluttered with fever to a new spiritual rhythm and where there had been so much life, there was only white.

To excise the beach and his memories, Ebo ran all the way home, as if what he felt he could sweat out of his system. In the backyard, he peeled off his T-shirt and stood beneath the hose for longer than he needed to. The initial thrust of warm hose water soon ran cool over his face. His bird was now on the brick steps of the coop, waiting beneath the shade of the awning. Without the sound of feed clanking against the metal troughs, the bird hadn't been called through the one-way trapdoor that funneled into the loft.

Ebo knew he couldn't kill it, had somehow always known. He turned off the hose and shook the water out of his hair. Determined to put a brick at the opening of the fly pen to keep the bird out, he would teach it the cruel lesson of having no home. Then it would be like the strays nobody wanted, or even liked. Just a rat with wings.

He shooed the bird into the plumeria trees and went about loosening the brick. The brick had been there for years and was embedded in grooves of hard earth, so it took some effort. When at last it came free, Ebo stood with it in hand only to find his mother behind him, peering into the coop at an unnecessary distance. He set the brick down, unsure of what she wanted.

"Show me yo bird," she said.

Ebo thought that maybe she wanted to kill the bird herself, which made him hesitate protectively. She'd probably wanted it dead all these years. But his mother rarely asked anything of Ebo and he dutifully went about trying to locate it anyway.

His mother hadn't so much as glanced at the coop after Momo's illness, with some part of her needing to blame the bird to keep from blaming Ebo. He understood her reasoning. If the business of pigeons had never happened, that day wouldn't have happened. There wouldn't have been the river, the bacteria, the fever, all of which reduced their atmosphere to the thin air of the aftermath. There wouldn't have been the attempts to explain, to name, to apply medical sense to what had happened.

Momo had had a cold, yes? *Yes.* The virus had weakened her immune system and allowed a secondary infection to take hold. *OK.* The circuitry of her brain could not withstand a fever that high. *OK. OK.* Words like *bacterial meningitis* were spoken. Words like *hyperpyrexia* and *apneic attack.* And when those words didn't register, there were apologies for the one thing that everyone understood: that Momo was not dead, but gone.

Ebo only knew that a stranger had come home to him from the hospital. Like an oversize infant, she went between a playpen in the living room and that sandbox Daddy had built for her in the yard. Ebo would sit with her, listening to her new language come out as guttural moans that would stretch and deepen into a sort of song. When she was given a blue-and-yellow helmet to wear for when she seized, her face was pinched beyond what little recognition Ebo had been holding to.

In time, doctors spoke of Waimano Home. Though it was located on another island, a world away, they insisted Momo would receive attention specific to her condition. They said Momo wouldn't know the difference between her home and Waimano, that she would in fact be happier. But the day she was taken away was the day Momo's song grew to its utmost, growing louder as the distance between her and her mother stretched wider. That distance now spanned two islands, with miles of ocean and nine years of time in between. It was a distance Ebo would travel in just under an hour.

He launched another rock at his bird in the plumeria tree. He didn't mean to hit it directly, but to scare it back to the loft. Like the first rock, this one hit the bird's branch and fell to the brittle leaves below, two thuds that sent the bird higher. With his mother waiting, Ebo grabbed a handful of smaller rocks with which to cover more area, but she called him back to the side of the loft, to where she stood next to the can of feed.

"Show me how," she said, knowing the feed was the way to the bird. Ebo ran a hand through his hair, frustrated that his mother had witnessed his not thinking straight. He hurried in and out of the coop with those things that fed and watered the birds—a foot-long metal trough and a milk carton gutted at the center. By using his thumb at the spout, Ebo showed his mother how to hose everything off.

"Gotta be clean," he said, and she nodded. At the feed can, he removed the lid and filled the scoop with the right amount. "Gotta keep birds little bit hungry. Dat way dey come back." She nodded again.

Though the entry was plenty high for her to walk through, Ebo saw his mother dip her head into the loft after him. She made circles with her eyes, pulled in all there was to see. "Long time," she said. "Look good." Ebo guided the scoop along the trough's opening so that the feed fell against the metal in a clatter. It wasn't long before they heard the clank of the fly pen drop back into place and the bird was pecking at the feed with its feathered tail raised behind it.

As they watched, Ebo felt the dusty air constrict, making the confines of the coop feel even smaller. He wasn't used to a second body's being in there with him. He also wasn't used to having his mother close like this, in an enclosure, where they might say those things they couldn't say elsewhere. He knew if there was ever a time to tell his mother exactly what had happened that afternoon with Momo, specifically his part in abandoning her, that time was now.

"You know I goin see Momo," he said as a means of bringing up the subject. He'd told both his mother and Daddy that seeing Momo was possible. But he'd kept from them that seeing her was the very reason he'd enlisted. He knew it was an impulsive and outsized decision that warranted, even deserved, criticism. They would have said to get a job, wait for money, then go to her. But he'd tried for a job; ten months he'd tried. He couldn't wait anymore and yet he couldn't explain his impatience. Because how could they know what he hadn't confessed? How could they understand the guilt within him, located somewhere beneath the ribs like a dark hunger he fed with secrecy? This guilt that defied reason, that kept its own time, made its own sense—how could he tell his mother about it here, like this?

She stood staring down at the bird with her arms crossed at her midsection. Had she heard him? Ebo wondered. Perhaps she had something she wanted to say to Momo, or for him to give her? Ebo thought maybe this might be the thing to ask his mother, was about to ask when she spoke first.

"Dis bird. Still plenny strong. Good fo my baby girl. You take dis bird to Momo."

When just a half hour remained, Ebo slipped into his new shirt as if he were putting on another skin. He buttoned the bottom button first, then undid it, thinking that way was wrong, the top button was right. He hadn't even needed to ask Daddy for socks, because his mother had either found two pairs for him or made Daddy give them over. He wore a pair now in his new shoes, which made his feet feel awkward with bulk. He wished he had pants to wear rather than shorts.

Ebo's mother appeared in the doorway. He thought she might be pleased with his new look, all of it owing to her sacrifice, but she was distracted, barely noticed. She muttered something Ebo couldn't hear. When he asked her to repeat it, she shook her head, looking at the ground as if she'd dropped the words she had wanted to speak.

"Ma—jus talk. Say what you gonna say."

She looked up at him, emboldened: "You and me. We go O'oka."

"O'oka? Why O'oka? I gotta go airport."

"Jus come. Fas kine. Real fas."

It was the last thing Ebo had expected, his mother suggesting they go to the grocery store down the street. Still in his new shirt and shoes, he trailed her from the house as reluctantly as he had when he was a boy. Grocery shopping bored Ebo both then and now, but especially then, when it was his job to keep Momo from touching everything on the shelves. Back then, Ebo would put his feet at the center of the tiles and avoid stepping on the lines, encouraging Momo to try to copy him—a little game. Now he had to focus on keeping up with his mother. In the midday heat, her cotton dress stuck to the skin of her back. She didn't break pace, nor did she speak. Ebo worried he'd ruin his new shirt with sweat and billowed it for breeze.

Once in the air-conditioning of O'oka, he relaxed. But his mother was still intent on something. She took Ebo by the elbow, stood slightly behind, and urged him forward. They moved up and down the aisles in this way. If he had still been a boy, she would've had him by the scruff of his neck.

Of course he knew this fierce focus in his mother. He glanced back at her as she scanned the faces of other patrons, moving on the moment they were not what she wanted. But what she was after was not in the store. When they moved past the entrance again, she happened to look out the door and finally see. Ebo felt a tug at his shirt and lowered his face to his mother's. He breathed in her sweet and sour as she outstretched her arm and pointed toward the parking lot.

"You see dat man?" she said. "Quick. You see him?" She did not look at Ebo, but he looked to her when she said, "Dat man, he yo real daddy."

Ebo stood perfectly still to take in everything that moved. What he had seen was an old man in an orange vest gathering shopping carts, wearily pushing them forward and out of view. The old man had been all there was, so Ebo waited for someone else to see. He waited as people continued to shuffle past, as a voice spoke over the intercom, as registers pinged open and groceries were rung up. Ebo waited until the sounds became for him a sort of silence.

It wasn't until he'd arrived at the airport, checked in, and sat down in the terminal that Ebo looked into the brown paper bag his mother had given him. In it were mochi balls she'd made, as well as Spam musubi that was still warm to the touch. He turned one musubi over in his hand and saw how the rice was stained brown with shoyu, how the dark green nori wrapped around the sliver of Spam and held it in place. This food he had taken for granted he now studied like a keepsake.

Airport time felt different from the experience of time elsewhere, and Ebo, who had never flown before, worried he would somehow miss his flight. But no one around him seemed bothered the way he was, all these people whose travel purposes were so different from his. None of them noticed Ebo, who was going to war on their behalf. No one noticed him until his bird began to stir in the silver carrier at his feet. The woman seated next to him located the source of the fluttering, leaned over to peer through the bars.

"What's dat stuffs . . . ?" she asked, putting her fingers to her nose to ask after the clumping at the pigeon's beak.

"Called cere," said Ebo quietly. "Like nostrils." The woman nodded and looked away. Soon she was among the many who were standing in a hurried response to boarding call.

Everywhere Ebo looked, the words PAN AM could be seen scrawled across the body of the plane, printed on a little white bag in the seat-back pocket, embroidered into the edge of the hats the stewardesses wore tilted to a lean on their heads. Though he tried to be casual about it, Ebo watched closely as a stewardess demonstrated safety procedures. He pulled the tail of the strap too tightly across his abdomen and gripped the armrests during takeoff. He was amazed at the feeling of suspension and closed his eyes to feel it fully. When he opened them again, the plane was airborne. Ebo looked through the window to witness his whole island come into view and simultaneously shrink in size.

The flight to Honolulu took thirty-two minutes, gate to gate. Just as Ebo was finishing the passion guava juice they'd served him, the plane started its descent. Deplaning gave Ebo a slight headache, how everyone crowded him, how all of a sudden there was only one way out. In no time, he had followed the flow of passengers to baggage claim and found himself presenting his case to a taxi driver. He needed to go to Waimano Home and he only had eight dollars—would this be enough? The taxi driver shook his head, but opened his door to Ebo just the same.

As they drove along the H-1 freeway in the frenetic pace of pau hana traffic, Ebo rolled down his window and put his face to the wind. He was unsure of how he'd manage a ride to Fort DeRussy by day's end, but figured he'd deal with things as they came. Before long, the taxi exited the freeway and the glut of cars simply fell away. They drove switchbacks up the mountain along a narrow road skirted by tall pili grass and monkeypod trees. After a time, Ebo worried the driver had misunderstood him, but then he saw it off in the distance: a building, austere and feather white. Closer still and Ebo could make out the steel bars along the top-floor windows.

The taxi dropped him off at the front of the building, but Ebo walked away from it at first to see it against the mountain. Off in the distance was a pool drained of water, sloping from shallow to deep, where a number of stray cats had gathered. The kittens played amid dead leaves and trash while the older creatures sat there, watching Ebo. As he made his way back toward the entrance, he noticed the building's exterior paint was chipped and peeling so badly it made a pattern. State-owned and -operated, the building suffered from decay—not from negligence, but from lack. Ebo stepped through the doors and into the powerful smell of Pine-Sol that came at him like a wall.

After signing into the nurses' station, a middle-aged woman in pink scrubs said she'd walk Ebo to where he needed to go. She eyed his carrier and asked Ebo what he'd brought, saying, "We don't like to upset the residents, you understand."

"Jus an old bird," said Ebo. "Won't be here long."

He breathed through his mouth as they made their way, deciding there was at least a sterile sort of cleanliness to the place that he could appreciate. Along the walls were chicken-scratch drawings in crayon and chalk. Within the corridor were disabled patients, some whose eyes followed Ebo. Others sat in their crumpled bodies, waiting. "Dis place," Ebo asked of the nurse, "what is it exactly?"

The woman flicked her long braided ponytail over her shoulder. "At first, it was an asylum," she said. "Fifty years ago they called the residents 'spiritual morons' if you can believe it." She kept moving, skittishly on alert. "On good days, we think of it as a sanitarium. On the best days, a home." The nurse then pivoted on her thick-soled shoes to face Ebo briefly. "You must have memories of Miss Momoyo before her mental status change. How old was she again?"

"Momo was five," said Ebo.

"Well, what amazes me—and what you'll see too—is how intact her nature is. In all her sweetness, she is perfect. Isn't she, Billy?" The nurse said this as she patted the shoulder of a man with bulging eyes and jaws that went in opposite directions. She then pointed up a set of stairs, and left Ebo to go it alone.

He took his time going to the third floor. At the last step, he leaned forward and looked to his right. Momo was where the nurse had said she'd be, at the end of the hallway with a mop in hand. Mopping, he'd been told, gave her a sense of duty, and of home. But even without the mop, Ebo knew it was her in the helmet, now red and black. He approached slowly, soundlessly, and sat on a bench along the wall with his elbows tacked to his knees. Ebo saw that Momo, at fourteen, was taller than their mother. He saw that her hospital gown fell to her calves, where fine downy hairs grew undisturbed. From her full lips hung a short thread of spittle, and as she mopped the tiles, Ebo saw she did so within the lines.

"Momo," he said, and she stopped her work to slowly look up. He said her name again to bring her gaze to him. When she at last settled on Ebo, it took her some time to register a presence, then more time still to register it as familiar. All of this Ebo mistook for blankness and he looked away, feeling foolish for having hoped she would recognize him. But when the mop handle fell to the concrete floor, he looked again at Momo, whose delight he'd forgotten had always found expression. The shaking of her hands, the stamping of her feet, the insistent whimper, everything lacked articulation that Ebo made up for by standing and reaching for her, by using his feet to dance around her, by shaping his voice into words—"Ebo here, Momo! Ebo here!"

. . .

He'd been told they could sit outside for a short time. Ebo led Momo by the hand with the other gripping the carrier. When they came to a bench beneath a bottlebrush tree, he swept off the tiny red needles from the surface. Before them was a view of Pearl Harbor, the inciting place of another war, a war different from Ebo's.

In the thin-aired silence, the bird cooed to be let free. Momo heard it and again took her time locating its source. Ebo lifted the lid to the carrier, and the bird, sensing the distance from home, the long journey ahead, struggled against his grip. He held the bird in front of Momo and she raised a curious hand. Ebo waited for her finger to reach the bird's body and when it did, he made it so that it was Momo who tapped the bird free.

Ebo knew the bird was too old to make it home, knew that it would die a watery death trying. But as it circled them now, climbing higher and higher, he let go of everything he knew. He craned his neck to track the bird as it became just a curl of calligraphy against a cloudless sky. All the while, Momo looked across the ocean in the direction of home, waiting for the bird to dip into view.

Sarah Shun-lien Bynum

Julia and Sunny

OUR FRIENDS, our very good friends, are getting a divorce. Julia and Sunny, lovable and loving, whom we've adored from the beginning, when we were all in medical school. The past few years have been difficult, we know that; we've known that for a while. It's not news to us that there've been problems, some counseling. A furnished short-term apartment. But still: it is a shock. Julia and Sunny, both in our wedding. And the same with us, for them. All those ski trips, the late-night card games, the time we hiked the Inca Trail and threw up repeatedly in the high altitude. There are kids now, and if any of us went in for that sort of thing, we'd be godparents; that's the kind of close we are. Or were? There are moments when we feel as if we don't know them anymore.

Julia's family owns property in New Hampshire, right on a lake, a place the four of us have been going to for so long that we can't help but think of it as ours. When we were in school it was close enough that we could go up any time we wanted, but now, with Julia and Sunny living in Missouri and us in South Pasadena, it's no small feat to get there every summer, as we have. The last week of July, without fail.

It was at the lake house, two summers ago, that Julia began talking about letting some air into the relationship. Those were her words. She sat on the splintery bottom step, gnawing on a coffee stirrer and swatting at the blackflies, frowning, saying that she'd been depressed over the winter and started taking Lexapro. Lexapro? We tried not to let our eyes meet. Julia had always been so sparkly. And with all that energy! Loping off into the dawn, her orange nylon jacket bright in the mist. There was nothing she loved more than to run and swim, to travel impossible distances by bicycle, to sign up for half marathons on holiday weekends. She always wanted us to join her but never shamed us when we didn't. She never noticed when her running shoes tracked stuff all over the rug. But for an athletic person she was mystical too, full of superstitions and intuitive feelings. During our second-year exams, she brought each of us a little carved soapstone animal she'd found in a global exchange gift shop behind the pizza parlor and insisted that we give them names. Hers, named Thug, looked as if it could have been a tapir. With the help of our animals we managed to pass our exams, to do well on them, in fact, and we celebrated by having a dance party and eating too much Ethiopian food and then, years and years later, felt unspeakably touched to discover Thug sitting on the windowsill of their guest bathroom, looking fine. That was Julia—sentimental and fond, likely to invest inanimate objects with meaning, always sneaking off to exercise—the Julia we knew, and it was hard to imagine that person in the grip of a dark Midwestern winter, writing herself a script for antianxiety meds. She tossed her chewed coffee stirrer into the grass and said listlessly, "It'll biodegrade, right?" When asked what she meant by *some air*, she sighed. "I don't know. I'm still figuring that out."

Where was Sunny when she told us this? He must have been off somewhere with the kids. It's easy to allow that to happen: he's good with them, naturally, one of those rare people who manages to still act like himself when he's around them. Our son,

Henry, has formed a strong attachment to him, somewhat less so to their daughter, Coco, who is eighteen months older and a little high-strung. They don't always play well, so having Sunny there to facilitate was helpful, maybe necessary. He kept them occupied with owl droppings and games of Uno; he coated them in deet-free bug spray and took them into the woods hunting for edible plants that we then choked down as a bitter salad with our dinner. Wherever he might have been with them that afternoon, he wasn't there to add his thoughts on letting the air in. Julia was the one who started us wondering, and for a long time afterward, hers would be the only version we knew.

In a way, it was almost like being back at the beginning, back before there was a Julia and Sunny, back when there was just Julia, knocking tentatively at our apartment door, bearing bagels and cream cheese, rustling in her workout clothes, desperate to talk. She wanted to learn all she could about Sunny, who had kissed her briefly on a back porch at a party, and as the people who usually sat next to him in immunology, we were interesting to her. Among the topics we covered were his note-taking, which was haphazard; his penmanship, loopy yet upright; the scuffed leather satchel in which he carried his books; the silver ring he wore on his right hand; the involuntary tapping of his foot. All three of us liked the dapper way he dressed, as if ready at a moment's notice to spend a day at the races. We liked, too, the things he'd say to us beneath his breath during the lecture, comments that were off-kilter and often very funny. He was easily the handsomest person in our class.

This was the point at which Julia would kick off her sneakers and we would really dig in. That woman Sheri—now, what was that all about? Sunny had dated her at the very beginning of the year. She was a type that schools were eager to get their hands on back then: definitely not premed, but the kind who does something interdisciplinary, like East Asian studies, and then takes some time off and has life experiences. In Sheri's case, she had doubled in classics and dance theater at Reed. She didn't have any piercings, at least as far as we could tell, but she did have a large tattoo on her right shoulder of a woman who looked suspiciously like her. Same flaming red hair, same wide red mouth. But how could we be sure? Asking would be rude. And she was difficult to have a conversation with, precise and cold in her way of speaking but nervous in her body, a little twitchy, her eyes darting about. Yet Sunny had wooed her, had undoubtedly slept with her! That haughty kook. At Halloween, they dressed up as a garbage collector and a bag of garbage. She was the hottest bag of garbage we'd ever seen, all silver duct tape and clinging black plastic, wobbling slightly in a pair of bondage boots. Soon after Halloween she and Sunny split up. "And a good thing too," we pointed out, given the accidental comedy of their names. Julia had never noticed this before, and now she laughed and laughed, with genuine delight. "Sunny and *Sher*-i," she repeated, eyes shining, and stretched her long limbs in the morning warmth of our apartment, already perfectly at home.

We liked it when Julia dropped in on us unannounced. She made us feel romantic. She'd peer at the photographs lined up along the mantel of the bricked-in fireplace; she'd compliment the ceramic salt and pepper shakers, shaped like French roosters, and open the flimsy kitchen cabinets to admire the plates and cups within. Settling back into the recently acquired club chair, our secret pride and joy, she propped her feet up on the matching ottoman and cried out, "I never want to sit in a papasan again!" It pleased us to no end. We were new to this, and sometimes just the sight of our clothes hanging companionably in the closet, or our large and small shoes jumbled in a heap by the door, would be enough to send us falling onto the nearest sofa in a sort of diabetic swoon. With Julia around, we wanted more than anything to while the day away discussing Sunny, and never have to send ourselves to the library, or class.

Julia alone, whose soft knock on the door used to make us so happy, now fills us with a feeling similar to—we hate to say it— dread. Sometimes when she calls, we do not have the wherewithal to answer. We're afraid that the conversation will go too long, or that she'll bring up Robert again and want to be affirmed. Sometimes we let her phone calls go straight to voicemail, and then allow a few days to pass before we even listen to the message.

"Aren't you going to call her back?"

"I think it's your turn. I'm pretty sure I did it last time."

"Are you keeping score?"

"Keeping track is not the same as keeping score."

"Seriously?"

"I just don't want this to become exclusively my job. Like what happened with the pool."

We can't help wishing that maybe one of these days Sunny would give us a call. Before we even really knew him we liked him, from afar we liked him, and sitting next to him in class we were charmed by his sudden way of smiling and his jaunty haircuts, which he received weekly from his octogenarian landlord, who in a former life had been not only a barber but a classical music deejay. This was the sort of information he'd occasionally divulge, each casually offered aside accreting into an ever more subtle, complex, and absorbing picture. He enjoyed reading fiction, especially Nordic detective novels. He'd once played lacrosse at a very high level, and done massive amounts of hallucinogens. He'd gone to a good boarding school but a mediocre small college, spent much of his twenties trying to save his family's electronics business, and now here he was, making his comeback in medical school, where by all accounts but his own he was doing very well, with seemingly little effort.

We liked him, too, for not continuing to kiss Julia at parties.

We appreciated the clarity of his intentions, and the way in which it flatteringly reflected our own: because what sane person wants to keep messing around at this age? That was what the undergraduate experience had been for, those four short and sweaty years. Now it was time to relax into something real. "He asked me on a *date*," Julia said in wonder. "That's actually the term he used." We suggested she wear her hair down.

She had brought over some different outfits to model for us. It was like watching a parade of past Julias: a kittenish little number she'd worn during her year singing a cappella; a pleated skirt and sweater set that had been her daily uniform as a temp. She retreated modestly into our bathroom between each costume change. "None of this is working, is it," she called from behind the door. We had a glass of wine waiting for her when she emerged again, plucking at the neckline of something cheap and brightly patterned, the kind of pretty dress found for half price on a sidewalk rack. She looked with longing at the wine but didn't take it.

"Will you drink it for me?" she asked. "I'm already nervous that I'm going to have too much at dinner. And wine turns my teeth purple, so I've decided that I'm just going to stick with gin and tonics for the night. The lime always brings me to my senses." She hiked up the skirt of her dress and climbed unceremoniously into the club chair. "Oh no. Do you think this place is going to have a full bar, or just beer and wine?"

As we searched the bookshelf for our restaurant guide, Julia recounted tales of other boyfriends she had had. She didn't want to make any of the same mistakes again. One ex had followed her down to Ecuador during her semester abroad and camped out for two weeks at a nearby youth hostel, watching her morosely from an Internet café as she walked in the mornings to the local clinic. And then, the year after graduation, she had become embroiled with a Ph.D. student who was supposed to be supervising her at the lab where they worked, doing gene sequencing in a mild stupor. He was already engaged to someone else, which had made things extra heated and complicated between the two of them. She'd trained for her first marathon with him, and it was really more the running than the lab that had gotten them into trouble, and even though the relationship had ended in disaster and she was relieved, *glad*, that it was all over and done with, sometimes even now she found herself crying a little as she ran.

At least there was a full bar, according to our guide. "The crispy cod cakes come recommended. Also the short-rib ravioli."

"I'm not saying that going out to dinner automatically makes him my boyfriend. I'm getting ahead of myself. Way ahead of myself, as I have the tendency to do."

"Did the fiancée ever find out?"

"Oh, sure. It was kind of inevitable. I think he was just looking for a way to avoid getting married and there I was. Literally sitting right next to him, day after day. I had the whole convenience factor going for me, which can be a powerful source of attraction," she said plainly. Sitting cross-legged in the chair, she planted her elbow on her knee, and then her chin on her palm. She gazed out the window at our air shaft, where the daylight was already starting to disappear. "Do you realize that Sunny is the first guy I've liked *before* he liked me?"

We stopped listening for a moment to wonder which of us had liked the other first, and how, when things happened so naturally and fast, was it possible to tell?

"Which seems significant somehow," she was saying. "Even if nothing comes of tonight, even if he never asks me on a date ever again. I'll still feel hopeful. In a general sense. About me and love." She inhaled. "Please forget I said that word." And then, recalling her audience, she smiled at us trustingly. "But you probably use it all the time."

We did, of course, and contrary to what we thought, it didn't necessarily make us authorities. We believed strongly and without any particular evidence that Sunny had liked her all along, even back in the days of Sheri and the garbage bags, and we told

her so. From where our confidence came we couldn't have exactly
said, but it struck us as indisputable, the rightness of Julia and
Sunny, and on this feeling alone we were willing to stake our new
friendship with her, and to not say a word when she leapt out of
the chair and put on her coat while still wearing the cheap dress,
which wasn't nearly nice enough for the restaurant where he was
taking her. We experienced not the slightest protective urge as we
sent her out the door.

In fact, the wrongness of the dress only served to further endear
her to him, as did, we were to learn soon enough, her half-drunk
insistence upon paying her share of the bill and her less drunk
attempt at getting him to sleep over. Julia had predicted correctly
that he would never ask her on a date again. It seems miraculous
to us now, the quantity of mistakes we made, mistakes that should
have sunk our romances straight off from the start: the hasty tumbling into bed, the disproportionate demands, the declaration of
feelings. How did we manage to stay together despite all of those
offenses? Today young people are so *cagey*. Always keeping their
options open, hedging their bets. Sure they have a lot of sex with
near strangers, but that's not the same as being heedless in love.
Not like us! Before we knew it, Sunny was making dinner for
Julia most nights and cleaning up afterward. He was, he is, a terrific cook: cassoulets, curries, the most remarkably ungreasy fried
chicken. We had never liked lentils before trying his. The card
table set for four, the yellowish glow from Julia's thrift store lamp,
our textbooks, open to the same page, spread like stepping stones
across the floor, the steam rising from whatever rich, soupy thing
Sunny had just placed in front of us . . . It was a very sweet time.

Incredibly, he liked us back. That was the great, unhoped-for
gift of it all, that Sunny—whom we had admired from both near
and far, from our plastic seats in the lecture hall and over bagels
at our apartment, who had so enchanted us with his distracting
good looks and breezy style and eccentric remarks—appeared to
find pleasure in not only her company but ours. It now seems

negligible, his being six years older, but then the difference in age felt meaningful to us, as if we were being paid a serious compliment. Often, he would send us into spasms of private delight by doing that thing that comedians do, a callback, he was so good at doing that, plucking out of thin air some throwaway line we'd mentioned days earlier and then making it sound hilarious and intimate by referring to it again. He was listening, he was remembering! Even his impatience made us happy. Once, we were driving home from a camping trip in the mountains, and after sliding up and down the radio dial a few times, he finally landed on something he liked, turned up the volume, and then swiveled around to grin at us from the passenger seat. It was a song we hadn't heard before. Neither had Julia, clearly. She was driving with her eyes fastened on the road and a small, polite smile on her face. "Guys. Really?" Sunny looked at us in despair. "It's their best record. With the kudzu on the cover?" He let out a low groan. "You probably weren't eating solid foods yet."

So much of that is irretrievable now. The papers haven't been signed and filed yet, but Julia and Sunny, as a couple, are over. We've needed to keep reminding ourselves of this fact, only because it is so easy to slip into the habit of hoping otherwise. Our hope has remained quite stubborn for the most part.

"I met him at that physician wellness conference," Julia told us, and started to cry. This announcement occurred in Utah, about six months after our last time at the lake house. We were chopping things atop the kitchen's glittery granite counters while the children, stripped down to their long johns, watched television upstairs, and Sunny drove back to the grocery store because he was making turkey chili and the rental didn't have any cumin. His name was Robert, and he was in radiology. He lived in San Diego. His first email had just been friendly, Julia said. A regular old *great meeting you hope our paths cross again* kind of email. No more than two sentences, and a signature featuring a long list of his various titles and affiliations. They had exchanged business cards after eating a complimentary buffet breakfast together at the hotel, at one of those big, round banquet tables where solitary conference-goers are herded into each other's company. She had had a yogurt and watched him polish off a plate of warmed-over scrambled eggs. After the perfunctory exchange of cards, and after being slightly sickened by the spongy look of the eggs, she was then surprised to experience a little surge of erotic feeling when he stood from the table and she registered how tall he was. Not just tall, but big. Visibly strong through the chest and shoulders, and with thighs that looked like they could belong to an Olympic speed skater. Briefly he had loomed over her.

He was not her type at all, not by any stretch of the imagination—and yet she had been moved to reply. "Take care" was what he'd written in closing, and though every rational part of her knew that this farewell was, if not electronically generated, then at least his go-to phrase when signing off in casual correspondence, Julia couldn't help but feel that there was a hidden message for her in the words he had chosen, as if he had perceived, and was tactfully acknowledging, that she might be in need of some care. So it seemed reasonable to answer, "Thank you for your kind message," and somehow just the typing of that one word, *kind*, released the series of sentences that followed, which began lightly enough, with a humorous account of the delays she had faced when flying home from the conference, but then made a sort of unexpected but lyrical turn toward the prospect of another long winter, the ineffectiveness of Lexapro, and the pain of watching one's only child struggle socially at school. Off it went, off into the ether, and a several-day silence had followed, long enough that she thought for certain she would never hear from him again, an idea that didn't really bother her once she realized that simply the act of writing those sentences down had helped her, and that maybe she should just start keeping a journal like everybody suggests, or at least consider combining some talk therapy with the medication, when bam! There in her in-box one overcast morning: the most wonderful, wonderful reply.

The sound of the garage door churning open caused us to drop our knives and circle helplessly around the kitchen, but Julia, pausing, promised us that Sunny already knew about the radiologist. "I'm committed to being transparent," she said. "And nothing has actually happened. I haven't even seen him since the conference, which is strange to realize. But I feel like something might happen. Soonish." She said it ominously, and all of a sudden looked as if she might cry again. "I just wanted to keep you updated. The thought of telling you guys was almost worse than telling Sunny." She tore a paper towel from the roll and swabbed her eyes while we tried to keep our faces still. We wished that the children would appear, demanding snacks and a different show. What were we to do with this information, except pretend that we hadn't received it? Sunny, smiling, came inside with the cumin, cheerfully unaware that we'd had this talk, and what a relief it was when Henry pulled his groin on the slopes the next day and we had to head home early.

Back in South Pasadena, under the safety of our own duvet, the conversation turned inevitably to Julia and Sunny. And now this new person, this Robert. A *radiologist*, of all things. It was impossible to conceive of the attraction, despite his size and his flair with email. The simple fact was that no one could compare to Sunny, who was sensitive without being spineless, capable but not controlling, funny, affectionate, generous, a highly respected doctor, a hands-on parent, and still so staggeringly handsome. He was aging better than the rest of us. True, they had landed in a city that was a bit off the beaten path, it was hard to get direct flights, the school options weren't terrific, he had persuaded her, for Coco's sake, to adopt a small hypoallergenic dog that she hadn't wanted, her father was showing signs of dementia—but still, on balance, in fact by all imaginable measures, her life was good. Wasn't it? We sank into bemused silence for a moment, and then got sidetracked by a disagreement over who had made the greater professional sacrifices for the other, Sunny or Julia, and in a fit of sulkiness stopped talking, only to wake up in the middle of the night to have intense, heartbroken sex that resulted in our sleeping through the alarm the next morning and Henry's being late to Chinese school.

A phone call from Julia soon followed. "My mom wants Coco to stay with her over the summer. And though my initial response was to say no, now I'm thinking it could be good for both of them." She was calling from the car, on her way home from the hospital. "Coco can be an uplifting presence when she wants to be. Even if she's not, just her being there will keep Mom from dwelling and, you know, fixating. She was always a worrier but it's gotten so much worse with my dad." The ticking of a turn signal punctuated the roar in the background. "The great thing is it'll be a chance for Coco to train with my old swim coach. And she's never ready to come home when we visit. She always wants to stay longer. I think she's kind of starved for an environment that isn't dominated by freeways and Chipotles. A place where you can walk to the corner drugstore." Julia's parents live for most of the year in Rhode Island, in one of those flat-faced colonial houses that stand a little too close to the road. "Does it sound like I'm rationalizing? I'm really not. I really think this will be beneficial for everyone. It's an adventure for Coco, and it gives us a little space. A little room to breathe. Do you realize that Sunny and I have not taken a single vacation without her since the day she was born? I know—you're the same as us. I don't need to tell you. And I know it seems easier with just the one to bring them everywhere, especially when they're this age and they're good travelers, but it's actually not easier in the end, it takes its toll, and we have to remember how important it is, to have time alone as adults—" A getaway! Just the two of them and their swimsuits. It was exactly what they needed. The Azores, or Cambodia . . . "Well, what I meant was time *alone* alone, not together alone," she said gently. "Sunny has signed up for a cruise, believe it or not, because he's short on his CME credits. Then he'll stay on in Alaska for a few weeks to see the fjords and do some camping. You know how he gets about *Grizzly Man*. It's still his favorite." And what would she do? All by herself? With that long, luxurious stretch of unencumbered time? It felt dangerous to ask. "Oh, I'm staying put. Cranking up the air as high as I want and working some extra weekends. Someone has to be here with Peaches."

There was no mention of Robert. And no mention, conspicuously, of the lake house. Months later, in a semiapologetic text, it was confirmed that we wouldn't be gathering there in July. But we have managed to get together with Julia twice this year: first at a Houston's off the 405 in Irvine, roughly equidistant between San Diego and our house, and the second time, also in Orange County oddly enough, for a long, hot, glazed-over day at Disneyland with the kids.

We should acknowledge that Robert ended up not being as bad as we were prepared to think he would be. The meeting up at Houston's had been his idea, according to Julia, and as we drove south we couldn't decide whether this choice was considerate on his part, our drive being ten minutes shorter than theirs, or whether it implied a sort of finicky exactness, an insistence on making everything "fair" instead of just sucking it up and driving to South Pasadena as Julia had most likely wanted. Then again, maybe Robert's plan suggested depths of sensitivity that we hadn't expected, allowing him to intuit that we weren't yet ready to have him hanging out at our house, his very presence polluting the home in which Sunny had cooked countless pots of dal and relinquished so many hands of Hearts. And the fact is, we were not ready, not at all. Which was nice of Robert to anticipate.

Once we all got settled in the leather booth, however, it quickly became clear that none of these factors had played a role; Robert just really liked eating at Houston's, and before we had looked at

our menus, he'd already ordered the spinach dip and grilled arti-
chokes for the table. When we asked for margaritas, we learned
that he was sober. "Three years and eight months," he said with
simple happiness. It was hard to reconcile this large, ruddy person
with the radiologist we'd imagined, the bloodless Lothario who
had destroyed our friends' marriage. As much effort as we had put
into hating him over the past many months, regularly enraged by
the thought of him, our insides roiling at the sound of his name,
Robert was, we had to admit, probably beside the point. We pro-
tested a little when he reached for the check, but eventually gave
in and said thank you. He and Julia had been careful to leave a
few inches of space between them throughout dinner, and as we
watched them cross the parking lot, we saw her take his hand and
kiss it.

The more recent trip to Disneyland was, on the whole, less successful. Julia had persuaded Coco to try a weeklong marine biology
camp on Catalina Island, and apparently her reward for surviving
it was a weekend at the Happiest Place on Earth; the proximity
of all this to San Diego was not lost on us. But it had been such
a long time since the kids had seen each other. We didn't want to
take the high road at the expense of Henry, who'd been lobbying
to do the Jedi Training Academy for a while now, and despite our
discomfort with Julia's self-interested itinerary, and some deep-
seated misgivings about supporting the Disney empire, there was
no graceful way to avoid going. And we should say up front that
the bulk of the blame for what happened at the end of the day
falls squarely on us.

The real problem was the lack of Sunny, of course. We hadn't
sufficiently prepared Henry for the shock of this—we'd mentioned
it plenty of times on the drive to Anaheim, but the reality of Sunny's not being with us was a different thing altogether. Without
Sunny around, the full extent of our children's incompatibility

was free to reveal itself: Coco wanting to do nothing but get her autograph book signed and have her photo taken with princess reenactors, Henry gloomy and lagging behind, unable to recover from the brief high of being a Jedi trainee, which had required us to register as soon as the park opened and then lasted all of twenty minutes. Their only shared inclination was to ask wistfully for "mementos" while stopping to examine the merchandise at gift shops. Neither of them seemed particularly interested in the rides; both of them were unsatisfied with the food options. All of us felt somewhat stunned by the heat and the long waits in line. None of this was helped by the fact that Coco had shot up in the past year and now towered incongruously over Henry.

While shuffling slowly forward we tried to ask Coco questions about her time on Catalina, but she offered only vague, incomplete answers, made more difficult to understand by a metal appliance that had been installed inside the roof of her mouth. "It's called a palatal crib," Julia murmured. "I know it looks like a medieval torture device, but there was no other way to stop her." Coco was a hardened thumb sucker, grown furtive and resourceful over the years. "The orthodontist said that we couldn't even think about braces until we achieved 'total extinction of the habit.'" She widened her eyes at the terminology. "And normally I wouldn't have taken such drastic measures, especially given what's going on right now, but did you see? She's already chipped her left front tooth. Her teeth are sticking so far out of her mouth that the dentist says they're 'constantly vulnerable.' We had to do something—Sunny felt the same way."

We must have perked up at the reference because Julia stopped talking about the crib and instead continued warmly on the subject of Sunny. "I mean I knew this before, obviously, but he is an incredible coparent. That hasn't changed a bit. We are completely in sync when it comes to Coco, really clear at communicating about her needs. And completely on the same page in terms of making this transition feel OK for her. We have dinner as a family now three nights a week, all of us sitting at the table, focused, and we never miss it or let anything get in the way. It's actually more than what we did when we were still living together." It was odd to hear Julia talk this way, using phrases that sounded borrowed from a parenting book. She wasn't bothering to speak in a lowered voice anymore, and Coco seemed undisturbed by the topic, staring agreeably into space, as if she were already accustomed to hearing it discussed in her vicinity.

"That's great," we said to Julia, meaning it. "That's wonderful." We told her we were glad but not surprised. How like the two of them to approach divorce not as a dissolution, but a kind of renovation, a rebuilding into something new. "Yes!" she said. "Something new. And better. With more room for all of us." She smiled at us radiantly.

"And she and Robert"—we nodded at Coco—"they're hitting it off? That's going well?" We were smiling too—at Julia, at the kids, at the other people waiting in line—feeling that maybe we'd been wrong, and that maybe, in defiance of our fretful predictions, everything would turn out all right in the end. But then Julia's lovely face froze into an expression of pure alarm just as Coco, without missing a beat, asked—in a perfectly distinct, piping voice—"Who's Robert?"

"He's a colleague, baby," she said, "you haven't met him yet," and from her backpack she handed out sticks of mint gum to all except Coco, with her mouth crib, who received an energy bar instead. We chewed in silence. No subtle means of changing the subject came immediately to mind. "Watch where you're stepping," Julia warned as she steered the children around a pat of bright pink bubblegum glistening on the ground. "That is definitely not sugarless," Coco noted, and then craned her neck to see if she could guess which person in front of us had spit it out, Robert apparently forgotten.

But as awful as that moment had been, it wasn't as bad as what we felt later that night, after we had dropped off Coco and Julia at their Disneyland-adjacent hotel, and after we had made the trek back to South Pasadena and pulled into our driveway. We turned around and there in the backseat was Henry, sound asleep: head cocked and mouth gaping, arms spread in surrender, a light saber in one hand and a small square of silky, pale blue material in the other. Oh God. We knew immediately what it was. We would know that silky scrap anywhere. It was Coco's. It had started out years earlier as the satin trim on a fancy chenille baby blanket, a blanket she had loved, her favorite thing to do with this blanket being to pile it up on one side of her and then take the very tip of its corner and press it against her nose, where she would stroke it voluptuously with an index finger as she sucked on her then-permissible thumb. Without the blanket she refused to go to sleep; also, she refused to read or be read to, watch a movie, take a time-out, ride in the car—and each summer at the lake house, when Coco emerged from the back of the Subaru, the blanket would appear a little further diminished, until at last it had disintegrated into this one remaining relic-like bit of trim, no more than three inches square. For a few long minutes we sat there in the driveway staring at Henry, feeling sympathetic and sort of furious that he was acting out in this weird way.

When questioned the next morning, he was not very forthcoming.

How did he end up with Coco's wubby?

She was playing with it when we drove them back to the hotel.

But how did it come to be in his possession?

She put it in the cup holder when Julia told her to pull her sweater from her backpack.

And after she put it in the cup holder?

They got out of the car.

Did he tell Coco that she'd forgotten her lanyard, and hand it to her?

Yes.

So why didn't he tell her that she'd left her wubby in the cup holder?

He'd forgotten to mention it.

Did he know how much it means to her?

At this, Henry merely shrugged. He was glowing with resentment and by now crying hard. We discussed the logistics of driving to Anaheim and catching Julia before she left the hotel for the airport, but soon enough came to our senses and made Henry draw a card, first in pencil and then more carefully in pen, which we enclosed in a self-sealing business envelope, unable to find anything cuter, along with the little blue remnant. While it wouldn't quite beat them back to Missouri, Coco would be reunited with her transitional object in just a matter of days. So what an unwelcome surprise it was when the business envelope and its contents appeared in our mailbox several weeks later, looking battered. How stupid—the wrong address! But to us it was the right address, and would always be the right address: the house to which, for years, we had sent holiday popcorn tins and joke gifts and small belated offerings to mark Coco's birthdays. There were now two new addresses, though still in the same zip code, and we hadn't had the chance to update our contacts list with either.

It goes without saying that we did repackage the whole thing, making sure to write down Julia's new house number and street and also including a set of flavored lip balms designed to look like macaroons, which was meant as a mea culpa to Coco but which also necessitated a larger, padded envelope and a trip to the post office in order for it to be weighed and affixed with the correct postage. Little did we know that due to operating budget shortfalls, the post office now closes early on Saturdays—so the padded envelope went into the backseat of the car, and then it migrated to the trunk when Henry and his friends Noah and Griffin had to be driven to basketball practice, and there it stayed for quite a while until a long-overdue Costco haul, when it was discovered again and placed inside the capacious French shoulder bag that's intended to collapse into chic origami but, as the repository for seemingly all of the family's cough drop wrappers, parking tickets, reusable water bottles, school newsletters, store receipts, etc., is never empty enough to do so.

An absurdly long delay—but we did keep Julia posted on our efforts and having looked hard at ourselves can say that it truly was a case of two parents working full-time, a kitchen remodel going sideways, their kid trying out for the travel team and actually making it, and life just being the breathless, nonstop circus that it tends to be these days. After a month of being toted about in the bag, the envelope became part of the furniture, as they say, and encountering its puffy presence while fishing around for a permission slip or the car keys came to feel sort of reassuring. In fact, the envelope was still inside the French shoulder bag when a last-minute trip to New York proved unavoidable, a parent's knee finally needing to be replaced, and who of all people should materialize at the Muji store near the food court in JFK's Terminal 5—full head of hair appearing above the rows of tiny Japanese containers, lean frame moving down the aisle—but Sunny. Our Sunny. Wearing a slate-gray coat and a bright, beautifully striped scarf, looking as marvelous as ever.

It felt unbelievably good to hug him. He smelled of coffee and fig shampoo. Both the scarf and the coat were cashmere, and though it's possible that he had an extra layer on underneath the coat, he didn't feel as thin as we'd been worried he might be. Inexplicably, he seemed an inch or so taller. Never before had my head fit so neatly under his chin. I must have held on for a second too long because he gave me a little pat on the back, letting go.

He was coming from Glasgow, of all places, where he'd been invited to give a talk. He said it went well, and that he'd been traveling more in general. Gracious as always, he asked after us, after Henry in particular, inquiring about school, the basketball season, whether he was still interested in Houdini. He laughed when he learned about Henry's ongoing efforts to raise enough money to buy a straitjacket. As we talked, we browsed through the selection of soothing organizational items, unable to stop touching things and weighing them in our hands, and I chattered about the knee replacement and holiday plans and staffing changes at the hospital, trying to resist the urge to hug him again. It was just so good to see him. It had been such a long time, and he looked so exactly himself, which was a relief to me, a great comfort and a relief. Finally, I admitted this aloud and pressed my face against his shoulder, adding how glad I was to hear that they were all doing so well. Sunny turned to look at me. "We are?" His surprise seemed real. He picked up a pocket notebook and began thumbing through its pages. "Julia told you that?" He shook his head. Then he smiled crookedly at the notebook. "I think it's safe to say that she's speaking for herself."

The notebook ended up going back on the shelf but he did hold on to a clever stapler and hovered over the rainbow array of gel pens, asking if I thought Coco would like them. His question reminded me, for obvious reasons, of the package I had been carrying around with me all this time, the package addressed to Coco; I dug it out of my shoulder bag and held it up for him to see. As soon as I did so, I felt ashamed that we had used Julia's address and not his. Yet it somehow seemed not only an apt correction but an act of fate that he should be the one to deliver it. I imagined the look of amazement on her face when her father walked through the door, bearing his prize: I could picture the appliance glinting in her slightly opened mouth. What serendipity that I hadn't had the chance to make a second trip to the post office! For once I felt good about being harried. I gave the padded envelope to Sunny and explained what was inside.

"Disneyland," he echoed, and then realized: "Which was in August."

I didn't want to bore him with the convoluted story. He had a flight to catch, and still another one after that before he reached home. I knew from experience that he didn't like to rush. He seemed to have changed his mind about the stapler and the pens, maybe because a short line had formed at the register or maybe because—this was my pleased, ridiculous thought in the moment—he already had something special to bring back to her. Outside the store we hugged once more, and this time Sunny was the one to give an extra-long squeeze, and the last thing he said was "Be sure to tell Henry I said hey," before he adjusted the beautiful scarf and headed for his gate.

In other words, we ended on a very warm note, and I turned dreamily in the direction of my own gate, still glowing from the encounter with Sunny but already starting to feel a familiar melancholy at the thought of their divorce. The truth is that my sense of loss has not abated, as I originally believed it might, with the passing of time. *Tincture of time*—a phrase I had first heard while sitting beside Sunny in immunology, his foot tapping away. I think it was my sadness that made me glance over my shoulder to steal one more look at his gray coat, growing smaller as he retreated down the bright, polished corridor, and this is how I happened to see what he did then, which was to take the padded envelope from under his arm and drop it into a large putty-colored trash receptacle. He did it without stopping, in one swift motion, a gesture so fluid that I almost missed it. But this was unmistakably what he did.

Of course I was surprised, actually quite shaken, and I spent the flight home flipping from one free movie to another and trying to analyze the act that I'd not been meant to see. My first hopeful thought was that Sunny didn't want to reintroduce a crutch after Coco had learned to live without it. Entirely possible. Less probable but also consoling was the idea that he objected to the artificial additives in flavored lip balm—I had mentioned the little gift we'd included—or the marketing of beauty products to preadolescent girls. Maybe he'd never liked the blanket and was just as glad to have it gone. Gradually, though, my theories grew darker, and on the drive home from LAX to South Pasadena, I find myself wondering if his treatment of the envelope is a reflection of how he feels about us.

It's well after eleven when I pull up to the house. They've left the lights on for me, but my first impulse upon stepping inside is to turn them off. Upstairs they are in their rooms, asleep, which makes the house feel very still but also full. In the darkened living room, I pick my way to the club chair, now twice reupholstered, and as I sit down, it occurs to me that though I will certainly describe running into Sunny, I'll keep the other part of what I saw to myself. Now that I'm home it's clear that there is no need, really, to bring this abrasive bit of mystery in through the door with me.

Our months of conjecture, our lengthy, circular conversations with Julia: they have left us exhausted, not to mention irritable with each other, and with no deeper understanding of why she doesn't love Sunny in the same way she used to. We ask ourselves, Is there something she isn't telling us? Is she protecting us, out of kindness, from disturbing truths—about Sunny? or herself? As much as we try, we can't bring ourselves to believe what she keeps insisting on, which is simply that she wasn't happy. Simply that her feelings changed. Because this is inconceivable to us, when ours have remained so constant. We love them, Sunny and Julia, as much as we did in the beginning.

Sometimes it happens that in the early morning, we shuffle out onto the landing at the same time—my snoring has gotten worse, so lately I've been sleeping in the guest room—and without speaking we keep shuffling forward until we're touching, resting on the other's upright body, and almost magically, Henry opens up the door to his bedroom, and out he shuffles too. The three of us lean into each other, and it's not exactly a group hug but more like the kind of huddling that animals do in the cold, our flanks rising and falling with our breaths. We stand there sleepily for a minute or two, and once in a while, I'll think I smell something faint and intoxicating, similar to the fancy shampoo that Sunny must have used at his Glasgow hotel; I'll sniff Henry's hair, sink my nose into my husband's T-shirt, trying without success to find it again. Then, as easily as we came together, we break apart and go about our business, knowing that soon enough we'll be bumping up against the same bodies, whether on the landing or in the kitchen or somewhere else. Just knowing that, it seems to me, is plenty as it is.

Stephanie Reents
Unstuck

Liza wasn't sure when things began to change. One day it was the bed: made when she wasn't one for making something you were going to unmake hours later. Another time, it was the walk, swept, and the dead bird that had kamikazeed in the front window weeks earlier, vanished. Then, the kitchen sink looked cleaner. Years of grease scoured, the drain as shiny as a new dime. It seemed as though someone had even taken a toothbrush to the spigot and the handles for the hot and cold. The heaped-up recycling: vamoosed, too. Even she couldn't ignore a clean sink. She called her boyfriend Lloyd to see if this was his doing while he waited to plunge his coffee. Every Monday morning, he left at the crack of dawn to drive back to Phoenix, where he worked at a big accounting firm. They spent weekends together. This arrangement, going on fifteen years, was fine with her. Liza liked a little elbow room.

"No, nope," Lloyd said, "it wasn't me."

"Strange," she said. "I washed the dishes, that's all."

"I seem to recall martinis," he said.

"They make me want to do handstands," she said. "Cartwheels and whatnot. They don't make me want to clean."

"You never know," he suggested; but she did.

She went into the Arizona Room—nothing in its place there— back through the kitchen and into the living room, where everything was as she remembered. Her computer was open on a stool, her coffee cup on a poetry volume—*Small Animal Diagnosis*—that she'd wound up using for the past decade as a coaster. Someone had lent it to her, though she could no longer remember whom. For most of her adult life—she'd be fifty-seven at the beginning of April—she hadn't believed in things like coasters or soap dishes, or even bath mats for that matter. They seemed too specialized. Why buy a soap dish when you could use the edge of the sink? Or a large oyster shell? Or even the lid from a pickle jar? She pulled aside the thick quilt that she'd hung at the entrance to the hallway and went halfway down and into her office. Her breath bloomed. In January, it dipped into the blessed teens at night, and these houses built with little insulation and shit-for-nothing furnaces got so cold you had to get resourceful. Before he left, Lloyd flipped on the mobile radiator in the living room. Then Liza pulled it behind her like a dog, heating only her immediate vicinity.

She was looking for something, but what suddenly escaped her. This was where she kept books, boxes of decorative papers for bookmaking, paste, the computer modem, a busted printer, climbing gear, her mother's old Singer. Was she looking for a book? Her eyes inched across the uneven spines, mostly poetry, most of it from a period of her life where she'd had the patience for caesura, compression, broken lines. It was weird, now that she thought of it, but she'd stopped reading poetry completely after almost getting stuck in a slot canyon in southern Utah. She couldn't concentrate. That was nine months ago. To say she'd almost been stuck wasn't quite accurate. She'd been stuck. She was leading the way on a canyoneering trip through the Middle Fork of the Leprechaun. She knew the canyon would be tight; the night before, several of the bigger men in the group had decided to detour. But Liza was tall and lean and way under 180 pounds, which the canyoneering guide warned was the upper limit for safe passage. The rocks scraped her shoulders in several spots, and she had to climb off the canyon floor and scoot, with her back pressed against one wall and her feet against the other, to pass. She was feeling good, making good time, not that time was relevant in these tight spaces. It swept by. You could come to a technical spot—a spot where you might test dozens of different handholds, make thousands of minuscule adjustments to the angle of hips and shoulders—and an hour whooshed by. Then, without her really noticing, the canyon was suddenly so narrow above her that the space tunneled. Dropping to her hands and knees, she crawled until she ran out of room for crawling and had to lower her belly to the rock. She squirmed, tucked her chin, lowered her head, squirmed some more, tried to relax her shoulders. Her hands, straight out in front of her, frantically felt around for a nub or crack so that she could pull herself forward. She kicked with her legs. She was stuck. She couldn't move forward, and she couldn't move backward. "I'm stuck," she yelled, hoping someone coming right behind her—her friend Carl, or another guy named Jim—could grab her by the ankles and ease her out.

That's right. She was looking for sunglasses. She was sure she had an extra pair with her climbing gear. She'd misplaced her everyday ones. They were probably in the car, but she hadn't been able to find them, though she also hadn't looked very carefully. In the closet, among her mess of backpacks, carabiners, chalk bags, and climbing shoes, her ropes hung coiled from a hook. She never hung up her ropes. She slid the closet door back in place. In the living room, she opened the novel she was reading, had a sip of coffee. It was cooler than she liked, but she couldn't risk going back into the kitchen and noticing something else amiss. Best to stay put.

·   ·   ·

From the very beginning seventeen years ago, she'd disliked the house. She'd bought it because she was sick of the landlord she had back then. Sometimes he showed up in the middle of the night, too high to remember that he no longer lived there. Sometimes he came by to fix something and his dogs, two Dobermans, broke something else. The last time, the dogs were barking at the foot of her bed, and her landlord was yelling, "Goldilocks! Goldilocks!" when she woke up. Her mother gave her $17,500, and within a month she was out. The house was located in what was at the time a new development west of the city, the streets named after women (Shannon, Jennie, Sheryl) and famous racehorses (No Le Hace, Riva Ridge, Flying Fox). This was long before the resort and golf course went in. She could walk five minutes to the end of W. San Juan Drive, which was an exception to the names rule, and be in desert. This was the only thing she liked.

The house itself was a nondescript desert ranch with three bedrooms and one and a half baths. It had a carport and a paved driveway. In the front yard stood a saguaro and a blue agave that eventually shot up a twenty-foot-high flower and died. This seemed ominous. A screened-in porch ran along the back. The poured-concrete floors were covered in linoleum, except in the master bedroom, which was carpeted; the ceilings were popcorned; the windows rattled in their metal frames when the front door was opened. The builder had spared no expense, installing a cheap electric stove, hollow-core doors, ugly fake-wood kitchen cabinets, laminate counters, and a plastic bathtub. The rooms were small and claustrophobic; the flat roof was covered in black tar. Even the exterior bricks were fake—just a scrim of stone applied over Sheetrock.

She valued her house so little that she couldn't imagine anyone else buying it. This, along with other idiosyncratic habits of thought, was how she wound up staying for so long and letting so many things go. She rarely vacuumed, and she never scoured the whole tub, only the inside, because she did enjoy a good long soak.

She didn't dust. She didn't wash the windows, didn't wash the sliding glass door between the kitchen and the screened-in porch, she neglected the grout around the kitchen sink. Water dripped into one of the closets, but she never fixed the crack in the plaster. When it rained, which wasn't too often, she just moved a garbage can into the closet and tried to ignore the irregular ticking. Her mother would have pitched a fit; she was the kind of woman who dusted her lightbulbs and cleaned the refrigerator once a week. But her mother only came to visit once, and that was long before the kitchen linoleum grew brown and sticky and her utensil drawers became so chaotic it could take ten minutes to find a garlic press.

She had coffee with her friend Jan at a coffee shop that had changed hands several times. The French country loaf and baguettes were good but the carrot cake and other desserts had gone downhill. That was the problem with living in a place for a long time. You saw that change almost never truly represented progress, just trade-offs.

"I think my house is haunted," Liza said.

"Yeah?" Jan said, sounding not especially surprised. She tipped a straw of sugar into her cappuccino, but did not stir. She liked her foam to have crunch. She and Jan had been having coffee for decades, and there was almost nothing they hadn't talked about. They'd met at the university swimming pool, where each dutifully swam seventy-two laps every morning. Jan sometimes wore two suits to create more drag, which impressed Liza, even though she would have preferred to do her workout naked.

"Little things are weird," Liza said. "Someone took out the recycling and scrubbed the sink."

Jan snorted. "You have a ghost that cleans? Where do I get one?"

"You can laugh," Liza said, "but I'm seriously freaking out. What if it's the same one that . . ." It was the first time she'd made the connection. Something mysterious had happened in Leprechaun Canyon. She preferred not to dwell on it.

"Your guardian angel is back?" Jan said.

"More like meddling angel," she said. "I like my house the way it is."

"You like your house? That's the first positive thing I've heard you say about it in years." Jan suddenly smiled and waved to someone over Liza's shoulder.

"Who was that?" Liza asked.

"Bill," Jan said, her face resuming its natural state.

"Oh jeez. Is he coming over?"

"I don't think so," Jan said, "but so what if he does? He doesn't bite."

"He owes me money," Liza said.

"What?"

"I didn't tell you I lent him $2,300?"

"When was this?"

"Months ago. He needed to rent a truck that he could drive across the border. He was picking something up in Oaxaca."

"For $2,300?" Jan asked.

"What's he doing now?"

"Talking to a woman. The new girl who works behind the counter."

"The old new girl? Or the new new girl?"

Jan laughed. "The one with the snake tattooed . . . Oh god."

"What?"

"He just kissed her."

Liza still hadn't turned around. "Bill's been a horndog since the beginning of time."

"He's probably got thirty years on her."

"Go, Bill, go!" Liza said. "Get it up!"

Jan groaned.

"What do you care?" Liza asked. "You're a lesbian."

"It's just such a cliché: the old guy and the girl. And the girl's thinking, *This is no cliché, we're different than everyone else.* But they're not. Her guy is just like every other old guy—he wants to stick his pecker in some yummy, preferably hairless pussy."

"Whoa," Liza said. She thought she knew Jan, and then Jan would come out with something so totally surprising. This was another reason they'd remained friends for as long as they had. "I dated an older man once, but I wasn't particularly young. Does that count?"

"It's all relative," Jan said. "When I was thirty-one, I dated a guy who was forty-eight. You know what he told me? He said, 'You're the oldest woman I've ever been with.' Then he stuck a pencil under my breasts to prove they were already sagging."

"You dated men?" Liza said. "I thought you'd always been a lesbian."

"Basically, yeah. Except for a couple years in my early thirties when I decided that women were such head cases. But it turned out to be a grass-is-always-greener kind of thing because men are head cases, too. And they're assholes. And their stuff is bigger and takes up all the room in the dresser. And they have penises."

"I think it's peni."

"Seriously?"

Liza giggled. "No, not really. I made that up."

"The only thing that men have on women is that they're better at fixing stuff."

"I wish Lloyd were more like that." Lloyd was handy enough, but he preferred sorting out people's problems with money.

"But now your ghost or guardian angel has followed you back to Tucson," Jan said.

"Don't laugh," Liza said. "The whole thing is unnerving."

"Maybe you've been cleaning things in your sleep."

"Are you kidding?" Liza couldn't believe how upset she was, even though Lloyd had suggested as much. "I hate cleaning."

. . .

Liza was reluctant to go home. A handful of other times things had spooked her, and she'd wished she wasn't mostly on her own. A fire at the house diagonal to hers had killed the old man who lived there. For weeks afterward, if she wanted to go for a walk, she went out her back door and took the long way to the path that led out into the desert, but there was no detour when she was driving, and it required serious discipline not to stare at the charred La-Z-Boy and cowboy boots that remained in the driveway. Another time, a white pit bull found its way into her fenced yard—she never could figure out how—and killed her cat, Stelley. She told people that she'd had to stand by and watch the whole sickening thing. But the truth was that after she called 911, she crouched in the closet.

The most unsettling thing was also totally mundane: those times, especially over the past year, when she'd wake with no idea where she was. Nothing looked familiar—not the French wardrobe that she'd inherited from her mother, not the red stool that she used as a bedside table, nor the room itself with windows on one side and a mirrored closet on the other. She'd look at a shape in the wall, wondering what it was. It might be dark or light, depending upon a number of factors. When sense trickled back and showed her that the rectangular shape was a door, she'd puzzle over where it might lead, whether someone might come through it. It was terrifying to feel so disoriented, so in the wrong place. She blamed the house; it had never been quite right.

To kill time, she went to Whole Foods, a store she loved to hate, but as soon as she stepped under the buzzing fluorescent lights and heard "Purple Rain" playing in the background she couldn't think of a thing she needed. She was surprised management hadn't done a study that showed that playing Prince so soon after his death was a bummer and dampened middle-aged women's desire to buy $14 pieces of blue cheese. Was she even middle-aged? She didn't want to think about it. At the front of the store, a man was giving away free samples of mint-flavored water. It was dumb to use plastic cups the size of thimbles, but Liza grabbed one anyway, took a sip, and promptly spit it out.

"You don't like it?" sample man said. He had a John Deere cap and one of those big bushy beards that were favored by hipsters. The Sunday funnies were tattooed on his arms.

"What's the point?"

"Refreshment," the man said. "Enjoyment."

It was hard to read his tone: Ironic? Sincere? "It tastes like cheap gum."

His beard bobbed up and down as he frowned. "Look, lady, I'm just the messenger."

"When did plain water stop being refreshing?"

"Consumers' taste buds have evolved."

"Boy, you drank the Kool-Aid," she said.

He looked blankly at her.

"Never mind," she said, handing him back the cup. "You're too young. Be sure to upcycle that."

She left the store with two apples that she hoped would be crisp, a handful of firm red grapes that she knew were good because she'd sampled them, a small block of really sharp cheddar, and walnuts.

When Liza arrived home, she was thinking about how irritated the checkout people at Whole Foods became when they saw that she had not bagged her fruit. They also despised her for using paper bags for bulk and not writing down the bin numbers. (They had to make themselves useful in some way.) But plastic bags were overrated and ecologically hazardous, and what was the point when she could stash the grapes in her crisper or even a bowl with a plate for a lid. Or leave them on the counter, because the more she read about refrigeration, the more she was beginning to think it was overrated, too. After she put away the groceries, she poured herself a glass of water (it was filtered water, okay, she wasn't perfect) and threw herself down on the couch. By midafternoon, she was better off dealing with fictional characters who were more interesting and less predictable than actual people. She couldn't remember the name of the novel she'd been reading that morning—that happened a lot, it was annoying, she had to write things down—but it was about a man who believed that his wife was poisoning him. They'd had a long and happy marriage, though lately the man, who'd quit working earlier than most (just like she had) and had started building exquisite little wooden boxes in his many spare hours, suspected his wife of having an affair. When she went to the grocery store, she wore a dress. When she came in with the mail, she was smiling. Most damning, she told the man day and night that she loved him. He had no real proof she was poisoning him, only that she'd started serving him soft things like chocolate mousse and lemon pudding for dessert, and his mind often felt fuzzy. It wasn't Liza's usual kind of book, but it was entertaining. She had a hunch the wife wasn't having an affair, and the husband was losing his mind. But that also seemed too obvious, especially since she was only midway through. There had to be a twist. She sometimes worried that Lloyd had a lady on the side. She didn't really know how he filled his free time up in Phoenix. But then she thought about how much they loved each other, and the idea seemed ludicrous. As she'd grown older, she'd gotten better at wriggling out of the grip of her fears. She sat up to get her novel, but it wasn't there (on the side table, on one of the three stools she used as ad hoc coffee tables, anywhere where she would have normally left it). Now that she looked around, she saw that all her books were gone. Her novel. The other books stacked in a precarious pile. Vanished. They were library books, damn it. They were overdue, yes, but she'd worked out a deal with the circulation librarian where she brought Mexican wedding cakes, when she remembered, and her fines disappeared. Now what would she do? Tell the librarian they'd been carried off by a mysterious intruder? She called Lloyd.

"It's back."

"The orange-breasted hummingbird?"

"No."

"What?" he asked.

She was silent.

"I can't hear you," Lloyd said.

"It's the ghost," she said. "Why would I call you about the hummingbird?"

"Because you would," he said, "and you have. It's a cool bird."

"I have a ghost, and you want to talk about a hummingbird."

"Calm down," he said. "Open a beer."

"At three p.m.? Do you not know me?"

"You've been known to drink a beer at lunch. Or after hiking."

They kept arguing, first about Liza's drinking habits and second about Lloyd's desire to solve everything, until Liza began to cry. She rarely cried. The last time had been Leprechaun Canyon. Lloyd immediately offered to drive down after work, even though it was a Wednesday, because Liza would be too afraid to go to sleep. What if she heard something in the middle of the night? She didn't believe in anything, except that luck was blind, and when you were dead, you were dead.

"I'll be fine," she told Lloyd, blowing her nose into a paper towel. "No need to burn a boatload of fossil fuel just because the house is getting cleaner."

"I have a Prius, sweetie. Remember?"

"Oh, right," she said. "I forgot. That's weird."

"You sure?"

"Are you fucking with me?"

"No, I meant are you sure you're okay."

"Of course, I'm okay," she said. "I'm so okay, I'm spiffy."

That time she'd been stuck in the Leprechaun, after an hour or two had passed, she thought that maybe this was it for her. End of the line. There were plenty of places where the canyon divided. She was certain she'd been going the right way, but being right wouldn't matter if Carl or Jim had headed down another branch. Maybe their way would peter out and they'd turn around. Maybe it wouldn't. She tried to distract herself by singing but could only remember marching songs, and it was too depressing to sing about moving when you were stuck. What if it started to rain and the canyon flooded? Then her mind swung around, and she wondered how long she could survive without water. Her mouth got dry. She thought about how Native Americans danced for three days straight without food or drink. Jan had done some ritual like that once. That was the thing they tiptoed around—spiritual shit. Jan, for all her pluck, was a believer. Maybe Liza could last six days if she wasn't moving or sweating much. It was lucky she wasn't claustrophobic, or she'd probably perish from fear. What if something came along and attacked her? A mountain lion. A bear. A snake. Bees. It wouldn't matter if she survived then. She'd lose it, go out of her mind. Could she literally be stung to death? What if nothing happened? No one came, and nobody found her.

"Hello, Nobody," she said in a quiet voice. "It's nice to meet you."

"Nobody, this is No One," she said, "No One, this is Nobody."

The ground was starting to get cold, and her left leg tingled with sleep. Her arms ached from being stretched out in front of her. She tried to shimmy forward for the hundredth time but her shoulders were too broad. Then she tried to push herself backward but she couldn't lift her arms high enough to get any leverage.

She screamed and tried to struggle, but there was not enough room. Her hip stung as though she'd scraped it. Maybe she was bleeding. That was not good. Fresh blood would draw animals. Even bugs. If she felt something crawling on her, she would seriously freak out.

"Stay calm, Liza," she said, and hummed a bit. Her voice, vibrating at the back of her neck, was friendly and soothing.

Stay calm. Calm, Liza. Calm. Stay calm. If she lost her nerve, that would be the end of her. She thought about making decorative boxes, one of her hobbies. Measuring the cardboard. Cutting it. Measuring the paper. Covering the cardboard with a thin layer of paste, applying the paper. She put the pieces between wax paper and placed them under tall stacks of heavy books. She constructed little hinges. When the boxes were finished, she lined them up on her bookshelf, each one empty, each one waiting to be filled. This was one of the few things, besides climbing and canyoneering, for which she had the patience to be precise.

"Help," she cried. "Help."

She called out for five minutes and then rested. She had enough sense to preserve her voice.

It grew colder and then dark. She had no idea how much time had passed. Night came much earlier in the canyon. It could still be hot and bright up above. It could be cocktail hour. Maybe Carl and Jim were mixing camp margaritas. Lloyd loved tequila. Liza loved Lloyd. The only reason he wasn't on this trip was because some bigwig was being audited. The other guys would be opening their Nalgenes of scotch. She licked her lips, pretending she was sucking the salt from the rim of a margarita glass. She was so thirsty. Her whole body was sore, her left calf was cramping. She flexed her toes as much as was possible in her boots. Would it get cold enough that hypothermia was a risk? The instant she thought about trying to stay awake, her eyes were closing.

The things that kept happening, inexplicable and also mundane. A cocktail shaker appeared. (She and Lloyd found that a mason jar and a fine sieve were adequate.) A six-pack of beer vanished. The silverware drawer seemed more organized. The toilet looked cleaner. When a new packet of wheat biscuits went missing, she went to Whole Foods the next day, clutching her receipt for the wrong date, and accused them of sloppy bagging. When she couldn't find something, she wasn't sure whether to blame herself or the ghost. Then something would show up that she hadn't seen for years: a photograph of her grandmother in a halter top; a small bowl carved from black walnut; her mother's engagement ring. She'd suffered intensely when she'd lost that ring. She was wearing it, and then she wasn't. She was impulsive. Unappreciative. Crap at taking care of things. Lloyd took apart the kitchen sink plumbing just in case it had slipped down the drain, but all they recovered was a slimy wishbone. And now some seven years later, it turned up in her top dresser drawer inside the case meant for her mouth guard, except she had lost that on a backpacking trip years ago.

"Are you sure someone's not sneaking into your house?" Jan asked several weeks later over tacos and horchata at the one taqueria that was authentic, but not too authentic for white people. Liza had never seen the point of eating cactus. "Isn't the side door always unlocked?"

"Why would anyone sneak into my house?"

"Why wouldn't they?" Jan said.

"I would never sneak into my house."

Jan said nothing.

"What?" Liza said.

Jan sighed dramatically, "Never mind."

When she woke up, and she didn't remember where she was, and she tried to move, and she couldn't, and she tried and she couldn't, and she tried and she couldn't, she really lost her shit. She was stuck in a canyon somewhere in southern Utah. She screamed, and because she could not move she dug her fingernails into her palms until the skin broke. It was pitch-dark, and she couldn't move, and no one had come for her, and maybe no one ever would. She struggled to stay awake, but sleep pulled her back into oblivion again and again.

Finally, conscious as light sifted down into the canyon, she heard the hopeful crackle of twigs and pine needles catching fire and then tumbling rocks that gradually morphed into the sound of footsteps. "Hey," she cried. "Hey, here I am. I'm here." The sound seemed to come from in front of her. Though her neck was stiff, she lifted her head and in the distance saw a pair of boots and red-socked ankles coming toward her. "Thank god," she said. "I've been here all night. I'm stuck." She rested her head for a second and when she lifted it again, the boots were gone. "Where did you go?" she screamed. "I'm here. I'm right here. I'm stuck. Please help. Somebody, please help me!"

Before she realized what was happening, someone had grabbed her ankles and was pulling her out. "Take it easy," she cried again as her body scraped against the rocks. "Thank you, but take it easy. There's no rush, right?" And then she was freed, except that it was like she was still stuck because her body wasn't working. She lay there for who knows how long, trying to move her limbs. Her breath suddenly sounded very loud, and she realized she was panting. "Carl?" she said, but no one answered. Turning over to her left side, curled like a shrimp, she tentatively bent one leg, then the other. When she got back to civilization, she was going to have a chocolate milk shake. And a large order of fries covered in ketchup and mayo. She heard someone talking about sweet potato fries. Onion rings. "My god, I'm happy you came along," she said. "Dinner's on me." When she finally managed to sit up, she was alone, the smooth canyon walls rising on both sides, the pale blue sky slashed above her. Someone had dragged her from her rocky tomb. She didn't think about everything she would do differently. She wept, and while she was weeping, she popped a stone into her mouth, a trick she'd learned for making more saliva, and started the long limp back, still crying until her body stopped producing tears.

.   .   .

Here she is in the Arizona Room, lying on a red couch that belonged to her mother and used to be nice until the cat scratched it up good. The room seems less cluttered in some way that Liza can't quite put her finger on. Are the screens cleaner? Are there fewer cobwebs hammocking the corners? Where has all the dust gone? She thinks back to Leprechaun Canyon. Maybe if she had stayed in the canyon, the ghost wouldn't be here. Does the yard look different? Is the air cleaner? Someone bangs on the side door and then it is opening. The windows chatter in response.

"Scram!" she yells. "Amscray!"

Grabbing a brass candlestick that she's been using for a doorstop and a broom that is collecting dust, she steps into the house to confront her intruder, to fell him, to tell him to leave her the hell alone. Stop your meddling. She likes her house just the way it is, thank you very much. She winds up to swing the candlestick, but the man, dressed in a plaid shirt and khakis, is busy pulling a carton of half-and-half from a plastic bag. Plastic bag! She hates plastic! Why didn't he bring his own bag, or at least get paper! And how does he know her half-and-half went sour that morning so that she has been drinking her coffee bitter and black all day?

"Shit, are you trying to kill me?" The man takes off his glasses and rubs his eyes. "Shit. Shit. Shit."

"Lloyd?" Of course it's Lloyd.

"I told you I was coming," Lloyd says.

"You did?" she asks.

"I think I should move in." He reaches and pulls her into a big Lloyd hug. "It's about time."

"You want to move here," she says, "into this haunted shithole. You think it's going to improve, but it's not. It's all going to fall apart."

"Funny," he says, except that it's not funny, not for now at least. The house is changing so much, she barely recognizes herself.

Alexia Arthurs

Mermaid River

THE SIGN READ, WELCOME TO MERMAID RIVER, and in smaller print, NO SWIMMING, THE ROCKS ARE SHARP, but my grandmother remembered when the river was just a river. Nobody called it any name or took photos in front of it, and the rocks were sharp but it wasn't anything to keep anyone from swimming. When my grandmother was a girl, the river used to be fat. The day I sat with her across from Mermaid River, it was thinned down and half dried up. And the stones were sharper, angrier than my grandmother remembered, as if the river rebelled when the resort wanted to stretch and the surrounding land was bought up. The river became Mermaid River, and what wasn't bush to be chopped down were houses where country people lived. The houses were torn down, replaced by vacation cottages. But I haven't seen Mermaid River in years, not since I left Jamaica. I only have my memories to go on.

These days I ask for fried plantain between two pieces of bread for breakfast. Sometimes I ask for scrambled eggs on the side, or an egg sandwich with fried plantain on the side. I always drink tea. The cereal boxes sit on top of the fridge, barely touched. They are the sugary kind I see advertised on the television. My mother bought them four years ago as one of many introductions to America. Sometimes, after she's put my breakfast in front of me and I sit eating alone, my eyes will catch on the boxes sitting on top of the fridge and it will occur to me to throw them out. They must be expired by now. But I never do, I always forget, and now they almost seem to belong in our kitchen.

My first morning in this country, I ate the bowl of cold cereal and drank the glass of orange juice my mother put in front of me, and my stomach cramped and pained and finally I vomited. The night before, sleeping in my new bed, all of it felt strange, as though I had stepped out of my skin and was watching myself from outside myself. When I was little I used to show off to my classmates that my mother was in America and would soon send for me. But the story began to seem far off, less true, almost as though it belonged to someone else, so I stopped telling it. That first night, the woman who resembled a woman I used to know— that's how my mother seemed to me in the early days—showed me to my room. She opened a closet and showed me new clothes. She rubbed her hands against the dresser, pulling out drawers to reveal new socks and underwear. She explained that the entire bedroom set was new. In the woman's face, I recognized the roundness of my grandmother's face.

My second morning in this country, my mother asked what my grandmother usually gave me for breakfast. I didn't tell her porridge, which my grandmother prepared every school day, ignoring my complaints. My grandmother believed porridge was "proper food" for learning, since it was the kind of meal that kept a belly full until lunchtime. But I hated how full cornmeal porridge left me—I liked to run to school and it interfered with my speed. I also disliked the lumps and the fact that porridge always made me need to go to the bathroom in the middle of my morning classes. I hated shitting in school, because if you took too long somebody would always make notice of it and ask what you were doing, and then everyone in the class would start laughing.

So I told my mother what my grandmother made on weekends, and since then I've basically eaten the same meal every weekday morning. On weekends my mother prepares pancakes from a box—another "introduction to America." I would prefer plantain and bread and eggs, but I don't want her to feel bad. She already worries what I will eat when I start college next fall. She says if I can get a little hot pan in my dorm, she will ship me plantains if I end up someplace where I can't find them. I tell her she doesn't have to worry. I will eat American food when I have to.

I have on my coat, my hat, and I'm pulling on my gloves when my mother walks down the stairs. She has rollers in her hair, and she's wearing the lavender nightgown. Months ago, when my mother stood in front of the nightgown rack at the department store, she was running her fingers along the pink version of the lavender nightgown. She asked me which one she should get, and since the pink reminded me that there was already too much pink in her closet, I picked the lavender one. Not long after, my mother was drinking a cup of tea while I ate my breakfast. When she got up to wash the breakfast dishes, my eyes were pulled to the back of her nightgown. It took me a moment to realize that I was looking at blood. And it took me another moment to realize it was probably period blood. I quickly turned my face away, begging my mother to see the blood herself because I didn't know how to voice those kinds of things to her. I heard her walk up the stairs, and before I left for school she had changed into another nightgown. Whenever she wears the lavender nightgown, I always remember the blood, and sometimes I look for evidence, the dull imprint of an old stain. There isn't any. My mother comes over to put some money in my hand, as she does every Monday morning since she knows I like a beef patty and a cream soda from the Jamaican restaurant after school. She also gives me the letter to show my teachers. I fold it without looking at it and put it in my coat pocket. Then she is wrapping her arms around me and whispering a quick prayer because she watches on the news the ways in which America can swallow black sons. She still worries, even though I've done well in Brooklyn for so long already.

Last night it snowed but only left a dusting. I watch where my boots make prints in the snow. The thing I hate most about winter, besides the cold, snow, and extra clothes, is how dark the mornings are. Because there isn't light shining through my window, I stay in bed longer. I'm always tired until spring comes. The first year, I explained how tired I was and my mother thought maybe I had worms, so she bought a special drink for me. The drink was meant to clean me out, which is why my mother asked me if I saw any worms when I used the bathroom. I told her I didn't see anything, and because she asked when my stepfather and I were eating dinner, he began to choke because he was laughing so hard, and it took him a long time to finally say, "Why are you asking the man his business for?"

There is an old woman in a wheelchair waiting at the bus stop, smoking a cigarette with gloved fingers. There are also the regulars, a mother with six children huddled up next to her. All of them look exactly like each other, and nothing like her. The oldest boy helps the mother huddle the smaller ones, since her arms are busy holding the smallest one. All their names start with "Jah"— the mother is calling their names because the bus is pulling up. "Jahzalia. Jahmalia. Jahmajesty. Jahmarie. Jahzal. Jahdan." The oldest boy is hauling the stroller onto the bus and the mother calls the names of all her children, worried that she will lose one of them. The eyes of everyone on the bus are forced wide open because the mother is loud and everybody is wondering at those names and all those children.

The bus stops at the L train station. Just before the doors open, the oldest Jah hollers bye to his brothers and sisters, and his mother pulls him down to her to kiss his cheek, smashing the youngest one between them. It is loud and very dramatic. Even the bus driver is looking through his rearview mirror. I get off too. The family does this every morning, as if they don't live in the same house and see each other on a daily basis. Then the youngest is crying and the mother is holding him up to the window so he can see the brother, who is standing on the sidewalk waving one last good-bye.

On the subway platform, the conductor speaks on the inter-com, asking people to please let go of the doors. He says that another train is pulling up in two minutes, and people causing a delay are endangering themselves, but nobody pays him any mind. One lady holds the doors open for a whole group of people, including me. Now a man is holding the doors open for the last stragglers.

Every morning the same old lady walks up and down the train car, preaching and giving tracts to anyone who will take them. She always seems to pick the fullest car, the last one, weaving her way through and around people and never bothering to break her sermon to say "Excuse me." After preaching, she prays for us and then she breaks into a hymn. The woman next to me hisses her teeth and says it is too early for all of this. Two girls, maybe two years younger than me, are leaning against the doors and laughing into each other, probably because the singing is so bad. The old lady tries to give a tract to a couple with dreadlocks, but the man takes one look at the tract and says, "A white Jesus you a gi mi? Mi no bother wid nuh white Jesus." The woman he is with laughs. Most everyone else is folded into himself or herself, sleep still in their eyes because they are holding on to the last free moments before work or school.

I touch the letter in my coat pocket. I imagine the tidiness of my mother's handwriting and the polite way of her words.

When I was little, my grandmother and I lived in the house I was born in. The bed my mother used to sleep in when she was a girl was the same bed she gave birth in, a bed I claimed as my own for the eight years my mother left me with my grandmother. My placenta and umbilical cord were buried under either the ackee tree or the breadfruit tree. My grandfather buried them deep, so no dog could get to them, but he died when I was a baby and my grandmother couldn't remember which tree it was. She always wanted to say it was the ackee tree but she really wasn't sure.

My name was supposed to be Sylvia if I turned out to be a girl or Roy, after my father, if I turned out to be a boy. But when my mother pushed me out, my grandmother said that no one spoke for a moment, and then the midwife, a woman with aging eyes, asked, "A light 'im light so?" No one who had seen how dark my father was would have asked that. "Samson," my grandmother said. "We a go call 'im Samson." My grandmother said she looked at my albino skin and knew I would have to be strong. That's why she named me Samson instead of after my father, whom she called a "cruff" whenever his name came up. Because the labor pains silenced my mother and my grandfather wasn't interested in what they named me if it wasn't after him, no one argued with my grandmother. My name is Samson Roy Johnson.

When I lived with my grandmother, she used to take me with her down to Mermaid River. But I soon became tired of sitting around while she and the other women took care of business— selling the food they prepared, talking people's business, and whatever else old women did that bored me. I was freed when my grandmother started leaving me at the house of a woman who watched children, and then I started school. After that, I hardly bothered to make it down to Mermaid River, and then, when I went of my own accord, it was because of what Roger Boxx said.

A man went mad down in Porus and chopped his wife with a machete, which was how Roger Boxx came to be in my class, since his people took him and his little sister to live with them. Everyone had heard about the woman who was chopped. My grandmother and I were eating fried fish and watching the evening news. She paused from picking a fishbone out of her teeth to say, "Jesus," elongating the word and almost whispering, in the way she did whenever she heard something painful and surprising, or sometimes, miraculous.

Roger Boxx was the shortest boy in our class. He took over from Clement Richards, who had been the shortest boy in the class but made up for his height with his voice, which sounded like he was copying after his father, who was a Seventh-Day Adventist minister. Nobody paid Clement Richards's height any mind because they were invested in the way his voice sounded, in the highs and lows, the drama of it. Roger Boxx didn't seem to have anything about him to level out his height, so nobody paid him any mind. He took up a space next to those of us who were never invited to play cricket. Silently, except when it came time to cheer, we watched the games from the edge of the field.

After a week or so, Roger Boxx and I were paired up as spelling partners. As soon as he sat down after pushing his desk next to mine, he told me that he had a Game Boy at home. I told him I had a three-legged dog named Delilah who ate the pears that fell from our pear tree. We became inseparable.

I remember how one time Roger Boxx said that he wanted to see Delilah but when we got to my house, she was nowhere to be found. This was because, as I suspected about the Game Boy, I didn't have a three-legged pear-eating dog named Delilah. In fact, a man who lived down the road owned a three-legged pear-eating dog he called Trouble. The first time I asked about the dog's name, the man told me Delilah since he knew my name was Samson. I didn't confess any of this to Roger Boxx. We walked around the yard calling out Delilah's name, and I told Roger that sometimes Delilah walked all over the district and then she might come home with somebody's fowl in her mouth.

This was how Roger Boxx and I, tired of looking for Delilah, came to be playing marbles in the front yard when he looked up and asked, "Who is dat ole woman?" I looked up quickly to see who was walking into the yard and my mind got stuck on the word "ole" when I saw that he was talking about my grandmother. I never thought of her as old until he said it, maybe because she raised me as if she was my mother since my own mother had been in New York for eight years already, working and making a way so that she could send for me. Or it could have been because she was big and tall, and even with gray hair she never seemed weak. Old meant weak to me then. The word surprised me, offended me, and put a fire under my tail. I decided that since my grandmother was old, I had a responsibility to help her more.

I get off at Broadway Junction. The preaching woman gets off too, hauling two big bags with her. Just before the train stopped, she abruptly ended the hymn, gave everybody a last word about Jesus's coming again and getting our lives right, and quickly stuffed the tracts and Bible into one of her bags. We go up the stairs and then the morning crowd swallows her. I follow the crowd that gets on the down escalator, then walk a little way to the stairs that lead to the A and C train platform. The A train is pulling off but that's okay. It's really the C I need to get on.

I sit next to a young couple sleeping on each other. It's the only free seat. The girl's legs are spread out across the guy's lap, his arms are wrapped around her, and they look to be completely lost in sleep. Across from me a woman is looking into a mirror and putting on her entire face. My mother's voice comes into my head, so I smile. She would call the couple sleeping and the woman putting on her makeup "slack." She would be horrified. She would say that Americans don't have any shame, and she would warn me, "Please, Samson, I didn't bring you to this country to tek up dem ways."

.   .   .

The morning after Roger Boxx called my grandmother "ole," instead of running off early to watch the cricket games in the schoolyard, I stayed behind. After I had eaten my porridge, washed my face, brushed my teeth, and put on my uniform, I stood behind my grandmother in the kitchen with my hands in my khaki pants pockets. Standing around was the quickest way to become involved in whatever needed to be done around the house. "Here," she said, bumping into me as she turned around in our small kitchen. "Yuh look like yuh wan' someting fi do." She gave me a pan filled with big pieces of coconut to cut into the little pieces she used to make coconut drops. That morning she had thrown the coconuts against a big rock behind our house because it was the way she busted them open. I'd heard the coconuts being flung while I ate my porridge.

When I got to school, Roger Boxx and the other boys who nobody wanted on their team were watching the last minutes of the game. Roger held his arms up as if to say, "Where were you?" I only shook my head, because explaining I had willingly stayed behind to help my grandmother cook wouldn't make any sense to him. I took my place next to him and we watched the rest of the game together.

After school, I told Roger Boxx that I couldn't play marbles because I had to help my grandmother. He looked at me as if I wasn't making any sense to him. After I walked out of the schoolyard, I turned around to see that he was playing football with a marble. I couldn't see the marble from the distance where I was standing, for all I knew he could have been kicking a small stone, but I knew it was a marble because we played football that way sometimes. I almost went back to play with him. I'd told him a half lie. I didn't have to help my grandmother and she wasn't expecting me. My plan was to go down to Mermaid River to help with the selling and, when the sun began to set, the packing up of the leftovers and bringing it all back home.

In front of a yellow house was a tree and under the tree were three women standing huddled close to each other. I saw my grandmother before she noticed me. A big-boned tall woman, she was hard to miss. She was picking at something wrapped in a piece of foil, and then she, Mrs. Angie, and Mrs. Wright were laughing loudly, the kind of laugh that made their whole bodies dance. For a moment it seemed as though the woman laughing as if she didn't have one fret in the whole world wasn't the same woman who quarreled with me. Then she saw me, and I saw myself in her eyes, a twelve-year-old boy prone to trouble since I sometimes didn't know what to do with myself. She started walking quickly toward me and I could see the questions in her face. She wanted to hear what happened, what trouble I had gotten into, since I never made it down to Mermaid River after school.

"Wah 'appen, Samson?" my grandmother asked when she was close enough to call out.

"Nothin'." I shrugged my shoulders.

My grandmother stood in front of me wearing a faded church dress and an old purse, the handles of which were tied around her waist. I knew the purse was where she kept the money she made from sales and the mints she sucked on when she felt for something in her mouth. I grew up hearing her say, "Mi feel fah something," and then she would look for the purse so she could suck on a red-and-white-striped mint. I hadn't seen the purse in some months, and I missed it, because I used to take money when I wanted to buy a suck-suck at the shop, or a mint when I too felt for something in my mouth. I had been taking money and mints from that purse my entire childhood and I always suspected my grandmother knew, but when she finally caught on she said, "O Lawd, O Jesus, O heaven cum down an fill mi soul, di bwoy a thief fram mi!" and then she started keeping the purse somewhere in her bedroom. Although it occurred to me to look for it, I hadn't built up the ambition, especially since the last time I went into my grandmother's bedroom to look for something she hid from me, I hit upon the pail she used in the nights when she couldn't make it to the bathroom. Usually she emptied it out in the toilet before I even climbed out of bed. She had forgotten, that morning, and as I looked down at it I realized that I was seeing the entire meal she had eaten and drunk the night before. I couldn't say why I was so annoyed at being greeted with her bowel movements. At first, I thought it was her negligence that upset me, but then I realized, plain and simple, that I was angry she had created the opportunity to disgust me. At the time I didn't understand why my grandmother was so angry when she came home to meet my annoyance and scorn. It was the complaint I greeted her with when she walked into the house. She wanted to know what I was doing in her bedroom, and if the pail bothered me, why I hadn't emptied it myself. She asked why I left the pail in her bedroom for the entire day for her to come home and throw it out. She wanted to know how I could scorn the woman who had cleaned my vomit and wiped my behind and changed the sheets when I used to wet the bed. The whole incident bothered and embarrassed me, and my grandmother was so angry that she left me to prepare my own dinner.

"Wah yuh doin' down 'ere?" My grandmother wanted to know down at Mermaid River. I remember she was looking over me carefully, and using her hand to shade her eyes, which made the bangs on her wig scrunch up. She braided her hair in little plaits but I only saw them early in the mornings or late at night because she wore a wig everywhere.

"Oh, I just come down to help you." This made my grandmother look at me hard, as though I was telling her stories.

But she looked happy to see me, too. She could show me off to Mrs. Angie and Mrs. Wright, telling them how I always brought home the highest marks in school. She offered me the piece of foil she was eating from. It was a piece of jerk chicken, still warm as I used my fingers to break the flesh apart. Mrs. Angie was roasting jerk chicken in a steel drum and Mrs. Wright was roasting yam, saltfish, and corn in another one. They were across the road from

Mermaid River, under a tree where everything they needed was laid out: chairs for sitting, an umbrella, paper fans, and a Bible and church hymnal and other necessities I can't remember. The tree was in front of the house where Mrs. Angie lived with her husband. On one of the two front walls of the house were painted the words WE SELL HOT GOOD FOOD, big enough for the people in passing vehicles to make out. Every morning my grandmother woke up early to prepare various sweets, like tamarind balls, coconut drops, and plantain tarts. Then she walked down to Mermaid River to sit under that tree with her two friends. On the days it rained, if the rain was very bad, they all stayed home. But if it was only a drizzle, Mrs. Angie would get her husband to tie a piece of tarpaulin under the tree.

There are three black students in my chemistry class, and then there is me. When I told my mother this, she said I shouldn't worry with those things. The *and then there is me* part was supposed to be funny, but she didn't get it. My mother wants to keep me strong to make sure I do something important with my life. My stepfather is a garbage collector, which must have been a disappointment to her. Once, I heard her telling her friend that she never wanted to marry a man who came home with dirt under his fingernails. The irony of my mother's marrying a garbage collector, the exact kind of man she didn't want to marry, filled the next moments with laughter. But my mother says my stepfather's job is very good money in this country, and nothing to be ashamed of, and she says this to convince the both of us, and to meet our surprise, because where we come from, nobody with any shame would willingly collect people's garbage for a living.

When class ends, I walk up to the chemistry teacher to show him the letter. He is an old white man with thinning hair, who smells of cigarettes and something else we can't put our fingers on. He is known to make at least one student a semester, usually a girl, openly cry. He is also the only teacher who cusses in class, saying, for example, "I don't give a rat's ass" whenever someone gives him an excuse. Now he says to me, "I'm sorry for your loss." This is a surprise to hear from him, but how he says it feels appropriate since it's the uncaring way he always speaks. He must have lived a hard life—that's what my mother says about people who are miserable. Then he says it's okay that I'm going to Jamaica, but make sure I get the notes from someone when I get back. I thank him and leave the classroom.

I show the letter to all my teachers. Mrs. Cunningham, my French teacher, looks very sorry for me because this is the kind of person she is. She looks like she is about to hug me but she remembers herself, so she only puts her hand on my shoulder. My classmates want to know what's in the letter because they are nosy. I see them looking at me.

The day I went down to help her, my grandmother and I sat under the tree, waiting for customers. She started telling me about old times—how the river used to be fat, how it used to be unnamed. Eventually a tour bus pulled up across the road, everyone disembarked, and a guide began talking to a group of people. Then the tourists were taking photos and a few crossed the road to our stand. One woman bought a dozen coconut drops from my grandmother, explaining that she was taking them back home with her. As afternoon pushed into evening, cars pulled up alongside the tree. Mrs. Angie and Mrs. Wright would get up to take the orders. I collected one of everything my grandmother prepared and held them out by the top of the plastic bags she tied them in, so customers could see what we had for sale.

By the time the second tour bus pulled up, I had learned that as little girls my grandmother and her friends from primary school tied up their uniform skirts to wade in the river. One time, they got it into their heads to wade in their drawers, so that's how they were, all four of them, and then they wrung out their drawers and hid them in their schoolbags and walked home holding down their skirts in case a heavy wind blew.

Sometimes someone would go home with a busted-open foot, a sharp stone having made its mark. The time it happened for my grandmother she was walking softly on that foot when her mother asked her, "Wah wrong wid yuh foot, gal?" "Nothing, ma'am," my grandmother said, and then she tried to walk normally on the foot, just until her mother shifted her attention to something else. Later my grandmother was made to reveal the foot, to lift it onto her mother's lap, because her mother once again noticed how lightly the foot was touching the ground. Somehow my great-grandmother knew the cut was from a stone in the river, so even while holding my grandmother's foot on her lap, she smacked the side of her daughter's head, hard enough for tears, because she wasn't allowed at the river without somebody grown watching. Later, though, my great-grandmother found a piece of aloe vera to rub on the cut. And that day under the tree, the memory of the whole incident made my grandmother smile.

My closest friend is a Chinese boy named Jason. His real name is something else. Every time we have a new class, the teacher will try to pronounce his Chinese name and Jason will say, "Just call me Jason." We met freshman year in literature class because we sat next to each other, so we were always assigned to work together. When Jason asked where I was from and I said Jamaica, he complimented my English and asked what language Jamaicans speak. I laughed. That question is what I remember when I think about us first becoming friends.

We are the same: quiet, loyal, but mostly our commitment is because we were each other's first friend in a new school. Sometimes we forget each other. Jason will hang out with some other Chinese boys, and I will hang out with the smaller amount of black boys in our school. The black boys like me, especially because sometimes what I say that isn't meant to be funny is funny because I say it. Since I don't want to bother with the pizza they are serving in the cafeteria, and I see Jason with some other Chinese boys eating pizza, I go to the gym to watch the basketball game.

Since the game has already started, I sit on the bleachers and watch. Nicolas looks up and asks if I want to play. "Next game," I say, knowing that by the time the next game starts it will be time to head back to class. Before I moved to Brooklyn, I'd never played basketball before. I like that they want to include me and I've grown to enjoy watching them play when I have nothing better to do, but usually I try to get out of playing, because I know I'm no good.

If I could play basketball better or liked watching it more, my stepfather and I would get along better. We get on fine. Nothing is wrong. I just know I am not the son he was hoping for. Sometimes he sees me studying and says, "I could have used a little bit of that when I was your age," but I know he is also saying, "You are not how I was expecting." Sometimes I'll sit for a while to watch a game with him and I can tell my presence pleases him. When he and my mother picked me up from the airport, he touched my shoulder and smiled; later he would laugh at my accent. My mother told me that because he is older than she is, he didn't want to bother with any babies, which is why he was glad she already had a son. They married just before they sent for me, since my mother didn't want me to think of her without respect. She said she couldn't bring me into any living arrangement with a man she wasn't married to. She is always telling me everything, even what she is ashamed for me to know. This is how my mother kneads the eight years away.

Sometimes I want to lie on my bed in the middle of the day, which is another thing my stepfather doesn't understand about me. I just lie there thinking, with my hands folded under my head, and sometimes I fall asleep. When I lived with my grandmother I used to sit up in the mango tree to think, or when I had to memorize something for school. One time, my grandmother told me that the man next door complained that I was sitting in the mango tree because I wanted to peep on him. But when she told me this, she was smiling like she really wanted to laugh at the man. Because she did things the old way, she didn't want to laugh at him in front of me, because she didn't want me to forget I was a child. I smiled back at her, because this old man was known to be miserable and forever convinced that people were stealing from him, or watching him, or talking his business.

All those years later, my grandmother still went back to Mermaid River, though she hadn't let the water touch her in years. All her life, she only called one place home, and she watched it build up and change so that some parts didn't bear any resemblance. As a little girl walking to and from school, she'd become familiar with the concrete-and-zinc houses whose backyards dipped into the river. In the afternoons a woman used to sit on one of the verandas discreetly breastfeeding a fat baby. Next door lived a couple that seemed to enjoy cursing each other at their gate. A cherry tree leaned out of one of the yards, which attracted schoolchildren. When the houses and the inhabitants were gone, the government finally looked about the potholes in the roads. My grandmother packed her basket every morning and walked the twenty minutes to the river, where people will remember her, if they remember her, as an old woman selling food from a basket when they got off the bus, or stopped their car to see Mermaid River, maybe to take a photograph by the sign. Perhaps they heard the story given by the tour guide, or read it in a pamphlet, or knew it for themselves: an old-time story about how old-time people used to see a mermaid combing her hair on the bank of the river. The mermaid is said to have jumped back into the water when she realized she was being watched. WELCOME TO MERMAID RIVER and in smaller print, NO SWIMMING, THE ROCKS ARE SHARP. Always, someone will dip his or her foot into the water, since the sign only forbids swimming.

Only now does the history of that river sit on me. I realize that my grandmother had a world all her own, one that excluded me because I'd never thought of her as a little girl or as anyone other than the woman who took care of me until the real woman who should have been taking care of me was set up good enough to send for me.

The day after I helped my grandmother down at Mermaid River, I still had the fire lit under me, so I flung the coconuts against the cement at the back of the house. I cracked open tamarinds and, following my grandmother's instructions, folded them into little balls with sugar. I got to school a few minutes early and was shocked to see Roger Boxx playing cricket. That was how he would level out his height; he turned out to be the strongest cricket player in our school. And he brought me along. He convinced the other boys to look past my overall mediocrity and my subpar batting skills, and then my mornings and afternoons were filled with cricket. The first few days, I felt guilty when I thought of my grandmother, an old woman, whom I should have been helping. But guilt often loses its flavor, I've found. My grandmother shook her head when I raced out of the house in the mornings. She said she should have known it was too good to be true, but I knew she missed me. The morning I started leaving early again, I left the coconuts on the dining table. I left them even though I knew they were laid out for me to crack.

I close my eyes on the plane. I see three old women under a tree, laughing a dancing laugh. My mind doesn't recognize who they are and still I want to tell one of them, "I never seen you laugh like that but once the whole time I knew you." I open my eyes and I can't say whether I was dreaming or remembering, maybe both.

My cricket days ended when the school year came to a close because my mother finally sent for me. She had married a man for love. It also solved the problem of getting her papers. Now I am back, finally, for my grandmother's funeral. In the city, the heat feels as if it wants to knock us down; that's what my mother says, she says the heat wants to knock us down. I have been craving the sunshine the whole time I've been away. On our way from the airport, my mother convinces the taxi man to stop in the city. All because my stepfather wants oxtail from a restaurant he ate from when he visited the island with another woman long before he knew my mother. My stepfather says he has been thinking of the oxtail for the past seven years. I see my mother look at him because she cooks oxtail in New York whenever he wants it. I see the look she gives him and I understand because I am her child. The look passes, and then my mother is telling my stepfather to buy enough oxtail for all of us.

This is how my mother and I are alone in Kingston, Jamaica, such a small place on the globe in my world history class that if you aren't careful you can easily miss it. At that market, there are so many people, most of them trying to sell us something. There is a man selling string crafts, he has them stacked up on top of his head and he is shouting that the crafts are patterned into the hummingbird, the national bird. There is a woman selling bammy from a basket on her head. There are fruit stands and men roasting meat, corn, and yams. My mother's head is turning to look at everything and everyone because she so badly wants to use the spending money she budgeted.

Long after my mother and I have eaten, my stepfather is still sucking the oxtail bones.

The taxi is driving my mother, my stepfather, and me to my grandmother's house, where we will meet relatives before the funeral tomorrow. Even though I'm waiting to see Mermaid River, I almost miss it, because on the other side of the street, there is a tree, and behind the tree is a blue house that used to be painted yellow. There is no longer a sign that reads, WE SELL HOT GOOD FOOD. There are no old women laughing a dancing laugh.

I can't remember this, but my grandmother used to say I would sleep on her breast after my mother left. I cried when she put me in bed by myself, so she put me in bed next to her. She said I used to fall asleep with my head on one of her breasts. This embarrassed me because it was a story that my grandmother repeated often to her friends and I realized early that old-women breasts were something I should stay far away from. I didn't know what about the story pleased her to retell it. Now I think maybe she was trying to say "Listen, to how this boy loves me."

Valerie O'Riordan

Bad Girl

Miss york—the school counselor; a meddling, newt-faced wench—gave my stepdad, Simon, the flier: a therapeutic speech and drama course in St. Richard's Church Hall, Cleaverton.

"He's very good!" she said. "It's all about confidence, you know: forming positive attachments with one's peers! Right, Cheryl?"

I grunted. This was Parents' Night, eighteen-point-five months since Ma's funeral. I was down on the school's records as *withdrawn/hostile/uncooperative*, but mainly, in block capitals, *ABSENT*. According to the deputy head, it was therapeutic speech and drama or bust, and Simon was panicked.

He flipped the page: on the other side was an ad for *York's Hypersexual Disorder Support Group*! "What," he said, "in case the attachments get too fuckin positive? How confident are yeh hopin she'll get?"

York reddened, glanced at me. "That's not really—"

"Ah, God," he went, "I'm jokin, amn't I? She's barely fifteen." He scratched his beard. "Well. I suppose we could give it a shot. Eh, Cher? Pet?" He slapped my back. "Lady Macbeth, innit?"

York smiled anxiously—first at Simon, then at me. The deputy head was surveilling our table from his podium at the far side of the assembly hall.

"All right," I went, at last. Fed up. "Fine! God, whatever."

So: me, Mondays, four thirty p.m.—Malachy Mahoney's *Am Dram Family*.

Malachy was a dramatherapist and an RSC fanatic. According to York's sales pitch, he took referrals from shrinks and teachers across the city, although, after my first session, I wondered if any of them had ever actually seen him in action—romping sweatily about the overheated hall, trilling in Ye Olde English at his "behaviorally challenged" students to *emote!* And the students! A sorry band of also-rans, I thought; a social services wet dream.

They were rehearsing *Pygmalion*, Malachy explained, and he stuck me with this gawky sixteen-year-old lump from Overhulme College—Arthur Leese—to run some lines. But as soon as Malachy had pranced off, Arthur ditched the script; he wanted to tell me about insect reproduction. This, he explained, was his calling.

"It's f-fascinating," he said, "it's all about organ p-palpation!" He clutched my arm.

"Ew, bug-face!" A girl, tall, a little older than I was—Arthur's age, maybe—and wearing, like me, a Cleaverton Comp cardigan, planted herself between us: she flicked her chin at Arthur. "Get your mandibles off her, hey?"

He flushed, scowled, scuttled behind the drop curtains. The girl laughed. She had a high forehead and pocked cheeks smoothed out with thick cream foundation, and her hair was chopped to ear level: her breath was sweet, like sugared-up Irn-Bru; her vowels drawn out like strawberry gum.

"So," she said, "Chloe says you live in a pub?"

Chloe? I glanced around. Chloe Regan: of course. Chloe was on her third go-round in Year Ten up at the Comp; this time, we shared a form tutor. I'd heard she'd drunk her own piss once to get out of a maths GCSE paper.

"Uh, yeah," I said. "The Glory Hole. But, like, not *in* it—above it? My dad—my stepdad?—he's the landlord."

"Amazing! And, what, your mother's the barmaid?"

"Well, no," I said. "She's actually dead?"

"Got hit by a bus, din't she—Cher's mam?" said Chloe, bouncing up to us, ignoring my scowl. "Like, *smack!*" She drove her fist into her other palm.

I nodded, curtly, though I wasn't so sure about the *smack*: I'd seen Ma's arms flying up, is all, one of her shoes coming off as the bus carried her along, pure terror buckling her face. We'd been on the way to Tesco's—we'd been rowing about packed lunches and she'd stepped off the curb without looking.

"Oh, fuck." The other girl had started to laugh. "Oh, man, I'm sorry! Oh my *God*."

And that's how I met Tan. Tania Malone. It turned out Tan was lacking in "positive attachments," too; her da'd been jailed for, like, fraud—he'd brought down a charity, or something; it'd been in the papers, according to Chloe. Anyway, Tan's ma had pulled her from the über-swish St. Fidelma's Grammar in Scranton and sent her instead to scummy old Cleaverton Comp for Girls—and now Tan had York on her case, as well; like me, she was flagged as "troubled." The difference was, Tan was psyched to be here, in Malachy's Academy for Misanthropic Freaks: she wanted to act. She was going to LA, she told us; she'd get Golden Globes, she'd feature on *E! News*—she wasn't clomping about bloody *Cleaverton* forever, like an absolute spod. She said this glaring at Arthur Leese, who was sitting alone on the edge of the stage dissecting his egg sandwich.

Then, my second week, she invited herself round the Hole for tea.

Simon was exuberant: "I fuckin *knew* it, Cher—look at yeh! Visitors! Yer fuckin blossomin!"

He raided the carvery, laid us out a greasy binge of onion rings and pork chops, shepherded Tan around the Hole on the Grand Tour: the keg store, the snug, the Smoking Hole (a rickety balcony over the bin yard with a corrugated plastic roof).

"We do karaoke," he said, "an there's a Singles' Night, an—"

"Amazing," said Tan. "And, Cher, what do *you* do? Like, mix cocktails?"

"Oh," I said. "Yeah, well, I—"

I looked to Simon for help—it was embarrassing enough I had to live here, without admitting that all he'd let me do was soap the floors—but he looked flummoxed. She gazed at us, we both floundered, and then the buzzer sounded—a delivery. A delivery! I snatched the docket book from the bar.

"I liaise with the suppliers," I said. "For the deliveries. Don't I, Si?"

"Oh," he went, "well, if yeh—I mean, yeah, that's what—"

"Super!" said Tan. "Very *real-life*."

She followed me downstairs, to where old Jim Lanigan, the butcher, was rolling a fag as his apprentice, Fredek, a shaven-headed skinny Hungarian lad in dungarees, heaved pallet after pallet of bloody lamb shanks out of the truck and into our freezer.

"Cheryl! And Cheryl's friend, hello!" Jim jumped up, spilling his tobacco. Sometimes he'd offer me a smoke: I'd always refused, but today, I thought, I might—

Only this time he wasn't asking; he was ogling Tan, and then snipping at his helper: "Fredek! Say hello to the girls, will you, for fuck's sake!"

Fredek was snaggletoothed, twentyish, with a shiny bruise on his left cheekbone and a long, thin nose. He looked us up and down—Tan, anyway; I was old news—and twitched his upper lip. A smile? A grimace? I couldn't tell and I didn't care; he was a freakoid perv, a meat-stinker. I saw Tan note his name tag—*F. Rijj*—and grin.

After they'd gone, she gave my cheek a pinch. "Seriously, girl?" she said. "This place is the absolute bomb. You have it *made.*"

Well, I thought, maybe, actually, I had. That night I felt unexpectedly jaunty. And Simon was jubilant:

"There yeh go," he cried, "positive fuckin attachments! Just like yer woman said! Yeh see, Cher? We're fuckin laughin!"

Within a fortnight, Tan was sleeping over twice, three times a week—begging Si to teach her to pour porter, borrowing his laptop to watch Method-acting tutorials on YouTube, asking me for loans of knickers and pads. Simon wanted to know if all this—the pub, the overnights—was all right with her ma, but Tan, who never spoke about her family, just shrugged, and he let it pass by: I was going into school again, wasn't it? I was, like, *smiling.*

And then a spate of boyfriends broke out, like mono, across Cleaverton Comp, and Tan got distracted. Abruptly, in Years Nine through Eleven, it had become de rigueur to hoik some gray-faced troll called Tony or Daz up the Big Wheel in Piccadilly Gardens on Saturday afternoons. At Malachy's, Chloe recited painful accounts of Mo Smith's tiny left ball and the way Tom Ketter yanked at his earlobes when he came. And Tan started scouting punters at the Hole: old, *no*; bald, *no*; meth dealer, *no*.

"But, I mean, even if you found some guy," I told her, "you'd just have to lug him around, and, like, *talk* to him."

"Jesus, Cher," she said, "how juvenile are you?" And she flounced off home early, leaving me to retreat in a mardy strop to the flat upstairs, ignoring Simon's entreaties to tell him what the holy fuck was up.

Then she ambushed Arthur Leese. She tugged him round the side of the church hall after Malachy's next session, and they huddled there muttering for almost fifteen minutes before he finally beetled off, his face and neck and even his hands a deep, heart-attack red.

Tan, too, tried to sneak out, but I waylaid her. "Oh my God," I went. "You're *not*. Not with—"

"Shut up!" For a minute, she looked sheepish. "Anyway, he's totally into it." She was meeting him later at the Overhulme Park playground; he was bringing "the things." She said, "He was all, *OMG what time?*"

I winced. "Arthur Leese, but! You can't. I mean, you can't."

"I can if I want, girl."

"I know you can! But it's Arthur. Like, what's the point? It's not like anyone's going to be impressed, like all, *Oh wow, Tania, you're so lucky!* Or"—now I couldn't look at her—"it's not—I mean, you don't *like* him?"

"Oh my God," said Tan. "Oh my God, Cher."

"Well, you're the one—"

"It's a rehearsal! It's a practice. Like, you know, in First Aid. What are you, nine years old?"

"Hey," I said, but she'd already stomped huffily away ahead; I trailed her in silence as far as Bargain Booze, where she'd turn left and—as usual—I'd turn back.

Tan's old house in Scranton had had seven bedrooms and three whirlpool baths. Her dad had driven a Porsche; Tan'd had her own en-suite, her own laptop, and her own Netflix subscription; she'd seen *Les Misérables* and *Wicked* eight times each in the West End. And now she lived in this straggling estate squished between the dual carriageway and the rubbish dump, in a two-up-two-down box that didn't even have a telly. I felt dead bad for her, but I'd never say so—I mean, I'd heard none of this from Tan herself; it was just that Chloe's ma swept hair in Curl Up & Dye on Clea-verton high street, and there wasn't much that Chloe didn't know or wouldn't tell about anything that went on locally, Tan included. I knew, even, that Malone wasn't her actual name, but her ma's

maiden name. The point was, though, that we—me and Tan—
were meant to be mates: she pretty much lived round mine and
yet I'd not met her ma or seen inside her bedroom. I wanted, suddenly, to yank her shiny hair; I wanted to scream, *Fuck you, if you
think you're better than me!*

But I didn't. I couldn't. Instead, before she walked off for good,
I said quickly, "So—I suppose you're getting palpated by the semi-
nal vesicle tonight?"

She grinned. "My dear," she said, "I think you'll find it's called
the *spicule*," and she poked an invisible set of glasses up her nose.
"Anyway," she said in her normal voice, "you can drop the act—
you know you're gagging for a good palpating."

"Oh, haha, yeah." I pretended to retch. "Utter dejection without it, like."

She gave me the finger, but kept grinning.

I walked back alone. The Hole was deserted—we didn't open
until six p.m. Mondays—and even Simon wasn't at his usual off-
duty table; his Sudoku book was tucked away behind the till. I
got out the mop and sludged a bucket of suds over the floor, but
I couldn't really concentrate. Each slap of the wet yarn was going
Arth—ur—Leese—Arth—ur—Leese, no matter how much I tried
to put him—put *it*—out of my head. It felt like I'd choke. Finally,
I dropped the stick and ran upstairs—I'd distract myself, I'd have
a soak—but Simon had locked himself into the bathroom.

"Give us a minute, pet!" he shouted, when I yelled at him to
get out. "I have to show yeh something!"

"Fuck's sake!" I roared back. I sat down instead at the foldout
dining table and opened my geography homework.

Q.1: Trace the spurs along the Teesside flats.

My pencil raked gouges through the copybook. They'd have
gotten started by now, straddling the slide in the adventure playground: Arthur mishandling Tan, haw-hawing like a frantic goat,
and Tan hissing, "Not there—Jesus, Arthur, *there*!" She'd have
loosened her hair; he'd still have the Overhulme blazer buttoned

all the way up. He'd be scared of her bra: Arthur was scared of the *word* bra. What did she want him near her bra for, anyway?

Q.2: Sedimentation, erosion, deposition.

Practice, I thought, *Christ!* We could've, like, watched porn; Simon had a box of DVDs in the loft—

My pencil snapped. I threw it at the wall.

"All right!" He came out of the bathroom. He was wearing his good shirt and tie, and he'd shaved: his chin looked rough and sore. He'd gelled his hair for the first time in months.

"Oh God," I said, "we're not getting inspected?"

"What? No!" He laughed. "Jesus, pet. It's just, well, I'm going— I've got a date, Cher."

"Oh," I said. "Perfect." I ripped the torn page from my copybook and scrunched it up.

"So," he said, "tell us. I mean, am I all right, or what?"

Or what, I thought. *You're fifty-two. Your dead wife's* withdrawn/hostile/uncooperative *daughter lives in your flat and listens to you crying in the shower. Of course you're not* all right. But instead I just lifted a shoulder: he could make as much of a tit of himself as he wanted. He wasn't my actual dad. So did I give a shit if Simon Reyniss was *all right*? No. I did not.

"The thing is," he said, "the, uh, she—well, yeh know Tabitha?" And when I still said nothing: "Tabitha York, like? From yer—"

"What?" I stared at him. "Not, like, *Miss* York?"

"That's the one—who'd've thought, eh?" And he grinned, like we were all together in this twisted little conspiracy, all three of us.

I got up and shoved past him, into the bathroom, and bolted the door. I sat on the lino, wedged in between the toilet bowl and the stem of the sink. I wasn't going to cry. He shuffled about for ages—apologizing, excusing himself, blethering on about *connections*—before, at last, I heard the bouncing *thud-ud* of the flat door slamming shut. Then I picked up the toilet-roll holder and pitched it as hard as I could at the wall. The steel left a cracked dent in the plaster. *Miss York*, I thought. The boggle-eyed try-hard. Ma would have clocked him one for even looking at her.

My phone beeped: a tiny animated thumbs-up from Tan. *Ugh*: I switched it off and started picking at the crack in the wall. When I had a neat little cairn of plaster dust, I made a fist and flattened it.

Next day at school, Tan was sitting alone on the assembly hall steps; she jumped up when she saw me, and went, "So!"

"So?"

"So!" She rolled her eyes. "You want the blow-by-blow?"

"Ew. Not, like, especially." I didn't stop. I didn't want to loiter; it was only half ten, and I'd already had to duck York twice—she'd come at me between classes, waving hugely, like her having shared a biryani with Simon made us besties.

"Oh, come on!" Tan fell into step beside me. "What are you, Our Lady, the Holiest of Cheryls? I'm seeing him again tonight."

"What," I said, "so, like, it's a proper thing now? You and Arthur?"

"No! God." She shrugged. "It's just convenient, is all. But here, look." She unfolded a leaf of lined A4 and passed it to me. "He gave me this."

"*Sublimity*," I read. I stopped walking, turned the page: there was verse after verse. "*Epidermis, dermis / I feel / the layers of you.* Oh my God. He's going to flay you."

"It's an ode. He did it right there while I was doing up my top. I'm devo," she added, but she looked far from devastated; she looked triumphant, like she'd already gotten her BAFTA nomination. She took the poem back and folded it away, and laughed—a daft, fake titter that was as much like Tan as Arthur was like an actual man.

And that's how it went for the next three weeks: Tan texting me from the playground or from the abandoned Dip A Door unit by the bagel factory, complaining that Arthur had dirtied her suede skirt, that he'd bought himself a McFlurry but none for her, that he'd given her a blister "in a place you wouldn't believe"; in school, she'd grab me in the corridor and, smirking, flash me her phone: a close-up of Arthur's nipples or arse cheeks. She said she wasn't *into him*, but she wasn't what I'd call detached, either: in mid-February, a new girl turned up at Malachy's, a twitchy little bulimic Year Eight from Overhulme who kept gawking at Arthur as he hunched over his back issues of *American Entomologist*, and Tan blanked her.

"Bitch," she said, when we got back to the Hole.

"I thought you didn't even like him."

"I don't! Wow, Cher, you're obsessed." She'd decided that I was jealous of her "awakening" and that I needed one of my own; she reckoned she could find me a decent "starter specimen," and she started listing candidates: the stumpy little server at the petrol station, the skater boy who practiced falling over in the Tesco's car park.

I retorted that I certainly wasn't jealous—that, actually, I was bored, and that the last thing I needed was some dumbo, greasy cretin grabbing at me, and that if I did need that (which I didn't), I definitely didn't need it from any of the knob-head lurch-arounds *she* was talking about.

Tan said I ought to check myself. "What you *need*, Cher, is to just get the whole business over with. Like me! Here, for instance." She took out her phone. "I'll show you what I had Art do on Saturday. It was unbelievable. You need a teapot and—"

"Shut up!" I glanced around: we were sitting in the snug—I didn't want Simon overhearing this. "I don't want to know, do I?"

"Oh, please." She folded her arms. "So what did Saint Cher do all weekend? Ironed her socks?"

"No!" I folded my own arms. "I've a life, too, don't I?"

"Yeah? So?"

"So what?" For a moment, I hated her: she was just like York—*snooping*.

"So," she said, "what did you do? Or, here, I'll guess: you met some lawless young bruiser and did it behind the kegs! Am I warm?"

"God, Tan, that's—"

She grinned. Sneered. "That's a no, is it?"

"No! I mean, *yes*—I mean, like, it wasn't—" I slammed down my geography book. "What," I hissed, "it's *that* hard to believe, is it? Like, Arthur Leese can go out and do it, but I can't?"

She sat back, holding up both hands, like *Whoa, girl, chill!* "All right," she said, "so who was it?"

Who was it? God. I stared out across the room. Leaning against the bar was the usual crew of moody old gets; to their left sat the woman who'd run the pound shop down the street before it went on fire; squished up beside her, a fat boy not much older than me, drinking Coke; next to him, Shane the Tweak, who, according to Chloe's ma, sold crack in the park. *Who was it?* How was I supposed to know? I felt clammy.

Then the toilet door opened: Fredek Rijj, the apprentice butcher, came out, wiping his hands on his T-shirt.

"There," I said, "him. Him there."

She craned. "What—*Fridge*?"

"Don't stare!"

"No way," she whispered. "He's old. He's like twenty."

It was my turn to smirk. "Think what you like."

We watched Fredek return to his table—he walked draggingly, frowning, like he had a grudge against the carpet—and pick up his apron from the back of the chair. He was heading for the door. That meant he'd pass us. Never mind clammy; I felt outright sick. What if he looked at me? What if he didn't? What if—

He'd passed. He was gone.

A pause. Then:

"Oh—my—God, Cher!" Tan clapped her hands. "Amazing! So, what now? Is it *on*?"

What? "On?" I said. "No! It was just—"

"Quick!" She picked up my phone and put it in my hand. "Text him."

I stared at her. "Who, Fridge? Why? What would I even say?"

"Oh my God, Cher. You *know*. Something foul. Keep him boiling!"

"No!" I shook my head. "No way."

She rolled her eyes. "Give it here, then." She took the handset, tapped at the screen, passed it back. "Start simple, see?"

I read: *i wanna c ur drty cOck*

I dropped the phone. "Tania!"

"If you can bite it, you can write it." She grinned. "You've got his number?"

I didn't want to say no. I looked again at the message—*i wanna c ur drty cOck*—and imagined it somehow getting back to Simon.

"Come on," said Tan. "Ticktock!"

"All right! Jesus." I hunched over the screen, my body shielding it from her view, and tapped out a random number. *Save as: FREDEK. Send.* "There!" I said, sitting up again. "Happy?"

But even as I spoke, I could see the blue message status changing from *Sending* to *Delivered*. Then, *ping*: a reply. A picture-message. I almost moaned aloud: that wasn't supposed to happen! But still, intrigued, I looked—

"Fuck!" I knocked the handset halfway across the table.

Tan reached for it. "What—oh, *dude*. He's keen."

I snatched the phone back and fumbled to delete the message, but the little trash icon wouldn't respond; I thumbed it again and again until, at last, *Delete message?* Yes, yes, *delete* stupid *message*!

"Oh my God," I said. I shut my eyes, but all I could see was— well. I opened them again.

Tan was beaming. "My, my," she said. "Cheryl Reyniss. You dirty little tart."

. . .

Arthur had written her another haiku sequence. We sat on the lip of Malachy's stage as I read it:

You, the specimen / I, the rapt observer of / all that you reveal.

"He's abject," Tan said. "He's started calling his gear his *membrum virile.*"

You've not ditched him, but, have you, I thought, but I said nothing,

Malachy had cornered Arthur and the new girl to size them up with a measuring tape and an armload of fabric swatches for the Summer Show—*Pygmalion* mashed with *Wicked,* set in Moss Side.

"So," said Tan, "tell us: any messages?"

There was, in fact: I'd gotten four more texts in the last twelve hours—three fuzzy close-ups of the dude's *membrum virile* and a video of his hand stroking it.

Tan flicked slowly from one to the next, zooming in and out. "What did you write back?"

"I dunno." I shrugged. "Nothing." And, because she was staring at me, "Oh, come on, Tan!" then: "I'm out of credit, anyway. So."

She shook her head. "God, Cher, you can't just drop it—this is *huge.*"

"Yeah," I said, "but—"

"Tania! Dude!" Chloe was clambering up to join us. "Look!"

She'd found a flier pinned to the Tesco's classifieds board. A music video was being shot right here in Cleaverton, and they were casting:

GIRL NEEDED

YOUTUBE HIT GUARANTEED

"Oh my God," said Tan. "Like—oh my *God.*"

"But won't it be singing?" I said. "Not acting? And, like, you're not a singer?"

"Fuck off! You think I can't sing?"

"It's not her voice they'll be looking at," said Chloe; she yanked at the neckline of Tan's jumper and pretended to drool. Instead of flinching, Tan giggled, and Chloe clapped her hands: "Come on, bitches," she cried, "training montage!"

So while Malachy fussed about with Arthur's inside leg measurements, the two of them started sucking in their stomachs and trilling off-key verses of Chloe's favorite track: Whitney Houston's "I Have Nothing."

Tan was exuberant. "This is *it*," she kept saying, and she tried to drag me onstage with her; when I objected—I didn't want to dance, I didn't *like* to dance—she said, "My God, Cher, can't you get over yourself? This is, like, my moment!"

I wasn't so sure that it was; Malachy had spotted the commotion and was scampering in our direction.

"Ladies," he cried, "we have a show to produce! Focus, please! Ladies!"

"Hey, man, keep it down!" yelled Chloe. "We're rehearsing!" She'd loaded the Houston track onto her phone; she turned the volume right up, and nodded at Tan, who dropped my arm, took Chloe's, and started to bellow, loudly, tunelessly: "*I'll never change all my colors for you!*"

Malachy was shrieking, "Girls! Girls! I won't have this carry-on!" He pointed to me—the closest. "Cheryl Reyniss, get down! Get out—now! Go!"

I climbed down. Well, what did I care? I hated Drama; I didn't care if I never came back. Tan had linked arms with Chloe—they were spinning round and round. As I reached the door, Chloe sang out, "Hey, Cher! Who's a bad, bad girl?" And Tan laughed.

Malachy had mounted the stage; he grabbed the phone off her and switched it off. "Regan!" he snapped. "Malone! The pair of you—out! *Now!*"

Tan laughed again. She and Chloe staggered to a dizzy halt, and Tan gave the rest of the gawping am dram brigade a deep curtsy. Then she hopped off the stage and strode to the back of the hall—Arthur came scampering after her, going, "Tania! W-wait!," but she didn't wait: she paused at the door just long enough to send it crashing into his face as he tried to chase her outside.

By this point, my phone's storage was maxed out with close-up studies of the fake Fredek's groin; Tan insisted she inspect every shot before I hit *delete*. Plus, she wouldn't stop hassling me to "follow through, Cher, for God's sake!" Of course I'd followed nothing through and so I'd been vague and defensive each time she'd quizzed me, but now—with Chloe kicking about in the wings—I started wondering if it wouldn't be better, after all, to, like, try to appease her. So I started saying, *Yeah, I called him—yeah, I saw him*. And I started to describe what we'd supposedly done—these, like, mini-scenes that Malachy would have loved; he'd have called them *tableaux*. There was me and Fredek squished into the Hole's unisex toilet cubicle after school; me and Fredek grappling in the hold of the meat-delivery truck; me and Fredek in the back alley, in the rain, in our pants. For maximum authenticity, I looked up the Hungarian for beautiful (*gyönyörű*) and "I love you" (*szeretlek*), and got her to repeat after me: *John-you-roo, serret-leck*.

"Fucking hell, Cher," she'd said, like I'd turned up to school in a basque and silk suspenders.

"Yeah," I said. "And he's, like, really into licking my toes?"

I knew she was properly impressed because she talked: she told Chloe, and Chloe, of course, told everyone else. Becca Jameson from Year Eleven pushed me against the lockers and hissed, "Hobag! Foot skank!"

I'd turned scarlet, but Tan had been exultant: "You're made," she said, "you're absolutely fucking *made*."

I didn't feel made, though; I felt fishy and exposed. Whenever I saw Fredek—which was, like, all the time: he came to the Hole most evenings with Jim for their dinnertime fix of marrowfat peas and Blue Tit IPA—I'd turn even redder. And, worse: he'd clocked the attention and started winking at me convulsively; now I was worried he actually *would* talk to me.

The Saturday before Tan's YouTube shoot was Simon's birthday. When Ma was around, we used to get steak from the Caribbean takeout and watch old Eurovision clips online; this year, Simon grilled pork loins and invited Miss York for tea—and Tan, too, to keep me sweet. And, for the first time in weeks, Tan was actually free: she said she had a water infection ("It burns like fucking chilis down there, Cher") so there wasn't any point in dragging Arthur down the Dip A Door. Really, though, she was avoiding him—she'd been muttering for a week now about looking for an "upgrade"; she'd started pestering me about Fredek's friends.

Anyway, Saturday: the four of us sat squished around the fold-out table. I sawed and sawed grimly at my food while Tan kicked me under the table and York went, "Oh, girls, I'm so glad you're both doing so well!"

Simon clanked his can against my beaker of Coke. "She's a little star, en't yeh, Cher?"

Tan leered. "Oh, Cher's *totally* making connections."

"Shut up!" I kicked her back.

Simon grinned at Tan. "Yer doin all right yerself, but. Tabs, did yeh hear this one's goin for an audition? For a film, is it, Tania?"

"A music video, actually." Tan preened.

"Fantastic!" York beamed. "How absolutely wonderful!"

"It's an open call, but," I muttered.

"Did I tell yeh"—Simon slopped us each a celebratory extra dollop of mash—"Cher's ma was in a panto once? Judy, like. Wallopin poor auld Punch."

I looked at York, but instead of going decently quiet, she put her hand on the stubbly back of his neck and said, "You know I used to do a spot of improv myself?"

"Yeh didn't!" Simon leaned back into the crook of her arm. "Did yeh?"

"Oh, yes. We used to just fling ourselves about the stage! It was very expressive"—she threw her free arm up, dramatically, knife in hand—"very rousing. I wanted to dance, you know, but of course I was terribly bowlegged—like a little frog. Not like *you* girls."

"Cher can bow her legs," said Tan, "can't you, Cher?"

I put down my fork.

"Tania," said Simon, frowning at me, "why don't yeh show us yer audition bit?"

"Oh," cried York, "that's a lovely idea!"

"What," I said, "like, now?"

But Tan was already on her feet and fiddling with her phone: it tooted the opening bars to Queen's "Who Wants to Live Forever," and she started to belt it out ("There's no *ti-ime* . . .") so loud that you could see Simon flinch, but he tapped his foot anyway, and beamed at her.

I got up and stomped out. Banged my bedroom door shut and waited. Nothing. Except, of course, a beep from my phone: a picture message. *Delete.* I got under the duvet. Hunched up. Waited—waited—

A knock on the door. Quickly, I sat up—but it wasn't Simon, or even Tan; it was just York. *Ugh*, I thought, and lay back down. She'd started talking already—harping on in her softly-softly psych voice about *family* and *needs*. *I* need *you to go*, I thought, but she didn't—she sat down on the bed. When she reached out to touch me—to stroke my hair—I snatched the hem of the duvet and yanked it so hard she almost spilled off the mattress.

"I—*need*—to go—to *sleep*," I said, and I rolled away from her and shut my eyes.

When I opened them again, she was gone. And then I must really have slept, because when I next opened them, the flat was silent and Tan was sprawled snoring across the mattress in just her bra and pants, one leg flung on top of mine.

"Get off," I hissed. "Tan! Go home, will you?"

Nothing. I sat up, poked her hard in the ribs, but she didn't properly wake: "Art," she mumbled, "stop it."

So I got up, the duvet gathered in my arms: I'd sleep someplace else. In the bar, if I had to.

I went downstairs. It wasn't as late as I'd supposed: the last of the drunks were still picking themselves up, the dishwasher was humming. Damo, Simon's part-timer, was out in the Smoking Hole with the mop—though it didn't matter how often you scrubbed, how hot the water or thick the Shake n' Vac, the Hole always smelled like burnt rasher fat. I liked it: it reminded me of Ma, who'd hated it. When we'd moved in with Simon she'd gotten me, age six, to help her paint over the tobacco stains on the walls. I wondered, sourly, if York was handy with a roller.

"Ello!" I jumped: Fredek. He'd lurched up from the snug, pint glass in hand, pea stains down his dungarees. He winked at me. "Is time for bed, yes?"

"What?" I looked down at the duvet. "Oh! No! I mean, I—" I stopped.

He'd come to a halt very close to me; I could smell his breath. Cheese, parsnips, ale. "I think," he said, "is yes?"

"No!" I swallowed—a grotesque gummy click, my tongue sucking against the roof of my mouth. "I didn't say that—definitely not yes."

"Yes," he said, nodding, and he slipped a hand under the duvet; he found my bra strap and tried—failed—to unhook it from my shoulder.

I froze. I was thinking, *Slap him, knee him in the balls*, but also: What if Tan was right, and I should just get it over with? Like, let him do whatever it was he wanted, and then we—me and her—would be even. Wouldn't we? I didn't move; I let him carry on. He wormed a hand under the cup of my bra; he found my nipple and pinched.

"Ow!" I twisted away, but he kept hold of the gobbet of flesh: this time, then, I did kick him. "Let *go*," I went, "God!"

Then Damo was crossing back toward us with the bucket. "Fred," he called, "mate! You ready to go?" And now, finally, Fredek dropped his hand; now he stepped out from behind me and said, "Yes! Yes, we go?"

"I just gotta get locked up first, yeah?" Damo rattled his keys. He clicked his tongue at me. "Yo, Cher—you all right, babe?"

"Perfect," I said, tightly, and I gathered up my duvet and headed for the stairs.

Monday—audition day—Tan didn't turn up to school. She called me at lunchtime: her mother had dragged her to the GP's to give a urine sample for her UTI, and the doctor had told them there was nothing wrong with Tania's kidneys—that, in fact, it sounded very much like she had chlamydia.

"He took a *swab*," she howled.

"God," I said. "What did your ma say?"

"I'll kill the fucker, Cher. I'll string him up and bloody Bobbittize him!" It took me a minute to realize she meant Arthur. "Chlamydia, like! I mean, where would he even go to *get* chlamydia?"

"Do you want me to come and get you? Is your ma still there?"

She wasn't listening: "I'll tell you what, Cher—he can take his greasy, contaminated arse, and—*and*—" And with an exasperated, guttural wail, she hung up.

Fifteen minutes later, she called me back: Arthur had dumped *her*.

"Wow," I said. Then: "You're not—are you, like, crying?"

"No! God. I mean, it's not like I care! He's a gimp, I never—" A pause while she snuffled and sighed, and then she said, "I swear to God, Cher? If I don't get this part? I'll tear his bloody *cock* off."

"Right," I said, but she'd put the phone down again.

We'd already arranged to meet after school, in the McDonald's toilets, where I was to help her prep for the audition, so that's where I headed at four o'clock. On my way I passed Arthur coming out of Tesco's with his arm around the waist of the twitchy little Year Eight girl from Malachy's. I didn't even know her name. I stopped—they hadn't seen me—and I thought about yelling at them: *Whores! Septic mutants!* But at the last minute, I changed my mind: what did I care who Arthur hooked up with? I wanted Tan back, was all. So I scurried on; I ran the rest of the way and got to McDonald's early.

Tan, who was never anywhere on time, was there already, bent over the sink. The whole left side of her face was bruised—she was troweling concealer over it like you'd ice over a burnt cake.

"Oh my God." I stared, then thought I shouldn't, but kept staring anyway. "What happened? Who did that?"

She'd not heard me come in; she started, scowled, ducked her head—went *dab-dab-dab* again, furiously, with the sponge. "Excuse me?"

"Not, like, *Arthur*?"

No reply. *Dab-dab-dab.*

"I'm just asking, is all," I said. "I'm just saying if it *was*, then you should—"

"Should!" She turned around. "What should I do, Cher? Tell me!"

"I don't know! What about your ma? Should I call her? Does she know?"

"*Does she know.*" Tan laughed. Barked. "Yeah, Cher, great idea. You tell her all about it, will you? Or, like, you could just shut the fuck up?"

"What?"

"*What?*"

I frowned. "Okay! God, I'm sorry. I'm just—"

"*Just* drop it, will you?" She tossed the sponge in the bin and shut the makeup case. Then she got changed: wriggled into a leather skirt she'd borrowed from Chloe and a gold crop top I'd borrowed from Ma's drawers that Simon hadn't yet sorted through. There was another yellowish bruise on Tan's rib cage, but I kept my promise; I shut the fuck up. And then we set off.

The audition was in the old Scout Hut, a dumpy, window-less, pebble-dashed extension to the Tesco Express by the railway tracks, where once I'd gotten a Brownie badge for starting a fire in a bin lid. A handwritten sign was taped to the door: FLIM SET.

"So far, so good," I said.

But Tan had stopped; she bent over the bonnet of a battered old Skoda Rapid parked outside, and looked like she was going to puke. "I have to get this, Cher," she said. "I *have* to."

"I know."

"You don't!" She thumped the hood of the car. "You don't know even the stupidest little thing! Jesus!"

"What? What's that supposed to—oh, shit. Wait." My phone was ringing. Simon, I thought, after I'd told him we were—

But it wasn't Simon: the screen said *FREDEK.*

"Here," said Tan, "if that's Ar—if that's *him*, tell him he can go fuck himself."

"No, it's not—it's—"

"Oh, God, whatever! Come on." She checked her costume—plucked off a nub of lint, smoothed her hair—and, without wait-ing for me, slammed through the Hut door.

The phone was still ringing.

Hang up, I thought, *throw it down a drain—or get Tan back, make her answer it!* But then I'd have to explain, wouldn't I, that *FREDEK* wasn't Fredek, and where would that leave me? And if I hung up, well, it'd just keep on going, wouldn't it?

FREDEK. My hands were trembling. I pressed the green but-ton. I said, in a dry croak, "Hello?"

There was an intake of breath, and then: "Karla? Is that *Karla?*" A woman. My stomach flopped. "He's with you, isn't he? Jonny!"

"Jonny? No, I d-don't"—my voice was shaky, puny, a kid's—"I mean, I don't know who—"

She was crying. "You must think I'm so dumb—but I seen what he's been sending you! I fuckin seen it!"

"No," I said, "it's not—I'm not like that!"

I'd sagged against the Skoda; I was staring at the backseat den of takeaway containers and umbrella frames, a green scarf winding along the floor like the dead skin of a snake. "It was just a sort of joke," I whispered.

"I'll give you a joke! I'll find you, I'll fuckin kill yous both—Jonny! *Jon*—"

End Call. I jabbed the red icon and dropped the phone; I heard a *crack.* I picked it up again: the glass was fractured in a great jagged fork, but the phone still worked, because immediately, he—she—called again. I switched it off this time, and then took out the battery, but it still seemed to vibrate. I shoved it in my coat pocket. *Breathe.*

It's all right, I thought, *forget about it—block the number*. I wiped my eyes; I stumbled toward the building. *Tell Tan, she'll—*

I pulled the door open.

—she'll what, exactly?

The Hut's tiny anteroom smelled like Plasticine and wet socks. There was Tan, alongside a woman in her twenties in a floral catsuit and a scowling boy in a tight yellow dress, all three of them sweating; they looked up as I came in—the two strangers raising their eyebrows at my school uniform, then resuming their nonchalant poses like I wasn't there at all.

"Tan," I said, uncertainly, but then a short, balding, ponytailed man barged through the door at the other end of the lobby, followed by a younger, reedier chap with a clipboard: "Right!" barked Ponytail. "Let's get a look at you all—quick now!" He scanned the three of them, frowned, then went, "No! Wait!" He strode toward me and took my chin between his finger and thumb. "What's this one—seven stone? Tom, what do you say? Jailbait, or—?"

"Uh," said Clipboard, "no?"

"All right!" He snapped his fingers. "Get her in costume, will you? People, thanks for your time, much appreciated, lah-di-dah, good evening!" He crashed back into the main room, and Clipboard beckoned to me. "All right, love, come on."

"Wait," I said, "I didn't—" but Tan cut me off; she'd rounded on him.

"The fuck?" she said, in a high, rattled voice. "What do you want her for? I mean, God, look at her!"

The boy in the dress nodded. "Uh-huh."

"Hey," said Clipboard, putting up his hands, "I'm not the creative here. You, now—quickly!"

They were all looking at me now. Again. Sneering. I was looking at Tan. I'd been about to back away—I'd been going to protest, say they'd made a mistake, that I was just the moral support—but now I was thinking: *Look at her?* What did that mean? Why shouldn't he want me? There wasn't anything wrong with me—how come everything always had to be about her? So I looked at her and I shrugged. I said, "Well, I guess I'm up! Wish us luck, Tan, yeah?" And when I let Clipboard tug me away, I didn't swing round to grimace at her like I was joking or like I was sorry, and so I didn't see what expression she had on her face—if she was raging or shocked or jealous or sad—before the door fell shut between us. I did know, though, what I was thinking: for once, I thought, Tan could just go fuck herself.

Two days later. Three. More: a week. I stayed off school; I told Simon I had a stomach bug and couldn't leave the flat. He kept asking how Tan's gig had gone: "Fine," I'd said, over and over, "I *told* you," until I thought I actually would vomit. In fact, I kept checking YouTube to see if they'd uploaded anything, and rejoicing when it seemed they hadn't—then five minutes later I'd feel nauseated again and I'd have to run the search over. I kept remembering Ponytail's caw of hilarity when he'd seen me in the bikini that Clipboard had produced (two brassy shreds of sequined polyester that had cut into my belly and gaped at my chest); he'd sprayed driblets of spittle over my shoulders.

"All right," he'd said; "so you just keep on looking awkward, yeah?"

The lighting techs had swung their lamps around on me. They'd cleared the hall of the Scout troop's plastic chairs and wobbly trestles, hung a huge black felt drape over the mural of Baden-Powell, and replaced the lot with a glaring copse of light stands and hairy booms: I'd stood in the midst of all this and looked at the floor. A dead ant lay by my big toe, its thorax crushed beneath a strip of yellow tape.

"Rolling?" yelled Clipboard. "Speed? Okay, and—ACTION!"

Somebody hit *play* on a PA and a scratchy recording of a man's voice blasted out: "YOU—GOT—THE—MOVES, *GIIIIRL?*"

The idea was that I hadn't—which was, like, true—and so, all evening, I'd wiggled my thorax as instructed and leered at the cameraman in fright until somebody yelled, "CUT!"

Now I lay in bed knowing that Tan, too, would be searching online for evidence of my humiliation, and that as soon as she'd found it, she'd share it across the entire Comp, and I'd be destroyed. *Tan*, I thought, *Tan, Tan, Tan*. The whole week she hadn't called, or messaged, or emailed, and all I'd gotten in the post was a curt note from the deputy head reminding me of my "probationary status." And Simon was losing patience: he was talking about dragging me down to the doctor's if I wasn't on my feet soon, and York kept sticking her head around the door, asking if I needed "an ear."

"Get a grip, Cher," I told the mirror. "It's just Tania."

All week, I'd been practicing this: it was just Tania! Like, of course I could face her! It wasn't like I'd actually *made it*; it wasn't like she'd actually missed out. And by Monday, I was (sort of) ready: I *could* face her, I decided. We'd laugh it off. I'd explain, even, about Fredek—we'd be single together, just like before.

So, at ten to four in the afternoon, I got dressed and headed down the High Street, thinking I'd cut her off on the way to Malachy's.

And I did—that is, I saw her. Not hurrying down the road from the Comp, like I'd expected, or coming out of the newsagent's with a bottle of pop, or even detouring up toward the Hole to see me, to make amends, but sauntering out of Lanigans chatting—like really casually chatting, as if they were solid mates—to Fredek.

I stopped. They were maybe ten yards away. "Tan?" I said, hesitantly, and then I was raging; I was screaming, "Tan! Hey, *Tania!*"

She didn't reply, but she turned: *Fuck you*, she was saying—the arms folded, the shoulders back, lips thin as she glanced around at me. *Look what I've gone and picked up.*

Fredek glanced around, too; he saw me, winked, put a hand on the small of Tan's back, his fingertips slipping behind the waistband of her school skirt.

No, I thought, *don't*—

But I didn't say it aloud, and she took his other hand and tossed her head at me—like, *We're done here, bitch.*

I spun away and walked off quickly, almost trotting until I was safely around the corner, and then I sat down hard on the footpath, my feet splodged right in the sludgy overspill of a blocked gully. I heard—I thought I heard—Tania going, "Cher?" but she didn't come after me. *Don't*, I thought, *don't cry, don't be such a fucking gom.* That was one of Ma's lines: *Don't be such a gom, Cher.* Well, I wasn't: I mean, what was there to cry about? Fredek? Tania? I barely even *knew* Tania.

"Cheryl? Cher, is that you?"

York—it was York, not Tan. York, trotting toward me, gabardine coat flapping, her face all agape, work satchel in one hand, a pint of milk in the other. She dropped the milk as she knelt beside me; it burst all over the two of us but she didn't pause to mop it up—she blotted my face with her coat sleeve.

"Cheryl," she went, "oh, pet. Look at me." All this in her stupid counselor voice. "Oh, Cher. Oh, my love."

Patricia Engel

Aguacero

I REMEMBER THE SKY had been dark since morning, as if pro-
testing the start of another day. Rain held off till afternoon,
then started heavy, long gray water shards dropping like scissors
on the pavement. I'd just left my therapist's office without an
umbrella and stopped for a pack of cigarettes in one of those midtown shops, the size of a closet and smelling of nuts and tobacco,
because nothing makes me want to smoke more than a visit to
the shrink.

I remember the only other customer was a boy of about fifteen
paying for rolling papers and a lottery ticket he told the cashier
was for his mom, and after, I stood outside the shop, my back
pressed against the glass window under the cover of the black
awning, trying to decide if I should make a run for the nearest
subway all the way over on Eighth Avenue. I hated city rain. The
kind that sticks to your face, stiffens your hair, makes you stink
like a dog drenched in its own piss. Nothing like the gentle purify-
ing showers you see out in the country or by the sea.

One of my cousins in Bogotá once taught me a trick: light a
cigarette, hold it out with your hand, and an available taxi will
appear, guaranteed.

I opened a flame and extended my cigarette arm to the curb. For my cousin, the trick never failed. For me, nothing.

I retreated to the shelter of the awning, watching the rain slashes, the glossy street current rush toward the sewers.

"You're Colombian."

This came from a guy I hadn't noticed standing next to me. Something about urban living makes it so you don't even feel when your arm is pressed against a stranger's.

"How would you know?"

I didn't speak much in those days unless I had to, so my own voice sounded strange, defensive, even to me.

"You have an Andean face. Also, you just tried to call a taxi with a cigarette. Only Colombians do that."

He asked if I could spare one so I pulled another cigarette from my pack and passed him my lighter.

I watched the guy sideways as we both smoked. Late forties, maybe. Clean-shaven and pale. Small eyes behind square glasses. Sweatered, with hemmed jeans and brown suede loafers. He smoked vigorously, like a guy who'd been deprived, talking about how this rainstorm was like those of the Amazon, blinding and impossible to navigate. But, he said, rain sounds the same no matter where you are, and he could close his eyes and almost forget this was New York if not for the midtown smells, the song of car horns and screeching brakes.

For the first time in a while I wanted to talk, but felt my tongue curl into the back of my throat like a sleeping mouse. That very day, my shrink, a guy I'd been seeing three times a week for the past two months and who barely ever said a word even when challenged by my silence, told me I should push myself to talk to a stranger, to make conversation, to *connect*.

When I was down to a nub, I flicked it to the street and lit up another. The guy had the nerve to ask for a second cigarette too. I thought about telling him he could go in the shop behind us and buy his own pack, but just handed one over. He seemed to sense debt accumulating between us and stared at me as I held the lighter out for him.

"Can I invite you to wait out the rain with me over a coffee?"

I said okay because I didn't feel like going home and had no other place to go. On afternoons like that, during the lull between therapy and the night, I often rode the train to the end of the subway line and back just to eat away a few hours, and because it was a way to be with people without really being with people.

We ducked into a coffee shop a few doors down. The exposure was enough to soak the back of my jacket and top of my head. We found a table along the wall. He went to the counter and ordered us two coffees, both black with no sugar. I remember we sat opposite each other as if we'd been assigned to one another for the afternoon, with duty and resignation. He didn't seem particularly curious about me, just that he preferred company to being alone, and maybe it was the same for me.

His name was Juan and he was Colombian going several generations back. This much he revealed on that first afternoon. But he'd abandoned Colombia for Europe a decade earlier, and now lived in Madrid with his girlfriend of twenty years and their daughter, who was six. He didn't ask much beyond my name and my instinct was to tell him a fake one—Sara. But by the end of our coffee, when the rain started to lift, he asked for my number and I gave it. He said we could meet for another coffee sometime. Maybe a walk in a park. We were speaking only Spanish together at this point—I don't recall at which point we'd made the shift—his with a heavy Bogotá monotone. Without my asking, he admitted he'd recently turned fifty and I responded that I was twenty-five.

"Look at us," he said, "both partial markers of an incomplete century."

It was only a day before he called. I hadn't worked in three months, though nobody knew this, since a strange June when I was no longer able to sleep. I'd spent entire nights sitting on the stoop of my apartment building watching people come in and out, pass on the street, waiting for dawn, when my eyelids would finally surrender. I'd manage only a two-hour nap every twenty-four hours, and then my heart would begin beating at high velocity, vibrating through my gut and in my throat, and I would fall into a corner on the floor, place my head between the crease of two walls, and weep.

I didn't want Juan to know where I lived so I agreed to meet him at a café on Elizabeth Street and looped around the whole block so he wouldn't know from which direction I'd come. He appeared even older to me in the September sunlight, face laced with small wrinkles, and the lenses of his frames looked even thicker. He asked if I worked or was in school, so rather than admit I spent days hiding in my apartment, only venturing out to sell my best clothes at consignment shops as my only income, I took the opportunity to lie again, something I used to feel very guilty about, and invented a whole other life, said I was completing a Ph.D. in anthropology—ridiculous since the only anthropology class I'd ever taken, I'd dropped midsemester. He asked what I was specializing in and I said the indigenous peoples of the southern Americas, specifically the Sikuani tribe in Colombia because I'd just read an article about how many of them had been massacred by paramilitaries.

I impressed myself with my ability to lie on the fly. It was easier than being honest.

He told me he'd been a lawyer in Colombia, and in Madrid worked as some kind of legal consultant, but he'd given that up last year to pursue his dream of writing a novel, which he described as a time-travel supernatural saga about a twenty-first-century Colombian man who travels to ancient Europe and discovers the secrets of destiny, or something like that.

We talked about movies, then books, then about the city; museums and parks and specific streets we each liked to walk. He said he liked to explore neighborhoods at night and I said I did, too.

Then he let slip: "I'm not really supposed to be in this country right now."

"What do you mean?"

"Well, my girlfriend thinks I'm in London. My family thinks I'm in Paris. But I'm here. In this café. With you."

"What are you supposed to be doing in London?"

"Research for my book. That's what I told her. But I was really planning on spending the month in Paris. I have another girlfriend there, you see, and she's been pressuring me to spend more time with her. But when I went to the airport, I canceled my ticket and instead bought one for New York. Nobody knows I'm here."

"Your family knows about the second girlfriend?"

"Yes. They know I've been planning on leaving my girlfriend in Madrid for a long time. If not for our daughter, I would have left years ago."

"I can't imagine spending twenty years with someone, then leaving them."

"You're young. You will live through plenty of things you never could have imagined."

"I guess you're off the hook because you never took vows."

"A child is a kind of vow. That's why I've come here. To think."

"Maybe you should see a therapist."

"I don't believe in that shit. I've spent years in therapy and it was useless. My sister is a psychologist and people pay her a fortune even though she's a lunatic whose own life is a disaster. It's a crime, the industry of therapy. We are all fucked no matter what and when you finally understand that—poof!—you're cured."

When we left each other that afternoon, he kissed me on the cheek in that casual way of every other Colombian on earth, but it felt different, suspended, and I was suddenly aware of his prickly stubble on my cheek, tiny hairs otherwise invisible in daylight.

. . .

The next day he called to invite me for dinner. He said he would cook. He was staying at the apartment of a friend near the news-stand where we met. I had an appointment with the shrink and would be in the neighborhood anyway so I agreed but didn't tell him that detail. During my session, I talked about meeting this new stranger.

"You might even call us friends at this point," I said.

The shrink asked if I was experiencing feelings of attraction toward Juan. I said no. Besides, he was old and already had two girlfriends and I found men who couldn't make up their minds kind of pathetic.

He was staying in one of those cramped old Hell's Kitchen buildings with fire escapes down the front and back, where you can hear everything happening in every apartment from the hall. Kids squealing, televisions buzzing. A man yelling that something wasn't his fault.

Normally, if going out with a stranger or to a guy's house for the first time, my friend Thea and I would tell each other exactly where we were headed with names and addresses, but today I hadn't told her or anyone anything. My shrink had gotten me to admit a few weeks earlier that I was harboring anger toward Thea because she'd been the only person I told what happened and her response was that he was my boyfriend, he was *allowed* to do with me what he wanted, and I was the girlfriend, so I had to take it. "It's not a tragedy," she'd said. "All women go through it. You need to forget it and move on."

I knocked on the door marked 302 and Juan swung it open, an apron tied around his waist. He led me into the apartment, a rectangular studio with a queen-size bed pushed into the corner, a small living area along the long wall, and most other walls lined with bookshelves, framed posters of old European films, photo-graphs and postcards thumbtacked to vacant patches of Sheetrock.

I sat on an armchair while Juan dipped into the tiny kitchen and returned with a bottle of wine, which he poured into a pair of glasses already set on the coffee table. He toasted to meeting new friends, to the unknown, and we both sipped, though I kept my lips pressed tight so no wine would slip into my mouth.

Juan cooked pasta. We ate from plates set on our laps. He said he loved cooking but their chef in Madrid never let him, and the girlfriend in Paris always wanted to go to restaurants. He'd learned to cook the few years he'd lived on his own in Bogotá. In his childhood home, men weren't allowed in the kitchen.

"Why did you leave Colombia?"

"The same reason everyone leaves. Colombia is a rabid dog."

"Do you miss it?"

"Sometimes."

"Why don't you go back?"

He reached for a pack of cigarettes on the coffee table. This time he'd bought his own and offered me one, which I accepted.

He took a long drag.

"I can't go back."

"Why not?"

"Either they'll kill me or I'll kill myself."

I couldn't tell if he was being vague to provoke intrigue or if I was crossing a line of discretion. So I pulled back, my gaze bouncing around the room from books to photographs and the bed made with boarding school tucks and folds.

"Whose apartment is this?" I asked.

"A journalist friend. He's not really a friend, more of an acquaintance. I hate when people use the word 'friend' so liberally. He's Dutch. I met him through another acquaintance. We once had a pleasant conversation about the Basque resistance and he offered me his apartment in New York and I offered him a room in our place in Madrid."

"I was in Madrid once," I said, "but I had a stomach virus and stayed in the hotel room throwing up for four days and by then it was already time to leave so I saw nothing."

"A reason to return."

"Most cities make me ill, New York included."

"When I returned to Bogotá after several months in the countryside, I developed a terrible case of asthma."

"You became allergic to your hometown."

"So it would appear."

He stood up abruptly and asked if I wanted coffee. I told him I never drink it at night.

"I'm sorry I didn't think to get us dessert."

"It's fine. I should go anyway."

In truth, I had nobody waiting for me anywhere, only a sense that I should keep things in motion, not linger anywhere too long, so I'd leave Juan's place and migrate along city streets, probably walking the fifty blocks home rather than taking the subway or a cab. By the time I got to my building it might be midnight. The nights were still warm enough that I could sit out on the stoop with a light jacket and not feel too cold. Sometimes I brought a book outside with me though I didn't have the concentration to read. Sometimes I tried to write in my journal, but my hand would go limp after only writing a sentence or two.

Juan walked me downstairs to the street. I thanked him for the meal.

"I hope it wasn't too terrible," he said.

I started to feel crowded by his body so close to mine in the doorway so I walked away without that kiss on the cheek that had become our hello and good-bye custom since yesterday. I didn't think much of it but seconds later, as I crossed the street, he was at my side.

"Sara. Did I do something wrong?"

"No. Why?"

"You just seem, I don't know."

"You don't know because you don't know me," I said.

We were on the corner now, standing by a garbage can as pedestrians passed close.

"I want you to know something. I'm not sure why I want you

to know it. I left Colombia because I was kidnapped. They held me for five months. When they released me, I left the country within a week. I will never go back. Maybe this makes me a bad person, a man with no loyalties, no character."

"I'm sorry that happened to you."

"It happens to many, and usually much worse. Some they take to the jungle for years, so long their own families forget about them. And when they're freed, they don't think to leave their country. I'm lucky in comparison, yet I ran away."

"Survival requires different things of different people." I don't know where in me this came from. It was something I hadn't even begun to understand for myself.

"Can we spend some more time together? I feel comfortable with you. I can't explain it."

I nodded. I felt the same but wasn't yet ready to say it too.

I'd known other people who were kidnapped. It's not only a Colombian thing like newspapers and movies want you to think. Guerrillas and paramilitaries didn't invent or even perfect the art of secuestro. Governments have always done it much better.

Back in my hometown, a Jersey suburb where everyone had eyes on each other, a girl from my high school was kidnapped by the young couple she babysat for when they went on the run on account of credit card fraud. The girl's parents hired a detective, who tracked her down in Jacksonville three months later. She was hooked on pills and heroin. Our mothers were friendly, so I overheard whispers that even after rehab the girl was never the same, and my father never let me babysit for gringo families after that.

In college, the mother of a girl from my Twentieth-Century Art class disappeared while walking the dog on First Avenue. The professor canceled class one day so we could all help post signs with the mother's picture around Central Park and the Upper East Side. Months passed with no clues and people muttered the husband should be a suspect, though he was never charged. With the spring thaw, a jogger spotted the mother's body on the banks of the East River, fully clothed, still wearing her wedding ring and her gold watch. Police never figured out who did it. The dog was never found.

I heard a television shrink once say the easiest people to hurt are those who've never been hurt before.

They're the ones who never see it coming, and afterward, it takes a long time for them to understand what's been done to them.

"He loves you," Thea said. "You have to forgive and let go."

I wondered why it had become my burden.

He once told me that, as a kid, when his father was upset with him or one of his brothers, he would take them alone to a tool shed at the far end of the house property. He'd have the boy sit on a folding chair, tie his arms with a rope behind him, blindfold him, and whip him with a power cord, going much harder if the boy cried. This would last an hour. Maybe two. When it was over, the father would untie the son, fall to his knees, and cry over the child's lap, saying it hurt him to have to do this to his own flesh and blood but he'd had no choice.

I'd come home from a party with Thea, barely able to hold my head up or walk straight; a reaction from a couple of cocktails mixed with antibiotics for strep throat I'd finished the day before. He was waiting outside my building when we pulled up in a cab. He must have been there for hours. Thea handed me off. "You take care of her," she said. He helped me up to my apartment and into bed. I remember feeling grateful for him in that moment.

Juan said he'd never smoked his entire life until he was taken, when the guards started giving him cigarettes to stave off his hunger. They came for him while he was in a taxi, which is why he still felt a reflexive terror whenever he got into a yellow cab. At a red light on a quiet road on the way to visit his parents in Los Rosales, a car parked close behind them and before he blinked, a machine gun had already poured into the taxi driver's skull and another man was pulling him out the door and shoving him into the other car. Juan reached for his wallet, told them to take all his money, but they laughed, said they didn't want his money, they wanted his life.

They were kids, he said. Boys who'd been born and bred to die young, who spoke in indecipherable slang and code, whom he'd get to know by their voices since they'd never let themselves be seen without masks. They made him lie on the car floor, slipped a pillowcase over his head with slits for his nose and mouth, and held their boots tight on his back and neck while another drove for what felt like hours, far enough that when he was pulled out of the car, the air was different, fresh and wet like the sabana air at his family's finca in Subachoque.

They put him in a windowless room the size of a pantry, and now, he said, he felt most comfortable in small quarters, like the apartment of the Dutch man and his second girlfriend's tiny chambre de bonne in Paris. There was a bare mattress on the floor on which he spent most of his day. There was a lamp in the ceiling and they would often remove the bulb to taunt him or to control his waking and sleep patterns. At night, the guards sometimes led him into another room where there was a window with curtains drawn, and a radio and a TV, and he saw his picture flash across the news as the presenter reported there was still no clue of his whereabouts. On the radio, he heard the voices of both his parents pleading to his captors for his release. The masked boys laughed, lifting the fabric that concealed them only enough to bring a joint into their lips. They were high much of the time, Juan said, but still had rules, like that Juan had to bow his head and raise his right hand for permission to speak or use the toilet. The first few weeks they beat him regularly. Then they went for stretches in a kind of peace, cohabiting, eating the same crummy mushed rice and bean slop for every meal with an occasional sausage, bringing Juan a pillow and a blanket for his mattress. But then they would get a visit from a superior, or they would get drunk, and would burst into his cell and beat him into a corner, pull his hair, poke their fingers into his eyeballs, spit in his mouth, or piss on his face.

We were in my apartment when he told me this. I had called him this time. It was late and I knew another long night was ahead for me. He arrived quickly. I put out a bowl of chips and made tea. We sat on the sofa along the window, cracked it open enough to let out our smoke but not let in too much city dust or noise of fire trucks roaring from one end of Fourteenth Street to the other. He spoke calmly, often pausing. He said the boys told him that in these cases, when a person is held captive alone, it's because they're going to be killed. Otherwise he would have been placed in a house already holding two or three others, which was easier for them to manage until their release.

"So you're going to kill me," he'd said, and one boy punched him for speaking out of turn, removed the lightbulb, and locked him in his room.

I got the feeling Juan was waiting for me to ask why he'd been a target. There must have been a reason they saw him as valuable. But I didn't ask.

Finally, he said, "My family is, well, a word for it would be 'prominent.'"

"Like drug dealers?"

He laughed. "More like presidents and senators, on both sides."

I wondered which presidents he was related to. Most of the recent ones weren't anything to brag about.

The day of his release, the boys drove Juan to a parking lot behind some warehouses near El Dorado airport, that same pillowcase around his head, and told him to count to one hundred very slowly before taking it off. He was so scared he counted to five hundred, sure they were watching and waiting and this was some kind of test. But when he removed his hood, he saw he was alone and heard the rush of nearby traffic. He walked until he came to a boulevard and asked a shopkeeper to use his phone. He called his mother.

To this day, he said, his girlfriend still threw in his face that Juan hadn't called her first. That was another reason he'd stayed with her this long: guilt.

"So why didn't they kill you?" I asked.

Juan shrugged.

"Either I was worth more than they thought, or not worth enough."

I remember it started to rain so I closed the window but Juan asked me to leave it open a crack. He said when they were holding him for two or three months already, he built up the courage to ask the guards for permission to look out the window in the room where they kept the TV and radio. He could hear the soft drum of rain through the walls, feel the humidity in his bones, but he wanted to see the rainfall, he wanted to smell it. The boys agreed to part the curtain for him only this once, and let Juan sit on a chair by the open window, his hands tied tightly behind his back and with duct tape covering his mouth so he couldn't scream. This is how Juan understood his prison must be in a populated area even though from the window all he saw was a small field surrounded by a high wall, and above it, the rise of the Andes in the distance. And it was on those mountain peaks, that charcoal open sky of equatorial dusk, and on that smell of rain on grass and trees, that Juan meditated for two or three minutes until he was sent back to the hard edges and walls and darkness.

We'd smoked the last of the cigarettes and had been listening to the radio so long the station was repeating songs for the third and fourth time. Even the street had gone quiet. Juan's narrow lids were drooping; he rested his head on an elbow propped along the back of the couch, his body turned to me from his end while I leaned against the opposite armrest.

I stood up, went to my bedroom, and returned with a pillow. I pulled a spare blanket, one I only ever use in winter, from a closet and placed it on the cushion beside him.

"You can sleep here. It's a good couch. People like it."

He gave me a tired smile and nodded as if he'd known this is where we were headed all along. I said good night and went to my room without turning back. I locked the door behind me but stood by the wall that separated us for a while listening for movement, but there was nothing.

That night, I slept. It didn't happen right away. I lay on my bed, my spine resisting the flatness of the mattress. I pulled the blanket over me, pushed it off, then pulled it back on, over my shoulders and head to block out the white streetlights streaking through the blinds and across the walls and ceiling. My face grew hot, so I pushed the blanket back down around my waist, wondering what I would have done in Juan's place, if held captive, if upon being freed my absence would have made my family and friends love me more.

Sometimes I sat at a table with my parents and brother, surrounded by the circus hum of a crowded restaurant, hating that they could not see into me. They'd ask why I was so serious all the time, why so quiet, tell jokes to provoke me to smile. It wasn't their fault, really, that particular blindness. But I couldn't explain. It would break them to know they'd protected me with their lives and failed.

Juan said his parents had prayed to la Virgen del Socorro to protect him so when he was released they made him promise to name any future daughter after her to show his gratitude. But during captivity, despite having prayed more than ever before, he'd become a complete atheist. His girlfriend didn't care to keep the promise either. So when their daughter was born they'd named her Azul, simply because it was their favorite color, and his mother cried for days because they'd given her granddaughter such a meaningless name.

"It's so easy to break a parent's heart," he said. "I keep a distance from my daughter for that very reason. I'm afraid she'll hurt me the way I've hurt my parents. One day I will regret it, I'm sure, but it's the best I can do for now."

I don't know at which point my thoughts turned to dreams. Only that they led me to the hazy consciousness of morning and I realized I had slept more that night with Juan in the next room than I had in months.

It was the last of the summerlike days before the thorny autumn turn toward winter. Juan and I were on a bench on the riverside watching the sunset over New Jersey. The sky, graffitied with purple and fuchsia and smoky blue clouds, reflecting off of the Hudson. It hadn't rained in days.

For weeks, we'd made a routine of sleeping in the same apartment nearly every night. Mostly at my place, Juan on the sofa, curled on the cushions in his trousers and button-downs, only taking off his shoes but never his socks, and me in my bed, finally inhabiting full hours of rest. A few times, I went to his place for dinner and he allowed me to sleep in the bed while he leaned back in the armchair. Once, I sat up in the early hours of morning and saw him hunched over a pillow on his knees, and told him he could get in the bed too, it was okay with me. But he only shook his head and closed his eyes and somehow went back to sleep.

He told me on one of those nights that after sleeping in the small room where they held him all those months, he could sleep anywhere. He'd trained himself, he said, because sleep was the only escape. Now he could have an equally satisfying slumber on a train, a plane, or even while standing on a street corner and holding his eyes shut for a nap of a minute or two.

He would be leaving for Madrid the next day via a connection through London so as to keep up the lie when his girlfriend arrived to meet him at the airport. We'd spent twenty nights together and I'd never once heard him on the phone with either of his girlfriends or even his daughter. I never even heard his cell phone ring.

He invented these ways to disappear, he said, because he'd learned all those years ago how it felt to be forgotten, and in some perverse way, he'd grown to like it.

When it was dark, we started the walk back to my apartment. He held my hand at times, the length of a block or two. I wondered what passersby thought when they looked at us, what was their immediate impression. A man and a young woman twenty-five years apart, though we shared no resemblance so there was no way we could be father and daughter. And yet there was still a distance between us, a raw awkwardness that never dissipated despite all our shared nights that would make it obvious to anyone that we could not be lovers.

The farewell was not a farewell, really, because he'd planned to come back to New York in late November and I had no plans that would take me anywhere else.

"We'll see each other again soon," he said.

We exchanged contact information and it was only when I wrote out my email address for him that I realized I still hadn't told him my real name.

He wasn't mad when I confessed. Not even surprised.

"I'll still call you Sara," he said, "if that's okay with you."

In the ten years since, I have often wondered if any of what Juan told me was true. The taxi secuestro. The months of imprisonment. He could have gathered those details from any news report or documentary about real kidnapping victims. There have been so many.

I couldn't even be sure the story of the two girlfriends was true. I'd never seen pictures. But then I'd feel bad about my skepticism. He was a man who claimed to have been forced to give proof of his life through an audiocassette with a machine gun aimed at his head, while reciting headlines from that day's *El Tiempo*, and recalling the names of his favorite stuffed animals from childhood so his parents would believe it was him.

We never saw each other after that September. November came and I didn't hear from him. I sat at my computer some nights, running my fingertips over the keyboard, wondering if I should send him a note, but I never did. I could have searched the Internet for archived details of his kidnapping, but neither of us had told the other their last name.

A year later, I left New York. I moved to Miami, where I slept heavily through the night and awoke to the sound of doves outside my window and the aroma of sweet morning dew. Here, it rains often, and I welcome the tropical aguaceros, letting water run over my face, drip off my chin, tasting it on my lips, salty and cool and soothing like bits of ocean. I remembered Juan's telling me that when he was released and finally returned to the safety of his parents' home, the first thing he did was go out to the garden and rub dirt on his face, run his hands over the bark of the trees, crush bunches of leaves in his palms, and smell the air, which, while dusty and polluted, was at least not the stale air of that windowless box of a room. He'd lie for hours on his back staring at the open sky, even as allergies and asthma kicked in, and even as police came to interview him over and over about his captors. When it rained, he let himself be soaked, eyes closed, remembering the months he'd had to beg for a shower, when that room he existed in might as well have been a desert. He had never felt freer, he told me, but with night came the cold and he had no choice but to go indoors, where unrelenting panic returned, and it was quickly decided he and his girlfriend should leave for Spain, where his parents and the police agreed they would be safer.

A few years ago, while in Madrid for the wedding of a friend, I sat by a fountain in El Retiro one afternoon and was sure I saw Juan walking by, looking older, thinner, grayer. I followed him several meters but as I approached, I realized it was someone else.

I thought of calling him or writing him, though he'd never done so, but convinced myself that if we were to see each other again, neither of us would have anything to say.

After a recent visit, my mother left some Colombian magazines behind for me on the kitchen table. It's there, while thumbing through an old issue of *Semana*, that I recognize a face printed in color on the page. The rest of the spread shows shots of a funeral. Women dressed in black, wearing dark glasses, exiting a church with arms linked. I read that the funeral is for a man named Juan who died of a pulmonary embolism while vacationing in Marbella. The photos of the mourners are captioned with the names of his parents, his longtime companion, and his daughter, Azul, now sixteen.

The article says that despite having made his home in Spain for the last twenty years, it was the wish of his family that Juan's body be returned to Colombia for burial.

It listed his famous relatives, presidents and senators, as he said, and made reference to the months he spent in captivity followed by a heavily negotiated release.

I never thought to ask if a ransom had been demanded for his freedom or if it had been paid.

He was fortunate to survive, the article said, when so many others don't.

What stayed with me most was when Juan told me that even though people called him brave for having endured his imprisonment, he considered himself a coward because he hadn't had the courage to try to escape. Instead, he'd spent months waiting for permission to be free, and the shame of this truth, he said, would never leave him.

Kenan Orhan
Soma

T HROUGH THE HILLS sprout white turbines, lofted over fifty meters into the air. In the breeze they swing languid arms in arcs across the sky, dipping the tips of blades beneath the horizon and pulling them back up like the strokes of a swimmer. They are propellers anchored to the earth, carrying it through its leisurely orbit. They are bright in the sun, these turbines, and at night their rotors glow from red safety lights, and we can't see the pillars or the blades, just the hubs sprinkling the air like cigarette butts.

And the miners walk in the release of the moon, heading with their meals in pails and plastic bags, heading with their hardhats heavy in their hands, heading to the shaft elevator that extends some two thousand meters underground, where they will work in golden pockets of electric light while the sun begins its sweep across the sky. After six hours they will ride the elevator up, stopping shy of the surface to let their eyes adjust before they breach once more into the world above.

As a boy I woke with my father, and watched him pack his breakfast of *sucuk* and boiled eggs, and struggled in his arms as he lifted me and kissed my cheek, stamping it black with coal dust carried always between the fibers of his moustache. Then my mother would wake and wipe my cheek clean and perform her own ablutions, and still hours before sunrise I would go to our apartment's balcony and wave good-bye to the miners. The moon so big and bright I waited all night for it to explode.

I still wake a little after four and go to the balcony with my coffee while my parents sleep. I wave to the miners as they walk through our village, and I make jokes: "Lock up your women. I'm on the prowl." They shout back: "Get a job, useless."

The file of men disappears behind the curve of the road, a scythe through the hills. For a half hour, at shift change, the town streets are empty and dark; the breeze shakes the homes of absent men, as if the village needs only a little encouragement to leap up into the air and ride the wind far away.

Now those done with their shifts creep up the road quietly in a long column; the only sound is the shuffle of their feet. At the edge of the village they break ranks and slip over stone streets to their homes, to their beds. I wave at my friend Mesut, who comes to the base of my building wearing his smile like a shard of porcelain in the dirt. I finish my coffee, grab my bag, and hurry down to him. Through the slopes of our village, I follow him, asking about the soccer match, about his shift, about the movie I lent him. The sun is on its way and I am restless.

We sneak out of the dawn and into his parents' apartment. The kitchen light displaces darkness, and from the hallway rolls his mother's snoring. Mesut goes to rinse the grit out of his hair so I sit at the table, take out my test-prep book and start working on the mathematics practice problems. Unable to focus, I pick at the seams of the plastic table cover decorated in daisies, coming undone. Mesut's mother keeps in a small white vase on the table a purple orchid—plastic stem, paper petals. I tap my pencil on the book, I flip the pages back and forth. I watch the way the windows grow full of light.

Mesut shoves my book off the table, replacing it with a plate of pasta his mother cooks up each night. "Swallow a big gulp before saying a big word."

I pick the book back up and set it next to the pasta. Mesut's a year older than me. He dropped out of high school and has been working the mine for the last year.

"Win this race first, İzzet, then you can worry about entrance exams."

"I need both," I say. I tell him they don't give scholarships to idiots, no matter how fast they swim. My father can't afford university, not on his pension. I'm jittering my leg like I do every morning, waiting for the water. Everyone in the village moves in smooth, simple motions, their muscles spent from hours underground.

Mesut sits next to me. His father has already left for the mine. From the bedroom, tremble snores growing louder, a testament to sound slumber. Mesut used to work the night shift with his father, but when one night someone ran off with a neighbor's bicycle, Mesut's mother cried worries of thieves and rapists. Now Mesut's father works by day to spend his evenings at home with his wife. Mesut tells me all their time together strains their marriage.

Mesut crumbles feta cheese over my pasta and gets a plate for himself, and this is what we do each morning: fork cold pasta into our mouths like we're furnaces.

Mesut's mother sleepwalks through the kitchen and into the TV room. She watches the local weather reports until after we leave, until she wakes up, then she cleans away the dishes, the evidence of us, and goes to cook more pasta.

I clean my first plate and pile up another. We finish our meal in the silence of smacking lips and digestion, then I fill a plastic container with another helping, and go change into my swimsuit, and pack my book back into my grocery bag with my goggles and towel, and I follow Mesut to the shed out back. The sun is up and already heavy in the sky so that it droops, long like an oval.

We climb into his dad's car, a relic from the sixties, and Mesut drives us out of the terraced village on narrow roads. I imagine calculating the village's slopes with my graphing calculator under the great expanse of mountain-fringed sky.

"Take the 240," I say.

"At this hour it will be slow."

For the last two months we've said this each morning, and I enjoy Mesut's route through Darkale, the winding descent. The way we travel is a delay of the sun, a delay of my eager nerves, my return to easy strokes. We take roads that cleave the mountains, roads from which we can count all the tumbledown shacks and hovels of the province falling over slowly, roads covered in shade, roads with streetlamps still on though the sky is lightly blue. Retaining walls squeeze our path, and we skirt around rocks fallen into the road and piles of trash people leave but no one picks up. And then before us opens the mountain range for just a moment, revealing Soma like a secret, tucked into the crevices, atop flat peaks, surrounded by gravel summits, potholed roads, telephone wires, and black trees that dance in the breeze. Far away are rain clouds. Half-finished houses in gradients, their terra-cotta roofs like steps into the air. TV dishes pimple up along the skyline. The minarets are ablaze with muezzins. The streets are built over top a number of buildings; all are curved like funnels flowing down the slopes through paths of least resistance. At a stoplight a man shoves bottles of water through my open window. Mesut runs the light.

"You could have ripped off his arm," I say.

"He's got two."

We turn east and head toward the thermal power plant. We curve around the field where squat cooling towers pop up in neat rows of six—olive trees growing in the shade of their steam clouds. Smoke drifts from the three slender chimney stacks attached to the plant like beautiful cigarettes. The plant fires the poor lignite dug out from the mine by Mesut and his father and every other able-bodied man in our village. The furnaces produce kilos of bottom ash every minute. The ash is mixed with water in a pump and sluiced away from the plant in eleven oversized pipes. We turn at the end of the olive grove and follow the pipes north out of the factory grounds. To our left are the eleven outgoing pipes, to our right are seven incoming pipes. Beyond these are the vineyards and groves and power lines and rusted-out cars and derelict houses, and farther still are the shops and restaurants and apartments and mosques of Soma, where no one is yet on the street— all still ambling through their dreams. I practice my breathing exercises.

Mesut slows—ahead there is a dog with valleys in the space between its ribs, with gray hair around its snout, with shoulders sliding up and down like oil derricks as it crosses our path. A car behind us honks, reminding Mesut we aren't alone, and he gooses it so we speed down the track of road that runs away from the plant in a beautiful line, the kind of line that's in my textbooks, the desire line, the most efficient line you ever saw, and I swear I can hear the water coursing through the pipes.

These pipes empty into a man-made dam to the north of town. Its bottom is covered in cement to keep toxins from leaking into water supplies. The ash separates from the water and settles along the cement like multicolored oils in chemistry. The empty water is filtered from the top and pumped back to the plant. We park at the road that runs along the side of the reservoir. Because of the ash and cement, the water is bright, turquoise, as beautiful as the Ottoman palaces of Istanbul, covered in electric-blue arabesques.

A wall separates spare water from the filtration area where the slurry settles. I stretch, shaking my limbs to get the blood flowing. Mesut sets up a lawn chair in the gravel and begins drinking. I dive into the cold water. I backstroke toward the middle of the pond, keeping my eyes on clouds slicing the blue same as me.

"Keep your eyes closed, İzzet."

I close them. Open-water swimming depends on bearings,

straight lines, knowing your way without looking. Mesut shouts when I begin to drift and says nothing when my vector is straight for the telephone pole on the opposite bank.

Other days I have practiced taking off while treading because Mesut says they might not provide a diving platform. He wouldn't know, but it is good practice.

Before that, I practiced turns. He had me swim around buoys he set up while he watched my strokes underwater.

Before that I practiced swimming in groups. It's hard to navigate a race with hundreds of people cutting through the same small stretch of water. We'd made planks with short rudders and rope tails. Mesut rigged them all up into a network. I positioned myself amid the wooden swimmer-substitutes, and swam toward Mesut while he pulled the flock of planks along, keeping pace with me.

Now there is only sighting left to work on. I keep conditioning, but I'm in good shape for the race. Mesut drinks his beers and falls asleep while I incorporate sighting into the rhythm of my strokes. When Mesut wakes, he takes notes of my timing, my pace.

Nothing is jittery in my mind, my nerves are cooled by the water. Mesut shouts to me, his voice crashing with the crest of the water in my ear. I can't hear what he says. I reach the dividing wall and push back from it. I backstroke for the beach, for the car. In the middle of the reservoir I look directly up, the blue of the sky converging with the blue of the water in my peripheries so that I am a point in an ineffable expanse of buoyancy. Here I have no thoughts. My limbs negotiate with the weight of the water through which I become weightless. I am deprived of sensation save for the color of the sky. I am miles in the air. My heart steadies. My strokes slow. The beach is close though I can't feel it.

We pack everything into the car. My muscle cords twitch and scream beneath my skin. Mesut takes the 240 back to town because he knows I like to watch the turbines while I cool down, because I like to watch the great turns. We don't park, but he drives slowly. There's not enough of a breeze today; the turbines hang in disuse over the clefts of hills and fields.

"I'm going to be up there," I say.

Mesut gives a tired laugh. He's been awake, he's been working, he's been drinking.

"Right there." I point. "I'm going to straddle the rotors."

"What's the difference, eh?"

Instead of descending into the dark, I will climb into the bright day, into the sunlight.

"The same thing is done up there," Mesut says, "the gathering of electricity. So you are in the air, or in the ocean, or underground, whatever. I want to be flatly on the ground. Safe. I wouldn't mind taking in a little sun across a bed of grass, or under olive trees."

He drops me off at my house, then he's off to bed. There are friends of his who go straight to bed after work, and most of the year they never see the sunlight.

At home, my parents watch television. In the kitchen, I study some more. My mom comes in. She cuts up a watermelon and leaves a plate of slices next to me. She sits across from me, watching the flicks of my pencil.

"I'm so proud of you, you know," she says.

What do I say to that? I could tell her it's not a sure thing. I could tell her I haven't even taken the exams, I haven't even swum the race, but what are these things to her? She looks at me, marble eyes heavy with pride.

"Is that watermelon for everyone?" my dad asks.

She takes it out to the living room, and they call for me to join them. On-screen is an American show. The cigarettes and cans of beer are blurred out so every few seconds the characters take swigs from pixelated rectangles.

"Have they asked you what you want to study?" my mom asks.

"I haven't turned in my application yet."

"You ought to get into architecture," she says.

"He's going to be like his father," my dad says, rosy glints of melon pooling in the corners of his mouth. He does this more and more, says I'm going to be a replica of him—like I haven't been training, like I haven't been studying, like the turbines are the same as the mine.

"I will be an engineer," I say.

"Do they work inside?" my mom asks.

"Four years of school just so you can wear a bigger hardhat? If you're going to fantasize don't do it on a budget," my dad says as he stuffs another slice of watermelon in his mouth.

They eat watermelon and laugh at the television. My mom goes to the kitchen to start tea. Without looking from the television screen, my dad says: "What's that worth?"

He means *What can I do with it?* He means *How far will that take me from the mine?* He means he wants the distance in kilometers that I will escape into.

"I could be a technician for those windmills," I say. "Mom would like having me around as you two grow old."

"Who's planning on growing old?" My dad laughs a little. "Who wants to keep you here?"

"They make a living. It isn't the mine."

We sit like that until my mom brings out the copper tray of tulip glasses. We stir in cubes of sugar, the tinkle of teaspoons tickling our silence. The television is turned way down. My mom falls asleep. The engineers make six times what I would make in the mine. They live twice as long, I hear. They have suntans.

"It isn't the mine," my dad says, trying the words out for himself.

"There's a program that I could do. It specializes in . . ." But I don't know what to say. It's too late, and I can see that. My dad doesn't care about the windmills. We sit close to each other on the couch, the rough fabric scratching our undersides like bark. I'm jittering my leg. I'm feeling my body sink into the cushion. I want my dad to ask me about my swimming, how training's going, what Mesut thinks of my speed.

"I don't think you know what you're talking about," he whispers. "It *is* the mine."

There are cookies and a bowl of nuts on the tray. I swallow the tea as easy as sand, and my throat feels swollen. My dad keeps eating, plucking almonds from the bowl with sticky-glazed fingers from the watermelon. I think about going for a walk to get out of the house, but there's nothing to see in this town except retired men huddled around small tables at street corners, playing cards and *tavla*, drinking tea and coffee, their skin drooping like time because of their underground lives. There's nothing to see in this town but quiet women, running errands, beating dust from rugs, clipping cotton sheets to clotheslines, dripping soot from their hair at the bounce of each step. There's nothing to see in this town but coal-stained children like feral dogs through the streets, their lungs sucking all the ash from the air.

I go to my room instead. I try reading but I don't like the book and I'm a slow reader. Everyone I know is asleep or in the mine, like I'm a fugitive, like I'm the only unclipped bird in an aviary. I go to bed as well, with the sun in my window. When I wake, the sky is dark, the clouds cover the moon. I take my coffee on the balcony and shout to the miners until Mesut returns and drives me to the reservoir. We do this for two more weeks. I study when I'm not training, though I am exhausted and unable to focus. I think of every face in town. I book a small room at a hostel near the Dardanelles. Mesut gets the day off so that he can drive me to the race. The website claims over six hundred registered entrants.

The morning of the race is here, and splitting across the sky comes a crash you can hear in your bones. It's flat, monosyllabic. The ground doesn't falter, the air is clear and blue, the grass shudders only in the breeze. If you could listen to the scrape of tectonic plates, if for just a flash of time there was the great flow of mantle and crust caught in your ear, it wouldn't sound like this. It's not at all like an earthquake. We know those here; you grow up knowing them. We know this too: the silence, the absence of aftershocks, the snap of energy is a single, released moment, the space between heartbeats. It can suffocate you if you're not careful—the mine.

I've never seen the streets so full as they are now, though no one hurries. They compact themselves into one another, press close, hunch. More people from more homes. I break from my mom's grasp and run down to the street, her shouts chasing after me. Still we all pack tighter, our closeness brushing black dust from our skin. The crowd shuffles now, searching with stamping feet for the path to the mine. People talk in hushed voices, careful that their words are not picked up by the wind. The mine, everyone whispers, the mine. No one runs, no one shoves, no one steps on toes or heels. We walk deliberately down the curved path to the mine, our voices extinguishing as we near the mouth of the shaft. For a long time, long enough that clouds have moved to cover us, we stand there watching from afar a dozen or so men scraping at the pile of earth obstructing the main shaft—scraping with their hardhats like shovels.

I see Mesut come away from the mouth of the mine and run to him. His face is black and he doesn't recognize me. Behind me people start running for things, for shovels, for carts, for oxygen tanks, for picks, for stretchers, for a defibrillator, but we don't know what we're doing, we don't know what's going on.

Exasperated, Mesut shouts for help, shouts that the slope to the mine is blocked by boulders and soil. I follow him back down the ramp to the shaft elevator, my arms swinging wildly as I try to keep up. The keys to his dad's car must be in his pocket. People swarm around us, with buckets, with handcarts, with helmets, with outstretched shirts in vise-fingers. Others shovel rubble and dirt into every cart, every helmet, every palm to be carried away, up the tracks and into the sun. Everyone is shouting, cutting at the great barrier of earth between us and the shaft elevator with frenzied limbs. A scream of sirens, and the crowd breaks for a line of ambulances and the police chief's car. Mesut is throwing boulders large as my torso into carts, up and down, up and down, like a piston. I'm bobbing my head up and down beside him, screaming that there's no time to waste, there's no time for digging. There's a race up the coast, there's a race we must get to.

"Grab a shovel," he says between grunts, between heaves.

"Can I take the car?" I ask, because what else am I going to do? It's all set, it's my life at stake too.

He doesn't hear me. He shoves his fingers into the soil and unearths rock after rock like potatoes plucked for boiling.

"Do you have the keys?"

Mesut looks at me, confused. He keeps digging with his hands. He doesn't say anything. He scratches at the black soil with callused fingertips. He's bleeding from a few cuts on his arms, between his fingers. There are hundreds of people now, a number of trucks with emergency lights, a bulldozer, an excavator, a dump truck. More people arrive, some with pots to help scoop dirt. No one's crying yet. I notice it, that no one's crying yet.

"Can I take the car?"

Mesut throws a stone back into the rubble. Screaming, he grabs me by the shoulders and shoves me into the pile. He yells to get a fucking shovel, to start digging. With difficulty I pull myself up from the rubble and rocks, a stray point knocking me in the spine, and then there is Mesut's fist, fast and fleshy, striking me squarely in the jaw. I can't see for a moment in my right eye, the way the sight goes when I am swimming too long underwater. There's a pounding moving from the exploded capillaries of my face, through my jaw and temples to my ears. Mesut is on top of me as my sight comes back, his dirt-caked face shouting at me through the fizzling little dots on my peripheries. I grab at his collar, I try pulling him to the side, but he's bigger than me, pushing my chest into the dirt, shoving my head back so that I can feel the soil spill down my forehead. Desperate, I kick him off. No one around us seems to care. They are all singularly busy in their efforts to remove the rubble.

Mesut drags me off the pile and onto the cart tracks. He throws the keys to his dad's car at me and goes back to ripping at the rocks with his fingers. All around people are tearing into the mine. But I'm already packed, I'm already enrolled. I go to the car and drive away, north through the stalks of windmills. I listen the whole way for another explosion. I leave the radio off, and for the four-hour drive I listen carefully for another explosion, promising myself that if it gets worse I will turn back, but the four hours don't take long, not really, and I'm in Çanakkale, with a view of the Dardanelles from a square window in the hostel. There's an Australian named Bruce in the bunk next to me who asks me if I'm excited for the race tomorrow, who asks me if I got that bruise on my face from swimming.

I don't say anything, not to him or anyone else while I lie in my bed until morning, thinking about the route I must take to cross the channel, thinking about the landmarks I will use for bearings, timing out my breathing with imaginary strokes. In the morning, I have a small breakfast very early and ride the ferry to the other side of the Dardanelles. I sign in and look around the beach for a good spot to start from. The water is choppy. It will be difficult to navigate. Where the strait begins to narrow, near Çanakkale, it is only a kilometer and a half wide. The current there is inexorable. I set up at the north end of the beach, go as far as I can, an extra two or three hundred meters up from most of the other swimmers, all in their Speedos and caps and goggles, lubing themselves with Vaseline, slapping their muscles and shaking their limbs. I've done my preparations in the hostel. I don't like this bit of showmanship beforehand. The novices take places as far south as they can squeeze, as close to the first marker as possible, without room to maneuver with the current. The man next to me is very old for this race, beside him is a woman a few years older. They are married and from Liverpool. I ask what it is they are putting in their mouths. Salt tablets, they say, they are good for preventing cramps. They give me some. I take them with water and start up with my little ritual of splashing water from the sea on my forearms, shins, thighs, chest.

There's a starter's pistol, but we don't hear it this far away, in this much wind. We take the cue of the hundreds of bodies diving into the water, cutting at it with frenzied limbs, violent lungs, combustion engines inside thoracic cavities. I dive in and aim directly across, aim straight for Asia though the finish line is a few kilometers down, past Çanakkale. It takes some time to escape the breakers, and I haven't paced myself well, but soon enough I am out striding through the open water, I am beyond the sounds of shore, I am above a blur, a void, an ineffable divide. When I take a breath, I adjust my line. While I stroke, I gaze below me, watching the bottom until it dissolves behind the opacity of depth. But it is an illusion, the bottom is only a hundred meters at its deepest. There are men trapped now in a tunnel over two thousand meters underground, and their lungs must be deflated balloons.

Most of the swimmers, especially those that started farthest south, are taken by the current of the water emptying into the Aegean. They broke too late, their lines too direct. They will not make it across. I make my turn and let the water carry me. In a long sweep I've aimed for the beach like a celestial body exiting orbit. There are a number of other racers who have done the same as me, there are a good number of them. But I am fast, I am calm, and I scrape at the crest of the water, I grip and tear and cut through it. Past the narrow I don't bother looking around me, I don't worry for nearby kicks or slaps. I don't bother opening my eyes beneath the waves. I look only during breaths, I look only at the expanse of blue above—I think only of my breaths, conscious, measured like the breaths of men who must worry over the factor of oxygen. I am not any distance above or below; my elevation is zero. I am on the flat of the earth. Every few strokes, as I turn my head, there is the boom against my eardrum from the breeze. I listen below me, I listen for explosions in the earth but can't hear anything over the slap and kick of a thousand hands and feet.

I ride the breakers to shore. A man takes a picture from the beach as I slip through the glinting surf. I can taste the salt in my smile. My back is burned from the sun and the iodine. There are others in the water, the other swimmers. I am the only one on land, and my body feels heavy, the fibers of my muscles drip from my skeleton under the pressure of gravity.

Before my feet have a chance to cake with sand, a committee brings me a ribbon and a bottle of liquor. I ask for water and let someone drive me back to my room in Çanakkale, where I pack my things and send a text to my mother telling her I'll be back after dinner.

But when I get back no one will ask me about what I've done here, what it means for me. Will they think me vile? When I pull the car back into Mesut's shed, I check his house but no one is home. It's evening, the sun is an orange radiance spread just below the mountaintops. I walk through an empty village, my hand out, reaching for the sides of houses, brushing them with fingertips until I'm outside my own home. I walk up to my room. No one is here. Lights are not coming on in the other houses. I fall asleep and don't wake up until a truck honks in the street the next morning.

A procession of black cars curves around the truck, on their way to the square not far from Mesut's house. I splash my face with water from the tap and look for my parents. They are out somewhere. Maybe at the mine. Outside, I follow a small group of people walking after the procession of cars. I ask them if they have any news. If there's anyone still underground.

"They aren't sure if anyone's still alive. Already they've hauled fifty bodies."

"How are they breathing? How are they breathing that deep?" I ask.

A machine is still pumping air down the shaft like a large snorkel, the few miners left alive are struggling to sip from it. They are stuck, trapped, some with bodies broken in a dozen places they tell me. They've pulled a few survivors from the mine, in a trickle are the miners, surfacing.

"Is it a funeral?" I ask about the cars.

President Erdoğan is visiting. He's speaking in front of the old *bey*'s mansion. In the square, usually so stuffed with *döner* vendors and coffee drinkers, are all the people I have ever seen in my life, every face to haunt the little village. More than that, even, more faces, more people from other villages, from the city of Soma not far away. They're hoisting banners, picket signs. They shout while the mayor introduces the president. He's taller than you think, with eyes like coal. He tells us that mining accidents are typical, they are to be expected. He tells us of incidents in Britain and France in the nineteenth century, talking to us like we are anachronistic, like we are suspended in the past. Since the mine was privatized, the cost of producing one ton of coal has dropped over 80 percent. Our mines kill us at rates five times greater than in China, three hundred and sixty times greater than in America.

Looking around, I am wrong. This is not everyone I have ever seen. This is only the semblance of the village. This is only the people not part of the mine. The people chant: *Murderer Erdoğan*. All around are men, some wearing suits, some in construction uniforms, some in miner's coveralls, some in firemen gear, some with hardhats on, some with shovels over their heads. The women are in their living rooms, at the funeral homes, in morgues identifying bodies they barely recognize.

The president steps off the platform and immediately his bodyguards wrap around him. His limousine is blocked by the crowd, so the guards escort him to the lobby of a bank at the corner while rocks fly through the air. I pick up a rock as well and think about throwing it, but I don't deserve to, I don't belong here with a rock to throw at a car. The rocks these men throw are dug from the mine, from atop the bodies of their friends. A guard fires his rifle into the air. The crowd parts for the limousine, though their chants grow louder. The president is ushered into his car and driven away. A man tears from the crowd and runs for the car.

It's Mesut. He kicks the wheel. He kicks the fender, and right away two bodyguards in fatigues with rifles at their shoulders grab him and throw him onto the pavement. The motorcade takes off, cutting through the crowd of mourners, protestors, locals. They throw rocks at the bodyguards. The two men in fatigues try to wrestle Mesut's arms. A presidential aide in a suit pulls one of the bodyguards away. Fire in his mouth, he swings a sharp foot into Mesut's side. He swings again, he swings a third time, kicks Mesut in the ribs while the two bodyguards in fatigues hold him down on the cold pavement. They will arrest Mesut, and hold him for weeks, maybe months, without charging him. His father, if he is not in the mine, will not find work. His mother will spend mornings in the prison visiting him until she is detained as well. I do nothing. I don't stand out from the crowd. I've just won the race. I will pass my entrance exams. I go from the street full of people, down an alley, and I walk for a long way through a village I don't recognize, until I'm not far from the cemetery they've been taking the coffins to in truckloads.

Along the low stone wall stand relatives in long lines. A few politicians have stuck around, maybe they're from nearby, maybe they're up for reelection. The coffins are all covered with the flag, like the dead were soldiers, like they've just come back from the east, shot to bits.

They've brought in digging machines, three of them. The undertaker and his two sons can't keep up. They cut little rectangles into the dirt, long rows of them, you can't count how many, you wouldn't need to, the number will be in the headlines. The space between the graves is slight, out of necessity.

I think of the speed sound travels through water. There's a difference between salt water and fresh water. There's a difference between loamy soil and geode. Supposedly sound travels fastest through solid objects, but that can't be true. When I press my ear to the earth I still hear the whisper of methane, the crack of each molecule combusting, the slow fizzle. I can still hear the explosion in process.

Am I so different? Am I not just the other side of the coin, the man who will climb up a shaft two hundred meters above the ground, and tinker with machinery so far from the surface, tinker with the things of power, of energy? I will tell my children stories of my work the way my father has told me. I will tell them of the world of light, the world without gravity.

My father's moustache still leaks black powder, but mine will not. My children will ask me of the mine, will crawl onto my lap and ask why the fathers of all their friends have moustaches of pitch, have backs like mountain ranges, have stories they share, they know by heart, they lived through side by side. I will tell them of my life in the sky and they will ask me of the men I left in the earth. Perhaps they will ask me of the mine when they've outgrown sitting on my lap, ask me why the men of Soma walk like phantoms of soot through the dawn, and I will tell them of my love for the slow swing of turbines. Perhaps they will ask me of the mine when they've just come back from it, hands caked, cracks of white on their faces, ask me why I'm not down there with them, why I'm still climbing ladders upward bound. Perhaps they will ask me what I did during the explosion, and I will tell them about the race, about the beautiful strokes of the windmills.

Sarah Hall
Goodnight Nobody

JEM HAD SEEN THE DOG the week before, the day after her birthday, while she'd been breaking in her new shoes. It was a small dog, a Jack Russell or a terrier, not something that looked dangerous like the muscley Doberman and the mint-eyed Alsatian further down the street. She'd seen the man walking the dog by the weir, and she'd seen it tied up outside the Saracen's Head. It didn't choke its lead or drool or go for people. The man was hard-faced though, hair buzzed to the scalp, tight jeans he was too old to wear, dark red boots laced up his shins. He had a tattoo on his neck. A web. Or a net. Something stringy. Mumm-Ra said tattoos outside the collar and cuff meant people were beyond civilization. Mumm-Ra saw a lot of tattoos at work, in all kinds of hidden places. She often told Gran about them. Once a woman with only one breast had had one where the other breast wasn't. A rose.

Outside the man's house there was a police van. It'd been there all morning. The lights and the engine were off, but it was very noticeable, very nosey looking. They would be taking the dog away soon, Jem was sure. The kids on the street had been trying to climb the backyard wall for a look-see before it was destroyed, even though it was the same dog it'd been the week before, nothing extra special or with superpowers.

Destroyed made the dog sound like a battleship in a war game. Jem wondered how they'd do it—a gun, maybe, or by injection, like criminals in America. The dog would twitch and go to sleep and then its heart would stop. They'd been learning about the heart in biology. The heart was the last piece of equipment to keep going in a body; it worked the hardest. One cell told all the others what to do, and if the main cell died another normal cell took over. She'd shared that piece of information with Mumm-Ra and Gran. Gran had said it sounded like socialism. Dictatorship, more like, Mumm-Ra said. A vet might come to the man's house and put the dog down, the same as if the dog had cancer or a broken leg. The dog wouldn't know what was happening, so it wouldn't be scared, although dogs did understand, they could sense things.

Martin, Jem's dad, had had cancer. He was extremely lucky. He had one lung and he'd had chemotherapy while living in his caravan in Catton Park. It'd taken months for him to get better and during that time Jem hadn't seen him much. He'd said, before he'd been told he would be fine, that if he wasn't going to be fine he wanted to be put down. Before he started to mess himself. He wanted sleeping pills or to be dropped off the bridge into the river. After the chemotherapy Martin's eyebrows didn't come back.

He still smoked sometimes, at the pub, and after tea. Mumm-Ra said he was an imbecile and would be seeing her soon enough if he didn't stop—she'd be zipping him up. Mumm-Ra worked in the mortuary at the hospital. She wore blue scrubs. She looked like a doctor, but she wasn't one, even though she'd taken exams as part of the job. A practical exam and a written exam. After she'd said the thing about Martin, Jem had wondered for a while about people being zipped up, as if they were bags. She knew it meant something else. Jem didn't like to think about what Mumm-Ra did at work, which involved glue and chemicals, and not crying while other people cried.

Mortuary. Mortuary. Sometimes words got stuck in her head, usually if they sounded a certain way—strong, important.

The street had been busy all morning. It wasn't raining. People were standing about with their front doors open and their arms crossed and they were talking about what had happened and waiting to hear more. Before Gran had gone, Jem had been standing around too. The rules about who you could talk to, when, and where, had been suspended. People she didn't know had said things to her like, What a tragedy, and, Oh my Lord. She'd even missed watching *ThunderCats*, which was her favorite program.

The baby had been a tiny baby, a newborn. No one knew if it was a girl or a boy or what its name was. Maybe it didn't have a name yet. People on the street had seemed angry there was no name and were tutting a lot. She wondered if that meant the baby wasn't a proper person yet, or was beyond civilization.

Jem's brother hadn't seemed like a proper person until he'd been given his name. Mumm-Ra had been too sad to give him a name in the first week because his dad had gone back to Yugoslavia. For good, because of the war. She'd also had a cesarean so she couldn't come downstairs. Cesarean. Mumm-Ra had a smiley scar that was hidden by the hair there, and a skin fold, not that Jem saw that part much. Gran had had some serious words with Mumm-Ra and then they'd taken Jem's brother to the town hall. Her brother was called Sava. It was a name from his dad's country—Gran had found it in a book. Everyone called him Sav. Jem couldn't really remember Sav's dad, except for his red checked shirt and jars of sweet pickled seafood that he ate on black crackers. Mumm-Ra and Martin had chosen Jem's name together before they'd split up. Jemima. Jem hated it. Posh, or a duck, were the bullying options. Everyone called her Jem, luckily, but that didn't stop people not liking her at school. Mum had become Mumm-Ra after *Thunder-Cats* Series One and the big argument over Jem's bike and because of her job. Jem never said it out loud though. Gran's real name was Marcy. You couldn't write a report at school about a book unless you said why the characters were called what they were and what it meant. Naming humans was complicated, and went wrong really easily, and people fought about it, so Jem hadn't minded if the baby didn't have a name. It was neglect, people were saying, poor little mite.

People were also saying that the baby had been left outside in a basket in the yard, near the kennel. It'd been crying for hours. Dogs didn't like crying babies. The man's girlfriend was very thin and hadn't even looked pregnant. Then she was holding a screechy bundle outside their front door and there was a big party and the next day there were bin bags full of bottles and cans on the pavement. Jem didn't know their names, the man and his girlfriend. They lived thirty-two doors down. That was very close. If what had happened had been an asteroid, it would have hit Jem's house too, but asteroids were rare and they usually hit deserts.

The baby had already been taken away in an ambulance. The man had been taken away by the police, because he was the dog's owner and responsible. Possibly he was also drunk. Someone who had passed by the house had looked in and said that the girlfriend was sitting at the kitchen table, not crying, just drinking a can of lager. Someone else had said that she was hysterical; she'd screamed and hit the policeman who'd arrested her boyfriend. Hysterical. Jem had thought that meant "funny."

It was hard to know what to believe. She didn't have any friends on the street. Deborah Mason lived a few doors down, but she and Deborah were not friends. Deborah called Sav a half-caste commie bastard. She called Jem duck-fuck. She said once that *ThunderCats* was a stupid television program, why did they have blue faces? Jem tried to explain they didn't, only Panthro, and actually his face was gray, which had made things worse. She'd ended up with a horse pinch on the arm that was red and sore for a week. Deborah was two years older than Jem and at a different school, but they took the same bus. Deborah was always talking about her periods, but she called it red-eye or painters or the blob, and her Tampax was always in wrong and uncomfortable, and it made the whole thing sound horrible.

Deborah had talked to Jem earlier on the street though, in a normal conversation, without any insults. She'd said the baby had been picked up by the neck and shaken to death. The dog had bitten right through the baby's neck. Decapitated it. Then it had licked up all the blood. Deborah's mouth looked horrible when she said this, glistening and dramatic, and her tongue tip came out between her teeth. Some of what she said might have been true, but a lot definitely wasn't. Jem had nodded and tried to look impressed. You made the most of it when the rules were gone. But after a second or two, Deborah's face had gone blurry, as if she were underwater in a swimming pool. Jem's stomach had sent a bile bubble up to her mouth, which popped and tasted disgusting. Gran had called her in not long after that to mind Sav because she was going to the social club and Mumm-Ra wasn't back from her night shift.

Mumm-Ra was home now, looking withered and baggy in her uniform. She was moving around the kitchen slowly. She was, Jem knew, capable of turning into a monster if everyone wasn't careful. Night shifts were killing her, Gran often said, but Jem knew her mother would never die, just like actual Mumm-Ra, it was impossible. She was far too powerful. There were probably a lot of evil spirits where she worked, which might help summon her strength. Jem didn't really believe in spirits and thought the séances some of the girls in her class had done in the store cupboard were stupid, obviously fake. Night shifts paid well though, especially at weekends.

Mumm-Ra was opening a tin of tomato soup, while Sav flicked bits of baby food all over the floor. Mumm-Ra had cut her hair very short last year because Sav was a puker and she was sick of washing sick out of it. Other mothers got perms and crimps. From behind, in the uniform, she looked almost like a man.

Sav was nearly two. He was extremely strong and didn't like to do what anyone wanted him to do. He liked to prod eyes and to smash down towers of objects he'd stacked. Steering him along to the newsagent's to get sweets or collect Gran's paper was impossible. If the man's dog had gone for Sav, he probably would have blinded it.

It's not the dog that should be put down, Mumm-Ra was saying, quietly. Some people should have to get a license to breed. She was up to speed on the situation, even though she'd only just got back. Maybe she'd seen the baby. Maybe she'd actually been handling the baby. Putting it back together. Making it look not so bad for the relatives, with powders and cream. Cosseting, it was called. Gran said what Mumm-Ra did was sort of what a beautician did, but much harder.

Jem never talked about Mumm-Ra's job. If people asked in school, she always said a hospital orderly or a nurse. The source of all Mumm-Ra's power probably came from her ability to do what she did to bodies, which didn't scare her, though Gran said it certainly took its toll. Because death, and people's grief, were exhausting. Morticians often had to stop working. Some went mad, really mad, with roaring in their heads, or they disappeared and were found in the woods. Nerves of ice, Martin said about Mumm-Ra.

Martin wasn't able to pay much money toward Jem, some months nothing at all. He did get a disability benefit for having only one lung though. And the house they lived in had belonged to Martin's mother. Useless, is what Mumm-Ra said about Martin, a useless lump, but they were quite like friends. Martin had even put his arm around Mumm-Ra when Sav's dad left and had offered to stay. Mumm-Ra said no. No, no, we're the opposite,

Martin, the absolute opposite. Sav's dad was a roofer, an expert roofer; he'd worked on the repairs on the prison in the castle. He'd worked legally. Then he'd gone back home because men especially were needed. Unlucky in love, Gran said about Mumm-Ra. She likes the leavers, your mother. If a man won't marry you before the babies come, Jemima, he'll be gone after. That fellow will have a family, I bet, never mind any war.

Gran had bits and bobs of wisdom about men. Her husband had died before Jem was born. He'd been called Leonard. Gran had burgundy hair that was white at the roots. She drove a green Maxi and could fix the fan belt herself when it squealed. There were always soft mints and a packet of Merits in her purse. She slept in Mumm-Ra's room overnight when Mumm-Ra was working.

Mumm-Ra stirred the tomato soup. Sav put his dinner bowl on his head and orange goo smeared into his hair. Then he flung the bowl at Mumm-Ra and a splattery streak went up the back of her scrubs. Hell's teeth, she said, without turning round. Sort him out will you, Jem. Your gran'll be back soon. But it's Saturday, Jem wanted to say. She didn't say it because Mumm-Ra turned round and gave her a look that involved not blinking and the kitchen light dimmed a bit. Mumm-Ra could sense things coming like a dog could. She took the soup upstairs on a tray.

Jem decided that when Sav was having his after-lunch nap, she'd go out again and see what was happening. Sav was a good sleeper, an hour at least—you could stick pins in his forehead and he wouldn't wake up. He wouldn't be left alone really if there was an emergency; Mumm-Ra would be in the house. If Gran arrived, Jem could say she'd had to nip to the chemist for some more of something. That seemed sensible. She was always being told how sensible she was. It was annoying, especially as she was only just not eleven anymore. Today she wanted to see what was going on, like everyone else. The baby and the dog would probably even be on the news.

She did Sav a nappy in the bathroom and put Vaseline on his bum, shielding herself from a wee spout with a towel. He loved weeing when his nappy was off. Men loved weeing up against trees and in the underpass and in the park and they started very young. Jem was getting good at nappies. She could do them much faster than Mumm-Ra. It was mostly Gran and Jem that looked after Sav though so there was plenty of practice. Jem put the dirty cloth in the dirties basket, which was getting full. The nappy man came on Sunday nights and Wednesday nights, but Sav had gone through quite a few with a bout of something runny. The nappy man was a stupid old-fashioned person and it was embarrassing to have to open the front door to him, hand over a smelly bundle, and get a clean bundle back. Even though a lot of people were using disposables, he was still in business. Mumm-Ra said disposables were expensive and it was better to keep a person in work. She snapped at Jem when Jem asked who made the disposable ones then? Why do you have to be so contrary, madam? Contrary.

Jem hated the nappy man, partly because what kind of man wanted to wash poo for a living, partly because he had a van that said MR. NIPPY NAPPY MAN on the side like a giveaway, but mostly because he had a funny eye. He had an eye with a golden gash in it, like a gold disease of some kind. The eye didn't move about much. His other eye was blue and normal. She sometimes wondered who had the worse job, the nappy man or Mumm-Ra. Mumm-Ra, probably.

Jem carried Sav back to the bedroom, got his library books out, then sat on the beanbag to read to him. He squirmed into position in her lap and she fended off his pointy elbows and heels. Moon, he said. Sav was heavy and half her size already, who knew how because he didn't eat anything. Moon, he said. What about Ant and Bee? Jem asked. She hated *Goodnight Moon*. The colors were horrible. The little rabbity creature in pajamas was horrible. The strange page near the end was extremely horrible. It gave her the same feeling as jumping down off somewhere high, or looking up at the sky for too long. She tried to slip the book under the beanbag but Sav spotted the cover. He scrambled to get it, took hold of Jem's hand, and made her hold it. Moon! OK, OK, mister.

She let him turn the pages as she read. Sav pointed items out in a slow, serious way as she said the words—toy house, mouse, comb, brush, bowl full of mush, quiet old lady whispering hush. She tried to flip ahead to the end of the book, past the weirdest bit, but Sav wedged his podgy fist between the pages so she couldn't avoid seeing

Goodnight nobody

Sav turned and looked up at her, frowning. He didn't understand, but neither did Jem. Who was nobody? Was nobody actually somebody, a person there but not-there in the room? Could the rabbity creature see nobody from its bed? That was like a ghost story for babies, which was very wrong. And if it was a joke she didn't get it, because it wasn't funny. It was exactly the opposite of funny, and opposites always created problems. The opposite of married. The opposite of love. The opposite of alive. She nudged her brother and blew on the back of his head. He smelled of milk and potato and nappy detergent. Come on, she said, turn the page, Sav. Sav turned the page. Jem read to the end of the book, then tried to lift him up and put him in his cot, but he grabbed her T-shirt and barnacled to her. Mooooon!

After three more *Goodnight Moon*s he let her put him down. He shuffled about, stuck his legs through the bars of the cot, kicked, yawned, then rolled onto his stomach and went to sleep immediately, as if someone had unplugged him. Under the sticky orange, his hair was thick and dark. He looked nice when he slept, Jem thought, loose and soft, not like the Lego-hurling, crusty-nosed monster he normally was. Sav always wanted things done for him and shown to him. Being the one who knew more was hard work; she often didn't like it. Maybe he dreamed of Yugoslavia when he slept. Maybe he dreamed of his dad, though he'd never met him, and his dad might be dead. Could you dream of a place or a person you'd never known? Gran said Sav would have a lot of questions when he was older.

Jem put a blanket over him. She thought about going outside. She thought about the little baby, lying in the basket, and pictured its neck like a chewed-on dog's bone. Mumm-Ra's bedroom door was shut. Silence and darkness behind it, like the Black Pyramid. Jem went downstairs and turned on the TV, but there was only motor racing on, flimsy cars on a noisy, skidding track. She got her book out and sat at the kitchen table.

The street was quiet by the time Gran arrived, just a few people coming back from the city with carrier bags and their hoods up. Drizzle had started. The police van wasn't there anymore. The dog had probably been taken away. Mumm-Ra had already gone back to work and wouldn't be home until morning. When she'd left the house she was pig-eyed and late and on the point of being extremely cross because she couldn't find her keys. She'd forgotten her box of sandwiches on the kitchen counter—she ate sandwiches for dinner at work as if it were lunchtime. Things always felt topsy-turvy when Mumm-Ra was on night shifts.

Jem walked down the cut between houses, to the football field, and along the backs of the yards. There were empty crisp packets skittering about, a flat, dented football. The back gate of the man's house was battered and blistered. There was police tape across it— the only sign anything terrible had happened there. Jem could smell dinners cooking, crispy pancakes and meat and gravy. She could smell rain on the bricks. People were inside waiting for the evening news. The baby might have a name and it would be announced. Could you name a baby after it was dead? Or maybe they'd use an initial, like the little girl who had gone missing from the park last year. Baby R. Rebecca, Jem had guessed, or Rachel. Gran was making cauliflower cheese for their dinner, which Jem didn't like because the cauliflower was usually soggy and the sauce had flour lumps and hardly any cheese. Gran would ask her about boys at school, which was embarrassing. Anyone look like that lovely Lion-y character? Jem never corrected her.

Mortuary. Decapitated. When you thought things, like words, it was because there was a voice inside your head that said the thoughts. Jem hadn't realized that before. The voice wasn't exactly your voice, but it wasn't anyone else's.

There was no point hanging around outside by herself. She walked back along the yard walls. If she were friends with Deborah she could go and knock on her door and ask if anything else had happened. Deborah's door was white plastic. In the upstairs window—Deborah's bedroom, maybe—was an A-ha poster. She could imagine Deborah's face when the door opened, a big how-dare-you sneer. The rules would definitely be back by now. Off on your own, duck-fuck? Where's your Yoogi brother?

Jem looked at her watch, which was blue leather and quite nice, a birthday present from Martin last year. He'd forgotten her actual birthday and had given the watch a week late. Overcompensation, Mumm-Ra said. It was quarter past five. She was supposed to be back by six. Sometimes Martin came to see her on Saturday afternoons for tea but not every Saturday. Jem didn't have Martin's surname, Steele, which he complained about, but it was too late now. He didn't have any other children—none that he admitted to, Gran said. Steele would have been a good surname. Martin was the only other person Jem knew who liked *ThunderCats*. He watched a lot of television, even cartoons; he said cartoons were ace and philosophical. *ThunderCats* hasn't caught on yet, he told her once. They're all too different from each other, too distinct. But they have the same emblems, she'd said, and they all follow the code of Thundera. Not the same as a uniform, he'd said.

Jem walked back down the cut. On the street a bus passed by with OUT OF SERVICE on the front. It never made sense when buses drove along out of service—they were still going somewhere and could drop people off and be useful. They were doing exactly what they said they weren't. She walked down the road toward the Saracen's Head, which smelled of beer and vinegar. A dog was tied up outside—a border collie. Its tongue was long and pink and tipped up at the end like a spoon with spit in it. She looked at its mouth for a while until she felt a bit sick, not with a bug, but a sort of strange worried sickness.

She turned and walked home. She opened the door and went through the front room into the kitchen, where Sav was playing with pots and pans on the floor, and Gran was having a cigarette at the table and reading the newspaper. Clouds of cauliflower steam billowed from the cooker. Hi, love, said Gran. Jem picked up the box of Mumm-Ra's sandwiches. I've got to go and drop these off, she said. Her face felt like it was glowing pink but she'd said it, matter-of-fact, like it was on a list of things to definitely do. Oh, said Gran, that's nice, you've certainly got a spur in your heel. Do you know the way? Yes, said Jem, get off at Ashton Road. Gran nodded. OK. I'll keep a plate warm for you.

Jem waited a moment. Sav held his arms up for a carry, but she ignored him. Her face felt very hot now. Her armpits felt hot and tingly. She waited for it to all fall through, for there to be a telling off, though Gran never told her off. Her heart was clapping, quite fast, as if it were applauding the brave performance. Mostly you didn't feel your heart, only after sprinting or when you were afraid. Gran turned the page of the newspaper. Bye then, Jem said. Bye, love, said Gran.

Sav wailed as she walked away. Jem got to the front door and opened it. She went outside. She walked down the street, past

Deborah's house, past the dog and the pub. When you were sensible, you were trusted to do things. You could look after your little brother alone in the house. You were allowed to find the hospital on the bus, even though you didn't know exactly where you were going. She had 50p in her pocket. She didn't have her coat. Gran hadn't even made her take her coat.

A bus was coming in the right direction. She half ran to the stop. The sandwiches bumped about in the margarine tub. She might have to stick them back together again for Mumm-Ra. She waved, and the bus stopped. Jem got on. The driver had smeary jam-jar glasses and didn't seem to care who she was. I have to get off at the hospital, she told him, Ashton Road. He nodded. She waited for him to say how much the fare was, but all he said was, Sit down then, Cuddles. The bus moved and jerked her forward as she walked down the aisle. There were no passengers except for a couple of women in brown cashier smocks and a man in a hat who was asleep against the window. Jem sat near the front, though the back seat was empty and she never got to sit on the back seat going to school, like Deborah did. She sat with the sandwich box balanced carefully on her knees. She could see a purple wrapper in one corner through the plastic. A biscuit. A fruit Club, probably. They were Mumm-Ra's favorite.

It took ten minutes to get to the hospital. She kept looking at her watch, the big hand ticking round. The town was dark silver in the rain, like pencil lead. The bus went past the prison and the castle, up the one-way system. People were already going into the pubs. A few umbrellas bobbed along. The streetlights were on.

She'd been to the hospital once before, not to visit Mumm-Ra, Mumm-Ra wasn't working there then, but to have a bean-shaped growth removed from her chest. She'd lain on a table covered with white paper and they'd given her a stinging injection to numb the patch and she hadn't felt them cut. She'd looked at the ceiling the whole time and a nurse had held her hand. She'd had eight proper stitches afterward, with thin black string because they couldn't use paper ones. She'd pulled the stitches out early because they were itchy and the hole had gaped open. There was a silky white scar on her chest now, a bit like a spider's sac, which her T-shirt covered. They'd done tests on the bean but it was harmless.

Jem got off the bus at Ashton Road. The driver didn't tell her where it was but she could see the hospital looming. She walked across the crossing. Ambulances were parked in a bay outside and as she walked toward the main doors one of them turned on its siren and whirling light and blared off. In front of the main doors, under the dripping porch, were a huge pregnant woman and an old man in a wheelchair with a metal stand next to him. A clear bag hung from the stand with a tube snaking down. It was rude to stare but Jem couldn't help it. The man didn't even look like a person. He was slumped over in the wheelchair. His bare shins poked out under his gown and his feet were purple and lumpy, like bruised vegetables. The gown was the same as the one Jem had worn, white with little blue diamonds.

Some patients died here, some died on the way here, and some were dead when they arrived. It didn't matter to Mumm-Ra, though maybe the ones who were dead or died coming were harder. They would have bad injuries, like motorbike smashes, and the baby attacked by the dog. They might be in pieces. Decapitated. Jem tried to stop looking at the man in the wheelchair. He would be going to the mortuary soon. The rain was very light again now; she could just about feel it on her nose, as if the rain were only thinking about what it was supposed to do. Most people thought working with dead people was a man's job, according to Gran. When the job had been advertised Mumm-Ra had interviewed and got it. She had the right disposition, Gran said. She's always been like that, your mother.

The Royal Infirmary was old, several stories high, with an even taller tower, but also new bits built on the sides. Hospitals had to keep getting bigger, because more and more people needed them and there were new cancers all the time. It was hard to picture Mumm-Ra anywhere, touching cold hands and faces, talking to relatives with orange baby food staining her back. She would probably have new scrubs on. Jem could picture her at home, on the sofa, tired, her head leaning on her hand, eyes closed, or staring at something on the other side of the room that wasn't really there. Mumm-Ra's staring always made Jem nervous.

The signpost of departments outside the main doors didn't list the mortuary. Jem could ask at reception. She could even leave the sandwiches at reception and someone might take them to the mortuary and Jem could go home. Probably they wouldn't even let her go to the mortuary, you might have to be eighteen, like for pubs and some fairground rides. She looked at her watch again. If a bus came in a few minutes, she could be back home by six o'clock, to Gran's cauliflower cheese, to Sav throwing water out of the bath and screaming when his hair was shampooed, to watching telly until later than normal because it was Saturday.

The woman on reception didn't seem concerned when Jem asked where the mortuary was. She pointed to a door on the other side of the building, described the way through the hospital, and then let Jem go, just like Gran had. Follow the blue line, the receptionist said, until you get to pathology, then turn right. Pathology sounded like a joke that actually was funny, though Jem felt too wobbly to laugh. She walked down a corridor, past several wards. A dinner trolley was going round. There were lots of old lopsided ladies. There was lots of coughing. She remembered the hospital smell from when she'd had the bean off; it wasn't as bad as everyone said. It was sort of aniseedy. A couple of doctors walked past and looked at her. One smiled. He had on a paper hat and a kind of paper apron, like a man who worked at a meat counter. Maybe he thought she was a patient. Maybe he knew Mumm-Ra, Jem looked more like Mumm-Ra than Sav did. People said they had the same eyes, hazel, which wasn't brown, and wasn't green, but was both mixed up. Gran said quite often that Mumm-Ra should marry a doctor. Not my type, Mumm-Ra always said. Exactly, Caroline, exactly my point.

Jem followed the blue line. She didn't get lost. The Royal Infirmary wasn't very big really. She went down some steps, then up some steps, out a back door, and past a few prefab huts until she got to a small plain building with a sign on the door. MORTUARY. Jem stood outside. The doors opened and a woman came out and she also smiled at Jem as she walked past. The woman didn't look like she'd been crying. Maybe she was a secretary. The door swung closed. MORTUARY. The building looked like a building where nothing important happened, like one of the humanities huts at school. She'd expected something frightening, tall, sooty, with ivy or broken windows, like a haunted house. This wasn't that.

Something caught her eye and she looked to the side. Next to the mortuary was a small car park with yellow lines painted on the concrete, which meant cars couldn't park there. Parked on the yellow lines was a long black car with an oblong window: a hearse. It was right there. She could see in. You were supposed to see in. On the back shelf was a coffin. It was made of dark, very shiny wood. Someone had polished and polished the wood. There were brass screws and handles and there was a smooth brass plaque with nothing engraved on it. No name. No birthday. Nothing. There were no flowers around it, like when hearses went to the church and made other cars drive slowly.

Another ambulance siren wailed in the distance. Jem stood outside the mortuary.

There was a rush around her, a feeling like jumping off a wall, like before throwing up. She wanted to sit down. She wanted to run back along the blue line, all the way to the bus stop, all the way home. It wasn't raining at all now. The rain had stopped. It was almost evening, almost six o'clock, the end of the day. But Mumm-Ra was working. She was inside the building, with the bodies of people who didn't exist anymore. She might be holding the little dead baby, carefully, combing its hair, buckling a tiny shoe strap, doing some makeup to blush its cheeks, or she might be holding the hand of a relative, the man who owned the dog, the man's girlfriend who people had said didn't care. Her mother would never die, because she couldn't, though all of this, all this, would be taking its toll.

Jem stood outside the door and held the box of sandwiches. She wanted Mumm-Ra to see her through the window and come out and put a hand on Jem's head, even if she was cross, and Jem couldn't really tell her why she had come here. Not the sandwiches. She wasn't even sure what the sandwiches were. Cheese? Fish paste? Egg? She didn't know. She lifted the lid and smelled inside the box. Egg.

Bryan Washington

610 North, 610 West

1

FOR A WHILE our father kept this other woman in the Heights.
It was tough luck seeing him most nights at best. He'd snatch
his keys from the counter, nod at all of us at once, spit something
about how he had business to handle, and of course he never
thought to tell us what it could be but we figured it out. We
adjusted accordingly.

This was back when Ma's sisters still checked on her weekly:
phone calls after dinner, drop-ins on Sunday. Before they finally
cut her off for hooking up with a spic. And those first few weeks
she waited up for our father, because she didn't want to see it, and
you know how that goes—kept Javi and Jan and I starving while
she cleaned the place solo, wiping and mopping and washing the
linoleum. Counting tips by the register. Refilling baskets of silverware. Then the four of us sat around bowls full of whatever'd
been left in the kitchen—pots of chicken and chorizo and beans
on the burners—and we'd stare at the plastic with our hands in
our laps like they'd show us whoever kept Ma's man out in the
world.

She's gotta be white, said Javi. He's already got a niggar. Otherwise, there's no fucking point.

She could be Chinese, I said. Or mixed. She could be like us.

My brother waved that away. He didn't even look up.

We spent whole days guessing. At what she looked like, where she stayed. Javi swore our father's *puta* was a model. Or an actress. But for the longest time I held out for something more domestic.

I painted her as a hairdresser. Maybe a dentist. A vet, although a year ago our father'd drowned the dog. These conversations usually ended up with Javi's smacking me down, pinching the fat on my ribs. Wondering how I could be so stupid.

Whenever summer hit, Ma kept us in the restaurant. Her usual staff begged off, blaming the lack of AC. Houston's sun had them out drinking 40s on Navigation, which left Javi and I sweeping, killing roaches, stomping the tile lining the doorway. Sometimes Ma just stood at the register, squinting, watching the two of us, and I'd wonder whether she saw her sons or replicas of her husband. But it only lasted a minute before her brow completely settled, and she'd point toward some invisible spot we'd missed right under the table.

Why the fuck would he be tripping over a mutt, said Javi, and when I didn't have an answer for that he chalked it up to dumbness.

She's definitely white, said Javi. She's definitely pale all over.

And she's probably got a fat ass too, said Javi.

Eventually Ma spoke up. Called our father a bastard. A wetback. And the one night my brother finally opened his mouth over breakfast, asking Ma why she didn't just drop him already, our mother reared back her elbow, crashed her palm into his cheek, before she settled her fingers right back onto the cutlery.

Javi slumped across the wood, crying into his knuckles. I sat beside him, kicking at the chair.

It was the last time Ma ever hit him. The one time I'd see him cry. But when our father saw the bruise in the morning, Javi told him he'd had a scrap.

We were prepping in the back. Ma was still in bed. We'd heard the shouts when he made it home, the fists smacking against the wall.

After enough time had passed that I'd forgotten about the lie, our father asked Javi if he'd won.

My brother curled his lips, testing the wound with his tongue.

Of course, he said. No doubt.

And our father cracked his wrists, staring into the sink.

Let me tell you a secret, he said. That's all that really matters.

2

Nowadays you wouldn't take her for one of those women who dupe themselves, but back then Ma wore it all on her face. That was the worst thing. You could spot it across the block. And not because he left us—that shit could happen to anyone—but for the years she thought she'd be the one to reel him back in.

My father was a handsome man. Wore his skin like a sunburned peach. He was someone who could sing, who actually had a voice worth listening to. He'd pace around the restaurant, beating his stomach like a drum, humming the corridos he'd never taught us way back when. He'd flip me over his shoulder if he found me at the sink, convinced that it was the last place a boy needed to be.

Es sólo para los mujeres y los maricones, he said, because the real men of the kitchen were out killing pigs or whatever.

But you, he said, you're like your old man. *Un hierba mala.*

Then he'd flip me back to my toes, kicking my ass with the flat of his foot.

Ma said that kind of wildness put boys on the streets. But then our father'd grab her, too, snatching her up behind the knees. And back when things were still good you wouldn't catch them again for hours, which left Javi and I up front, tending to the customers, counting receipts.

But the funny thing is, Ma actually had options—I can't even tell you how many men coasted through the doors.

Bald and young and old and hooded and thick and loose and hard, they'd whistle me to their tables. Offer me tips if I reeled her over. Once Ma found out, she told me to always, always agree—free money didn't get any easier. Sometimes she even slipped me a bill. Then she'd walk their way, beaming, asking if they'd enjoyed their ackee. Maybe setting a palm on a shoulder. Maybe laughing at a joke. And when the conversation turned toward her, and how she was doing, and how was my father, she'd wrap a hand across her chest, bringing the conversation to an end.

Ma shot all of them down. But never irreparably. Just enough to have them thinking they were always in striking distance. And if they'd paid me any more, I could've told them it wasn't worth it—but tell someone they want an impossible thing and they'll act like you've put out the sun.

3

Most weekends back then we caught the first bus to the market.

Javi slept in. Jan stayed out. Ma and I rode through East End, past Wayside, over Main, until we hit 610 headed straight toward Airline. You never saw any other blacks on the line—hair aside, I usually passed. But Ma looked like the thing that didn't belong. All the poblanos stared like we'd touched down from Mars.

One time this guy in an Astros cap actually grabbed her shoulder, told her the route downtown was the other way, pointing back toward Fannin.

In case you mistake, he said, smiling. His teeth were yellow, chipped around the cheeks.

He clearly meant well. Ma returned the smile. She wrapped her fingers around his hand, squeezing at the wrist.

Sí claro, she said, *pero no tienen lo que estoy buscando.*

And the man's face folded. He sat back down. The rest of the bus shut the fuck up along with him.

The market'd been around for decades, tucked way out in the Northside, where motherfuckers were born, lived, and died without coughing a word of English. The whole place smelled like rotten bananas and smog, and you couldn't stretch your hands without brushing somebody's junk. But through the elbows in our noses and the sandals stomping our toes, Ma wore a different face. The one she faked for her suitors.

Only now it was genuine. She really meant that shit. Whenever we hit the first tents, and the humidity kissed our cheeks, I felt her shoulders drop beside me like this weight that'd just slid off her.

She'd flirt with the little man hawking avocados. She cooed her peasant Spanish at the homeless kids guiding her along. We watched sons chop chickens in the shacks behind the tents, allowing the birds to pirouette before they finally snapped their necks, and the women at the bakery eventually called her doña, growing warmer once they decided we'd be regulars.

Mariachis shouted choruses to stragglers in the plaza. My father would've groaned, but Ma nodded along. Like she was the one who'd grown up with it. Bouncing in her flip-flops. Slapping at her thighs. And, once, this kid actually gave her his hand, and Ma'd smiled slowly, widely, before she reached out and took it— and then all of a sudden they were dancing, swaying, slipping and dipping across the sanded patio.

When her laughter finally came, it drenched the crowd. Some vendors on break clapped along with the bass. I sat on the clay, waiting for her to look back, and when the song came to an end she did.

. . .

We rode the bus home with the boxes of vegetables between our legs. Ma stared out the window while I slept in the aisle. The lights downtown glowed way beyond the highway, and the traffic clogging Shepherd blinked in and out like fireflies.

When we'd made it back to East End, shuffling through the door, Ma had me promise that I wouldn't mention the dance.

I told her I wouldn't. She pinched my arm until I swore on it.

I told her I'd keep it to myself.

4

My father was packing himself from our lives. That was his master plan. He could've been discreet, if he'd wanted, but he didn't. So he wasn't. His flaunting was a choice. The audacity made it deafening.

Clothes disappeared from the laundry. CDs from the shelves. A handful of photos evaporated from the walls. Even the one I couldn't help but look at whenever it jumped in my face: this half-torn Polaroid of Javi and I in the yard.

Someone must've taken it when we first bought the restaurant. Back when you could prop us next to each other without needing a Taser. He had me on his shoulders. My heels hit his chest. Both of us were glowing, smiling like we'd won something.

Ma only shrugged when I asked her where it went. She said everything left eventually.

And I opened my mouth to say that wasn't what I meant, but I didn't. I couldn't. I just let it go.

5

One day, Javi asked Ma if the place was haunted. And it was, in a way. By our father's other woman.

Even if we'd never seen her she floated over our space. We walked and talked around her. Made room for her at the table.

But Ma still asked my brother if he was the one hawking her shit, and he laughed in her face. He told her garbage didn't sell.

He'd started bringing his own girls back to the restaurant. The ones I'd seen around—leaning on windowsills, staring out at the road, slumping through dollar marts with their mothers. Ma raised a single eyebrow toward him, and our father only smiled, and neither of them said shit about it. It was just something that happened.

In the evenings, when the sun still had us grilling on our mattresses, Javi told me where he'd stuck it, and the noises they'd made when he did.

On your bed, he said, pointing above the headboard.

Right there, he said, shaking his head. Chuckling.

On slow days I heard the low squeaks through the walls. You could smell my brother in the hallway for hours. Javi never walked them out, but I'd wait until they finished, watching as his guests smoothed their skirts with their palms.

Most of his girls made a beeline for the door, but a few smiled my way, and one or two actually stopped to talk. They asked how old I was. Whether I got paid. They asked about my sister, where the fuck did she go all day, and I said I never knew, that sometimes I forgot she existed. They asked if the restaurant was hiring, and did I think they could get a job, and when I asked if I'd see them again you'd think I'd cracked the funniest joke. But when I told them I was Javi's brother those smiles were as good as gone.

6

Some days, it looked like our father'd given her up. He'd join us for dinner. He'd beat eggs in the kitchen. He'd spice the pork with Ma, cracking jokes over her head.

Mijos, he said, wiping the last of the plates, tell me about your day. Tell me what's been going on.

De veras, he said, when he saw we were low on rice. It's running because it knows your mother is going to burn it.

Stop fidgeting, he said, settling his fingers into Ma's shoulders, and they'd stand like that for hours, or maybe only a couple of minutes.

They actually looked natural. Like a thing that had developed. And Ma fought it at first, but of course she let him back in.

Still—none of us were used to having him around so often. It was this thing we all had to adapt to.

One night I asked Javi whether he was for real, whether our father was back. Or was he just bullshitting.

The AC had broken. It'd exhaled forever. We'd drag this busted fan around the dining room depending on where the customer sat. That left Javi, Jan, and I sopping wet back in our bedrooms, and the sweat stung my eyes, and our mattresses sank into shallow pools.

It means his *puta*'s left him, said Javi, which was a big deal since he never used Spanish.

He'd brought two girls back that day. Now he was barely awake. I brushed my toes across a pillow on the other side of his ear. When I asked him how he thought our father'd fixed things so fast, he kicked the side of my head.

You think that matters right now?

No, I said.

You learn anything in that crack-whore school you been going to?

Yeah.

Stop crying, he said. Shut your fucking eyes.

I asked Javi what did matter. He brought his hands to his face.

Idiotas, he said. That's what you and your mother have in common.

That's how I know you're her child, he said.

. . .

Our father loved Ma for the rest of the month. He mopped up behind her. Laughed at all her shitty jokes. He rubbed the tops of her knees when the silence overwhelmed us, and I wanted to drop a plate or throw a cup or crush his toes.

But after a while, Ma turned stone-faced again.

Her face changed. Whatever he'd shattered hadn't been fixed. Or maybe she wouldn't allow him to snap it again because she'd learned her lesson. So just like everything else, we watched it happen, we rolled with the punches, until one evening, after we'd set the table and closed the kitchen and settled in, our father looked at all of us, and he puffed up his chest, and he told us he was going out. Better we didn't wait up.

7

When it was finally just Ma and me, and I wasn't cruising Harrisburg, or stuck in the back room washing dishes, or out in Montrose fucking boys, I'd sit on one end of the sofa, and Ma'd settle into the other, and her knees would graze the edge of my thigh as she slept through the drone of the television. The AC was sopping. Our walls were still bare. Whatever bullshit we'd been watching hummed and buzzed across the room.

We filled the corners with our silence. It leaked into the hallway. If you didn't know us better, you might call us content. They'd built the strip mall behind us, and the sounds of the drunks rang through the windows. But mostly we had silence. The kind that seals your ears.

Sometimes Ma'd jolt awake, gazing like I wasn't there.

Sometimes Ma'd tell stories. Not to me, just to herself.

He was beautiful, she'd say, and I'd mute the television. Then she wouldn't say anything else, or who she was talking about, or what she'd meant.

Other times, I'd nod off, and when I woke up she'd be reading my face.

Qué?

Nothing.

And I'd close my eyes again.

But when I opened them up, she'd still just be staring.

8

He brought me with him once. Don't ask me why.

Javi was out whoring, and Ma'd been saddled with the night rush, and my father'd stepped halfway out the door when he told me to grab the keys.

He looked just as confused as I did when I handed them over. It was the same look he gave me when he'd watched me in the kitchen, or played dumb around Ma, or after Javi'd beaten my ass. *Como un pato*, he'd say, shaking his head, cracking his wrists, but now there was none of that. Now he was waiting on me.

East of 610 was clogged with commuters. It made the trip west more or less uneventful. He didn't ask how I was doing, or whether the air was too much for my face, but after I'd started to play with the radio he stopped me at a slow bachata.

You like this kind of music, he asked.

I didn't.

I nodded.

Of course, he said, grinning. Your mother does too.

The block we pulled onto was cleaner than ours. It had alleys and potholes, but there were blancos too. They tinkered with their yards. Walked dogs and checked mail. Some of them sat on their porches like plants. I looked at my father, like maybe he had some explanation, but he sat choking the steering wheel. Eyes on the road.

We pulled in front of this little blue stucco.

We stopped.

For a minute I thought we'd pull right back out again.

But then my father opened the door. He asked what the fuck I was waiting for.

Javi and I figured she'd be taller than Ma. Maybe a little slimmer. Blond, with curly hair. Javi said she probably had a condo by Reliant, and I saw her with two boys, brothers, just like us, and a daughter in the world, and a smile like nothing anyone'd ever seen in this life. And Javi called that stupidity—why would he leave home just to go home?—but eventually we decided that was a minor detail.

I guess that's all to say that I don't know what I expected. But when she opened the door, what I felt was disappointment.

She was darker than Ma. She wasn't black. Her hair was too long. Her hips were too wide. She had this funny nose, and her arms were a little fat, and she was plain—plainer than plain, enough to leave me blinking.

But she looked comfortable. That's the word for it.

That is what distinguished her.

When my father moved to hug her, she took him with one hand. She kept her eyes on me. She asked who I was. Before I could answer, my father called me his nephew.

He said he was babysitting. A favor to his sister.

I wanted this woman not to be an idiot, or to at least ask for follow-up, but all she did was smile.

She bent and touched my cheek. Asked if I wanted anything to drink. My father looked me in the face like I better not be thirsty, so I told her I wasn't. She smiled at that too.

Her walls were bright yellow like she lived in a preschool. Candles of the virgin were all over the place. Nothing looked too expensive, but it wasn't tacky either, and that reminded me of Ma. This was one thing that they shared.

They sat me in her living room, said they'd be back in a minute. But then an hour passed. Then another one after that.

Her dressers were cluttered: with empty coffee containers, with pencils. Plants hung in front of the windows, swaying above fans. The wood creaked beneath me as I stepped around the living room, and it was a familiar sound, and that didn't make anything better.

I found a photo by the bathroom of what must've been her. Smiling in the arms of two other men. They could've been her brothers, but maybe they weren't, and they stood in other pictures, too: smiling in a jungle, or hunched with a group in a parking lot, or huddled over a cake in a crowd at a restaurant, and that's when I saw the one of Javi and I, the picture I'd been looking for for fuck knew how long.

I'd given up on it. It'd been missing forever. And I was just about to snatch it when I heard the door open.

The woman came out in a slip. She wasn't hiding anything. She floated right past me, filled some glasses with water.

You look thirsty, she said. You should've said something earlier.

I thanked her, thinking she'd leave.

She settled beside me, crossing her legs.

She smelled like cinnamon. No makeup or anything else.

How is your mother? she said, and I fumbled with my tongue.

Fine.

That's good.

She thinks so, too.

I'm sure, she said, frowning.

It must be tough, she said. With you and the others.

I made a face, and she smiled.

Your brother and sister, she said.

Oh, I said.

I sipped from my glass. She watched me, smiling, growing warmer in her cheeks.

You know, your father's a funny man, she said.

Sometimes, I said.

Really, she said. He is. You'll see it when you're older.

It's just one of those things, she said. You know someone as well as you can. And then they say something that surprises you. It catches you off guard.

It's an easy thing to get used to, she said. You miss it when it's gone.

I looked at this woman, in her slip, and her comfort, and I wanted to slap her. I wanted to hug her.

Then my father moaned from the bedroom, a sound I'd never heard before.

The woman set a palm on her face. Like, what could we do. She told me her house was my house. When I was thirsty, I shouldn't hesitate.

Then she grabbed the other glass. She slipped out of the living room. I heard a lock click and I didn't see her again.

When the door finally opened again, I'd fallen asleep. It was just my father. He shook me awake. He didn't say a word, but he nodded toward the car, and I patted my pocket with the photo and then we were gone.

9

Ma was at the table when we made it back. My father stepped around her, and she didn't even blink.

Mijo, she said.

I sat at the table beside her. My father opened his mouth, but then he closed it. He disappeared.

Ma asked me if I'd eaten.

I said I wasn't hungry.

Ma asked if I felt sick.

I told her I didn't.

She kept one hand on my forehead, rubbing my face with her other one, and I couldn't meet her eyes. I couldn't do that for anything.

Eventually she told me I should probably get to bed.

So should I, she said, but she sounded less sure.

Back in our room, Javi smoked with the window open. The breeze was the first one we'd gotten all summer. I had already tossed my shirt, and rolled onto the mattress, and willed my eyes to sleep when he sat on my head. He ground his knuckles into my chest.

So, he said, what'd she look like?

I shut my eyes a little tighter. I asked who he meant. He sighed, like what he wanted to do was break my legs.

You know, he said. The slut.

I squinted into his thigh. My brother was getting older. Had hair creeping up his cheeks and down the sides of his ankles. A few months later, one of his girls would end up pregnant, and I'd only find out after she came around looking for him. Of course she wouldn't keep it, and he'd sulk through the house for weeks, but after that Javi was back to fucking whoever whenever.

She was beautiful, I said.

Yeah?

A real *belleza*. Just like you'd said.

No shit, said Javi. No fucking wonder.

White? he asked.

Like you said.

And her tits, said Javi. They were huge, right?

Right.

Fuck, said Javi. No wonder.

He sat on the mattress, kneading my shoulder. I could smell the smoke on his shirt. I tried keeping it in my lungs, but I couldn't do it. It slipped out just like everything else.

Then Javi stood up. Grabbed his cigarettes by the window. Once he'd pulled one for himself, he waved the box at me.

I shook my head.

Pussy, he said.

10

After we left the woman's house we didn't say much of anything, but I would not see her again and my father would not go back. I don't know where the fuck she went.

We'd made it out of the Heights but we hadn't reached the highway. My father inched us from block to block, running every other stop sign. We drove by the bayou on White Oak and over the bridge on Westheimer, and halfway down the East End overpass I noticed he'd been staring.

Qué, I said.

Es nada.

No. Tell me.

I knew he might smack me for talking smart. He'd turn it into a lecture on respect, or minding the ones that brought you into the world.

But he didn't do any of that. He kept his eyes on the road.

Then he let out a low whistle.

It doesn't matter, he said. *Estará bien.*

Just remember that, he said. Either way, it's all right.

And I didn't know what that meant. And I didn't ask him either.

We took the feeder down to Wayland. We slammed the doors in front of the house. The porch lights had been dimmed, but you could still smell the oil from the stove.

Estará bien, he said, and then one more time, and then we opened the door, and we were home.

Isabella Hammad

Mr. Can'aan

IT HAPPENED LIKE THIS. A week after the Six-Day War, Sam walked to the eastern bank of the Jordan River. He was working as a counselor that summer near Karameh, at a day camp for boys. Although the fighting occurred further upstream, camp activities had been suspended. Then came the cease-fire, and the usual schedule resumed: football in the morning, literacy after lunch, assorted games in the afternoon, orange juice and croissants in plastic wrap, and a bus to take them back to the city.

That Tuesday it was sweltering. After taking the register and sending the boys outside, the supervisor told Sam that a new counselor-in-training would referee the match that day, which gave Sam the morning off, if he wanted it. At first Sam considered hanging around all the same. He could watch the football and smoke. But the air was so thick with heat that even the boys faltered as they ran after the ball. By the time he set out, his shirt was sticking to his back.

The walk took perhaps an hour. He heard the river from some distance away, and when at last he climbed over the tussocks that crowded the bank and saw the water slicing through, a breeze reached him and the torrent sounded out in the clearer air.

He had arrived at a bend. The water coursed down over a natural dam of rocks, cascaded and slowed into a shallow pool, then fell again through a second, narrow channel and pushed on. As he stood there watching, something came into view. From around the corner on the far side, a long shape was carried forward beneath the low-hanging trees. He watched this enormous colored bundle transported downriver, and guessed, long before he could make out its features, what it was. He held his breath as the body sailed toward the rocks. The face was bearded, the arms flaccid. But the dam, alas, would not admit the cargo, and the body was caught. On either side, the water rushed white. A curtain appeared underneath, a solid curve reflecting sunlight. The curtain became wider and wider until finally, with one hefty surge, the corpse fell into the pool. It wore a white shirt. The parted legs wheeled.

Sam did not move immediately. He could see the mouth, though dunked momentarily underwater, was populated with flies. The stomach was bloated, the neck a dark bruise-blue. The hair on the head waved in the current. Sam removed his shoes and slid down the muddy slope, bracing himself against the water, which twisted like a muscle around him. He reached out and grasped the feet with both hands. The sodden plimsolls oozed under the pressure, and he resisted the urge to vomit. He fastened his grip on the ankles, the ribbed socks. He dragged, and finally hauled it up onto the bank. The white shirt was stained with red across the chest, still bright.

"And his eyes," said Sam. "They were open."

"And?" said Jibril. "What did you do?"

This was in Beirut, several years later. Sam and Jibril were sitting on the beach as the light faded after a long day of classes.

Well, of course he had buried him. He searched the body, holding his breath against the smell, found in the back pocket a wallet and an Egyptian document folded into a half pulp that showed the man was Palestinian. Then he removed his own shirt and ripped it into pieces, used the pieces to stuff the orifices. He performed the ablutions with the same water that had brought the corpse, the abdomen huge and white, the hairy navel visible in the stretched gaps between the shirt buttons. He shrouded the torso with his keffiyeh as much as was possible, then left the body concealed under a bush while he ran back for a spade and one of the other counselors. They dug a grave on the hillside. They offered prayers and supplication with the sweat running down their cheeks.

Sam looked at Jibril beside him and waited for a response. He wondered if he should have told the story differently. Jibril said nothing. He looked out to sea, where an oncoming fog was starting to overwhelm the Corniche.

That was at the beginning of their friendship.

Sam and Jibril first laid eyes on each other in the basement of Penrose Hall, at the inaugural meeting of the Monopoly Club at the American University of Beirut. Sam was the shoe, Jibril the top hat. The other players were soon joking that the two of them looked like brothers—and it was true: Sam and Jibril had a similar build, similar eyes and mouth, skin a similar golden dark. So where did you guys grow up? the others asked; and which one of you's older? And everyone laughed, and Sam and Jibril rolled their eyes and exchanged smiles. In the way that the meaning of a name can occasionally appear to prophesy, or at least to have some influence on a person, the two young men had, after that night, become quite good friends. It turned out they lived in neighboring buildings in Hamra, and Sam caught sight of Jibril a day later in the supermarket aisle. He waved, blushing, as he picked a *mana'usheh* from the counter. Although Jibril studied history and Sam engineering, they began to cross paths before and after classes. Then Jibril invited Sam round for coffee, and the accidental became fixed: Let's meet here at six and I'll show you the lab.

I know a good new bar near the seafront; meet me by the market at nine.

Jibril Tamimi came from Haifa. He was the type of guy women smiled at on the street. In bars, Sam watched their eyes fall on his friend's glossy dark head and angular body. *They* approached him. At night, Jibril would sip a nightcap while leaning over the edge of his balcony, staring at the lights of Beirut, and tell Sam stories about his childhood. He described the sense of mission that propelled him and constituted the central theme of his life.

"There are five types of Palestinian," he said. "West Bank Palestinians, Gazans, East Jerusalemites, Palestinians in exile, and Palestinians from the inside. That's what I am. *Falastini fi dakhil*, Arab Israeli, whatever you want to call us. And we are the quietest type. Haifa is actually the most peaceful city in the region. Except for Amman, I guess."

Sam had spent his whole life in Jordan. He did visit Dubai once, for a holiday, stayed with a cousin, spent a night in the Marriott and sat by the pool—but other than to Beirut, he'd never gone anywhere. He had never visited Israel or the West Bank. Nor would he: when he saw Jibril over subsequent years, it was always in Amman. Sam and, eventually, his wife, Aziza, would insist on hosting Jibril when he traveled, or when there was an uprising or unrest, and took offense at the suggestion that he might ever stay somewhere else. When a Palestinian militant bombed a bus near Jibril's house, he came to stay at Sam's for three months, and flicked all day long between news channels. By the time he left, Aziza had renamed the guest room "Jibril's room."

As a child, Sam knew the Palestinian refugee kids at school by the cheap plastic sandals they wore. He first learned the nickname Beljiki in the school playground, when a child wearing these shoes asked for the ball and an older boy, resting his eyes on the younger's feet, asked with a sneer, Did he come from Belgium? Soon Sam heard the word from his own mother's mouth: she hissed it at poor boys walking the pavement, and later, stopped in traffic, at a well-groomed businessman whose little flag on his wind-shield lacked a white star. Everyone Sam asked about the name had a different theory, but most said it was because of European aid after '48. And yet in Sam's mind, the name remained tied to those cheap plastic shoes. They were Beljiki shoes. And to his later shame, when the fedayeen appeared on television, he shouted "Beljiki" at the screen and his uncle cheered.

But then here was young, bony Jibril Tamimi, standing on a Beirut rooftop, telling Sam about his relatives in the Jordanian camps and in South America without shame, and even with some pride. Freely he discussed his opinions of the different factions, positing pros and cons, explaining the guerrilla movements and Nasser and the splits in the PFLP. In a measure, this openness was at the heart of Jibril's charm, and Sam was just as captivated as the girls were.

Yet it was only that evening on the beach, when the sea was gray and fatigue had worn off what remained of their shyness, that, sitting on the sand, Sam finally told Jibril the story of the body. For once this was Sam's tale to confide, Jibril's to listen to. Jibril's to be convinced by, of Sam's commitment and goodwill. Or so, at least, Sam always hoped.

"You know, I think we are probably all obsessed with our own cities," said Jibril.

It was their last evening in Geneva. They sat, two silver men, sharing a steak frites near the Saint Pierre Cathedral. From across the square, the night brought the strains of a lone cornetist into the murmurs of the restaurant and the clinks of steel tines on porcelain.

"I don't know, I don't have that obsession," said Sam, dipping four fries in mayonnaise. They hung from his fingers like giant matchsticks. "Amman? That piece-of-shit town." He laughed.

"You never wonder about Amman, her history?" said Jibril.

"Not really. I have my home, my wife. My kids are in America."

"Well. You know, I think I envy you."

Sam did not seem to notice Jibril's irritation. He patted his chest for a lighter.

"Come on, man," said Jibril. "We're still eating."

Until last month, Sam had worked at the same engineering firm in Amman since graduating in 1974. When he called to announce his retirement, Jibril, who was already planning this trip to Switzerland, invited him along to celebrate. This, therefore, was Sam's first journey to Europe. Nor was it insignificant for Jibril: he was on the hunt for a man named Mr. Can'aan, who he hoped would be the final source of information for the book he had been "finishing" for the last ten years. The working title: "Haifa, An Arab History."

Sam sucked on his cigarette and stretched an arm across the empty chair of the adjacent table, as if relaxing at a café in Weibdeh. Jibril's phone made a noise. He looked at the lit screen, stood up, and walked out into the darkness of the square.

Sam beckoned the waitress—could she tell him the Wi-Fi password? Snapshot of the café, its diadem of fairy lights. Another of the pink stucco wall and the chalkboard menu. Send—*Aziza*—delivered. *Kteer pretty!* she wrote back at once.

"That was Mr. Can'aan." Jibril set his phone on the table. "He won't be back in Zurich until Tuesday morning. Family emergency."

Today was Sunday. Their tickets to Zurich were booked for tomorrow at noon.

"Oh. That doesn't matter. I'll get us a hotel."

"No!" said Jibril. "No way."

Sam waved his hand at him. "Are you kidding me? You've brought me on this whole trip with you. It's the least I can do."

Jibril said nothing. For two days they had walked around the city, drinking melted sorbets by the lake and the Jet d'Eau, inspecting the clock made of flowers, the pillared cathedrals and museums, with Mont Blanc eternal on the horizon, ice-white under a blazing sky. Through it all, he watched Sam for any crack in his performance of ease. Nothing, bar the requests that Jibril translate a sign for him, or a custom. At most Sam might complain that it was all rather a lot at once, and perhaps they could sit a while longer in this café, have another glass of lemonade, are those macaroons? It annoyed Jibril that Sam refused to admit how estranged he felt: by the buildings, the voices, the texture of light. Jibril wanted his friend to feel uneasy. And he wanted him to admit it. He was the one who knew the terrain; there was no need for Sam to pretend he was his equal.

Now that they were in their sixties, Jibril was still almost as slender as he had been at twenty-three. Sam was heavyset and losing his hair, and where it sprouted on his jowls he shaved it imperfectly, leaving little wisps under his ears. He moved more slowly than Jibril and required frequent stops for narghile smoking, or, failing that, he would rapidly consume a couple of Marlboro Reds on a park bench. This was another source of irritation. Mild by nature, Jibril became exasperated as Sam asked passersby in bad French if they knew of any hookah bars nearby, or at least where there might be a newsagent. And now Mr. Can'aan was delayed, and Jibril could not even share his dismay, because Sam was waving it off like it was nothing.

As a local historian, Jibril spent half his time compiling catalogs of displaced Haifa families, their names, their professions, their houses, combing old newspapers for clues; drawing old maps of the neighborhoods, collecting oral histories, and so on. The other half of his time was spent writing applications to European bodies for grants. He was a figure about town, Jibril Tamimi, as recognizable from high up the mountain as from below on the beach: tall, sloping shoulders, tanned forehead, a shock of white hair; and up close, his slightly fanged teeth, his crow's-feet, his gentle manner—ah, the historian Jibril, they would say, the *angel*! Of course I know Jibril, of course I have his number!

He had spent forty years in this business. Was it even a business? These days it felt like more of a sad compulsion. Preserving fragments—what for, exactly? Making brass rubbings of what was still being washed away, even now, so that to walk around Wadi Salib was to miss any trace of the old "Arab Haifa" of his notes. Not to mention the murky longing which drew people out to sea and off to far shores and airport terminals. *How can you leave?* Jibril wished he could say to those who were packing their bags for Canada. *How can you leave Haifa? You actually have a house!*

As far as Jibril could ascertain, Mr. Can'aan had been a child when his family fled the "liberation of Haifa" in 1948. Unlike most families, the Can'aans seemed to have been blessed with a strange foresight, for with them on the ship they were alleged to have taken a number of photographs and several boxes of family records, the like of which had since become quite rare. Usually a family either believed what they were told—that their departure was temporary—and left everything; their libraries were confiscated, the contents labeled A.P., for "Abandoned Property," in the stacks of Hebrew University. Or else they did not believe the injunction, and remained steadfast amid the gunfire—as Jibril's own family had done.

Jibril had first heard his name from an elderly interviewee who recalled that, based on this family archive, Can'aan had developed his own interest in Haifa's social history. About fifteen years ago, this Mr. Can'aan came back to visit. Already an old man, he had gone around town in a taxi collecting testimonies and asking after letters and family papers. Although people gave their stories and showed him their photo albums, no publication seemed to have transpired from the enterprise: Jibril could find nothing of relevance under the name "Can'aan" on the academic circuit, or anywhere else on the Internet.

Mr. Can'aan's name had since begun to crop up with peculiar

frequency. First in a story about a café narrated by old man Floros, who died shortly after the interview. Then in a story about a French schoolteacher in the twenties who became involved with the Shehadeh family—the Can'aans of Haifa knew the teacher, they were neighbors, and Jibril should definitely talk to Sherif Can'aan if he could find him. Again and again this vortical name had reappeared, so that sometimes, when Jibril tried to attack a question by a different route, trampling through the woods in the hope that he might reach the back gate, he would still find himself at the foot of the same inscrutable name. But after two years of intermittent searching, he had finally found him through a cousin's cousin in Chicago who supplied Jibril with an email address, and voilà, here he was at last, on his way to meet the man, in the middle of Europe, among all this lavish greenery.

Except that Mr. Can'aan had called him on the telephone to say he would be delayed. Well. What was a day after years of searching? He threw Sam his windproof coat. They would meet him in the morning, at nine o'clock, on the corner of Anna-Heer-Strasse.

The concierge ordered them a taxi to the station. The train was on time, the cabin empty, and Sam and Jibril watched the window scene rattle past in silence. Flat green fields, livestock, rivers, back gardens of unhappy villages—the black mountain range always keeping the distance, wreathed with little clouds, phantom-close.

Sam had booked them a night at the Häberlin Hotel, two twin beds. They left their bags with the attendant and stepped out of the lobby into the old town, the Niederdorf. Colorful winding streets banked by café tables and tourists, baseball caps, toggle jackets. Above them the balconies spilled over with potted flowers; ahead a church pierced the sky with a turquoise steeple. The gold clockface showed four o'clock.

It was Jibril's turn to be exhausted. He smiled in spite of himself. "Narghile?" he said, with sheepish irony.

Sam clapped him on the shoulder, and Jibril turned to address a waiter in a café doorway, his arms full of plates. Could he tell them where to find . . . ? The man replied in Germanic French: The nearest was a taxi ride away. Turkish, couldn't remember the name. They served pizza.

They found the bar. The name was Kervan. Inside, it was tastefully decorated; flame-colored tapestries hung between ceiling-high mirrors, striped-cushion sofas half-mooned across the floor, sidelined by reflections that turned the little room into a vast hall divided by curtains. And the room was surprisingly full: all but two of the half-moon booths were occupied, and the noise of chatter nearly blotted out the voice warbling over tambours from the sound system by the bar.

They chose the booth nearest the window and ordered a grapefruit narghile. It was a real grapefruit—wonderful!—covered in foil, punctured with a toothpick. The waiter with his black shirt and skinny arms tonged the coals onto the silvered calyx, unwound the armored pipe. And a glass of arak? Two glasses. Celebrating! What exactly? Retirement, said Sam, and the end of all things.

Sam watched Jibril look around the room, suck the pipe, pass it back, exhale. After all these years, he thought, they two were just like siblings; sometimes they didn't even need to talk. He was moved when Jibril had invited him on this trip, and had tried to hide it. But looking now at his old friend, whose tired gaze was tipped to the ground, Sam felt a sensation of pity that was becoming familiar. Jibril's hair was so white. He had never married, was still working—if he had a plan for the future he never shared it with Sam. Who knew what would happen once he finished his book.

The arak, pearly with water, was strong. The clientele were mostly young people, Europeans. Sam squinted through the smoke at one of the long mirrors. He needed a haircut. He ran a hand through the wisps clouding round his skull.

The reflection showed a woman sitting behind him, by herself. She might easily have been Arab; black hair twisted into a plait, big eyes, olive skin. Green "Ciao Bella" T-shirt and skinny jeans, white around the knees. Early twenties he would have guessed, though she could have been older. No wedding ring.

"Lo samaht." Her voice behind him, he saw her reflected hand in the air. "Lo samaht!"

Sam leaned over the sofa back.

"Turks," he said. She turned round. "They don't speak Arabic."

"An jad. Min wain inta?"

"Jordan."

"*Urduni* Urduni?"

Jordanian Jordanian? No one ever asked that. Sam peered at her: she didn't look drunk. The dim lantern waved shadows over her face, colored in her top lip dark red for a moment.

"On your own?" he asked.

She blushed. "La', bas as-habi hunak." A couple whispered together on the far side of the room, their hands on each other's ribs. "Samira Abdul Salam." She extended her ringless hand.

Sam laughed. "And I'm Samir. Samir al-Bayati. And this is my friend—"

But at the other end of the couch Jibril's mouth was hanging wide open. He was asleep. His head was tilted back and sitting heavy on his neck, skull balanced, chin exposed and doubled. Sam was silent. The grapefruit smoke tasted sweet and clean.

"Wa inti?" he asked. "Min wain inti?"

"Falastin. Ghazze."

"Wa keef jiti hon?" *And how did you get here?*

"Minha . . . min aj-jam'ia. Ya'nni ba'd wa'et, tab'an."

Jibril was stirring.

"You feeling okay?" Sam addressed him. "You want to go back?"

"No, no. I'm just exhausted. Wow." And in French to the woman: "Hi, I'm Jibril."

"Mira."

"Arabieh?"

"Aywa."

"Your name," said Sam, "your name is important to me."

Mira laughed.

Jibril said, "What are you doing, man?"

"No—really. Not *Samira*." Sam shook his head jokily, already intimate. "No—Abdul Salam. It's a name I always remember. Because I once buried a man called Abdul Salam."

"Oh yeah," said Jibril. "Yeah, I know this story."

Jibril's tone was not dismissive: he had taken up the pipe with choral solemnity, assumed a thoughtful silence. Mira said nothing.

"So, at the end of the '67 war," said Sam, "I walked to the bank of the Jordan River. The eastern bank."

This story was passed on to me by a cousin of Mira Abdul Salam. According to that cousin, Mira's encounter with Sam al-Bayati at a hookah bar in Zurich ended a long period of mourning for the Gazan branch of the Abdul Salam family.

In 1967, Samira's grandfather Mahmoud Abdul Salam was martyred near Wadi Far'ah by the Harel Brigade of the Israeli army, and that loss was handed down through the generations. For years, Mahmoud Abdul Salam's children had petitioned the state of Israel to return his body. The state informed them it was already interred, in an unmarked grave in the Jordan Valley. Nevertheless, the Abdul Salam children embarked on a legal battle, which ended up lasting almost twenty years. It was a battle of endless forms, of the same questions, of small, overcrowded rooms with views onto building sides and the whitening sea, hours of waiting to enter a larger room of blank walls and high cameras, to meet another face behind a desk, to file another paper, to be told to wait. In 1987 they decided to stop trying. The Intifada had begun.

But the story of bereavement, and the duty, somehow, to give him a proper burial, was passed on. First to the eldest son, Mira's father, then to the second eldest, the father of my friend, and on down. My friend said he already felt it had fallen to him.

The moment Sam saw the look on Mira's face—that was for him a moment of near-religious ecstasy. He was transported back to that earlier scene, forty years ago, before the event became a story. He was there, the waters were rushing, the rapids swarmed toward him in a frenzy. Presenting to *him*, Sam al-Bayati, a corpse discolored verdigris and swollen with the Jordan River, the white shirt red like a symbol.

Jibril also witnessed the few wordless seconds that brought the story of the body to its crisis. He watched as the color left Mira's face, and realized at the same time as Sam did what it must mean for her.

"And then I dug with my hands," said Sam. "And a stick—I took a branch from a tree. And I placed him in the grave. And then I covered him with earth."

Jibril remembered this story well. And he remembered Sam's telling him how he ran back to the camp for help. He waited for his friend to correct himself. Sam simply continued gazing at the girl.

However, Jibril did not disturb them. In fact, he waited for Mira to weep, as in a film he knew the plot of. She was quite beautiful, with a prominent forehead and a warm skin tone and nicely shaped breasts contoured by the lettering on her shirt. But although her mouth fell open slightly, Mira didn't cry. This was in some ways a victory, he felt.

She spoke, and then Sam. Like newlyweds: cautiously, softly, reverently.

"Where is the body now?"

"By the bank, near Karameh."

"Is it marked?"

"It is marked."

"And you prayed?"

"Yes, I prayed."

"Will you draw me a map?"

"It was forty years ago . . . I . . . Well, pass me a paper—that napkin. I mean, I *hope* . . ."

"It doesn't matter if I can't find it. You prayed for him, he had a burial—that is all that matters. I can't . . ."

"I know."

"Thank you. God . . . God bless you, a thousand times God bless you."

And it went on like that for a while, until they had nothing left to whisper, and at last they shook hands good-bye.

Outside, it had turned cold.

"You didn't even ask for her number?"

"No," said Sam. He inhaled, as though to speak. Then he let the breath go.

The following morning, they had an early breakfast and placed their luggage in the trunk of a cab. They got out on the corner of Anna-Heer-Strasse and Beckhammer. On the pavement, beside their bags, they waited. Sam lit a cigarette and leaned on the handle of his suitcase. Both of them wore pressed shirts under their sweaters, and the stiff plackets showed beneath the wool. The sky above was thick with blue-shafted clouds; people in work clothes hurried out of the colored houses, holding briefcases, breakfast remnants in napkins. Jibril took out his phone and dialed the number for Mr. Can'aan, and a woman answered. Sam heard the voice faint from the receiver: Yes, she was saying, he is on his way, yes, I am sure he is on his way. They waited. They were close to the source now. The sun, already up, surged slowly overhead.

Weike Wang

Omakase

THE COUPLE DECIDED that tonight they would go out for sushi. Two years ago, they'd met online. Three months ago, they'd moved in together. Previously, she'd lived in Boston, but now she lived in New York with him.

The woman was a research analyst at a bank downtown. The man was a ceramic-pottery instructor at a studio uptown. Both were in their late thirties, and neither of them wanted kids. Both enjoyed Asian cuisine, specifically sushi, specifically omakase. It was the element of surprise that they liked. And it suited them in different ways. She got nervous looking at a list of options and would second-guess herself. He enjoyed going with the flow. What is the best choice? she'd ask him when flipping through menus with many pages and many words, and he'd reply, The best choice is whatever you feel like eating at the moment.

Before they got there, the man had described the restaurant as a "hole-in-the-wall." He had found it on a list of top sushi places in central Harlem. Not that there were many. So, instead of top sushi places, it might just have been a list of all sushi places. Be prepared, he said. Nothing is actually a hole-in-the-wall, she replied. Yet the restaurant was as the man had described: a tiny room with a sushi bar and a cash register. Behind the bar stood an old sushi chef. Behind the cash register sat a young waitress. The woman estimated that the hole could seat no more than six adults and a child. Good thing sushi pieces were small. Upon entering, she gave the man a look. The look said, Is this going to be OK? Usually, for sushi, they went downtown to places that were brightly lit, crowded, and did not smell so strongly of fish. But tonight downtown trains were experiencing delays because someone had jumped onto the tracks at Port Authority and been hit.

That was something the woman had to get used to about New York. In Boston, the subway didn't get you anywhere, but the stations were generally clean and quiet and no one bothered you on the actual train. Also, there were rarely delays due to people jumping in front of trains. Probably because the trains came so infrequently that there were quicker ways to die. In New York, the subway generally got you where you needed to go, but you had to endure a lot. For example, by the end of her first month the woman had already seen someone pee in the corner of a car. She had been solicited for money numerous times. And, if she didn't have money, the same person would ask her for food or a pencil or a tissue to wipe his nose. On a trip into Brooklyn on the L, she had almost been kicked in the face by a pole-dancing kid. She'd refused to give that kid any money.

You worry too much, the man said whenever she brought up the fact that she still didn't feel quite at home in New York. And not only did she not feel at home; she felt that she was constantly in danger.

You exaggerate, the man replied.

At the restaurant, he gave the woman a look of his own. This look said two things: one, you worry too much, and, two, this is fun—I'm having fun, now you have fun.

The woman *was* having fun, but she also didn't want to get food poisoning.

As if having read her mind, the man said, If you do get sick, you can blame me.

Eventually, the waitress noticed that the couple had arrived. She had been picking polish off her nails. She looked up but didn't get up and instead waved them to the bar. Sit anywhere you like, she said sleepily. Then she disappeared behind a black curtain embroidered with the Chinese character for the sun.

When they'd first started dating, they'd agreed that if there weren't any glaring red flags, and there weren't, they would try to live together, and they did. To make things fair, each tried to find a job in the other's city. Not surprisingly, the demand for financial analysts in New York was much higher than the demand for pottery instructors in Boston.

Huzzah, he texted the day the movers arrived at her old apartment. She texted back a smiley face, then, later, pictures of her empty living room, bedroom, bathroom, and the pile of furniture and things she was donating so that, once they were living together, they would not have, for example, two dining-room sets, twenty pots and pans, seven paring knives, and so on.

She was one of those people—the kind to create an Excel spreadsheet of everything she owned and send it to him, so that he could then highlight what he also owned and specify quantity and type, since it might make sense to have seven paring knives if they were of different thicknesses and lengths and could pare different things.

He was one of these people—the kind to look at an Excel spreadsheet and squint.

Before the big move, she had done some research on the best time to drive into the city in a large moving truck. She did not want to take up too much space. It would pain her if the moving truck was responsible for a blocked intersection and a mess of cars honking nonstop. The Internet said that New Yorkers were tough and could probably handle anything. But the Internet also said, To avoid the angriest of New Yorkers during rush hour, try five a.m. When she arrived at five a.m., he was waiting for her in the lobby of his building, with a coffee, an extra sweatshirt, and a very enthusiastic kiss. After the kiss, he handed her a set of keys. There were four in total: one for the building, one for the trash room, one for the mailbox, one for their apartment door. Because all the keys looked the same, he said that it might take her a month to figure out which was which, but it took her only a day. She was happy that he was happy. She would frequently wonder, but never ask, if he had looked for a job as diligently as she had.

I'll just have water, the man said, when the waitress gave them each a cup of hot tea. It was eight degrees outside, and the waitress explained that the tea, made from barley, was intentionally paired with the Pacific oyster, which was the first course of the omakase. The waitress looked no older than eighteen. She was Asian, with a diamond nose stud and a purple lip ring. When talking to her, the woman could only stare at the ring and bite her own lip. The woman was also Asian (Chinese), and seeing another Asian with facial piercings reminded her of all the things she had not been able to get away with as a kid. Her immigrant parents had wanted the best for her, so imagine coming home to them with a lip ring. First, her parents would have made her take the ring out, then they would have slapped her, then they would have reminded her that a lip ring made her look like a hoodlum and in this country not everyone would give someone with an Asian face the benefit of the doubt. If she looked like a hoodlum, then she would have trouble getting into college. If she couldn't get into college, then she couldn't get a job. If she couldn't get a job, then she couldn't enter society. If she couldn't enter society, then she might as well go to jail. Ultimately, a lip ring could only land her in jail—what other purpose did it serve? She was not joining the circus. She was not part of an indigenous African tribe. She was not Marilyn Manson. (Her father, for some strange reason, knew who Marilyn Manson was and listened to him and liked him.) Then, in jail, she could make friends with other people wearing lip rings and form a gang. Is that what you want as a career? her parents would have asked. To form a lip-ring gang in jail? And she would have answered no.

Tea it is, the man said. He smiled at the pretty waitress. She *was* pretty. The purple lip ring matched the purple streak in her hair, which matched the purple nail polish. Nevertheless, the man complimented the waitress's unremarkable black uniform. The waitress returned the favor by complimenting the man's circular eyeglass frames.

Oh, these silly things, the man said, lifting his glasses off his nose for a second.

They're not silly, the waitress said matter-of-factly. They're cool. My boyfriend couldn't pull those off. He doesn't have the head shape for it.

If the man lost interest, he didn't show it. If anything, knowing that the pretty waitress had a boyfriend only made the flirtation more fun.

Kids now are so different, the woman thought. She hadn't had a boyfriend until college. She wasn't this bold until after grad school. But the waitress might not have immigrant parents. Perhaps her parents were born here, which would mean different expectations, or parenting so opposed to the way they had been brought up by their own strict immigrant parents that there were basically no expectations. Another possibility: the waitress might have been adopted. In which case all bets were off. Kids now were not only different but lucky, the woman thought. She wanted to say to the waitress, You have no idea how hard some of us worked so that you could dye your hair purple and pierce your lip.

The man nudged the woman, who was sitting next to him like a statue.

You're staring, he said. The waitress had noticed, too, and huffed off.

The mugs that the tea came in were handleless. The tea was so hot that neither of them could pick up the handleless mug comfortably. They could only blow at the steam, hoping that the tea would cool, and comment to each other on how hot it was. Until now, the sushi chef had not said a word to the couple. But it seemed to irritate him as he prepared the Pacific oyster (which turned out to be delicious) to see them not drink the tea.

This is the Japanese way, he finally said. He reached over the bar for the woman's mug. He then held the mug delicately at the very top with two fingertips and a thumb. The other hand was placed under the mug like a saucer. This is the Japanese way, he said again. He handed the mug back to the woman. The couple tried to mimic the chef, but perhaps their skin was thinner than his; holding the mug the Japanese way didn't hurt any less than sticking their hands into boiling water. The man put his mug down. The woman, however, did not want to offend the chef and held her mug until she felt her hands go numb.

Now that the man knew the chef could speak English, he tried to talk to him.

What kind of mug is this? he asked. It looks handmade. The glaze is magnificent. Then the man turned to the woman and pointed out how the green-blue glaze of their mugs seemed to differ. The layering, he said, was subtly thicker and darker in this part of her mug than in his.

Hmm, the woman said. To her, a mug was a mug.

It's a yunomi, isn't it? he said to the chef. Taller than it is wide, handleless. Yes, handleless, with a trimmed foot. Used in traditional tea ceremonies.

The chef looked suspiciously at the man. Maybe he was wondering if the man was fucking with him, as people sometimes did when they encountered a different culture and, in an effort to tease, came off as incredibly earnest, only to draw information out of the person they were teasing until the person looked foolish.

He's a potter, the woman said.

The man quickly turned to her as if to say, Why did you just do that? We were having so much fun. Then he began to laugh, leaning back and almost falling off the barstool. I'm sorry, he said to the chef. I didn't mean to put you on the spot. The mug is beautiful, and you should be proud to have something like this in your kitchen. I would be.

The chef said thank you and served them their first piece of fish on similarly green-blue ceramic plates that the man promised not to scrutinize.

Enjoy, the chef said, and gave them a steady thumbs-up.

The man responded with his own thumbs-up.

The woman liked how easily the man handled everything. He never took anything too seriously. He was a natural extrovert. By now, the woman knew that, although he worked alone in his studio, he not only enjoyed the company of others but needed it. When out, he talked to anyone and everyone. Sometimes it was jokey talk, the kind he was having with the sushi chef. Sometimes it was playful banter, the kind he had with the pretty waitress. The flirting didn't bother the woman. Instead, it made her feel good that the man was desired. While he was not handsome, he had a friendly face and rosy cheeks. The word "wholesome" came to mind. He was someone who could have just stepped out of a Norman Rockwell painting.

Their first official date had been on Skype. It had consisted of each of them drinking a bottle of wine and watching the same movie on their respective laptops. He suggested *House of Flying Daggers*, and she said that she was OK with watching something else. Maybe something that wasn't so overtly Chinese and, no offense to the talented Zhang Yimou, so old-school.

What do you mean, "old-school"? he had asked.

I mean Tang dynasty, she had said.

She was fine with watching something more mainstream, set in the modern day, with story lines about non-Asians. She didn't need the man to make her feel comfortable, if that was, in fact, what he was trying to do.

But it's a critically acclaimed movie, he'd replied.

So they ended up watching *House of Flying Daggers*. The entire movie was in Chinese, with English subtitles. As they got progressively tipsier, the man asked the woman if the subtitles were all correct. I guess, the woman said, even though she understood only half of what was said and was reading the English herself. The man knew much more about Wuxia than she did. He also knew much more about the Tang dynasty, especially the pottery. During that dynasty, the Chinese had perfected color glazes. Most famously, they had perfected the tricolored glaze, which is a combination of green, yellow, and white. He even said the Chinese word for it, "sancai," and she was a little shocked. No, she was a lot shocked. You would know the glaze if you saw it, he said once the movie was over and the wine had been drunk. The next day, he sent her a picture of a Tang-dynasty camel with sancai glaze. It was the same camel that had sat next to her mother's fireplace for the past twenty-five years.

The woman asked some of her friends. Most of them were Asian, but she had a few non-Asian friends as well. A red flag? She did not want to continue with this man if he was interested in her only because she was Chinese. She had heard of these men, especially the kind you met on the Internet. She had heard of "yellow fever." She didn't like that it was called yellow fever. To name a kind of attraction after a disease carried by mosquitoes that killed one out of four people severely infected said something about the attraction. Her closest friends told her that she was doing what she did best, overthinking and picking out flaws where there weren't any, hence the reason she was still single at thirty-six. As a potter, the man would obviously know about the history of pottery. And he probably just liked *House of Flying Daggers* as a movie. One of her non-Asian friends said, He's a guy and probably just thinks martial arts are cool. One of her Asian friends said, He probably just wants to impress you.

We'll see, she replied.

For their next Skype date, he suggested a romantic comedy set in England. The following week, an American action film. The next week, a Russian spy drama. After watching, they chatted first about the movie and then about other things. He told her that he had been in a few serious relationships, the most recent of which ended a year ago. What was she like? the woman asked, but really just wanted to know if she was Chinese. The man said that she was nice, though a little neurotic. But what was she like? the woman asked again, and the man said, What do you mean? She was Jewish and tall. He didn't suggest watching a Chinese movie again. When they visited each other, they ate not at Chinese places but at French, Italian, and Japanese restaurants. She was excited that he was turning out to be a regular guy. He met most of her friends, who afterward found a way to tell her how lucky she was to have met someone like him: single, American—an artist, no less—and her age. By "American," some of her Asian friends also meant "white," the implication being that she was somehow climbing the social ladder. She hadn't thought any of these things before, but now she did. Or maybe she had thought all of these things before and was just now admitting to them. Eventually, the woman felt comfortable enough to ask the man why he had picked *House of Flying Daggers* for their first date. The answer he gave was even less profound than what her friends had said. It was a random choice, he explained. That day, the movie had popped up on his browser as something that he might be interested in watching. It was critically acclaimed, he said again.

So it was settled. The big question of why he was dating her was out of the way. Her Chineseness was not a factor. They were merely one out of a billion or so Asian girl–white guy couples walking around on this earth.

The sushi chef worked quickly with his hands, and the woman couldn't help but be mesmerized. From a giant wooden tub of warm rice he scooped out two tiny balls. He molded the balls into elongated dollops. Then he pressed a slice of fish on top of the rice using two fingers, the index and middle, turning the nigiri in the palm of his hand as if displaying a shiny toy car. As a final touch, he dipped a delicate brush into a bowl of black sauce and lightly painted the top of the car. For certain pieces, he wrapped a thin strip of nori around the nigiri. For others, he left the fish slices on a small grill to char. The woman was impressed. This chef looked as though he belonged at the Four Seasons or the Mandarin Oriental. Between courses, he wiped down his cooking station and conversed with them. He spoke softly, which meant that the couple had to listen carefully and not chew too loudly. The man told the chef that they lived only a few blocks away. The chef lived in Queens but was originally from Tokyo. The man said that he had seen the chef working here before. The chef said that that was impossible. The man insisted that he had. He said that he walked by this restaurant every day on the way back from his studio, and though he had never come in, he peeked inside every now and then and saw a chef—you, he said—working diligently behind the bar.

The chef chuckled and said, That's impossible.

Why do you say impossible? the man asked.

Because this is my first day working here.

Oh, the man said, but, refusing to admit that he had been wrong, pushed on. He asked if the restaurant was a family-run business. He might not have seen the chef, as in *you*, but he might have seen a brother or a friend. And surely the chef must have come in for an interview. Perhaps when he peeked in that day the chef was actually there, learning the ropes from the previous chef, who might have been the brother or the friend. At this point, the woman put a hand on the man's thigh.

The chef chuckled again, longer and louder than before. He looked at the woman, and she felt herself unable to meet his gaze. It was not a family-run business, he clarified. He did not know the previous chef. He had been hired yesterday and had interviewed by phone.

The man finally let the topic slide, and the woman was relieved. If he'd continued, she would have had to say something. She would have had to explain to the man (in a roundabout way) that he sounded insensitive, assuming that the chef he'd seen in the window was this chef and then assuming that the chefs could have been brothers. The roundabout way would have to involve a joke—something like Oh-don't-think-all-of-us-look-the-same—and the man would have laughed and the woman would have laughed and the chef would have chuckled. It would have to be said as a joke, because the woman knew that the man hadn't meant to seem insensitive; he had just wanted to be right. Also, the woman didn't want to make a big deal out of nothing. She didn't want to be one of those women who noted every teeny tiny thing and racialized it. And wasn't it something that she and her closest Asian friends joked about, too—that, if you considered how people are typically described, by the color of their hair and their eyes, it did sound as though they all looked the same?

But joking about this with her friends was different from joking with the man.

For a moment, the woman felt a kinship with the chef, but the moment passed.

After the couple had finished their tea, the waitress came back and started them on a bottle of unfiltered sake. She still seemed miffed from earlier. She spoke only to the man, explaining that the nigori had herbal notes and hints of chrysanthemum. The woman tossed back her sake and couldn't taste either. The man hovered his nose over his cup for a long minute and said that he could smell subtle hints of something.

Alcohol? the woman said.

Something else.

Chrysanthemum?

Something else.

The woman wanted to add that perhaps what the man was smelling was bullshit, because the waitress was clearly making everything up. How the woman knew was that she had read the back of the bottle, which said the sake had a fruity nose with hints of citrus.

What's wrong with me? the woman thought. She was getting riled up over nothing. This was nothing. The man leaned over and rubbed a finger under her chin. She felt better, but not entirely right. The chef smiled at them while slicing two thin pieces of snapper.

When enough time had passed, the man began chatting with the chef again. He was curious, he said. The sushi was delicious, and he was wondering where the chef had worked before. He must have had years of experience. It showed. Speaking on behalf of both of them, the man continued, he hadn't had omakase like this in years and they went to some of the best places in the city.

Like where? the chef asked.

The man listed the places, and the chef nodded in approval and the man beamed. The woman felt a need to interject. Many of these omakase places had been her suggestion. To be honest, when they first started dating the man knew what omakase was but had never tried it. He said the opportunity had never come up, and the woman wondered if this was code for I didn't know how to go about it, I didn't want to look like an idiot if I went in and ordered wrong. So, for one of their early in-person dates she had taken him to a place in Boston. She knew the chef, who was Chinese. Many Chinese chefs turned to Japanese food, as it was significantly classier and more lucrative. She spoke with the Chinese chef in Chinese about the Japanese omakase, an experience that she would not have known how to describe to her parents, who had been taught to loathe the Japanese, or her grandparents, who had lived through the Sino-Japanese War and did loathe the Japanese. Thankfully, that history was not part of the woman's identity. She had grown up in the States. She felt no animosity toward Japanese people, culture, or food. Anyway, the point was that, when she'd visited the man in New York, she had looked up the places he had just listed. She had taught the man that, in Japanese, "omakase" means "I leave it up to you." There was one more thing. She had paid. Not always but most of the time, especially at the more expensive places. And it made sense for her to pay. She earned more, and trying omakase together had become one of their things. She liked that they had things.

There was also that place in Boston, the woman interjected. Remember? The one I took you to. The first time you had omakase. While she was saying this, the woman wondered if she was being too defensive, but she said it anyway.

Of course, the man said without glancing at her. So where did you work again? he asked the chef.

A restaurant downtown, he said. He then gave the name, but it was not one that either the man or the woman recognized.

You might not know it, he said. It was a very exclusive place. Very fancy. We didn't open every day. We opened only by reservation. And to make a reservation you had to call a specific number that wasn't listed, that was only passed by word of mouth. When you called, you asked to speak with the manager. The manager had to know you, or else he would say you'd called the wrong number and hang up.

You're kidding, the man said. Then he looked at the woman and asked if she'd heard that.

She had heard it. The chef wasn't whispering. The man leaned over the bar, so that his upper body was now above the trays of nori and the bowl of sauce. He was leaning on his elbows, like a little boy waiting for a treat from his mother in the kitchen. Adorable, the woman noted, and momentarily felt fine again.

So I'm guessing you got tired of that, the man said. Dealing with all those rich folks.

No.

It was probably the stress. I bet a place like that made you work terrible hours. All those private parties. People who have nothing better to do with their money.

No.

And not being able to make whatever you wanted. What the customer wants the customer gets. A place that exclusive, you probably got some strange requests.

Yes, but that's not the reason I was fired.

Fired?

The man looked even more interested. Did you hear that? he said to the woman. To him, if a high-class chef had been fired that meant that the chef had a rogue streak, which was something the man tended to respect. Also, he was getting drunk. The sake bottle was empty, and the waitress had brought another.

Fired for what? the man asked. He offered the chef a cup of sake, but the chef declined.

The woman turned her own cup in her hands and stared at the wall behind the chef, which had a painting of a giant wave about to crush three tiny boats. The woman liked the fact that she and the man worked in completely different fields. It meant that there was very little competition between them, and what they had in common was something genuine. The man had no interest in money, and that fascinated her. He seemed a free spirit, but how was he still alive today if he didn't care about money? She, on the other hand, was much more concerned about money and where it came from. She liked her job, but she liked it most because it was stable and salaried. Although she could not say those things to the man, who sometimes said to his friends, Bankers, when she made practical remarks about how they were going to split the check. After he said that, he did one of those comical eye rolls to show everyone that he was kidding. It was funny. She laughed along. But later, when she asked him why he did that, he would put a hand on her head and say that she was overthinking it. He was only teasing her because he was so proud of her. She did something he couldn't in a million years do. Numbers, graphs— just hearing her on the phone made his head spin, but the work was clearly important and necessary. And you're able to do this because, well, let's face it, you're smarter than me. The man had said that. When he said it, the woman felt a happy balloon rise from her stomach to her mouth.

Fired for what?

The chef didn't answer. Instead, he washed his hands, which were now covered in red slime, and picked up a blowtorch to sear the skin of a nearby salmon.

A year into dating, she had taken the man to meet her parents. They lived in a cookie-cutter suburb in Springfield, Massachusetts. Her father worked for a company that designed prosthetic limbs. Her mother was a housewife. Back in China, they'd had different jobs. Her father had been a computer-science professor and her mother had been a salesclerk, but their success in those former roles had hinged on being loquacious and witty in their native language, none of which translated into English. Every now and then, her father went out for academic jobs and would make it as far as the interview stage, at which point he had to teach a class. He would dress as sharply as he could. He would prepare careful notes. Then, during class, the only question he was asked, usually by a clownish kid in the back row, was whether he could please repeat something. Her mother took a job at JCPenney but eventually quit. In China, an efficient salesclerk followed customers from place to place like a shadow, but no one wanted her mother to do that at JCPenney. In fact, her mother was frequently reported for looking like a thief. Nevertheless, her parents were now comfortable in their two-thousand-square-foot house, which had a plastic mailbox and resembled everyone else's. Perhaps her parents liked the sameness of suburban houses because, from the outside, you couldn't tell that a Chinese family lived inside. Not that her parents were ashamed of being Chinese, and they had taught their daughter not to be ashamed, either. You are just as good as anyone else, they'd told her, even before she realized that this was a thought she was supposed to have.

The woman did not know how her parents would react. She had brought home other boyfriends, and the reception had been lukewarm. The man was the first boyfriend she had brought home in a long time. Unfortunately, that made the question of race even harder to answer, as he was also the first white boyfriend she had brought home. So, were her parents being welcoming out of relief that their daughter wouldn't become a spinster or out of surprise that she, as her friends pointed out, had got lucky? As with every complex question in life, it was probably a mixture of both. But was it a fifty-fifty mix or a twenty-eighty one, and, if the latter, which was the eighty and which was the twenty?

Throughout the weekend, the woman felt feverish. Her brain was in overdrive. She watched the man help her mother bring in groceries and then help her father shovel the driveway. She was in disbelief when her father went out and came back with a bottle of whiskey. She didn't know that he drank whiskey. She then had to recalculate the fifty-fifty ratio to take into account the whiskey. For each meal, her mother set out a pair of chopsticks and also cutlery. When the man chose the chopsticks, her parents smiled at him as if he were a clever monkey who had put the square peg into the square hole.

That he could use chopsticks correctly elicited another smile, even a clap. Then they complimented him on everything, from the color of his hair down to the color of his shoes.

The woman was glad that her parents were being nice, as it dispelled the cliché of difficult Asian parents. Previously she had explained to the man that her parents had a tendency to be cold, but the coldness was more a reflex from years of being underdogs than their natural state. When her parents turned out not to be cold at all, the woman was glad, but then she wondered why they hadn't been more difficult. Why hadn't her father been more like a typical American dad and greeted the man at their cookie-cutter door with a cookie-cutter threat?

By the end of the weekend, her mother had pulled her aside to say that she should consider moving to New York. The man had thrown the idea out there, and the woman didn't know how to respond.

I'm not sure yet, she told her mother. But we're going to look for jobs in both places.

Her mother nodded and said, Good. Then she reminded the woman that a man like that wouldn't wait around forever.

For their last piece of omakase, the chef presented them with the classic tamago egg on sushi rice. The egg was fluffy and sweet. How was that? the chef asked. He asked this question after every course, with his shoulders slumped forward, and their response—that it was the best tamago egg on sushi rice they'd ever had—pushed his shoulders back like a strong wind.

The Japanese way, the woman thought. Or perhaps the Asian way. Or perhaps the human way.

Dessert was two scoops of mocha ice cream. For the remainder of the meal, the man kept asking the chef why he'd been fired. Another bottle of sake had arrived.

It's nothing interesting, the chef said.

I doubt that, the man said. Come on. We're all friends here.

Though neither he nor the woman knew the chef's name, and vice versa. During the meal, no one else had come into the restaurant. People had stopped by the window and looked at the menu but had moved on.

Management, the chef finally said. He was done making sushi and had begun to clean the counter. He would clean the counter and wash his rag. Then he would clean the counter again.

His purpose wasn't to clean anymore, the woman decided. It was to look as if he had something to do while he told the story.

What happened? she asked. At this point, she might as well know.

I was fired three weeks ago, the chef said. The manager had booked a party of fifty for a day that I was supposed to have off. Then he called me in. I initially said no, but the party was for one of our regulars. I said I couldn't serve a party of fifty on my own and he would need to call in backup. He said OK, and an hour later I showed up. But there was no backup, just me. The manager was Chinese, and said that he had called other chefs but no one had come.

The chef stopped cleaning for a moment to wash his rag. I'm not an idiot, he continued. I knew that was a lie. So I only made sushi for two people. I refused to make sushi for the other forty-eight, and eventually the entire party left.

Bold, the man said.

The woman didn't say anything. There was a piece of egg stuck between her molars and she was trying to get it out with her tongue. When she couldn't, she used a finger. She stuck her finger into the back of her mouth. Then she wiped the piece of egg—no longer yellow and fluffy but white and foamy—on her napkin.

I'm Chinese, the woman said reflexively, the way her parents might have.

The chef went back to cleaning his counter. The man cleared his throat. He said, not specifically to the woman or the chef but to an invisible audience, That's not what the chef meant.

I know, the woman said. She was looking at the man. I know that's not what he meant. I just wanted to put it out there. I don't mean anything by it, either.

The man rolled his eyes and a spike of anger went through the woman. Or maybe two spikes. She imagined taking two toothpicks and sticking them through the man's pretty eyes to stop them from rolling. Then she imagined making herself a very dry martini with a skewer of olives.

Sorry, the chef said. He was now rearranging the boxes of sesame seeds and bonito flakes. He was smiling but not making eye contact. In a moment, he would start humming and the woman would not be able to tell if he was sorry for what he'd said or sorry that she was Chinese. A mix of both? She wanted to ask which one it was, or how much of each, but then she would sound insane. She didn't want to sound insane, yet she also didn't want to be a quiet little flower. So there she was, saying nothing but oscillating between these two extremes. In truth, what could she say? The chef was over sixty years old. And the Chinese, or so she'd heard, were the cheapest of the cheap.

The man never called her sweetheart. Sweetheart, he said, I think you've had enough to drink. Then he turned to the chef. Time to go, methinks.

The chef spoke only to the waitress after that. He called her over to help the couple settle the bill. The woman put her credit card down while the man pretended not to notice. She tipped her usual twenty percent.

What was that? the man said once they were outside. It had got colder. It would take them fifteen minutes to walk home.

I'm not mad at him, the woman said.

And you shouldn't be. He was just telling a story.

Again, I'm not mad at him.

The man understood. They walked in silence for a while before he said, Look, I wasn't the one who told the story and you have to learn not to take everything so personally. You take everything so personally.

Do I?

Also, you have to be a little more self-aware.

Aware of what?

The man sighed.

Aware of what?

The man said, Never mind. Then he put a hand on her head and told her to stop overthinking it.

Caoilinn Hughes

Prime

W E'D ONLY JUST ENTERED Miss Lynch's classroom the summer after Johnnie died. Mister Lynch left, mid-funeral, on a boat. On the Atlantic too, but not facedown. He got on a boat and left. We thought Miss Lynch would do the same. Or be *let go* from the school to spare her the torture of our easy continuation. But she didn't.

In Clifden town, she swapped her wedding ring for a border collie that could fetch rabbits for supper. *You can teach a border collie sign language. How to tie a tourniquet. How to separate the dill from the fennel. But you lot?* She wanted more from us. We wanted more to give her. We made a bonfire on the beach of Johnnie's desk and chair. Splinters festered in us. The dog ate a feast of deadly web-cap mushrooms in the field and died. *Are there snakes in my hair?* she asked, on her ragged knees. It wasn't our place to act, besides rising above her expectations.

Death billows out like a stone plonked in water. We knew that. But we didn't know if the safe thing was to step back out of its ripples. We surrounded Miss Lynch like a net seven souls wide. She taught us from the east side of the room to the middle to the west. Shifting at the start of each year—fourth, fifth, sixth. Three years, three meters' lateral movement. The walls are a freeze-frame of slanting rain: the pencil evidence of our growth spurts. She logs our depth and breadth and height without saying what the figures add up to. We equal greatness. We are not quantifiable. We know how to be dealt an inch and to make a mile of it. But today is our last day. Out the window is the only lateral movement left.

We hear the wind whine at the glass. It lifts the whispery hair of our forearms. Our legs jiggle beneath our desks. Wild garlic Tara brought in for a thank-you bouquet stinks out the room from the sink at the back. The stuff grows rude and rampant in the graveyard soil so we all know where it came from. The spirit emits a smell as it leaves the body. The white-petaled bursts are the freeing of souls. Miss Lynch teaches us such things. Things that are difficult to know.

Out in society, she says. *Out in the wide world.* Light rain begins to sound like the rustling of someone drifting around a big empty house in a wedding dress. *You should all know by now that mercy is an artificial flower. It looks very convincing and nice. But it has no nectar.* Her eyes skim over us to the window panels. *Don't assume mercy to be real.*

Out of the seven in sixth class, she knows some won't bother with secondary school and will head straight for the till or the tractor or, for Liam that looks old enough, the quarry. Tara might sweep floors in the hairdresser's in town if her auntie'll have her. Queer sort of hay baling.

We bought Miss Lynch the biggest sunglasses on the whirly rack in the shop when she came to work after the funeral. When she put the glasses on, she asked if the insect they made her resemble (a big-eyed bug whose Latin name flew in one ear and out the other) was winged or not. Was it predator or prey? It made us ashamed, to see how fast and sloppy we did things. She wasn't trying to shame us. She was grateful for us. Today, she lifts the glasses from her marram-grass hair, folds in the arms and sets them on the desk. The sun's off gallivanting in another galaxy, we notice, so it's good to see the glasses: it means there's still light getting in that she wants to temper. Her eyes are bloodshot.

By the blackboard, the laminated WHAT TO DO IN CASE OF EMERGENCY is on the floor alongside its thumbtack. We try to be observant. Anything and everything can be symbolical and significant—can go to show how order isn't always the way of things. The centuries-old stone wall doesn't come natural to the farmer who wants the fertile soil on its far side, away from the rocks. To want such a thing all your life and never to get it because of paper. Deeds. Death certificates. Olden customs. *The challenge is to see cruelty and kindness not as opposites,* she'd said, *but as two sides of the same coin.*

Crystal.

Yeah, miss?

Could you take the wasp that's on your copybook outside? Miss Lynch smoothens her homemade clothes over her no hips. She's the shape of a long, straightish banana, so the main challenge of dressmaking is cutting straight lines in the curtain fabric. Avoiding moth holes. Her winter coat is made of carpet. When hems fall, she staples them up. *Oh to be a choirmaster!* she says, as the dulcet tones of Mister O'Malley's disciples come through the rear wall. (*Jesus saw something inside me that I didn't see inside myself . . .*) The commotion of our skittering stirs the wasp and it flies around berserk in this world of chalk and flesh and varnishes.

Duck, Bríona! shouts Shannon. *You're allergic—*

I am not!

—she'll go anafletic and even if we drive her to town it'll be too late!

Bright-red Bríona is standing on her tiptoes at her desk in fifth, willing the wasp to sting her. The pale brown wisps of her hair are a net. *I said HORNETS! Hornets can kill you!*

It's not your fault if—

Oisín whispers down the back: *Shannon has a thing for Bríona.* He does bashing scissor fingers. In response, Shannon slips a finger inside her veiny jellyfish cheek and makes a pop like soup in the microwave. Miss Lynch talks quiet so that only us who lean in can hear her: *The wasp doesn't understand this bland nectarless brightness—all this wasteful, contrary movement, not in the direction of the wind.*

Miss Lynch should have established order by now. Put fourth class to work so they don't get cranky. It's Father's Day in Ghana, she might say. Find Ghana in the atlas, then write cards, making no mistake as to where the apostrophe goes in your fathers. Make fifth class play Trivial Pursuit, where each team's given a set of encyclopedias and they're not allowed to pass on any questions and there's no time limit. (Her father was an encyclopedia salesman, so we have two full sets.) But today, she seems to be waiting for something. Denying orderliness. Or is she waiting for the hymn in the next room to end?

The fact of the matter is . . . , she says finally, *not a single child in this school will go to heaven, however angelic their voice.* She pauses. *Because every single one of you spends three years with me before you leave. Three is the magical number. The devil, though, has no horns. So you needn't fear him. He has no body at all. Only a shadow.*

The whole class hushes. Outside, the cloud cover thickens. Rain ups the ante. The wasp lands on Declan Quinlan's hand, which is delicate and lucent as suds in a bath. He shares the front desk in fifth with Bríona, who has stiff white snail trails down her face. Others will cry later at the notion of the Shadow Devil. Declan is breathing shallow and fast.

Now, Declan, Miss Lynch says. *You have a choice. Don't mind Newtonian mechanics.* She waits and takes a step forward, toward the wasp or the boy, and we're all too riveted to ask, What?

A THWACK announces a choice made. But it wasn't Declan's. The scream is his, though. Piercing and harrowing as a baby banshee's. Clasping our ears and eyelids tight, we see rocks shattering windows, which is the sound of suffering the consequences. Mister O'Malley is soon stood in the doorway, crying, *What's going on.*

Don't worry, Mister O'Malley. We wouldn't let you miss an exorcism. Miss Lynch doesn't take her eyes from Bríona, who'd brought her hardback copy of *A Wrinkle in Time* down with emotional force on Declan's hand, fracturing a network of bones inside it. The wasp is wasabi. *Declan Quinlan has been spared a wasp sting.*

Then why on earth is he bleeding all over his desk?

Miss Lynch turns to her coworker with a look of beguilement. *Was that iambic pentameter, Mister O'Malley?*

Is that disrespect, he wonders (readable as a tombstone). He huffs at the mounting evidence that her job could be his. The woman is clearly affected. He regards us like a rock pool full of periwinkles, determining if there's enough for a seafood linguini. *I'll get the first aid kit.*

You're very good, says Miss Lynch. *And would you mind taking fourth class for me, while we clean up here and consider the death of the wasp?*

Like ants, unsurprised by the load they've been given to carry, the children of fourth pack their bags and file out of the room, glancing sidelong as they go.

No, we inform them with our eyes. You won't be like us. Not in two years. Not in ten. You weren't with her in the pitch-black times. Through the boxes of what to keep and what to get rid of. By the flameproof wick, through the window, on the dwindling pile of rocks.

God is a circle whose center is everywhere and whose circumference is nowhere. Miss Lynch is short of breath from stooping down. *Have you ever heard such nonsense?*

We shake our heads at the egg carton of her spine as she draws a huge circle on the floor around all our desks in permanent marker. She'd tried chalk but it was useless on the linoleum. *Please consider the circle to be done in chalk, as permanency is not the point. Not at all the point. But a lesser point is that you make do with the materials at your disposal, so. And disposal brings us back to impermanence. Every thing in this world is cyclical. You'll find yourselves at the end of your lives thinking of the uterus, thinking of the buttons on your bedsheets, the conch you brought your ear to again and again like a lover's chest, and you'll be wishing, I bet my life on it, you'll be wishing you'd left a neat and perfect zero in your bank account.* She caps the marker and catches her breath. *Nothing and nowhere isn't worth saving for.*

We don't doubt it. We don't question the circle. It is very comfy sitting inside it. Rain on the windows sounds like rice thrown in a pot. Sure to swell.

On the other side of the room, fifth class is cloistered around a *Guinness Book of World Records* with the task of coming up with five of their own breakworthy records, each. Miss Lynch had asked them to give us space. Next year it will be their turn, they tell themselves. And that future—in which they will be her luminaries—is only one meter away. They could spit that distance.

Chewing on her cheeks, Bríona finishes administering first aid (the verb "to administer" is part of their lesson) and Declan's blood-heavy dressing sits in a bucket (from the kiddies' sandpit) so as to contain the mess. (The verb "to congeal" is a part of their lesson.) The bucket is in his lap and he's resting his head on his other arm on the desk, whimpering. He may go home if he so wishes, said Miss Lynch, who once relocated her own shoulder. He's staying put and his classmates are being gentle. They are offering him the low-hanging world-record fruit.

Liam, Shannon, Crystal, Tara, Oisín, Macdara, Stephen . . .

The rest of the room fades out now. All there is is Miss Lynch and the inside of our circle. Her teeth are an open matchbook, the front two twisted as though she'd thought of teasing them out and setting fire to something, but had changed her mind. *I'd like you to close your eyes.*

It's a kaleidoscope, the smashed mirror shards of our shut eyes. The crackle of readiness, heel lift and the whirr.

Envision an outdoors place, where you feel calm and content. A beach, a forest, a field of baled hay, a country lane, a currach in a still ocean, sitting perched on a cliff edge like a cormorant—an imaginary place or a real one, but you must be willing to be there alone. A place where you are self-possessed. Where you can take a measure of yourself. Away from people and duties and belongings, the external ways you understand your social standing. Are you there?

Humming. We are on rocks, connecting one beach to the next. It is our shortcut. We rockrun. Slant across the granite like the Milky Way across the universe. Like a Milky Way inside a Milky Way inside another one. From the band of us flashing to the freckle belt on our cheeks to the silver ways we alight in the rare sun. Outsiders go the long paved way. The road way. Only we know how the submerged stones keel and slither. We know where to step and where to jump.

Remember, you're alone.

How does she know this? That we'd been together in our heads?

You are alone and contentedly so. Aren't you?

We hear the stir of nodding over the rain.

See your place. With every breath, become immersed in your place. With every exhalation, it surrounds you. You are there. Where you need to be, for now. Your destination is very close. You have to move toward it. You can see up ahead where you want to go. The path is just wide enough for walking. It's unpaved. As you move slowly through it, you're a duck in water, leaving a V channeling behind you. That's your effect on this place. You're calm and the place is grateful in turn. Because you're so relaxed, you move easily. Your arms swing by your sides. It's cool but comfortable. You admire the scenery. It's calming. Nothing surprising. As you approach your place, you see a small wooden box, in a clearing. You continue walking through your place, keeping an eye on the plain wooden box. It has no keyhole or latch. There are no barriers here in your place. There's no need to keep any aspect of yourself out. You keep walking, approaching the box. The ground is springy as moss and you leave footprints. If there are trees, you smell bark, sap, lichen. If there is water, you smell salt. If salt had no smell, how would dogs know not to drink seawater? You smell oxygen. Oxygen smells very clean and good. It is what keeps us breathing. Any aches in your body disperse. You're cozily tired and heavy and glad to arrive at the box and to take it in your hands and, without thinking at all, to open it . . . Without thinking at all, you see what's there. You look at it. If you need, you may take it from the box to examine it, but there's no real need. It is what it is. You don't question it. Only see what's there. No need to change it. Do not change it. It's what you were meant to find and it is all that you've found. Now open your eyes.

Our eyelids flicker, like a song that wants to keep playing through the skips. Our cheeks radiate. Waiting for the words that should have come—the gentle carrying out and away as a stork lifts an infant: Notice the feeling of your clothes against your skin; turn your attention to the sounds of your environment; only when you are ready to leave this peaceful place, the awareness of your surroundings increases; as you reawaken, as you wiggle your fingers and toes, keep with you the feeling of calm and relaxation. She hasn't said this. But we fill it in. We open our eyes just a sliver, to see if those words will come. If her mouth is moving. If her wreathed teeth show. She has led us to such places before, toward the bonfire for getting rid of things. But she'd walked us away, after. She'd led us very far away. Slow and sure, she ushered us, until we no longer tasted smoke.

Miss? Tara says.

Liam, Miss Lynch says. *You may go first. You mustn't lie to your friends or to yourself.*

Liam frowns, glances at Tara. He does not yet individually understand, but we can help. She wants you to say what you found. Liam doesn't speak—not since. He writes things down. Our parents lose their minds over him. A sturdy, capable young man, voluntarily mute. Miss Lynch says it's a means of differentiating what needs to be said from what doesn't. She says it engenders something in him but we can't remember what because part of the lesson was the word "to engender." While we wait on Liam's report, Miss Lynch lingers over each of us, watching for alteration—signs of our brains doing the heart's work. We don't like having to tell her what we found with fifth class within earshot. But it's our last day and we know how we could hurt her by withholding. She is angling for a part in the rest of our lives. Beyond this room. Liam scratches dry skin from his jellyfish-stung arms. He washes in the sea when there's no rain because the Heffernans only have a water tank. This distresses Miss Lynch. Tara calls for attention again, pointing at Declan, who's begun to go a bit wan. Leave him be. We scowl at fifth. The loud rain makes the room sound like a tent.

Tara, says Miss Lynch. *Did you find a microphone, by chance? Or a mirror?* Tara lifts her pointy chin. Refocuses. No. It doesn't matter. *Make no mistake, Tara, your deepest concerns matter. But there's a reason I'm not asking you first. I know you understand.* Miss Lynch's closed lips stretched across her teeth resemble knuckles. We've seen how neatly her index finger goes there, in the philtrum nook. Key to lock.

Liam wrote down what he found and the note is traveling the tables. Miss Lynch carries a chair to sit among us. After soberly considering the note, we hear her swallow. Bunged guttering after a downpour. *A roll of them?* She asks Liam: *How big of a roll? Did you unspool it and count how many cards there were?*

No. This big. He makes the sign O. Smaller than a clam, bigger than a cockle.

What sort of cards come in a roll, we wonder. When it became clear he'd found scratchy cards, we were more buoyed than envious, because Liam deserves good things and because of what worse things it could have been and wasn't. We didn't understand Miss Lynch's expression. She seemed to be searching the note for something plain and ordinary. A naggin. A fillet knife. We suddenly recall her telling us: Being fortunate is not the same as being lucky. Good fortune has to do with providence, but luck is a fluke.

Is luck a sin, then? We hadn't braved asking. Are we better off with no chance at all?

Miss Lynch is making us nervous with the intensity of her focus. If it was a boat's radar, it would be too narrow and she'd thump rocks. She explains that one card represents one year of his life. One for every year. This line reminds us of the Seamus Heaney poem she taught us, where the brother (who is Seamus because poems are real) finds out while he's at school that his small brother's dead and when he gets home there's a four-foot box, a foot for every year. "To toll" had been part of the lesson. And how a hyphen is not the same as a dash. Our school has no bell though. Our church has no bell either. But before dinner at home we dip our heads and move our lips saying Hail Mary for the four-foot box and the boy in it. That's what we pray for. Providence. We try not to think of worms, but it's hard. But Liam's healthy as can be. If he'll only live as many years as there are scratchy cards, then he probably misjudged the size of the roll. One or two of us look across at him and smile. Let him see a small bit of our envy. It's nice to feel you have something that others don't and we want to let Liam have that because it's our last day and we might not get a chance again if he heads to the noisy quarry where there's no use for a voice. Gestures will do. We'll run along the limestone lip and wave.

Miss Lynch wipes her nose with her mustard corduroy sleeve that was definitely once a pant leg. There are sobbing sounds in fifth and the high pitch of voices competing with reason. We get hung up on a word she said—"portent" (without the "im-")—and miss the conclusion. Shannon's turn goes quick because she found nothing in the box and even though no one says it we imagine her running her fingers all around the box to see is there a small diamond she missed and then we're skittering again and Shannon doesn't give two shites but Miss Lynch looks a bit mauled and then we feel sick because we don't take this lightly.

Someone robbed you of it, Miss Lynch tells Shannon. *Someone took it from you, and you may know who and when.* She lowers her voice. *How dreadful.*

Shannon stops smiling and the blush drains. She holds Miss Lynch's gaze, turning her head slowly so that she's offering Miss Lynch her freckled cheek. Ever since Shannon found Miss Lynch taking the shortcut to the beach, facing off with a bull too far down the field to turn back, they've been bonded. A calf wobbling around behind the bull. Shannon gave instructions in a booming voice as she hopped the fence to help Miss Lynch out-bravado the animals. *No*, says Shannon. *No one stole enthin belongin to me.* There's no clock on the wall and none of us has a watch. Call it a minute before Miss Lynch says, levelly:

If you say so.

I say so.

And we're not sure if we want her to be so clipped with Miss Lynch. Anyone can see whatever Shannon's missing she'll live without. What was taken might be so worthless she'd never have noticed it gone. Like the dead ends Tara'll sweep off the floor of A Cut Above. Like taking clothes in off the line at the first lick of rain and putting out the ashes. Doesn't she want Miss Lynch to say what it is, for the knowledge of it? The advice she's doling out as a leaving gift.

Shannon's defenses are up, Miss Lynch says, looking at each of us in turn. *As is often the way of the burgled—*

Shannon bunches her hands on the table and Tara twirls her friendship bracelets made of catgut as though she's winding a watch. She blurts out: *I found a camera!*

We all beam at Tara. But Miss Lynch isn't done with Shannon— she can't send her out to the world unadmittedly burgled. *Look at me!* Miss Lynch says. *I'd know!* She wears a scooped smile, which she holds out like a bowl . . . then drops. *But not in here, with you. There's no call for defenses. When each of you walks out that door, you'll start to stockpile defenses. It'll be your main concern. Gather gather gather. You'll hoard them. Cars. Coats. Drugs. Tattoos. Gold claddagh rings. Perfumes. All shapes and sizes. But don't let them fool you into feeling safe. They're worth nothing. Nothing and no one can protect you. That fact is the only defense worth grasping.*

The wild garlic stench from the bunch in the sink is giving us headaches. We want to tolerate it, but a break would help . . . If there's to be no break, it feels like home time should be soon. Someone in fifth pipes up about Declan. He's asleep and should they wake him. Miss Lynch goes to inspect the hand for congealing. She looks into the blue plastic bucket and tips it to see how much blood is pooled in the bottom. A castle turret's worth. Evidently the bandage wasn't tight enough, so she redoes it and Declan wakes, whining, and Miss Lynch says fixing the bandage will sting but she'll phone his mummy to come and get him when it's done, and *Would you like a lolly to pep you up a bit?* Bríona gets a lolly from the cupboard and we all salivate at the pastel yellow-pink sherbet. When Miss Lynch is done with the hand and the phone call, she returns, asking Tara: *What sort of camera? And was the lens facing down or up?*

Immensely relieved about Declan, Tara tells us it was a disposable camera, lens down, that had been all used up—she'd checked by trying to roll the little wheel thing for new film.

Do you think it means I'll be a photographer?

Do you want to be a photographer?

The rain slants across the window behind, carrying a wet wind in it, as Tara thinks. There's only so much you can photograph drenched. *I want to work at Google.*

Miss Lynch looks to be sucking on something bitter since she gave Declan the lolly. He's zonked out on his desk and the blood bucket was emptied into the sink on top of the garlic and the wasp paste: a good basis for some potion. His-mother-is-coming-for-him-and-he'll-get-looked-after is the wrong message to send us away with. That is why Miss Lynch says what she says.

There is an undeveloped film inside that camera, Tara, and you won't ever see the photographs. You'll live with the vague sense of what's there—the latent rumor—but it won't ever clarify from the negative into a less-fogged image. Miss Lynch is trembling with energy and fifth class have stopped talking record-smashing and how really long fingernails coil into pigtails. The wind has moved the worst of the rain clouds along and it's easing, but there's a shade on the room the color of damp heather and it feels late. Mister O'Malley's classroom breaks into a hullabaloo, marking lunchtime, but we are not hungry. Miss Lynch continues:

A box is no use to contain it. You need to go back to the place and to dig yourself a pit, Tara. You need to fill the box with salt water or urine so the film spoils, then wrap the box in good strong skin and stitch it shut a thousand times. You need to bury the box in soil—not peat, that would only preserve it—and pack the earth like a suitcase before you stamp on it. Do you get the idea, Tara?

When Tara finally nods, a tear falls onto her desk, where it sits preserved on the lacquer. It reflects all the dots of us around her, like a ladybird.

We insert all manner of bad things onto the film. We feel bad to do this. But we think it's because Tara was his best friend. Miss Lynch might imagine it's a film of the friendship and she wants Tara to leave it behind in this room, not to take it with her.

But leaving behind memories is hard to do. We tried it. Some stay with us against our will. The poppy bruise stays. No one's hand is in the air but Miss Lynch says: *Yes?*

Macdara is holding two pencils like chopsticks, picking up a rubber. His fringe is a black feather pasted to his forehead. *Chocolate wrappers,* he says, uneasily, when Miss Lynch asks what he found in the box. His voice broke early when he was in third class, much to Mister O'Malley's annoyance. And today the depth of his voice sends shivers up our spines because it's not his voice that's out of place any longer. It's us, here. It's what's in store.

Quality Street, asks Miss Lynch, *or Roses?*

The rubber pops free of his pencil-chopsticks and plinks to the floor like a champagne cork at the end of a horse race with money on it. *Celebrations.*

Right you are, says Miss Lynch. *The party is over.*

The rain's stopped and it's white out. Break time's over and they're back in class next door, doing quiet lessons. We didn't eat yet but Miss Lynch sent fifth class to go with Declan to the gate and to sit there sharing their sandwiches till his mam comes. Our tummies grumble but in a good way.

Words that are part of our lesson: "To chaperone." "To divvy." "To soothsay." (Not the same as soothing.) We say to close her eyes. We slot her sunglasses on her, to help block out the afternoon that's getting bright. We say to think of an outdoors place where she feels calm and happy. A beach, a forest, a field of baled hay, a boreen with grass down the middle, a boat in a lake, the edge of a cliff where a storm petrel would sit with his wings wide. A make-believe place or a real one. She has to be there alone. With every breath in, to become immersed in her place. With every breath out, to be surrounded. She's there, in our circle. In her place. We grin wildly at each other, giddy at how kind and graceful we wield her, at all the better things an adult imagination will find. When she's arrived at the box, we bring her slow slowly slow back to her senses and try to sound ungreedy when we ask what she found.

An egg, hatching.

We all sip on the air. Some of us roll up our sleeves. Miss Lynch still wears her sunglasses but her eyes are open beneath them. She's searching for an empty chair beside us to rest her concern on but there is none, we make sure. *What sort of egg, Miss Lynch?*

Ovoid.

Avoid?

No.

A void?

A three-dimensional circle is a sphere. A three-dimensional oval is an ovoid.

O, we say, rolling our heads.

This matches all the things she's taught us and it's just as matter-of-fact. A two-dimensional life is a death. She'd said this to explain the sense of choosing ashes over casket: a strange sum of what lies above the earth divided by what lies below. We make our mouths oval. *Egg-shaped*, Shannon says.

Shhh, Shannon, with this small talk. Miss Lynch is holding an egg, hatching. It's our turn to explain it. What occurs to us, at first, is that she's breaking. Her responsibilities were sent down to the gate. She's passed the responsibility of herself to us like a bucket to be carried to the sink and tipped. She'd made us ready to handle such stuff. We brainstorm the moment. The image. Take turns expanding the sentence so that it goes all around the circle in a beginning a middle and an end: the meaning everywhere, the vocabulary nowhere.

Miss Lynch.

In the box there was an egg, hatching. Once upon a time there was a mother to lay the egg and tend the egg and hide it from the father, who was rash and would break it open early. The father would splash cold seawater on the egg to wake it up. To wean it off what's warm. Later, he'd splash cold seawater on the boy to make him a man. To make the boy better reflect him. Johnnie sat in our circle and made us complete. There were eight of us and we sat two by two. Johnnie sat with Tara and dipped Ghostbuster toys into her yogurt instead of spoons and licked the yogurt off like ghost-goo full of germs. Even though Johnnie was quiet as Liam before Liam went quiet, we loved him. We knew why. The yogurt was fruits of the forest, which is the same color as a poppy bruise and he had them. There was nothing we could do except to keep him out among the rock pools and streams, away from his father and his head. When he drowned we were down to seven, which is uneven, and it is also a prime number. That cannot be divided except by one and itself. We were only forming and our skin was made of thin shell. But now we are not so thin and breakable. Miss Lynch. You needn't take our measurements and compare them to his. We are taller. We are wider. Just look at the pencil rain on the walls. It goes halfway up the windows, so we can open them. Johnnie won't be missing tomorrow because we won't be here. You won't see us and count our uneven number and hear plashing in your head. In your box there was an egg, hatching.

Bubbles form in the corners of our mouths as we speak because we don't swallow or pause for fear of losing hold of the sentence. Miss Lynch takes off the sunglasses and because her eyes are wet and red the silver eyelashes are like slivers of moon. *It's you!* we say. *The egg. It's because you're ready to get out.*

Miss Lynch greets our readiness with the look of a fisherman arrived home from a storm. In one piece. Crates empty. Her limbs jut out of her center like a huge jigsaw piece with nothing to lock into. Mister O'Malley would tell her *Sing up!* if he heard the vibrato of her good strong voice:

I took it into my hands to watch life break the surface, she explains. *I felt warmth there, in my palm . . . A will to burst out into the air . . . but it cooled so fast. The cracking stopped. The fight petered out. There was a fissure large enough to fit my thumbnail into. And I did. I cleaved the egg open. And there was nothing inside?* The sunglasses on Miss Lynch's lap show us enlarged and reversed in their bulbous lenses. *Not even dust!*

"To cleave" is part of the lesson. "Peter out" makes us wonder: Who is Peter anyway? No one knows because he faded away. We each find explanations for the nothingness but our ideas don't really make a beginning-middle-end sense. It's just vocabulary. All circumference. To disentangle. To ghostbust. To mince.

From all the talk, we are thirsty. Shannon turns the tap on full blast and we dive our heads into the bunch of wild garlic and drink with our noses pinched, with the sight of a boy's maroon blood washing away. It tastes stony and cold and good. One of us takes a wasp wing on our fingertip and blows on it like on an eyelash. What did you wish for? The answer gets gobbled by water and we don't stoop down to recover the wing because wishes are hard to come up with. To recover. That had been part of a lesson when we were only young.

Outside, we take a hit of sunlight straight to the pupil. A fireball blooming in the void! We know it can blind us but our eyes will water and anyways we can blink. The clouds are on their way to America, like a flock of spooked sheep, and there's so much landscape to trace we don't need to think of the ocean. Wild yellow gorse for a road. Across the bramble and rocks, we form circles with our fingers and thumbs for the long-ranging whistle.

Because the sound we send out is real, because it assumes no mercy, all the border collies in Connemara come pelting our way like a legion of horses galloping for the Somme.

Souvankham Thammavongsa
Slingshot

I WAS SEVENTY when I met Richard. He was thirty-two. He told me he was a young man, and I didn't respond to that because I really didn't know what that was, to be a young man, if that was a good thing to be or a bad one. He had moved in next door to us, me and Rose, my granddaughter, in January. She was hardly home that summer. She had gotten together with a new guy and was mostly at his place across town. All my friends were in assisted living, but I wasn't. We didn't have the money, and besides, I didn't care much about going. I didn't want to be around people I didn't know.

Richard had parties at his place every Saturday. At first, it was just the housewarming, and then it was other things. His apartment was an open door, people coming in and out at all hours. Sometimes there were just kids, little ones, over there, with Christmas lights all over the floor. Other times it was middle-aged people crawling through some tent maze built out of cardboard boxes. He even had a party where people brought over their bikes, and we took a tour of the city with him. I did not have a bike, so he let me ride with him. I sat on the bar in front of the seat and he pedaled. He told us stories, personal ones, about his time living here. He'd been in the city for a few years. On the bike tour, he told us about a woman he'd loved once, his roommate. Where they ate in the city and skipped out on a bill, the places they kissed. The city became his with those stories. When I walked by that building, that corner, his stories were there, the way he told them.

"There's no such thing as love. It's a construct," Richard told me one day when I went over to his apartment. I had gotten a package of his in my mail. "You know anyone who is in love?"

I thought of Rose, who always said she was in love whenever she met a new guy and then would wait by the phone all day, crying. Then I thought of my friends and my own experience. We had all known it, but it was something that happened a long time ago, not something we sat around thinking about. It happened, and when it's happened, there is no need to think too hard about it.

"Maybe," I said, "you haven't had much time to know a range of people."

He told me he knew a lot of people. Thousands was the number he gave me. I got the feeling that what I wanted to say to him was about the quality of closeness, not what he was talking about. A few minutes passed between us, and he said, "People say that they are in love all the time, but they're not. I don't believe them. They think they should say it because it's what you say. Doesn't mean they really know what it is."

I looked around his apartment. There wasn't much in it. A few plastic chairs, a couch he had dragged back from someone's front lawn, a table, and a little anatomy man. The anatomy man had little plastic bits inside. I reached inside him and took out a small brown thing the size of a pencil eraser. I didn't know what it was and put it back.

.   .   .

Richard liked to talk about the women he had slept with. There were two he brought up a lot. The first was his roommate, whom he didn't talk to anymore, the one he told us about on the bike tour. The second was a woman named Eve. She lived in New York now but came back once in a while to visit. He said he wasn't in love with her, that they were best friends. They had, for seven years, been a couple, but then they weren't anymore. The chemistry wasn't there. When she didn't answer his emails or phone calls, he would google her. He always wanted to know what she was doing.

I asked him, "Do you think maybe you're in love with her?" He said no, to be in love, you should have sex with that person, and he didn't want that with her. He asked me if I'd had sex with anyone lately. I took my time to answer. I could tell he had no use for anyone who didn't have sex. I tried to remember the last time. I hadn't been with anyone but my husband. He died thirty years ago. A heart attack. Sudden. Thirty years is a lifetime for some people. As far as I was concerned, I hadn't had sex for such a long time that I could consider myself a virgin. I couldn't remember how it all happens.

Richard knew how. He was always talking about all the sex he'd had. Hundreds of women, he told me.

"It's easy. You just ask. And you never know. If someone tells me no, I don't get worked up about it. I mean, they said no. What's more clear than that? There are always others who want to. It's sometimes just athletic to do it." Richard was not a beauty but he acted like one. He said, "I'm not bad-looking. Anyway, looks don't have anything to do with it. Sometimes good-looking people don't do anything in bed. They just lie there. You want someone who has imagination, who is excited. It's the best feeling ever."

. . .

Richard had one of his parties. This party was different from the others. There wasn't any food, and it began later in the evening. There was a green glass bottle in the middle of the room. All his furniture had been cleared, piled on one side of the room. For all his talk, I had never seen him with a woman before. I knew what the bottle in the middle of the room was for.

I looked around the room, at the twenty-five or so people, to see if there was anyone I would hope it would land on. There wasn't, but I wanted to play. When I spun the bottle, it landed on a beautiful blond woman. A lawyer. She was still in her business suit, with the jacket. I kissed her on the forehead, like she was some child, and everyone laughed. Richard said, "Isn't she sweet?" I hated that he said that. I didn't want to be sweet. I was old and I knew it and I had been called a lot of words, but "sweet" really irritated me. I watched as those who were chosen by the bottle kissed each other. After a while, it got boring. The people at the party thought so, too, and started to file out. It was Richard's turn again, and each time it was, he always spent a long time with that person, kissing. There was a man with a beer belly whom he kissed, and a dancer. I didn't want to go home. It was the start of summer, and I wanted something to happen to me.

Richard told me, "You could go home, if you want. We're just going to keep playing this game. It might get boring." But I didn't go. There were three of us now. The other woman was named Lorrie. She worked at an art gallery. Lorrie behaved like she was a girl. Giggling, chewing on her long hair, blushing. When Richard spun the green bottle, it landed on me. He laughed, and said, "You don't have to. You can say no." But I didn't want to, to say no. He was sitting cross-legged on the floor, and I leaned over. He chewed spearmint gum. When we stopped, she was gone.

He said, "It's three in the morning. You should go home." He said it like a good friend who was looking out for me. I got the sense too that Richard didn't like me being there at that time, alone with him, like he was afraid of what an old woman wanted. "I don't want to," I said. I don't know why I said that. Just to see what he would do. He was a man, and I was bored.

His bedroom was clean and quiet. I said, "Can you take off your clothes? I want to see." It surprised me, how he listened. He didn't protest like I thought he would. He didn't say it was a bad idea. He stood there naked. He was beautiful, the way women are. He had hair on his chest and legs. I hadn't seen hair on a chest for a long time and so I reached out to touch it. He closed his eyes and breathed deeply. It was so easy. He sat down on the bed and I sat on top of him. He didn't go in deep, but held me there. I was supposed to lower myself. But I didn't. I could go as far as I wanted. The morning light came in, and he said, "We have to stop." I didn't want to. I liked looking at Richard's face when he held me there. He looked scared, or like he was about to cry. Then he lifted me off of him and turned around so I couldn't see his face. He said, "You have to go. I want to fuck you." And that's why I didn't want to go. Because he wanted that.

I didn't see Richard for a few weeks. He had his parties and people came and went. I heard their talk through the walls, and the women too. I wanted to know what it would feel like to have a sound like that in my mouth. But it was only the women. He was silent, breathing quietly, probably.

I asked him why he never made any noises, not even a grunt. "Concentrating," he said. He always talked that way. Easily. He told me what it felt like, for him, for a man, and what it was like having sex with a woman. I had never known that, but he did. He told me things I wished I could have asked my mother when I was a young girl, but this was better because he gave me facts. I wanted to know how he knew where to put himself, if it was the same each time, how he got them to come home to his apartment, how he undressed them. He always asked them, Can I do this? Is this all right? You're okay with this? The way he told it to me, it was like I had done it, too, had also been inside them, just like him, as a man. There was no metaphor, no seed and soil and growing flowers. Just the facts.

"What have you been doing all summer?" Rose asked me one afternoon when she came home. I knew how she would react if I told her. When she left for the weekend, I knocked on Richard's door. I tried the doorknob and went in. I could hear the shower going, and when he came out, he said, "You hungry?" Just like that. He was a good cook. I watched him cook. Bringing out plates, the pan, opening the cupboards, the fridge. He looked graceful. His long legs and arms. I liked that he wasn't mad at me for what happened last time, after the party, when we had gotten so close. "Why would I be?" he said. "Don't have sex with men who get mad about things like that." He smiled at me and said, "I liked that nothing really happened. We were close. That's the best part. To be that close. And to let nothing happen."

Soon after, we were sitting on the edge of the bed. I sat on top and I had Richard between my legs. We had been kissing. It started off really slow. And then I kissed harder. Then he pulled his mouth away from mine. His mouth was open, and he was breathing heavily. His head tilted back when mine leaned forward. We were so close, breathing into each other. Then I lowered myself onto him and said, before I pushed farther, "Do you want me to pull out?" I meant stop, but I didn't say that. He knew what I meant and why I didn't say that. He laughed, and said, "No, no. God, no." His lips were red, his cheeks pink. I wanted him to say it, even though I knew it wasn't true. "Tell me you love me," I said. "Even if it's not true. Say it." And he did. I wanted to feel what it was like to have someone inside me again, and I pushed him into me.

. . .

It was the end of August, and Richard didn't have his parties as often. We were spending more time alone together. He'd call me on the phone and ask whether I wanted to come over. I knew what he wanted me over for, and I wanted that, too. I went over whenever he called. Sometimes we spent the whole day together, not talking at all. And sleeping. We didn't have much to say, doing what we did. What I liked about the sex we had was how slow it was, and how long we could go, how he waited for my body to respond. When we began it was usually dark outside, and then we stopped when there was light. He told me, "You should get a boyfriend. I can't be your boyfriend." I didn't want a boyfriend, whatever that was these days. I wanted what I had. I didn't say anything. I just watched him put on his clothes. Then he asked me if I wanted to go with him to see Eve the next day; she was in town, and she wanted him to meet her new boyfriend. He said he didn't want to go alone. It was the first time I did anything with him outside the apartment.

I stood on the front porch of a house, on a small street, and Richard went inside to get Eve. She was in the back of the house, where the kitchen was. She called to me to come inside, waved me in. She had long, shiny black hair and brown eyes. She said her boyfriend was upstairs taking a shower and that he'd join us in a few minutes. Richard talked to Eve, asked her about this new man of hers, teased her about him, about being in love.

Then Richard said, "Well, I'm in love," and pointed to me. "With her." We laughed, Richard and I, as if this were our joke and Eve were outside it. You can do that with a joke, hide how you feel and mean what you say at the same time, and no one will ask you which it is.

Eve's boyfriend, Daniel, came down the stairs in a white T-shirt that clung to his chest and plain khaki shorts. "Hey, guys, how is everyone?" I didn't reply because it wasn't really directed at me. Richard answered for himself.

That morning, we played board games and charades. Eve and Richard had a way of talking with each other that made it difficult to join in. They made references and jokes and told stories about each other in bits and pieces that never came together because they'd break out in laughter. They never bothered to explain what any of this was about, always saying we would have had to be there to know. I had been around. I knew what was happening. Richard was oblivious to what Eve was doing with him. Playing the two men off each other.

I got up and went out to the front porch. It was only three in the afternoon. I thought of going home, and then Daniel came out for a smoke. He lit his cigarette and we watched the trees around us. The leaves were far apart from one another; they waved, darted left and right. Pushed by the wind, they looked like a school of fish in the blue sky. A thing out of place. We did not know what to say to each other. We were there at the same time and wanting the same thing, but from different people. If there was anyone else who understood what it was like to be on the outside looking in on those two, it was Daniel.

After a while, he said to me, "You ever seen a tornado before?" I told him I hadn't. He nodded and went on, "They destroy everything. You can see it coming in the distance. Most people would try to get the hell out of there. Some people see it coming and can't help but watch." I didn't say anything. He winked at me. I had only known him for a few hours that day. He saw me.

Afterward, Richard thought it would be a great idea to bike around the city. Eve and Daniel didn't want to go, so it was just us again. We arranged our bodies on the bike like we had done once before, me on the bar in front of the seat, and he pedaled. We went around like this, without helmets. I wasn't scared of getting into an accident. That's what it felt like then, to be with Richard. I didn't think about what would happen to me, what the future would look like. I was in it. I had had a life and had still gotten there.

Richard biked past the crowd at the ferry dock, and we followed the trail out of the city until we got to the lake. We weren't supposed to swim in it because it was polluted, but he did, saying there was nothing wrong with it. He swam far out but close enough for me to see him pretend he was drowning. His arms waved about and his head bobbed. Then he swam out farther and did it all over again.

We returned to his apartment. He told me his friendship with Eve was changing. She was getting on with her life, without him. She didn't drop everything to see him anymore. "I should marry her," he said. "I love her and I don't want to lose her." I did not tell him what to do about her. I did not ask what it would mean for me.

He took off his clothes. One by one, and then mine. The afternoon had changed him somehow. He had always been very tender with me but was even more so now. He put himself down on the bed and closed his eyes. I took him in. I did it slowly. "Yes," he said. I wanted to put something inside him that we could both see come in and out. I put a finger into his belly button, and he got so loud about it, like the women I heard him with through the wall of the apartment. I was quiet, breathing, taking everything in. Then he gasped like something was about to happen to him. He sat up and pulled me closer. He kissed me very hard and did not pull away. We continued like that, face-to-face. I love you, he kept saying.

He asked me to sleep over, but I didn't want to. I watched him with a sadness he couldn't see. I didn't want to be with someone who could do that—who could deny what I was. He had the time to have regrets, to be stupid. I didn't. And when he turned around, I don't know why I did what I did. I reached out and grabbed a piece inside the anatomy man. It was his stomach. A small plastic thing. It wasn't real, of course, but it was there, and it was something.

I went home and was surprised to find Rose there. She asked me where I had been, said she knew that I was spending a lot of time with that guy next door. She said, "He's never going to love you, you know. Have you forgotten how old you are? Look at all your wrinkles." That's the thing about being old. We don't know we have wrinkles until we see them. Old is a thing that happened outside. A thing other people see about us. I didn't know why she was talking to me this way. I didn't know whether she meant this about me or whether she was telling herself. I didn't say anything. It seemed to me she'd been drinking, so I let her talk. After a while, I didn't hear anything she said. My mind was somewhere else.

I did see Richard one last time, later that year, in October. It was at Daniel's funeral. Richard was there, with Eve, supporting her, holding her, like a partner. It seemed strange to me to have done the things people who loved each other did, so often, and for it to seem now like they had never happened. And it seemed strange to me to see him go back to her, to want so little. And what kind of person was Eve to see someone else's love and agree to see it wasn't there. But after a while, it didn't matter to think about it.

I looked over at the closed casket and thought of Daniel, how he died. He was a strong swimmer, in excellent shape, but it was very cold, he got a cramp, and he drowned. I thought of him and his whole life, how short it was. Forty. That isn't much time. I was there with him when he loved someone, and he was willing to wait it out. I wondered whether, in life, you get one big role, some message you need to deliver to someone, and when it's done, it's time to go. I thought of what Daniel said about tornadoes. He was wrong about me. What he said wasn't true. We weren't the same. I did not wait. I am not the kind of person who watches something happen in the distance.

Daniel's family and friends stood up and told stories about him. I did not tell mine. It was for no one to know, and I left. I looked back at the black everyone was wearing. I could not tell which one in the crowd was Richard. I was beginning to forget his face.

Once, walking down the street in front of my old building, Richard called out to me. I must have been closing in on eighty then. I looked through him and spun around. I wanted to be in the distance, beautiful and dark, spinning all by myself, in the clear. I didn't want him to come close. Nothing, not even the call of my name, could make me stop.

Liza Ward

The Shrew Tree

GRETEL'S FATHER did not want her to marry a farmer, but she thought she knew better what was good for her. Anyway, he was an older father who kept to his books, vice principal of the high school in Pattapan County. He had a paunch that draped over his belt and a beard from which flakes of sandwich bread sometimes fluttered away as he spoke, and after he chaperoned the school dance, he would come home with the tip of his necktie soaked in cafeteria punch. Going through her own awkward moments, she found these defects—results of cerebral distractions—especially embarrassing. In the time when her body began to change, strange hairs cropping up, her breasts aching, knocky foal legs starting to fatten, she felt it was some sort of physical betrayal she had committed against herself, coming closer to this humanness.

Then the boys would pinch her, shoulder her up against the lockers, drop things under her skirt to see how far they could get just a hundred feet from the vice principal's office as she walked the gauntlet, hugging the line of lockers so close, the locks clocking the metal doors. Nobody feared Vice Principal Varney. Had he administered the willow switch, he might not have been passed over so many times for a promotion. But there it sat, for his whole tenure, in the corner of his sparsely furnished office, untouched, because he could not bring himself to act violently toward anyone.

Instead, he flushed and stuttered, unsure of his viewpoint, and the troublemakers—*young degenerates with questionable futures*, he would call them later at the dinner table—always came away with the upper hand. Greasers racing hot rods at the fairground, he meant, or the sons of hired hands who'd spent so much time drifting from town to town, a lack of accountability had been bred right into them. And if, by young degenerate, he did not mean Karl Olson, that did not mean he believed the son of a farmer had a promising future, either.

Karl wasn't the kind of boy you noticed. Not at first. He didn't talk much in class and when he was called on, answered off the cuff, never exactly right nor wrong. He had a sense of what should be said even if he hadn't done the reading, and he always couched his half answers in "ma'am," doing just well enough to skate above the line beyond which nobody pushed him. He didn't have time for reading, or the football squad, either. There were chores after school, and by the time he arrived at the eight o'clock bell, he'd have burned off the fumes of breakfast a long time ago and moved on to a wad of mint gum. He'd been up since five, milking the cows and feeding the horses. You could read industriousness in the faded blue knees of his jeans, in his callused hands so unlike her father's. Hay and manure, leather harnesses and mint chewing gum. That was the smell of Karl Olson, and sitting in the close bright classroom smudged with chalk dust and the radiator clanking, she tricked herself into thinking those who had no time to think were maybe nobler, that she was closer to the rhythm of something truer and purer whenever Karl Olson was around.

It began that autumn her mother became so ill her father had to lift her from bed and carry her to a hot bath every morning just so she could straighten her knees and uncurl her fists. One September afternoon, Gretel and her father were walking home from school when a robin hopped onto the sidewalk and began fluttering in circles, flapping one wing because the other was gone. Something had torn it off—a high wind, or a hawk, or one of the cats that prowled the widows' porches in town. There was a seam of blood where the red breast met the brown shoulder feathers, coagulated around a nub of exposed bone. The bird kept trying to launch itself into the air, managing only to lift on the left, the wingless side holding it earthbound. Eyes shining like beads of mercury, it chirped the same note over and over again, a broken wind-up toy of persistence, as if all it had to do was keep trying to fly and eventually the situation would rectify itself.

"Do you remember that rhyme you were read as a child?" her father said, staring down at the wounded bird just as Karl Olson, who must have been walking ten paces behind them, caught up and stopped on the edge of the curb. "It was in that collection— deckle-edge first edition. Very fine illustrations." He raised his finger to his larynx and began, in a reedy voice, "*Who killed Cock Robin? I, said the sparrow, with my bow and arrow—*"

But before he could go on, Karl Olson dropped down to the bird and crushed it with a stone.

Something surfaced like a swimmer in Gretel at the sound of that smacking, as a single rusty feather fluttered into the street and all the birds in the crack willows stopped chirping in the same instant. Everything shifted, and the word *now* came into her mind. *Now*—like wind sweeping through the caverns in her body. Everything slowed except for the sky and the clouds drifting east toward the town green.

With Karl Olson bent over the stone on one knee in an attitude almost of supplication, she could see how violence had been the only course of action. What had they been thinking they would do with a one-winged bird anyway? Recite a poem over it? Place Cock Robin in a strawberry box and bring him home?

"No more to see here, Mr. Varney," Karl said, rising from his knees, dusting the thighs of his blue jeans. "No use in the suffering."

Mercy killing. That's what Karl called it. When an animal was suffering the best thing to do was put it out of its misery, but when it came to humans, you had to ferry the invalid through every unendurable moment.

Before the illness, her mother had enjoyed parties and dressing in clothes that elevated her beyond her station as vice principal's wife. Her nails were always painted bright colors to match the flowers on her clothes, and she brought Jell-O squares to picnics in which tiny bits of canned fruits were suspended like dark corruptions in perfect jewels. At high school dances, she had been known for taking a misfit's hands and leading him in a thin-wristed waltz under the streamers as the vice principal smiled wanly from the baseline.

Now she slept on the couch, knees drawn up, arms crossed over her chest, her body curled around her feverish thinking. She spent the day reading books or staring out the window, past the town and the cornfield, into her own thoughts floating somewhere out over the wood that flanked the west edge of the Olson Dairy Farm.

It was cold in the living room. The windows were open and the long white curtains swelled inward, before being sucked back against the sills, like the lungs of heaven expanding and contracting. They lived in one of those Victorian houses with high ceilings and rooms that opened onto each other, always so impractical to heat. Her father went to close the windows, but her mother stopped him. The high dry air did her joints good. "Besides," she said. "Do you want to know a secret?"

They came close to listen to what she had to say.

"I was sailing," she whispered, patting her hand on the *Atlas of Obscure Islands*. Her breath smelled sour for not having had a glass of water in hours. Instead she drank oceans of brine, marooned somewhere inside the atlas. It was a leather-bound book with thin, translucent pages. Her father had purchased it at an estate sale and it was worth quite a lot, but because it had given them so much pleasure, he could not bring himself to sell it. All the maps inside were blue with white spots for islands so accidental, smack-dab in the middle of vast oceans, they had only ever been discovered on the way to some other big discovery or scientific experiment, which was the human condition, wasn't it? her father had once told her—the winds blowing a person where he did not mean to go and wrecking him on the edge of a cornfield.

She took the atlas from under her mother's hand and opened it to an infinitesimal hunk of volcanic rock poking up from the middle of the South Pacific. "Pitcairn," she said, thinking of the stone Karl had used to crush the bird in mid-chirp.

"*You* must be sailing on the *Bounty*," her mother said.

"Then I guess it won't be long before we burn the ship and turn on each other," said Gretel.

"Oh, let's not," her mother said. "Not just yet. Let's keep our options open a little bit longer, shall we?—see where we end up. We might go to Easter Island from Pitcairn and then from Easter to Possession. Or *Charles* Island!—where they wear no clothes."

What would her mother look like nude, in the hard-boiled sun? A piece of driftwood, Gretel decided. As she thought of that body nudged and tossed by the sand-crashing waves, a hollow feeling came into her chest. Had someone tapped on her heart just then, it would only have been able to answer, *Nobody*.

"Tell me about your day," Gretel's mother said, patting the cushion beside her.

So Gretel sat there and told her, leaving out the crushing of the bird and the strange new matter-of-factness that had come over her.

Stepping toward the window, her father looked out into the long shadows falling across the sidewalk. "Who killed Cock Robin," he murmured,

I, said Karl Olson,
With my granite stone, I stoned him.
And all the birds of the air
Fell a-sighing and a-sobbing,
When they heard the bell toll
For poor Cock Robin.

The evening was cool, the stars bright, and after dinner they went out onto the porch to hear the birds grieving in the crack willows. For that was what they were doing, grieving the death of the robin. Or was it the end of daylight? Or the woman carried out of the house and placed on the porch swing with a cream blanket over her shoulders?

Just last season, she had been able to come and go as she pleased. Years before that, she had danced in the ballet studio downtown, pirouetting and pliéing, holding the bar and staring into the mirror at what she imagined to be certain fame as the clouds raced across the blue sky behind her. Then came the day when a fierce wind tore into town and slammed Larkin Varney up against the studio window.

There are things the dusk illuminates that nothing else will. The lines sharpen, wrinkles smooth into alabaster, the sidewalk's fissures deepening as the dropping sun steers the house on Vine Street right up against the end of everything. Gretel steps off the porch. She walks down the path toward the place where the town falls away and the cornfield starts, running to the wood, which arches its back against all cultivation. Closing your eyes, you might imagine you were on a ship, might imagine the rustling husks to be wind snapping the sails, and you, bound for that island of trees off the starboard bow. Pasture to windbreak to the farm where Karl Olson is bringing the cows back from the edge of twilight. Sea of swaybacks and paintbrush tails flick in the darkness. Pod of whales, her mother would imagine. Gretel, though, prefers things as they are. With seas of grass like this, who needs oceans?

She is prettier than either of her parents ever were, and it worries them, the way gifts like that can get girls who are unsure of themselves into trouble. Farther and farther away from the porch she strays, her steps no longer clacking on the macadam, until she stands frozen at the spot where the town's pavement surrenders to dirt and funnels into the cornfield. Pointing her toe, she brushes it back and forth across the tip of a weed, tempting a greaser out of the darkness. She turns her head and scrapes her chin along her shoulder, the side of her face nestled into her collar in an almost coy gesture. A conspiratorial little wind gathers out of the wood now, chattering in the corn before it dies, and then the night comes down hard, smothering every last glimpse of her.

Her father turns on the porch light to guide her back to them. Back from the degenerates standing behind the school, smoking like overgrown man-children. Back from the dangers that lie in wait for girls named after characters in fairy tales. The moths come fluttering in and the cat slinks up on the rail and bats them between her paws as the season's last crickets thrum in desperation. "A trail of bread crumbs," murmurs her father. "Rather poorly considered, I'd say, bread crumbs in bird country. Though of the pair, Gretel was always the industrious one."

Or was it Gretel who went into the oven—the first to pick candy from the house and bring the witch down on them? He moves his hand to his throat to choke out the idea of such an inauspicious beginning. A bit of dinner roll whispers out of his beard as the breeze kicks up and then the stillness sets in again.

"My, it was such a long time ago," the mother says, her wide eyes catching the glow of the porch light. "And it feels just like yesterday afternoon. Do you remember when she was a baby? How she used to cry and cry until we picked her up—and she always stopped right away. We'd never mattered that much to anyone. Who ever thought she could be so angry at us?"

"Too many books and blunders," the father says. "Books and blunders."

"And what blunders would those be?"

"Mine, my dear. All mine. One can't be forced into Melville and Shelley. And with all the resources allocated to home ec. and football, is it any *wonder* we've never had a matriculation to the Ivies?"

"Not yet! It isn't over, Larkin. It can't all have been decided," the mother says, lifting her eyes to the place where the cornfield drops off and the wood whittles away the black horizon. "She'll find she's more like us than she realizes. She can't help it. That's how come she's so angry. It's the things we can't help about ourselves we see reflected in other natures."

"You always knew more about her than I."

"See, I didn't feel that I knew anything, though—that's the thing—not until just recently."

"You could fill a book with all you know," the father says, staring out into the stars winking over the cornfield that seems to be playing a joke on him.

It's the loss of motion the bird grieves when it sings. Mourning dove. Barn swallow. Catbird. Thrush. Sparrow and starling. Sunrise bleeds into aimless afternoon. Gretel throws a ball in the air and swings a stick, the suck of missed contact whispering of disconnection. Sometimes the owl flaps up from her crook in the dead ash and floats out of the wood to haunt the garden. Other times she spreads her wings and flies over the cornfield, picking up mice as they scurry between the rows, bearing them back to the wood in her talons. From the wood to the cornfield and back again, she swoops and dives, snatches and soars, over and over again. The creatures struggle and writhe as she searches for gaps in the crowns of trees through which to thread herself and gulp down her quarry. Her eyes are deep black notches in a wooden face, her wings like a geisha's fan, ribbed and unbending. Those times she misjudges, her prey too heavy or her talons not sinking in far enough, the animal twists out of her grasp midair, hitting the earth at the edge of the cornfield with the lightness of a heartbeat to scurry into the crack willows where the cat lies in wait.

This is what must have befallen the rabbit: the cat hunted it, or the owl stole it and dropped it into the garden. A young rabbit playing dead in the middle of the first flagstone on an otherwise uneventful Saturday. When Gretel touched it with her foot, it leapt up and sat there puffing, trying to appear bigger than it was. How still the eyes were, like big glass beads catching the sunlight. Only the nose betrayed the fear, twitching to the rhythm of the creature's racing heart, its ears crunched tight against the head like flower petals. There was a deep gash in its side and one of the hind legs appeared nearly severed.

What is a rabbit without a haunch?

A dancer without joints.

A wingless bird.

A fish out of water.

"It's me," she said into the telephone.

Karl remained silent at the other end of the line.

"Gretel Varney," she offered helpfully.

"Right," he said, sounding far away. "The vice principal's daughter." Then swinging back, his voice solid, round: "Hi, you." He was doing something else as he spoke. He always would be. Drying his hands of the barn muck or getting ready to do the afternoon milking, his voice growing rich and full and fading out the next second as if the wind were always plucking him away right when you thought you were going to capture him.

"What are you doing right now?" she said.

"Oh, lots, Gretel Varney, and then again—nothing much."

She had not expected him to say something like, *Hi, you*, or to repeat her name that way, as if he not only remembered her now, but understood her maybe better than she could even hope to understand herself.

"Out of milk, are you?"

Burying herself between the staircase and the telephone table, the cord pulled tight enough to choke her finger, Gretel shook her head. "I've got something that needs putting out of its misery."

An hour later Karl Olson was standing in the front hall, chewing a wad of mint gum. His hair at its lightest parts was the color of hay, his jeans worn to white in the knees. Looking down, he froze. His boots! Suddenly, he crept back in his own footprints, knelt and untied the laces, then placed them by the door in a gesture she wanted to take as the gentlest intimacy, though it was only that the soles had manure in their grooves, that the toes had been soaked in cow piddle. Rising, he handed her a bottle of milk still warm from the udder. She opened the cap right there and drank the quart down in seven long swallows.

"Thought you didn't need milk," Karl said.

"Then why did you bring it?" she answered.

"Farmer's job to know what needs what without 'em having to ask for it," Karl said, and with his hands in his pockets, he followed her from room to room, past the clock that chimed once for the half hour. He stopped and ran his finger up a groove in the wood, as if he had caused the hand to shift, the pendulum to swing; as if Karl Olson was in control of everything.

The rabbit lay in one of her mother's hatboxes on the parlor table, next to a lamp fringed in tassels. Old books crowded the shelves, stacked sideways where they didn't fit. "Who does all the reading?" Karl said.

"My father sells rare books," Gretel said.

"Rare, huh?" Karl smiled. "Woulda thought he'd go for well done or something."

She laughed and covered her mouth with her wrist. "You know, first editions—signed, deckle edges. That kind of thing. He goes through dead people's stuff beside all the old biddies hunting for samplers and memory boxes. Says people don't know what they have half the time."

"Forty-two Herefords," Karl said, counting fingers on fingers as if he could not fathom a person who did not know at all times precisely what was in his possession. "Sixteen Plymouth Rock and four New Hampshire chickens. Two potbellied pigs, one Morgan horse, one draft. Two American quarter horses. The only kind of books at the farm are the cooked kind. Know what that means, cooking books?"

Gretel just stood there.

"Fudging numbers." Karl looked into the box. Once it had been home to her mother's Easter bonnet, and a piece of floral tape was hanging from the rabbit's whisker.

"You know, when you said *misery* to me, I thought you were talking about yourself." He lowered his hand, touching his knuckle to the rabbit's nose.

"Do I look that miserable?" Gretel said.

"I dunno. Bored, maybe."

"I'm *so* bored."

"Misery loves company," Karl told her, and picking up the rabbit, he snapped its neck.

She had never skinned anything before, but he talked to her as if she had, or might want to practice on this rabbit. The secret to skinning, he told her, was to slip the nozzle of a bicycle pump under the hide and blow it full of air, inflating it like a balloon so the pelt would come away without a tear from the rest of the body.

He told her how you could dig up a lilac bush and leave its roots exposed in the hot sun and when you planted it again, even after a whole season like that, it might still take if you were lucky.

Last night a calf had been born feet first.

When cows eat dandelions, it makes the milk taste bitter. That's why he had to go home straightaway to spray weeds before the ladies were turned out into the east pasture.

Maybe she was like that. Maybe she was a lilac that had been dug up and left in the hot sun and when Karl put her back in the ground he would press the soil around her feet and she would rise up, standing tall, and bloom because he'd watered her.

Only it doesn't feel like a blooming. More like a skinning, a pumping full of air that leaves Gretel raw and wanting. One afternoon that week when her mother takes a turn for the worse, Gretel finds herself walking up to the edge of the cornfield, the wood looming like the shadow of some giant hand just over her left shoulder. Things are moving in the wood, things she wouldn't want to know or have explained to her. Birds of prey keen in the snags. The owl sleeps, surrounded by pellets spat from her hollow tree, each one a piece of young rabbit or vole, a mouse with its bones and fur curled around itself the way her mother's infirm body cages her rapid thinking.

She reaches the pasture with her heart beating in her mouth, every inch of her tingling. Indian summer now. Insects surprised from dead leaves weave dizzy arcs on the edge of the shadows. She stands behind the barbed wire, watching Karl Olson crouch in the grass, one elbow on his knee, as he pulls up weeds to keep the cows from eating them.

In time, she will come to feel that a weed is a weed only when it grows where you don't want it to be—and who are we, besides, to judge the taste of a cow's milk? If a cow wants to eat a dandelion, why deny her the pleasure? Many years from now, these questions will bubble up from a place in herself she hadn't known existed. A voice will confront her as she stands over the stove in the predawn making Karl's breakfast, washing the supper dishes, or leading a bawling calf back home through a broken fence on the edge of the lot where her parents' house once stood. A voice will speak in her mother's tone, dazzled by mystery, and Gretel, pregnant and soaking owl pellets in water to reconstitute mouse skeletons, will wander into the pasture and press her cheek to a cow's velvet nose, shivering in ecstasy as the grassy breath tickles her. When she tries to explain to Karl why she can no longer cook him *ruminants*, he will rise slowly from the creaky chair and say, "*A what?*"

"Steak, Karl."

"Oh, I see. So you're a kook, now, hunh?—an *intellectual*."

But all this is waiting in the wings. Just a shadow haunting the trees, on the very periphery of the moment when Karl Olson catches sight of her and smiles, smiles as if he already knows everything.

"Hi, you," he says, wiping his brow with a cloth and sticking it in his breast pocket.

She presses the tip of her finger to the barbed wire, stealing a glance back over her shoulder.

"What's the misery?" Karl says, squinting past her into the distance.

The peak of her house rises behind the cornfield. Why has it always felt so lonely? No brothers and sisters. No chores. Not enough responsibility, maybe.

"They know where you are?"

Gretel shakes her head. "They don't know much of anything."

"Awful lot of books for not much, then," Karl says, doubtfully. He parts the wire for her to step through, and a barb catches her sleeve. He looks away. Pressing a thumb to the tear in her best blouse, she follows him across a pasture pocked with cow patties all the way to the windbreak, where old maples and oaks reach over a tangle of raspberry bushes to snatch scraps of the town and drag them into wildness.

Come back with me, she was going to say. *And what would you do then, Karl Olson? If you plant a woman in the ground like a lilac, will her ghost rise up and dance again?*

But the light shifts into a point of no return. She reaches for Karl's hand as charred leaves lift from the branches, stirring and twittering. A wave of blackbirds surges out over the wood, breaking around trunks and bracken to strand themselves high in the trees, each red wing as it spreads calling to that ill-fated robin.

In time, she will come to think it was the blackbirds that stole whatever crumbs she might have dropped to find her way out of Karl. She will remember being swept up in this destiny, the birds tumbling her dark blond hair out of its ribbon, untying the cravat at her neck, picking at her stockings, fluttering their red wings against her cheeks, marooning her on their way south in a middle-aged wintering. Not that any of this is here yet. Only the wood knows what is coming.

The wood, with its primeval stands of maples and oaks. Hemlocks. Poplars into which the Norse gods breathed souls to populate the emptiness. The tallest ash, bearing its scar to mark the year the milk ran blue, and Karl's grandfather trapped six mice and crushed each with a boot until he caught the shrew, then bored a hole in the wood with an auger, and immured her in the heart of the trunk to chew and scratch until she suffocated.

And do you know, Karl will say, standing over her one night with a branch in his hand after she has threatened to leave him, *that if you strike a lady with a switch made out of ash, they say your violence will never leave a mark on her?*

What will you do to me? the wood whispers inside Gretel, lifting her chin from her neck to expose the artery. She squares her shoulders and turns to face him under a bower of late September leaves so suffused in gold, it's as if she has come to stand beside Karl Olson in the belly of the sun.

"You weren't in English," she says.

Karl shrugs. "Don't go telling the vice principal." He slips his hand into his back pocket and offers her a stick of gum.

"He always knows," Gretel says, taking the gum, unwrapping it, letting the silver paper fall into the crevice of an old root ball. "Not that it matters any. What's he going to do about it? Whip you? Probably won't even give you detention." She leans into a trunk, sliding to the earth, strands of her hair combed up by the bark. "He'll be off reading a book and raccoons are breeding in the attic. Off writing a poem about the death of an insect."

She laughs at her own joke, covering her mouth with the back of her hand even as a shadow drops through her chest, taking root across her groin. For a moment, it feels like something is living inside the tree. Deep inside the rings, something is waiting for her, deep in the wooden heart of all things, trapped and restless.

"So there's the misery," Karl murmurs, as if feeling down a horse's leg to detect some hidden injury. When he says *misery* it sounds like *mystery*. *And what then?* Of course the horse will have to be put down.

On this particular day, she has no suspicion of Karl's own misery—that his father is drinking again, that his mother complains, as she hurls bread crumbs to the birds, that in thirty years of marriage the only Paris she's been to is the amusement park three towns over, with all the fountains and that fancy antique carousel. Gretel doesn't know that Karl's older brother is running away to the army, that the farm is tightening itself around Karl's neck, that English class makes him feel insignificant, because nobody gives a hey *what* he answers. That when the fence caught Gretel's sleeve and his eyes passed over the scratch, he had to stop himself from reaching for a hole in his own fabric to slip through.

He waves to a depression in the earth where fallen leaves have collected and started to brown. "We made it to the boneyard," Karl says, as Gretel searches the gray trunks and golden leaves for gravestones. "It's where we lead the ladies that can't be sold."

"Oh," she says, "it just looked so pretty."

"Pretty's a waste on a farm, Gretel Varney."

Nothing wasted. Not a word. Not even a quarter acre for a flower garden. What she mistakes for quaint from a distance will prove run-down once she's living inside it. What seems practical will become a poverty of imagination. For example, when one of the two oxen in the team goes south, the other ox is thought to be as good as useless.

She takes Karl's hand, which feels more like the one-winged robin than anything capable of crushing it with a stone. Tears well in his eyes and she hopes he is about to profess his love, but he just coughs, leans past her, spits out a wad of mint gum. *Can't say I didn't warn you,* Karl will tell her, the morning after their wedding, when he rises before dawn because the ladies will be aching.

Now a breeze moves through the wood, hurrying all creatures toward their final destination. Dried leaves blow over Gretel and Karl, bits of their clothes swept up, the buttons of her silk blouse clicking against his belt buckle. His body parts from hers and rolls lightly into the dirt. The sun drops behind the farm. A chill gathers in the wood. *Hurry up! Be quick about it!* Picking the leaves from their clothes, they turn away from each other, buttoning and buckling, and pulling up stockings snagged by twigs and thorns. Milking time. Time of the lady-aches. And what about Gretel? High time she placed Karl Olson at the center of everything.

"See you," he says.

"*Will* I?"

"Misery loves company, doesn't it?"

"I won't be if you aren't."

Karl stops and looks back at her over his shoulder. "That so?"

If she should lose herself in the wood alone, how would she ever find her way out? No bread crumbs. No pocket of moonstones, and leaves falling faster by the second to obscure every footstep. Karl would point to lichen growing on the north face of the trunk, or trails carved by errant calves, faces matted in burdock. Gretel, though, cannot tell north from south, or a spruce from a hemlock. *Can't find your way out of a paper bag*, Karl might say. Until he names it for her, she won't know a thing. An ash merely a tree. A shrew just a mouse.

Doua Thao

Flowers for America

Aʟᴡᴀʏs ᴀʟᴏɴɢ ʀᴜᴇ ʟᴀʙᴇᴏᴛᴛᴀᴅᴏᴋ, during unguarded
moments. This time on my way home from Mrs. Ketha-
vong's sister. It was almost dusk. But still enough light to see her
face was not among the orchid sellers crowding the street, calling for customers—*Sweetest smelling! Softest in all of Laos! For
you, the flower Asian!* Her face was not among the merchants by
their doors. Inviting, the way they stand. But always their looks
suspicious. Her face was not among the vegetable ladies, their
voices like a twenty-year smoker's from haggling. Her face was
not among the peddlers of jade animal figurines and combs and
full-belly Buddhas, always the whites buy and ask be wrapped
in paper. Gossip pieces for their walls and tables at home, their
vanities, about how they had visited Laos. Nor among the food-
cart cooks, whose grills scented the air, filling and cramping the
empty stomachs of the hungry. The cooks' loud voices, too, clash-
ing with the orchid sellers—food and flowers, flowers and food.
On Labeottadok they are one, a singsong of distorted echoes,
flower's food, food's flower. But right before the Royal Tea House,
when Houa, my old friend, stepped out from the alleyway, empty-
handed, instantly, I knew her.

"Why are you running—so quickly, Hnuhlee's Mother?" she called to me. So I stopped, of course, for an old friend. Her long hair folded and softly held on her head with a bright purple scarf. "You work too hard," she said, seeing the rice sack in my hand, after she had pushed her way through the crowd. In the sack were four fish wrapped in paper. One was a calf-sized frogfish, my favorite, and I was planning to steam it for dinner.

"Are you well, Shengcua's Mother?" I said, ignoring her question, walking still. *Lushest! Moistest! In all of Laos.* The top two buttons of her yellow blouse were undone, showing her pale, bony chest. Her red sarong covered her feet, stuttering her steps.

"Doing like yesterday. Hoping to do the same tomorrow," she said. Houa and I grew up in Fi Kha before the war. She had lived four huts over and is a sister by our Vue clan name. Forty-one years since our births, and here we were. On the same street. In the same town. Smiling at each other, each knowing the path of how the other got here, as if the other's was our own. *Orchids! For you the flower Asian!* "What happened to your leg?" she said, looking me over. On my right thigh, above my knee, was a bandage. A mean catfish had snapped back and stung me that morning as I untangled it from a net. "It's hard work *and* it's dangerous?"

"Every job has dangers," I said. "But I'm lucky to have this." *Come see Yellow Pearl Orchid!* Slowly I walked so she could keep up, and searched the oncoming faces. "You must be doing a little better," I said to my friend, speaking the way old Hmong women speak, which is to strike at the heart of the matter with the vaguest comment possible. The vagueness gives you space not to seem nosy, and space also for the other person to tell you what you truly want to know if she chooses.

"For a few months maybe," she said.

"A few months' calm of heart is worth it," I said. *The sweetest smelling.*

"You believe so?" she said, the left dimple marking her beauty emptied and filled before a stranger could notice it.

"For the heart to be calm, however short, is worth it. Even for thirty minutes. For the belly to stay quiet." Knowing I had a little more than my friend, I offered her my frogfish.

"Maiker," she said, feeling young again and comfortable, "you keep it. We will be okay for a few months."

"Oy, Houa. I caught with my own energy. I want you to have it." *Newly grown. You pick!* "It's a frogfish!" I said, as if that would settle everything. We had stepped out into the road and now were being pressed in by the flow of people around us, tourists, grocery shoppers, orchid collectors, laborers returning home.

"I don't want your charity," Houa said. "Don't pity me."

"It's not. I don't. I give it as a dear sister of a life we both knew from long ago." Stopping, I turned to Houa, and a body bumped into me before continuing on.

"All right," she said, accepting the fish I had taken out of my sack, "but only to help you sleep better." We walked on. *Purple Locust Orchid! Cheap!* But as I stepped into the intersection to cross the street, she was no longer by my side. When I looked back at her, four-five paces behind, she said, "Ask it." But who am I to ask? What do you say? Because I am a woman, I am fluent in vagueness but had no courage for bluntness. "You want to know how could I, right?"

"Anything for the heart to be calm," I repeated, knowing our existence here was lived closer to death than to life.

"You speak like it's opium. Something I need to do to survive the long day, to be able to face the world, to face you."

"It's not opium," I said. "But one must live, must try to go on. Believe me, I know it's not." But already she was in the street, crossing over to the next square, into the next group of vendors along Rue Labeottadok, never listening to the words I was never saying. *New orchid.* "Houa," I said, catching up to her, afraid to be alone with my own voice.

"All this time I've been wondering, Did she do it on her own?

Did her father and I force her? Did she have a choice?" *Blue-Winged Dragonfly.*

"It's done," I said. "Think instead of the two months you have to live and use it to prepare for the next two months."

"But—listen—it is *not* done. Never done unless you're dead. After two months, it might need to happen again." *Pink-Tipped Orchids. Come see.*

"Then you'll make the decision then."

"But it must be considered now," she said, shaking the fish in her hand as though swatting a small grease fire. She stopped walking and faced me. Her face was calm with the trouble of thinking, but having strong currents underneath. Did my old friend think I was naive? "Tell me what you think of me?"

"It's never easy," I said, "this life."

Trembling now, the fish in her hand. "You think she had no choice. Because if she had a choice, she wouldn't have done it?" I had no answer for her, but knew and was afraid she would take my silence wrong. "But what does that say about me," she said, "as a mother?" Because I did not know what to think of myself, I could not tell her what I truly thought of her as a mother. What would I think of myself if I were in her position? Of all things, this was the one difference in our paths. And now, it seemed, we were arguing about it. Besides, she had a husband, which left her decisions not so easily made. *Pink-Tipped Orchids, fresh and sweet.* A throng of people caught up to us, surrounded us. We quickened our walk, to let them separate themselves and hurry on, leave us behind. "However, if you think about it"—she stepped slowly and gingerly now, as though, with bare feet, walking on broken glass, *Purple Petal Golden Heart*—"she has many years ahead. And she could still get married."

"You want to know who gets to make the sacrifice?" I said.

"I want to know who gets to decide," she said. *Come see best orchids in Laos!*

"Maybe no one gets to decide," I said. "Maybe it was already decided long ago for us."

"I can't believe that."

"Maybe it was us who decided long ago, and those decisions are just now starting to show. Or maybe it has nothing to do with decisions. And choosing. Maybe it's just our luck. That we change. Forced to change. Everything changes."

"You have some luck!" she said. "Only one child, two mouths to feed. If your neighbor didn't pity you, how helpless you are without a husband, she never would let you fish with her." Her tone made me wonder if she wished her husband dead. Would she prefer that type of luck? *Blue Hooded Orchid. For sale. For sale, Blue Hooded Or—*

"That's true," I said. "That's my luck." We came to the end of the paved section of Labeottadok. Ahead was all red dirt and tire ruts, then home.

"Some luck, you don't get to change." Her knowing tone was an elder's, lecturing me before weighing me down with guilt.

"You're right, Houa. Some luck you don't get to change." My friend stepped into the dirt road, then, realizing her sarong was brushing over it, hopped back onto the paved street. "What were you doing on Rue Lab?" I said. Houa lived north of the city. There, the buildings thinned out, and more land was available for farming, where the popularity of Laotian orchids was making some farmers wealthy.

"Talking to myself about what was done and what to do," she said, then turned around, heading the way we had come, saying over her shoulder, "Meet you again," and fell in with a crowd walking back toward the heart of Labeottadok, the marketplace, and the orchid sellers. I knew I would again find her along this road, and maybe, someday, I would stop speaking to her like a woman who has been given space to remain silent about her luck.

On the road coming to my house, Bone and Skin slid out through the gate hole to warn me with their teeth, slowly backing as I came forward. I encouraged their barking at strangers and willingness to bite, but this had not been their usual behavior with me, only after I returned from the last time I saw Mr. Cha alive, as though, overnight, they had aged and were going blind and I now was difficult to recognize by sight. But always, when they heard my voice—Bone and Skin, I would say, because one is white and the other yellow, go home—they would quiet down and lead me home. This day, though, after seeing my old friend Houa and trying to help quiet the voices in her head, to reassure her of our decisions in the past, walking home, I remembered the disagreement I was having with Hnuhlee when my dogs ran out to greet me with their teeth and severed my thought, made me gasp, forcing a curse on my tongue, and for a second, I forgot how to quiet them down, to remind them it was only me, still me coming forward.

We now live in a house with two floors and whitewashed walls. To look like Modern Woman, as she calls herself, Hnuhlee has cut her hair short. All the reading she has done has made her need eyeglasses. She is pregnant with her first child. And this is the seed of our disagreement: whether we prefer a baby boy or baby girl. Hnuhlee said it does not matter, but I think it does, even for a modern woman.

And you? I had asked her husband.

Hnuhlee was born in 1978 in the Ban Vinai refugee camp. We had fled our village in Laos the year before without my in-laws. They believed things would not be as everyone feared when the communists arrived. When Hnuhlee was one, my husband heard from a new arrival in camp that his parents had disappeared into the jungle and were trying to join us in Thailand. He told me this at night as we lay facing each other, Hnuhlee asleep between us. He said he was going after them.

What do we do if you don't come back?

Why think that way?

What am I to think? I wanted to yell at my husband, but feared waking up our daughter. He turned onto his back. We had to leave fast, he had said after he returned from war the second time; he knew what the communists would do to us. Did he forget? This, the man, to become his wife, I had shouldered a *ker* for and fell in behind when he came through our village on his way back from war the first time. I wondered if still he was the sixteen-year-old who said to me as we came upon a stream during that march, I can be a horse, then laughed when I lost my footing on a slippery rock. Sitting in the water, I was angry at him for his man language—which I took to mean, then on, I will have to feed him, his horse's appetite—and his laughter at his clumsy bride. I was almost fourteen, but in the years since, I have come to understand his words to mean sacrifice, for me to jump on his back and ride across.

The small wooden shed the refugee people gave us had only a door. Between the wall planks were gaps allowing you to see the stars and brighter night sky, but the weak skylights did little to the darkness inside. I turned my husband's face and held it between my hands. His nose bridge was high and sharp: with enough light, I could pick out its outline in a sea of a million faces. I heard us all three breathing—Hnuhlee's deep and evenly spaced, mine shallow and hurried, my husband's broken now and again with sighs—and hoped in the morning the door would not open, that it would seal us in, and if we were to die in this wooden box, then it would be all right because we would die as a family, our breathing, finally, as one. He said, Follow your family to America. His words burned my insides like hot metal, and this time, letting go of his face, I turned on my back. I had married him and was part of his family. Saying that was like he wanted to divorce me. I breathed loud out of my nose because too much it was to use my mouth. He said, I'm their son. Do I leave them?

Each beat of my heart was a *yes!*-reply, a thump in my ear, but I let my silence speak, my breath scream. Hnuhlee started and stirred but did not cry; she knew to save her tears for later. Even in the dark, I could see what my husband was supposed to do: stay with his wife and daughter. But he was a man who walked the narrow path of a son—help your parents, protect your family, take a wife, have children, raise your grandchildren—and I knew my words would not enter his heart. Helping your parents was the first thing you learned to do and the first thing you got to let go. And long as they drew breath, their pull on him was strongest, and that night, briefly, I wished my in-laws dead.

The next night, I held tight my husband's arm and pushed Hnuhlee at him to hold, but he refused to take her. He pulled away and disappeared through the camp fence. In the dark of our shed, I cried and held my daughter's face next to mine, her cheek warm and soft, then my bitter tears, when they dried on her face, itched her, and she started to cry. Everything my mother had told me, it seemed, I was forgetting. She said to me once, Never cry on a baby's face. If your tears get in a baby's eyes, the baby will feel what you feel. So I put my daughter down on the bed and sat away from her, so I could cry by myself, and she by herself. I did not know how to stop for a long time. For a long time, I could not even hold my own daughter.

Seven months after my husband left, his parents arrived in the refugee camp. They were bones and walked slow. They explained to me this: They traveled with the last group of people from their village. My husband found them and led them through the jungle until the communists spotted them, and again, he had picked up a gun, making him a soldier. He drew the communists away from the group with two other men from the village.

You are so stupid! For many days, I said nothing else. Their assurances meant nothing to me, and I was a bad daughter-in-law to close my ears to their words, my heart to their suffering, too, and they had every right to beat me but could not find the strength to hurt. We all waited in silence. My husband was in the jungle, I believed, still fighting the war, and only waited for the perfect time to drop his gun and slip the communists and return. When my in-laws filed the paperwork to leave for America, I decided to stay. Don't make the mistake we did and stay too long, they said. But again, worthless words to me. They offered to claim Hnuhlee as theirs and take her ahead with them. But I told them no. She is mine, and she will wait with me.

Despite arriving in the refugee camp before my in-laws, my parents left two years later, watching and waiting on me, the last of their children in the camp. Mother said childhood is the length of your parents' lifetime; but I was only a daughter so did not believe her.

Grief has blinded you, Father said. Your in-laws, they have already left. They know your husband is dead.

They don't love him, I said.

Love? He left his wife and child.

His reason for leaving, I wondered, was it not a good reason? Would you have asked your sons to do the same?

If I made that decision, to stay behind, I wouldn't expect help. I wouldn't trouble my children. I've lived a full life, but my children have not. A parent's life is built on what you can give your children. You think about Hnuhlee. I was only twenty-one years old and knew there could be still many more years. We old people don't say this because we are afraid to die alone, afraid no one will remember us, but duty has an end date. Your duty to me, whatever you think it might be, should not dictate your decision now that you have a daughter. From this day forward, do not think of me when you think of her. Always, Father's words sounded like commands, and to disobey him was to disrespect him. Like my in-laws, my parents offered to take my daughter, but again, I refused. Only later, when Hnuhlee was twelve, would Father's words enter my heart.

The morning they left for the airport in Bangkok, Father spoke to me as his daughter for the last time. You have such a hard heart. Good for a man, but you are my daughter, he said before turning away to board the bus. I did not know if he meant I was brave, which is one meaning, or stubborn and thick-skinned not to think of my daughter, which is another meaning. Even now, I think, he meant both. Even now, the last image I have of my husband is his back, and he is walking away from me. For a wife who knows her husband loves her still, that should never be her last image of him.

In 1984, alone in camp, I thought about America for a long time, then I borrowed a cassette player-recorder and, for my family, recorded a cassette. I told them I had decided to go back to Laos. I sent them my words but did not wait for their reply. I took six-year-old Hnuhlee and, in secret, muffling her protests with my hand, walked out of the refugee camp in Thailand and followed the Mekong till I came opposite the shore of Vientiane, and hired a boat to take us into the city. While we waited for the boat, she cried, said she wanted to stay behind. I told her to be quiet, otherwise the Thai border authorities will hear us, and who knows what they will do to a young mother and her daughter. Or the evil spirits will hear her cry, seek her out, and make her sick and die, so her soul could be theirs. Did she want to be away from her mother? I held her hand tighter than when I held my husband's before he left. Don't you want to see your father? I said. What father? she said. Her father had died a long time ago because that is what everyone told her. Those words hurt me as much as if she had said she hated me. Again, hurt me like my husband's suggesting I return to my family. To keep from slapping her, making her cry louder, I had to be strong. But I wanted to go back and find my husband, and whatever I needed to do, my daughter was to go with me, even if it meant I must drag her until her knees showed bones.

I first saw Mr. Cha from behind. He had just turned out of his courtyard and was walking with his sons down the road. I had learned of an empty hut on the outskirts of Vientiane, in Phonda-chet village. I believed it was a woman I was looking at because of the long yellow hair reaching below the shoulders, a woman whose figure was hardened by work and square-shouldered like a man's. The Laotian lady in the hut across the dirt road caught me staring and shouted, He is a single man, you know? Her dark legs, round and fat as gourds, stuck out from her shorts.

That is a man? I said, hot with embarrassment when she nod-ded. I suspected, then, there were empty huts elsewhere in the village, but was told to come here for a reason. No, I am too poor to keep a man, I said to the Laotian lady.

Make him support you, she said, raising her chin, twitching her brows, a smile on her face.

Support me living in this? I pointed to Mr. Cha's hut, then to the hut across the dirt alleyway, which was to be my own. Our huts were made of wood—some planks, some posts. To hold up the thatched roofing, a middle beam, supported by a pillar, ran its width. This pillar, always in the center of the hut, seemed to cut right down the living space, and was either useful to hang stuff on or always in the way when you were in a hurry. Around each hut, people blocked off a small courtyard with wood poles, a private place to chop wood and husk rice and pluck chickens and gut a pig and plant a small herb or flower garden.

What is wrong with this? the lady said, sweeping her hand from one direction to the other. Not good enough for you? She rested her hands on her round hips. She was stout and strong, and my bony frame shivered from the fear of crossing her. Behind her were two girls and a boy.

No, I said. That is not it. There were a small, black fat-belly sow and six-seven piglets in a pen in the corner of her courtyard, and four hairy dogs tied to a sturdy post in the far back, all on their feet, looking at me, their back hair standing, trying to decide if I was friend or not. I said, For me, this is perfect.

. . .

Vientiane, being closer to ocean level, the dust and pollen floated even more, drifting from all the mountain trees and plants. But when the sun was near overhead, you could not make them out well, just a far-off haze, their presence only noticed when sneezing, because too much collected inside of your nose, or turning black in the folds of your body. Other refugees in the village had told me that with good luck I might talk to Mr. Cha about a job at the rubber-tree farm where he worked. Here, it is not polite to knock on the doors of people you do not know, so you try to catch them out in the open. I had heard music coming from his house. One day, while he was chopping kindling in his courtyard under the shade of a thin peach tree, I walked over.

How are you? I said from the dirt alleyway, a few feet from the gate door.

He leaned his long-handled sickle against the peach tree and tucked his yellow hair behind his ears. How are you? he said, walking toward me. I hear you have a cassette player—I held out my cassette—and was wondering if I can listen to this? Just arrived, I lied. It was the first tape my family had sent me, the only one I kept, the one with everyone's voices.

From who? he said. Boyfriend in America? Despite the dark of his skin, I could see the veins wrapped around his limbs, bulging like the rough bark of the wood he was chopping; dirt lined his sweaty arms, crosshatched in threads beneath his throat, embedded into the callused knuckles of his hands. Dark and dirty as though just come from the soil.

Family in America, I corrected him. I held out five kip, my way of being polite, certain he would not accept, otherwise I would not have risked giving away fifteen percent of my money. Hnuhlee was standing in the doorway of our hut, where I had told her to wait.

Mr. Cha invited me into the courtyard and offered me a stump by the door. When he returned with his cassette player-recorder, he asked if I had used one before. I nodded. Don't press the red button or you'll record over your cassette. But let me—he snatched the cassette from my hand. The sharp snapping sounds froze my heart, flooding me with anger and fear. Had he ruined my cassette? Was he trying to silence the voices of my family? I may have even yelped like a dog. Women, he said, shaking his head. Using his little-finger nail, he had broken off the corner tabs. That snapping noise, it was like he broke a little part of me, he a stranger I had trusted enough to ask something of. He started again his wood chopping, and I looked over my cassette, then yelled for Hnuhlee to come over, and we listened to past voices and words, fixing them to memory.

A long feather-filled coat was one of the first things my family sent me. They say, Here in America we need this coat to give us warmth. It can be squeezed into the size of a melon, but when you let go, again it puffs big. When first I put it on, it reminded me of the last time my family held me in their arms. The coat is in my closet now. Hnuhlee asks why, always, do I put it on when it never gets cold here. But my daughter does not know when I feel my family's embrace I see their faces—my brothers' and sisters'; Mother's and Father's, too; always, the face of my husband. And when I do his face is blurred by my tears, and I feel his body, remember the tone of his words, and I know I have returned to familiar arms, familiar sounds.

When my family sends me packages from across the ocean, also they include a cassette to tell about life on that other side. Usually, Mother would begin by telling me the month, day, and year—eighth month, eleventh day, 1984—then she would tell me how everybody is doing. Father never speaks on these cassettes, and only when I spend the money to phone my parents, if lucky and he picks up, do I hear his voice, which, quick, tells me to call back or fades as it yells searching for Mother. For me to stay behind, I know it must mean for him he failed, and failure is best left unheard. The next speakers would be my three sisters, starting with the oldest and ending with the youngest. They would tell me what is happening with their own families and about my parents, which I take to be more true than what Mother had told me, but on this tape from 1984, everyone agrees America has been good to them, so far. Then, in whatever order the cassette was passed on to them, my sisters-in-law would come on; my three brothers, speaking after their wives, would try to change my mind on America. It is my daughter I need to think about! They yell their words like Father used to do. I yell only to teach was his explanation. If I am not yelling, I don't love you. From them, nothing was said about the reason I stayed behind.

On the other side of the cassette were the voices of my in-laws. Sometimes, in a word used by my father-in-law, the way he spoke it, I would hear my husband, and my heart would quicken to tear up my eyes, and I would grow afraid with envy that, already, he was there, in a better place, that he had not waited for me. When this happens, always I find myself on the verge of cursing him, to knock him down, yank him back to this lower place where, for him, I waited with life to see his face again.

Every woman who speaks on the cassette weeps because, whenever they speak to me, they are reminded of the time in the Thai refugee camp, and my return to our old life in Laos. They remember how the general told us the Americans were pulling out after coming, staging a war, then losing it, and how he warned everyone to leave before the communists, in their turn, came. The country was never taken nicely, always violently, with guns at your head and bombs from the sky, with voices commanding Stopstopstop, don't run! Only after you were shot dead, or were looking at your legs ten feet from your body, or worse, were ravaged and the bleeding after the pullout was never complete, to save you by taking you from this life. Always it left enough so you would live, the memory a gun to your head, its presence always a heat behind you, a voice saying, Go on, hurry! Go on and be quiet! My family, when they record their words, is reminded of this land that no longer has a place for them to live, not in flesh or name, not even in spirit, reminded only of the reddened soil. But always, they wish me well despite their yells, and each tells me how much money, if any, they had sent. Maybe they believe the person who sent the most loves me the most, but I know they are telling me only so I will remember who to repay when I see them again.

Last on the cassette would be Grandma Joua. Often, her words are funny, full of truths and hidden feelings about everyone, which make me wonder if, before sending, anyone listened to the cassette. Or, if so great was everyone's respect for her, they allowed her words to remain as spoken, afraid to curse themselves or her by erasing any part of her. When Grandma Joua started speaking, Mr. Cha wiped his brow with a forearm covered in wood chips and dust, and turned his ears toward the cassette player. Grandma Joua sounds like she is in front of me and speaking only to me, so Mr. Cha, stopping to listen, made me feel I was giving up a secret. Grandma Joua says she is healthy but lonely in this tape from 1984.

All of them there and they allow her to get lonely? Mr. Cha said.

Everyone's lonely for the old country, I said. How we used to be, where the ones you miss could be run to.

Grandma Joua ends her message with a plea for me to come to America because she believes, soon, she might die. You are the only one I helped into this world that's still there, she says. Everyone else is a phone call away, but you, I have to record this old, sad voice and wait for a reply. It's like drawing upon a secret well of memory that I happen upon only by chance, never having learned the way to get there. I go as an orphan child, naive and ignorant, no one to lead me, but hopeful the spirits will look after me. I know why you've stayed behind, but if my words could pull you here, carry you across oceans, let them.

After the cassette ended, I asked Mr. Cha if he knew Grandma Joua.

Everyone knows Grandma Joua, he said.

Do I know Grandma Joua? Hnuhlee said, leaning back and forth in between my legs, playing with the cassette case. Mr. Cha smiled as I shushed my daughter, whispering in her ear it was not yet her turn to speak. The smell of her hair reminded me we both needed to wash.

This is my luck to be a war widow with a daughter, I said.

I have worse luck, said Mr. Cha. I am a man with two sons. He would have to find the money for his sons to marry, because sons were expected to take care of their parents in old age. That was their hold on a parent—best you try to give your sons everything and then hope. Hope they do not kick you out of their house. Hope they let you eat the moistest parts of meals. Hope they marry a kind wife. Hope they will clean you when no longer you can. There, hope is, always in a time to come, a rainbow you can see with your eyes, yet never, in your time, find realized, reacting to your every move, eluding your advances, only to vanish in sight, phantom in its makeup. Because one second into the future—right now—a bomb could fall on us and we would be dead. Our houses smashed and burning. And that would be reality and no longer hope. Hope is not Mr. Cha's wife dying eight years earlier from what the Laotian doctor said was poison in the blood. Before her death, Mr. Cha said, the family lived okay, had a little meat to go with their vegetables at mealtimes. But now, they ate only rice mixed with cornmeal. Sometimes with fish paste or sugar.

It was true, Mr. Cha's duties to his sons, but I checked my feeling sorry for him. I had not much for myself and my daughter to be able to give away anything, even pity. I was born with my bad luck, I said. I told him when I was born that dark early morning in the fifth month of 1962 I was not breathing. Grandma Joua was the village medicine woman and had delivered many babies before. I came out blue, she said, the color of death. She kept it a secret from my mother, who, after she expelled me from her body, had rested her head on the rag pillow. All blue babies that had fallen into Grandma Joua's catch already were dead, but she could feel my heart. She wiped my face with the hem of her sarong, then covered my mouth and nose with her own mouth, and sucked strong and deep. After three or four mouthfuls, she breathed into my body, unfolded my life, and finally, I cried. I did not tell Mr. Cha the part where, now as a mother and knowing how it looks when a baby is born, I once asked Grandma Joua if she was disgusted with me. She said she had no time to think. It was something any mother would do for her child. This is something a man does not need to know. Because my mother almost gave birth to death, Grandma Joua has kept watch over me, even though she is not my grandmother by blood. She said she needs to know when, again, she will need to breathe life into me.

See, I wanted to add, almost I was not born alive. I do not know now whether I was seeking pity or sympathy then from Mr. Cha, or if war has a way of muddling them and they become one metal, a feeling forged in war fires, hard to separate; only, I know nothing did I want to feel for him. Again, I offered Mr. Cha the five kip, but he shook his head. What do you do if you don't need my money? I said.

He told me he cleared the forest and burned the stumps out of the ground. Soon, they would start planting more rubber trees, and after that, he guessed, many of the workers would be let go. When we are done, he said, the forest will look different. The trees will be in a straight line, with paths between to drive a truck through. Him already worrying about being let go, I did not ask him if he might help me get a job with the farm. Instead, we talked about his sons, who were thirteen and twelve. They were at the age when they could help bring in money, and by saving a little, when they were about twenty, they might have enough for a wife. But to pull them out of school was hard for Mr. Cha to do. I thought to tell him, if he pulled the boys, he could save the school fees to pay for their wives, but, in time, decisions like these make out themselves.

You are a woman, he said. You have better luck than me already. A man is good for four things in this world. Hunting, lifting heavy things, fathering babies, and fighting wars, I was good at all of those. But now, I do only heavy lifting. What is a man in this broken country?

Why didn't you go to America? I said. Why stay here?

I tell you a story, he said, and, like Father when he began his stories that way, I was afraid he would speak to me in man language so I would not catch the meaning. One time while hunting, I walked into a tiger. I was watching my steps when, suddenly, everything went quiet. I looked up. Its face was there, among the shadows of the jungle—shadow and sunlight, that's the face color of a tiger. You know what I did? I flipped my hair like this—he flipped his long hair over to cover his face—to look like a spirit. And the tiger disappeared. Didn't even hear it run away. His eyes were slits of smiles, as though he found his own words hard to believe, squinting to see now, as he was reliving it, if there might be anything else true he might have forgot, all these years and miles walked from that life memory.

Did tiger disappear or you disappear? I said, wondering what to make of his story.

Perhaps the man did, he said, laughing.

The man that was you? Or perhaps the tiger never was there? Because everyone, when they talk of being brave, talks always of meeting a tiger.

Tiger is always there, he said. The sky was falling away orange by this time, and the fading light dusted the trees a rusty color and our houses a cheap gold. Mr. Cha leaned against the peach tree, which made a second back for a tired body. I hear in America, you get meat to eat, and everybody says you don't have to work, and the government won't let you starve. You put your feet up like a king. But if everyone is a king, there is no king. Isn't that same as the communists? If so, why were we fighting them? Why go to America when I can put my feet up where my father and grandfather are buried?

Here, you'll starve.

Here, at least, I'll need to work not to starve. That's something, no? To know this life is separated from death by a day's labor. That gets you up in the morning. My father used to say, Labor is ambition at work. The ambition of a biting sickle is to have firewood, to build a house, to clear a forest for farming. If not for work, aren't we all just kings?

That is why you stayed? Because you don't want to put your feet up?

My toes will be up eventually, he said, sure of himself. He straightened his body from the tree, the sickle hanging from a hand. His front side, which faced the setting sun, caught a fiery glow. But his back side, I could see, was growing a long tail of shadow, as though something was draining out of him and pooling away, distance distorting the shape of what once could have been the hard edges of a man.

How will you do that? I said, wondering what he planned to do to become comfortable as a king and still keep the choice of work, wondering if he would let me join him.

Days later, Hnuhlee at her four-room school, I walked into Vientiane. I asked merchants and storekeepers if they had any cleaning work, went to the wealthier neighborhoods to see if someone needed a housekeeper, but most wanted only single live-in help. I was willing to cook and sell food by the side of the road, stick my hands in wood ash and pig fat to make soap, dig through the trash for metal to sell. Sometimes, I waited by the Buddhist temples and saved the food the monks shared. A grandfather with a toy car for a left foot told me he knew people who recovered bombshells for the metal. Did I want to do that? You look light on your feet, he said. You just *bop-bop*, his hand fluttering like a broken wing, over the fields and not end up like me. A bull giving you full warning, he wheeled his left foot forward and backward in place, humming *hrmmm-hrmmm* from that part in his chest where war life needs a taint of humor, and following the sound—a cry, a complaint, a protest—is a laugh, and you can go on. But I was afraid to start digging up the relics of war when so many remained unburied, else they might explode in my face. Who would take care of my Hnuhlee then? One good thing to come out of my search for work was two stray dogs, Bone and Skin, following me home, by the ropes I tied around their necks and would not let go.

Bone and Skin should be glad I saved them, too. Once, on a trip back from Muong Long, Vietnam, to visit family, Father and I stopped at a creek for a drink. On the opposite bank were an old Vietnamese man and maybe fourteen or fifteen dogs tied to trees around his hut. All were yelping and barking, their tails like a water buffalo's swatting flies. So loud, the cries, that after ten seconds, I wished for them to be silent. The old man untied a red dog, maybe thirty pounds, and stuffed it into a sack. The dog struggled against the sides like a baby pushing against the mother's belly. The old man carried over a block of metal—what I now know to be a half of a motorcycle engine. Quick my hands moved to cover my ears, maddened by the noise, still the dogs shaking their rumps, swooshing their tails. With a grunt, the man heaved the engine, now tied to the mouth of the sack, into the creek. The splash stopped my breath, and I thought I had gone deaf but realized, as I brought my hands away from my ears, the dogs were silent. Maybe it was only ten minutes, but, for me, a lifetime of wanting to hear a dog bark passed before the old man retrieved the sack. Only then did the remaining dogs start to whimper, circling at the ends of their ropes, curling into themselves, and hiding their faces. Father did not yell at me when I asked why the old man did that. Quietly, he said, For dinner.

I first ran into my friend Houa on one of these trips looking for work, surprised she had not gone to America. It's my husband's decision, she said. Stubborn like a mountain. Afraid Americans would chop him up, steal his insides, and eat him.

This, the same man that makes war, I said. She laughed like she could not believe it either. I told her where I was staying and my bad luck in finding work. War leaves no work for the living to do, I complained.

Sooner or later, she said, we all become orchid farmers.

Is there money in that? This was the first time I heard of growing and selling orchids.

Of course, she said. Next time you look for work, go deeper in the city. That's where they mostly are. Watch for the small signs that say, WHITE ORCHID FOR ACHE, RED SILK ORCHID, LOCUST-MANTIS ORCHID. A grin appeared on her face.

How do you start?

Maiker, she said, laughing. Don't get too heartened. I'm speaking like a man to you—I know you could never do it. I felt naive next to my friend, who, from somewhere, seemed to have picked up the man tongue. Had she put a dare to me? She reminded me that I was my parents' laziest daughter and had escaped working out in the fields; that no food was ever gotten on my back. Which was true. While everyone was out farming, I did housework, and looked after the children, and massaged the pains of the broken elders in the village. So, yes, I did not know how good I would do to get my hands dirty. I had no knowledge of growing anything. Mother had said once, trying to teach me, there are some plants that do not even produce seeds. A drip of water, after hitting the leaf of such a plant and landing in the soil, could grow into that plant. Just that one miracle drop of water! Or some seeds refused to grow unless they were planted right next to the mother plant;

only the soil of the mother plant was good enough for the seeds. That is how stubborn and sensitive some seeds are!

Do you know how to grow orchids? I said, hoping that orchids did not spring from miracle water, that even a woman like me could raise them.

Maiker has lost her mind, Houa said, giggling now, like we were ten and secretly had learned something of our parents. Why was she laughing at me? Embarrassed, I told her it was getting close to time for me to pick up Hnuhlee from school. You better hurry then. Before you regret staying here too long. She turned me by the shoulder in the direction of my daughter's school and nudged me away. Go on, before she's lost to you!

A month into the dry season, but the lingering humidity left water everywhere truck tires had carved into soft earth, where motor-cycle tires were too thin for the weight they carried. To remain presentable while looking for work, always you must keep one eye on the ground, one eye on the road ahead, because, sometimes, the cleanest way forward means veering to the other side of the road; always your hands clutching and lifting your sarong to keep the hem from getting dirty, or enough to free your legs to jump over a muddy puddle. I was most jealous of the Laotian lady and her shorts on these days.

Three weeks into our lives in Phondachet, still without work, I picked up Hnuhlee and told her teacher I might have to pull her out of school. Hnuhlee looked at me, widened eyes and opened mouth, as though she was hollow—all hope cut down and burned, and her spirit abandoned her body, leaving only a skin shell. Those words in my voice and my daughter's emptiness convinced me, as mother, I was failing.

Not even a month yet, her teacher said. How is she to learn? He pulled me away from Hnuhlee. She is a good student, he said quiet into my ear, still holding my arm. You must do whatever you can to keep her in school. Warm were his words. I told him I had asked around for work until my throat was so parched I almost fell to my knees to drink water from a roadside puddle like some animal. Then consider becoming an orchid seller, he said. To convince me, he nodded his approval, proud of his suggestion as teacher, as someone with knowledge. I will buy from you, he said.

But to hear a strange man say those words suddenly made them mean something different: man language was made of words a woman should not question or dispute, but needed only to follow, give in to, act upon. If I hesitated and waited, I knew, he would think I was considering it. I snatched Hnuhlee's hand and hurried away. Most, though, I wanted to spit at his feet, call him dogface, tell him to die, but I did not want Hnuhlee to know something was wrong. To swallow down those words was hard—they hooked on my tongue, swelled heavy on my chest, smothering me.

Am I not coming back? Hnuhlee said.

New school, I said, keeping my words short to hide the shake in my voice. New teacher. Better school. Smarter teacher! You will be a better girl when you finish this school. School fee was paid to the end of the month, but I tried not to think of the lost days and wasted money. Else, I might turn beggar and allow her teacher to see me in my place.

I already have two friends, Hnuhlee said.

I handed her the red-bean bun the monks had given me. Eat this and be quiet.

Her teeth, she tore at the plastic wrapping of the bun while her little feet tried to keep up. You want me to save a little for Bone and Skin? she said. After the dogs followed me home, I had tied them to a post in our courtyard. At the same times each morning and night, I fed them what Hnuhlee and I could spare. I told her to go ahead and finish the bun, pulled on her arm, walking faster, not looking back. Never. After swallowing the last bite, she told me she needed water.

Swallow your spit. Unless you want to drink my piss.

I *really* need water, she said. You made me eat too fast. She started to hiccup, and I feared she would choke and die on me—and what type of mother would I be, then, if I let my daughter die in front of me?—so I hit her on the back three times. I dragged her toward the house, hopping over the muddy tire ruts, lifting her arm so she, too, would jump, as though mother bird teaching baby bird to fly, and Hnuhlee started to cry. The running only worsened her need for water, I knew, but, quick, we needed to get far away, get home. As last option, I decided to collect my spit in my mouth for her to drink. In that moment, though now it seems unclean, it felt natural that what came from my body would nourish hers, spit included, but the running allowed no spit to collect. Suddenly, Hnuhlee stopped and slipped out of my hand, gasping for breath like being pulled underwater, or squeezing her tiny body was a snake. I snatched her up in my arms to carry—but, oh, how she had grown in the few weeks we had been here—and I tumbled over. She staggered to her feet, looking at me like I was a man attempting to kidnap her to be my bride, and ran from me. To watch her escape, my seat on the ground, my sarong muddied—how fast she ran, I was hopeful.

When, finally, I caught up to her, we almost were home, but still she struggled to push down the food, and after hitting her three more times on the back, I looked up and saw the Laotian lady judging me from the open gate of her courtyard.

What she do that was so bad? she said.

She needs water, I said.

And you hit her?

I'm her mother, I said. I'm helping her.

By hitting her cause she thirsty? She called for her son to bring her a bowl of water.

As Hnuhlee tilted it to drink, the bowl caught a few of her tears. That sadness flushed into my belly and settled there, and I knew, then, orchids were raised on the backs and tears of women. I turned away from the Laotian lady and her fat body because I had no high seat in my life to argue from, and the thought of how she had put it shamed me. Even my body had failed to provide Hnuhlee the thing she needed.

Later in the evening, there were knocks on my courtyard gate. It was rude of the stranger, and at this time of night? Already, did a rumor get out that I was selling orchids? Bone and Skin disappointed me with their silence.

Husband said tomorrow you go fishing with me, the Laotian lady said, standing by my gate. Wake up early. There is plenty water on the river. She grinned, and again, I felt such shame, that grin a weight sinking me to live with the catfish and stingray. I nodded, though I was terrified of water. Because I am a woman, I never learned to swim; fishing was a man's job. To escape the communists when we crossed the Mekong into Thailand, I had convinced my husband to hire a small boat for us. I knew many people who died in the river when they tried to swim it. But since I took my daughter back to Laos, I had no other choice.

To Hnuhlee early the next morning, I said, You must wait until I can afford a new school. Work on what you have learned so far. Don't go outside. Do not open the door for anyone. This, you must do for me. Understand? I let my dear dogs loose in the courtyard, hoping on my return, still they would be there, waiting for me by the door to be fed.

On the new cassette, Mother says it is the tenth month, fourteenth day of 1985. She tells me they buy clothing in big black plastic bags from the thrift store for twenty-five cents each without knowing what is inside—they like the surprise and disappointment. For only twenty-five cents, they throw the disappointments away, or use them as rags and towels to wipe their feet with. Father is 182 pounds and one of my sisters has a new baby boy. Because of the baby, everyone says they have not much to send, but please do not think they do not love me with only ten dollars from each.

Grandma Joua says her son is in his second year at the university, but she sends twenty dollars because she wants my Hnuhlee to stay in school. Again, they yell at me for leaving the refugee camp. Stupid, they say. I should have stayed, so at least, still I would be allowed to come. But America had probably made them forget how, in the refugee camp, you could not even make a life like a maggot in waste. There are other ways to cross the ocean, they say. Think about yourself. Where will you live when Hnuhlee marries? Who will take you in? Still you are young, you could try to have sons here. But I did not want a man to tell my Hnuhlee she was to get married, have children, and not go to school, always to wear a sarong that would keep her legs close and never allow her a full stride when she needs to run. She would be disappointed in me, more so because I had dragged her back to wait for her father. She was to wear shorts and pants, if she wanted, to match strides with men, that way she would not fall behind, she would not keep them waiting; and should she err in her journey, an unfettered sidestep could right her way, an about-face would not trip her up; she was not to be like me.

Mr. Cha lost his job with the tree farm while I had good work as a fisherwoman. The Laotian lady, who told me her name was Keth-avong, and her husband owned two boats, long and only wide as a tree but with a five-HP motor attached to each. After seeing me hit my daughter that day, Mrs. Kethavong said she convinced her husband to let me help.

How did you convince your husband? I asked on the first day as we got into the boat.

We have two boats, she said. More boats, more fish, more money. Even my husband is smart enough to know that. Mrs. Kethavong and I worked one boat, her husband worked the other.

Thank you, I said. What to say to someone who might have saved your life? The first three months, I went out with an old inner tube tied to me. After making some money, I bought a small air vest. That vest protected me from causing a tidal wave of bad luck if I fell in the water. To think one wrong shift of your body is all it takes, it is a wonder how small things keep safe a life: Mrs. Kethavong's offer for me to help fish; the air vest, which would save my life so I could make my daughter's life, which, as it is doing now, is providing life for the child in her belly.

You work hard. That is all I ask, Mrs. Kethavong said. We trolled the wood boat out to the deeper, calmer breaks—this river is not the Mekong but a smaller river that brings water from a mountain lake to the Mekong, so when it is raining the water can be fast. Also, a wife has other ways of convincing her husband. Mrs. Kethavong stood up in the narrow boat, shifted her solid thighs from side to side like a dancer, upsetting the boat until I thought we were going to capsize and drown. She laughed loud at the fear on my face. Don't pretend you don't know what I am talking about, she said.

I am not pretending, I wanted to tell her. I could not remember many of the ways a wife can convince her husband.

Mrs. Kethavong and I dropped four nets and pulled them up every two hours. Usually, one net, we catch only seven or eight fish. Once, on our lucky day, forty-two fish. At two in the afternoon, if our catch was low, I hauled the fish in a cart to her sister's booth in the marketplace while Mrs. Kethavong and her husband continued fishing in one boat until nightfall. If we catch many fish, two or sometimes all of us will take the fish to market. What fish remained after three days on ice would be brought home and smoke-dried. The Kethavongs would give me a little to keep, and we would take the rest back to the sister's to sell.

One day, as we waited for the hour to come before we pulled in the nets, Mrs. Kethavong asked me why I have not remarried—I am still young, I have left a little beauty.

I said, I'm holding out for a rich Hmong-American. She laughed and shook her head, said that I was smart to do so, but she knew I was lying and only was giving me space. What can I do? I said. Already, I am married.

Yes, Mrs. Kethavong said. A lifetime ago.

No, this lifetime. But I knew what she meant—war makes a lifetime of a year. My marriage was a marriage of waiting. In 1985, my husband and I had been married for ten years, but we were together, I counted, only thirty-nine months. We made a life between the times he was away at war and when he found his way home, and always, he remembered to hide his gun in the jungle so no one would suspect he was a soldier. I was used to life without him, but always, I expected he would return and we would continue as husband and wife. I never told my husband I loved him, and he never told me. Wrong ears hung like leaves in the forest, and your words might give you away, so tenderly, my husband and I tried to treat each other, not be so rough when we talked. When we were together, we tried to be happy. That was enough. To Mrs. Kethavong, I said, What if I remarry, and he comes back? If I were a man, that would be okay, I could have more than one wife, but I was born a woman. And the thought of remarrying could never be on my mind.

I put Hnuhlee in the school of the three Kethavong children, deeper into Vientiane and more expensive, but there, they taught the students English.

Mr. Cha's sons started trading labor for money with the farmers in the countryside, and sometimes, he joined them. They were fed a handful of rice at lunchtime. Mr. Cha refused to ask his sons for their earnings to help with expenses. If they have need for money, he explained, they have in mind already what they're going to spend it on. Mr. Cha's hair was long to his waist by this time. When there was not enough work for father and sons, Mr. Cha would let his sons work, and he would walk to Vientiane, as I had the year before, looking for work.

One day, Mr. Cha returned with his gold hair muddied, nose bloodied and crooked, and lip fat and swollen as a sow's teat. This time I wasn't quick enough, he said. I plowed over a grandmother pulling a cart of vegetables—wincing as he pressed his bottom lip with his thumb and finger—and stopped to help her. I never imagined I would become a thief. He rubbed the bruise reddening along his right temple to the corner of his mouth. I steal only food. Nothing else. He was staring off behind me, but I knew he could not see anything in the distance. I let the cook beat me up afterward.

While I gathered a bowl of water and towel, he came into my courtyard and, kicking out his legs, sat on a stool. The five black hens I had managed to buy flapped their wings, could not get away fast enough from him. Up, I said, tapping the bottom of his chin. He leaned back, tilted his head. Since my husband left to find his parents, this was the closest I had come to a man. Strong on his warm body was the smell of salt and wood. I wiped away the dirt on the side of his face and saw, clearer, the bruise. The pain was blackening like a disease in his skin. His eyes were light brown, the color of green tea. To look into them made me uncomfortable, but I wanted to look because they were so different, and knowing this—that I wanted to look—made me shy and want to smile.

Close your eyes, I told him.

What for? he said.

So I can see your face better.

What about me? Then I can't see.

Close them, I said, impatient, a tone rarely used with my husband. There is nothing to see. I ran the towel across his eyes so he would close them.

What if I can't see and my hand happens to do this— His hand reached out and grabbed my outer thigh, and my body flinched, a lasting reaction from the war to gunshots and explosions, to loud foreign voices telling you to stop, a body gathering itself one last time before being hurt.

Stop it, dogface! I ground the towel into his lip. His hands shot up to grab my wrist, still my hands. That happens when you don't respect me. You get hurt. I pulled my arm away; faster were my heart and breathing. He opened his eyes to look at me, to see how my face was, to see if maybe I might be smiling, but I held still my face. The pain had put tears in his eyes, and I felt bad about what I had done, about how I was seeing this man cry. Close them, I said, and made my fingers into a fork to pretend to blind him until he lidded his eyes from my sight. With one hand, I cupped the side of his face gently. His skin was cooling from the water, and I was reminded of how I held my husband's face that last night. With the other hand, I pressed the towel into Mr. Cha's face firmly, so he would not notice how my other hand was holding him.

This is good pain, he said as I poured water down his hair, which I had untangled. Reminds me of the pain in the war when my feet were rotting with blisters, my shoulders ached from a pack full of rice, ammo, and water—all a man needs in life. You risk getting your foot stuck in a hole or rolling an ankle over a root. In war, to survive, you must be willing to do what the enemy is not. And sometimes that means going blindly into a thicket to sleep. And always you slept on the most uncomfortable ground because, there, the enemy rarely looks. War made for a tough life, but I felt like a man. This pain reminds me of that life.

I thought stealing didn't make you feel like a man, I said, squeezing my hands down his hair, which was softer when dirty than mine was when clean, this long hair, he told me once, his mother said never to cut because it was the only golden thing she could give him.

But this pain does.

Those who think like you are few. I handed him a torn and fraying towel. This isn't the cleanest. But you need to bathe before you can get a cleaner one.

I haven't complained, he said. He dried off his hair, wrung out the towel, and hung it over the top rail of my fence.

Since you are a thief now, I said before he left, go steal me a rooster. Recently, I had started letting my hens out of the courtyard when I was home so they could be covered by a neighbor's wandering rooster, but no luck yet. I will give you eggs to start a flock. Maybe it will help you steal less. Unless you like getting beat up and washed by a woman.

By 1990, about once a week, I would drop off a bag of four or five dried fish for Mr. Cha and his sons. He said to me one day, It's a good thing my wife died when she did. War makes you glad your loved ones are dead.

Only a man would say such a thing, I said. Only thinking about himself. I reminded him of his sons, how they needed their mother, even though they were poor, as Hnuhlee needed her father.

All these women making money now, he said, shaking his head, breathing loud a sigh. What's left to remind me that I'm a man? I can't find work. I am nothing. My usefulness slowly erased. But these women—cash in their waistbands, stuffed into their bras— they have so many ideas about life. New ideas, too. Even bossing their husbands around.

How would you know? I said.

Maiker, he said, looking down at his hands, again shaking his head. A dead wife is more demanding than a living one. He searched my face to see if I agreed with him. Now you can't even raise your hand to them. It's like, you raise it and it's frozen there, never coming down, never satisfying you for just that moment when it strikes her face. Every time a man raises his hand to his wife now, he is reminded of his own weakness. Every time he has to bring that hand down, it's with such shame to know he's powerless. Sometimes, you have to pretend you were only scratching your head so the bitch doesn't see you are incapable of it.

You want me to take back the fish? I reached for the bag I had placed on the small table in his house.

My sons wouldn't want that, he said.

Right, I said. Your sons wouldn't want that.

It was only morning, but he yawned, thinking about the long day ahead, groaned as he stretched like a man being pulled apart by horses, then scratched the top of his head before combing his hair with his fingers and tucking it behind his ears. I asked if I could use his cassette player-recorder, and he pointed to the pillar where it hung on a nail.

Does that work? he said at my back as I went to grab it. His question confused me. How much can you get from them?

I never ask for money, I said.

So that is how you do it. He nodded as though he had just come upon something that, all these years, had escaped him. Maybe it works because you are a woman—your sweet woman voice.

Mostly, the money, it is from my in-laws, I said. I think it is because of guilt.

A woman is a good cause for guilt, he said. Haven't I said that?

I'm no one's guilt, I said. Their missing son is their guilt.

I listened to the words on the cassette from two months earlier one final time. On the tape, Grandma Joua speaks of her son. He brought her so much shame in America, how he had run off with a girl. Mr. Cha shook his head when he heard this, saddened to learn America was teaching children to abandon their parents. What next, he wanted to know, parents will stop claiming their own children? Grandma Joua weeps, telling me this, and I could see the tears following the deep creases on her face. If tears could fill and smooth, all war women would have skin like a worn river stone; age and heartache would only affect them in spirit. Her husband, too, had left for war and never come back. Then, I did not know why, because of the tears maybe, Grandma Joua starts speaking fast, and it sounds like a different language altogether. This fast talk scared me.

What's she saying? Mr. Cha said.

I rewound the cassette twice before I caught on, as if shame, if ever it must be spoken, should be spoken fast so you can get through the telling of it. She regrets her own failure, I said to Mr. Cha.

The son running off?

You don't know? I said. Worse. Maybe.

I haven't seen Grandma Joua in a long time, he said. Not since my wedding.

I told him Grandma Joua wonders, on the cassette, if her life would be different. Would her daughter, if she were alive, have loved her more? And remained by her side, unlike the son.

I didn't know she had a daughter, Mr. Cha said.

I paused the tape and told him what Grandma Joua had told Mother and Father one day in Ban Vinai about the night in 1972 when she fled Long Chieng into the jungle with the Lee, Her, and Vang families. By then, she had lived there eight years after fleeing Fi Kha. Afraid Long Chieng soon would fall, it was safer, they decided, to wait out the war in the jungle or slowly try to cross into Thailand. When she walked away from the group to use the bathroom in the bush, she was captured and beaten. This, only the second night they were in the jungle. The dark was blinding, Grandma Joua said. She only remembers the stink of the man's breath, like sour milk, before she passed out. She did not scream for the others because she feared drawing them into an ambush. After that, the families hid during the day and moved only at night. When Grandma Joua gave birth months later, still they were in the jungle. They had run back and forth in the dark, then decided to get into Thailand but had gotten lost, and then wandered the long way down the country. Because the baby girl cried a lot those first two months, Grandma Joua used opium to quiet her, but had to leave the baby in the jungle. She needed to save her son.

That's the war, Mr. Cha said. We never knew the true faces hurting us. They hid in the dark, in the shadows. Sometimes they were the same faces you saw many times a day—you just didn't know. But I'd kill that guy if I knew.

Maiker, Grandma Joua says on the cassette before it ended, I keep all your cassettes because I am the last one to get them and no one else wants them. I listen to them when I am lonely for the voices of the old country.

I knew I, too, should save their cassettes, but I could not spare the money for even one cassette, and each time I erased their words and covered them with my own, I knew I was replacing causes for happiness—their voices, their love, their tears—with my complaints of a tough life in Laos. If I cried during a recording, always I made sure to muffle the sound. On the cassette I sent in 1990, I told my family that a few of those who left for America are now returning for a visit. In all of the world, I heard the visitors saying, the orchids of Laos are the best. And all around Vientiane now, orchids of all colors and fragrances are sold. *Orchids from Pha Thi. Centipede's Back Orchid. Orchid of Village 52. Cut Vein Orchid.* Many whites are also visiting Laos for the orchids, and they bring with them the green paper that can flip the communist mind. But Mr. Cha believed the communists are more accepting because the whites are not here to take over like before.

The orchid collectors are slowly starting to come out of Vientiane and into Phondachet, I said into the recorder. You see young whites as often as the old, and most do not look wealthy. The war widows, mothers, grandmothers, some wives, and even the young teenagers who are pushed by their parents to learn the business because it promised food—all who sell orchids now make more money than any man could make, despite some orchids' fetching only two thousand kip, about three American dollars, because there are so many sellers. But many survive only on what the orchids provide.

I said the Hmong collectors come dressed in creased pants, shirts with ties, gold watches. If they come around to our houses, trying to see who might have orchids, Mrs. Kethavong and I would untie our dogs. Collectors are scared of Mrs. Kethavong's four dogs because her husband uses them for pig hunting. Sometimes, the men would say okay, okay, they are hungry for fish to calm us down, and we would tie up the dogs and sell the men fish and charge them more. Always, they pay with cash that they take out of their back pocket, a fold in middle of the money so it looks more than it is. They smile when we look at the money, and ask where they might find the orchids no other collector has found yet. They would say, We take to show our wives back home. That is sometimes true because some collectors like to show off the orchids in front of their wives, to stab them with jealousy over getting to own such beautiful flowers, and oftentimes, they would breed them, the different orchids, but all are liars, I know.

I did not tell my family often Hnuhlee would ask why we could not go to America, since everyone who came back carried so much money. Nor did I mention the time she refused to go steam rice inside the house when I asked, forcing me to shove her and slam the door, latching it from the outside, while Bone and Skin ran to bark at three men approaching our house. After the men were gone, Hnuhlee said she only wanted to see their thick fold of American dollars—some girls at school had said always the collectors came with it. What is the wrong in that? Why can't we go to America? She was twelve and had recently started carrying around the clothes of women. A lot is the wrong in that, I wanted her to know, but did not say.

When I finished recording my words, I called for Hnuhlee to come and say a few of her own. Always, she said the same things, the same words I taught her when she was young and unsure of her own heart to know what to say: This is Hnuhlee, daughter of Yee and Maiker Pha. It has been a long time since I talked to you. I hope everyone is living well. We are okay, just the two of us, by ourselves, waiting for Pa, over here, after you left. Pa has not returned, but soon, we believe. I do not know what I will do when I see him. I do not know if he will remember me, or if I will know him. I am in year seven of school and would like to study English to be a translator, so when you visit I can talk to you in your language. I can read and write in English some, but I speak it slow. If we have just a bit more money, maybe I can make it to the next year. Maybe if I am lucky.

These, the only times my daughter said her father's name.

On the cassette from 1993, voices tell me to keep Hnuhlee away from the orchid collectors. Grandma Joua says evil spirits mostly like to steal the souls of young girls, and starts listing fifteen to twenty girls that died young, as though, always, they have been on her mind all these years—Phoua, Panyia, Gaosheng, Maizong—then this: Evil is everywhere even here in America, a man has arrived not too long here, why couldn't he have been buried in the old country because evil is at home in both countries, it can cross back and forth, it carries two faces, listen carefully, the truth is in and around their words, in that space their words carry many meanings, listen to what they don't say, go on, listen to me, remember what— On this cassette, before Grandma Joua can reach the last of her words, a girl's faint voice can be heard: Stop speaking like that, Grandma Joua. Tell me what it is. It is not good to frighten people. Just tell me. That young voice, still I hear it, those words seeking, as if, knowing, it alone could set right the world, there in America with both parents at the door.

That was the year Mr. Cha's oldest son, Bee, twenty-one, which was old to be without a wife, went to the Harvest Festival and kept another man's daughter too late. When Bee walked the girl home, the man asked him for his father's name. To keep her so late, did Bee intend to marry his daughter? Bee said sure, he would like to marry her, but he had no money, and they only were talking. But really, you do not know with children—they have their ways, like adults have theirs. The man went to the clan elders of the village, who settled disputes, righted wrongs, and restored honor. They determined that $75, about 55,000 kip that year, was the fine to be paid for soiling the girl and bringing shame to her father's name if Bee failed to marry her. For marriage, the father requested a bride price of $2,050. If Mr. Cha and Bee refused both choices, the father threatened to go to the Laotian authorities and say Bee had raped his daughter. The man could promise a little handout if they threw Bee in jail and knocked him around, as a lesson and to convince him to pay. Or if Mr. Cha was wealthy, he could pay off the authorities—and the clan elders—and have the problem gone, but that would cost more than the $75 fine because each authority and clan elder has more than two hands.

Mr. Cha asked what should he do, and I said did the children want to get married? The girl was a little shorter than I like, with dark skin. Her figure was delicate—narrow hips, thin legs, small breasts—I feared their children would go hungry. But she was a good speaker, respectful to the elders, and patient with everyone; in another world, she would make a good judge. I told him to pay the bride price. Why waste the money?

I'll ask for two years to come up with the money, Mr. Cha said. With father and sons working and a daughter-in-law taking care of things at home, or even herself working, they might need four years to pay it off, I thought.

Come up with half, I said. That might buy you more time.

Mr. Cha thought this over, but of course, for him, already the decision was made—only he was shifting numbers to see what was possible and not possible, and even in his mind, as it was in mine, his math did not show the possibility of coming up with half. Still, to marry the girl was the money-saving and honorable thing to do.

In one year, they were able to pay $620. Mr. Cha was confident, since they had been good to his daughter, the man would see they were decent, hardworking people, not slave owners who only wanted a water buffalo and brood sow. But just as Mr. Cha was feeling hopeful, after the man assured him there was no hurry, that Mr. Cha's name and promise were honorable, the son curse hit again. The younger son, Say, was caught being husband-and-wife with his sweetheart along the path that snaked into the jungle. At night, the girl had snuck out of the house under Say's urgings. The only daughter of a family with four sons, she was more expensive than Bee's wife. And unlike Bee, who met his wife at the festival and maybe a little too long into the night talked with her, openly Say and his sweetheart had courted for ten months. But rare are the marriages for love, even now. The father of Say's girl did not bother with the clan elders before setting a bride price of $6,500—so high that even Hmong-American men would not pay—though some people in the village said the father, knowing Mr. Cha could not afford much, had a good heart to fine them only $20 to restore his name. Say loved this girl, argued that whatever and however long it took he would come up with the money. But Mr. Cha said they could not afford it just then, maybe if he had waited four or five years. But that is men: when they want something, immediately they must have. All orchid collectors are like that. Worse, also, because men think parental love is a competition. So what one son gets, the other, too, must get. Else that means the parents do not love them equal. This time, though, while Say was off trading labor, Mr. Cha walked over and paid the fine to the girl's father.

One day not long after, the girl, Maida, came home and saw an orchid collector sitting with her parents inside their house. They told her the man was there to buy her orchids. He had heard she possessed the rare Eggplant Petal orchids, which resembled purple butterfly wings with a fiery floret between, but more valuable than the look was that her orchids could cure low energy and fatigue. She ran over to Mr. Cha's house, but they refused to let her through the courtyard gate; they feared being fined again. And like an innocent prisoner looking for a way, she shook the gate until it almost broke, then, knowing a woman in a sarong should never climb a fence to be loved by just a man, she walked over to our house when she saw Hnuhlee out in our courtyard staring. Maida was fourteen and had a good figure. She was tall, with a solid, wide frame to have babies easily and endure the many labors of a countrywoman. She told Hnuhlee she did not raise her orchids to sell to a Hmong-American man. She wanted only Say to have them, the man she loved.

What do you think, Ma? Hnuhlee asked. Would you do that? *Oy!* She and Maida walked into the house where I was poaching fish. I wanted to pinch her lips, teach her about saying things and asking questions at the wrong time. Instead, I said, Absolutely not. Maida is strong to love like that.

Only you two see only two ways in the world.

How many ways are there? I said, because there *are* only two ways in the world. The right. And all the wrongs. Hnuhlee was fifteen, and already believed she knew enough to survive without me. Her family isn't starving! I said. Is your family starving? I did not wait for Maida's answer because I knew enough about them. Her parents just want new things! Maida should get to choose who she loves! Who she wants to be with!

Hnuhlee turned away from me and Maida, and started walking out of the house. Why are you yelling at me? she said.

Your father wouldn't ask you to do that! Which, I was sure, was the truth. Sometimes it is okay to go hungry!

He can't ask me if he's not here, she mumbled, her back to me, but clear across the threshold, I heard her.

It's okay to go hungry, Maida, I said.

Later, Maida refused to go home when I urged her. Afraid Mr. Cha again would be fined, I walked to her house and told her parents she was in my home. That was when I saw the ugly man, who was more than fifty. Short, with three gold teeth, a big mole on his bald head. Some faces—how do I explain this—bring to mind certain things. Seeing this man, I wondered what Grandma Joua might have done to her daughter. These things about the world made me wonder why Hnuhlee's father, my husband, would keep away.

I fed Maida for two days before, by the hair, she was dragged home by her mother. Her parents had a new stove and bed. The man sat on a new armchair. Maida ran behind the curtain that made for her a private area in their small house and refused to speak to the man. So you have decided to watch your father *and* mother *and* brothers go hungry? her mother said. Remember, you're not the only person in this house! Remember whose hands you ate from all these years! To let Maida decide, her parents took the man to visit some of his distant family in another part of Vientiane: they hoped it would not come to them tying her down; they hoped it would be done by her will.

If she stayed, Maida knew, the man would have her orchids by morning. She wrote a letter, grabbed a paring knife, and walked past her brothers, who were keeping watch. Go on then! said the oldest brother, who was twenty-three years, raising his hands and backing away. From this day forward, this is no longer your home, we are no longer bound by name. I curse your oil-blood will no longer light your way to our people. The youngest brother, seven years, who would recount this to me years later, ran up to her, wondered if he could come with her. When she shook her head, he said, Be a good person, Mai. Go on before Mother and Father get home. Maida bit her lips and nodded and walked out of the house into the time at dusk when the shapes of people, still, you could make out, even as their details faded—the sharpness of their nose and eyes, the locations of scars and moles, the curve of the mouth in feeling; they were not altogether disappearing, but night was only exposing their shapes as hollow spaces in the world where they—their dreams for the future, the history of their love, their desire for life—had once been.

She gave the letter to Hnuhlee to give to Say. When Maida turned to go, she saw Say's figure standing in the doorway of his house. But it turned away because her parents had sent word to Mr. Cha that there was an owner of her orchids now. No one was to touch her. Maida yelled that he was a weak boy. Why wasn't he fighting for her? Wasn't he a man? But too young was she to know the war had taken our best men and left us only boys. And these poor farming boys, they could never hope to win fights against orchid collectors.

In a country where many had very little and love is still the one thing left of your own that you can give someone else, it was Say taking back his love from Maida, I am sure, that drove her to the river, because when you are poor, there is much honor to receiving someone's love. There at the river, Maida cut the lifeline of her orchids, slashing at the roots, and threw them in. As they floated away, she held on to them.

The cassette from 1995 contained only two voices. Mother says the Lee family, who takes care of Grandma Joua, has shut her in one room of the house. A sickness has left her with little energy to stand or walk. Grandma Joua's white hair has been cut short like a man's—they claim it is easier to clean. She is losing her mind, Mother says, screaming awful stuff about everyone. About her past. About her husband. Her son. For being an orphan. For being abandoned. Her memory, too, is fading and, with it, the right words. Grandma Joua, that fast voice, speaks even when nobody is near, like she is speaking to spirits. Mother says she tells everyone they should forgive Grandma Joua because she is old, and no more does she know what is right and what is wrong, what is real and what is past.

But when I reached Grandma Joua's section of the cassette, she says she has not been cursing anyone. She has chased away old spirits by accepting the words of the Bible, and only she is speaking to God. And no one visits her anymore. The Lees lock her in a room because they do not want to hear the Truth. They call her crazy. But I got no sense of that as I listened to her voice. She sounds as she did back when I was twelve. Her loud breathing, as she speaks her words, is strong as my pulse. Grandma Joua says only one person in the world cares for her now, the Lees' only daughter, but she is growing up, growing old, and soon will be gone, she is afraid, from her life.

The heart, use it enough, it thickens over. Same as your hands and feet, grows tough. And accepts new love, holds it without feeling pain. In the spring of 1996, Say found a new sweetheart. This time, I will kill myself, he said. By then, Mr. Cha had found a job driving a motorcycle cab. Mainly, his customers were orchid collectors seeking the untouched orchids of the remote countryside. It bothered him because he knew the countryside growers did not want always to sell, but sometimes, too much was the money. Quietly, some who did sell asked for buyers from Mr. Cha, and they would tip him if the collectors were generous. Sometimes, the buyers also tipped Mr. Cha if he led them to good orchids. But his savings was not enough to pay for Say's bride, whose price was $4,300—her father refusing to accept anything but full payment—though Bee's wife was finally paid for.

One early evening in the seventh month, Mr. Cha brought over his cassette player-recorder. He had heard I had received a cassette from America. I went to my corner of the house and searched in my bag for the cassette. When I came back, he was crying.

Who passed away? I said, because rarely men allow you to see them weep, except for the dead. Tears dripped down his bony cheek and collected into bigger drops at his chin.

When he caught his breath, he told me he had just made $400. I was so happy for him I, too, started crying—I did not make $400 in two years! I was glad these were tears of happiness. But I was curious, and because he was a man you do not give space to, nosy me said, Made, found, or stole? No person I knew made $400 in a day.

Made, he said. I earned it. He told me two whites, their hair the color of rice chaff, hired him to drive them into the countryside. Were they looking for orchids?

Please just show us the beauties of your country.

Opium? Heroin?

Keep driving, they said, fast. Get us a wind to cut this heat.

Far into the countryside, they asked him to pull over at a roadside grill stand. They requested he join them and bought him lunch. Afterward, they wanted to visit the Emerald Buddha temple in town, near Rue Labeottadok.

Where did you get your yellow hair from—is your grandfather white?

No, no, Mr. Cha said. We have yellow hair, too, going back hundreds and hundreds of years. He told them the story of a Hmong warrior who fought the Chinese. So courageous was he in battle, the ancestors' spirits rewarded him with gold hair. For however long you live, may gold grow on your head. Strange, I thought, because I did not recall hearing that story from my parents or grandparents when I asked about the yellow-haired Hmongs—always, their looks warning me I wanted too many answers. So I wondered if Mr. Cha had created a story because he was ashamed of his hair, this need for a glorious past so, without shame, he could live life in the present. As though life goes on only by one courageous act or decision, followed by another act, another decision. And on and on, allowing him to say, I got here because all these things happened exactly this way, and only this way. We are the seeds of the spirits, Father had said about beginnings. Only gods have no seeds.

Mr. Cha said one of the two men—the skinny, tall one—touched his hair. Then the other—older and balding—held Mr. Cha's hair in his hand like he was weighing the worth of it, he, solely from touch, able to know the quality and value of something.

You have beautiful hair, the tall man said. He held Mr. Cha's hair up to his nose and breathed it in. Mr. Cha felt the end of his hair get sucked into the wet inside of the man's nose. How would you like to have a drink with us at our hotel?

We'll reimburse you for any lost business, the old man promised.

If he did not need to drive in the humidity for the money, then
he surely was not going to. Mr. Cha thought they might buy his
hair, which he was willing to cut for the right price. They stopped
briefly at the temple, long enough for the whites to drop a sweat,
say they had seen it.

At the hotel bar, no more than two kilo-*may* from the temple,
Mr. Cha sat between the whites. The weather sank the liquor right
into his gut despite the lunch he had eaten. The whites spoke to
each other over him, sometimes looking at him, both touching his
hair. An hour passed. The old white asked if Mr. Cha would like
to make more money.

How much? Mr. Cha said.

Two hundred from me. Two hundred from him. Four total.

American dollars? Mr. Cha said.

Yes, they said.

What do I do?

In their room, the men counted the money and handed it to
him. Telling me this, Mr. Cha's shoulders started shaking, a few
words, now and then, sputtering through the tears on his lips.
Soon as his hand felt the money's weight, he managed to say,
knowing it was real, to keep it, he was willing to do anything
except die. Because he still had duties.

I did not ask what happened next, I did not want to urge him
on. I was quiet because I was thinking of my own husband. And I
stood and went to start dinner.

This too much for you? Mr. Cha said. You won't even let me
finish? I can't even go on—

Whatever you did, I said from across the hut, raising my voice,
wanting to be heard, it was for your children. You are a good
father. You try your best without a wife. Would my husband
believe I was trying my best for our daughter?

After a few minutes, when I did not return to my seat, when I refused even to face him, Mr. Cha walked out of my house, believing, I am sure, I had insulted him by lying to him. What he did not know was I had come to agree with him about one thing, and I needed to walk away, so he could not see me acknowledge he was correct: it was a good thing for him his wife was not alive to see this.

Days later, I told Mrs. Kethavong I needed a one-day break. You finally found a husband? she asked. He visit you while daughter's in school? When I did not answer, she said, Go on, but tomorrow you must fish. Tomorrow, all you must tell me. All was this that I told her—I added an ending to the story of my husband as my horse: Finally, I had seen enough to know how it would end, that the last river we must cross is wider and deeper than the Mekong. And, no wings to bear us above the burbling water, he could carry me only so far before tiring and sinking, having only human strength.

I went to Brother Pha, a village elder and clan brother to my husband, who knew the funeral rituals and who also played the *qeej*. I hired him to go with me into the jungle. Into my *ker*, I placed a dead chicken wrapped in a bag, boiled eggs, an arrow and bow, a knife, a small umbrella, cold rice, a small bottle of rice liquor, four small cups, two bowls, and sticks of incense. Hnuhlee shouldered a *ker* full of joss paper folded into the shapes of boats, money for her father.

When we started walking, Brother Pha asked me where we were going. The truth was, I did not know. Thirty minutes outside of our village, we entered the path into the jungle. Ahead of us, the feet of some animal scratched away, the sound of a straw broom sweeping a slate floor, startling me with its flight, unveiling a memory. My husband believed different animals can understand each other. When you go hunting, he said, it is not enough to be unseen to only the animal you hunt—all you must keep hidden from. Gibbons have learned to watch for the quick flight of birds, listen for their urgent, piercing calls; barking deer will raise tail at the ghostly howls of the gibbons; wild pigs will run with the deer, chasing squirrels to their holes. But not everything will run warning others of an intruder, giving away your location. You will have a bad hunting day if you are seen.

Travel this path long enough and it will start to climb, more brushes and branches in your way, black stripes barely visible against the dark jungle green, more fallen trees, their leaves yellowing, scattered, skin on the jungle floor, for you to step over, one foot and then the other, back onto the damp orange ground. In one hand, Brother Pha carried his *qeej*. His other hand held the gong, and tied to his back was a calfskin drum. I had no place in mind; I would let my heart tell me where to stop; I knew only I needed to get higher, closer to the mountaintops, to where they disappeared into clouds; I listened for the flight of birds.

My back and feet hurt, Hnuhlee said after two hours on the trail. Ma, you mean to cripple me with this weight?

I stopped, in the lead, and looked back at her. She was opening a bottle of water. Don't be disrespectful, I said. The money you carry is important. Don't curse it. Hnuhlee's hair was loose, hung over her eyes, her ears. She looked away when she saw me coming toward her, pouring water on her face. I wanted to yell, she was wasting drinking water. But she knew what we were doing, and maybe she was stopping, slowing us down because she refused to accept it. If ever a mother loves her daughter, it is in moments like this, when she knows for the longest they have shared the same dreams, stored away the same hopes. Hnuhlee, too, had waited all these years, keeping alive that image of her father's return.

I wasn't cursing it, Ma, she said. I wouldn't do that.

I held her face in my dirty hands, cleared away her hair so I could see her better. She is a head taller, dark skin like her father, but I see myself in her eyes, the flat of her cheek, the round of her chin. There was a time when I, too, had walked into the jungle with a *ker* on my back for this man.

Oy, Ma, Hnuhlee said when she saw me wiping away my tears. We have loved him long enough. Forever he will be with us. We respected his memory. I nodded. Hearing it from her, more than if it came from anyone else, made me feel better about my decision, made me believe this was right. I ran a forearm across my eyes. When I turned back to lead us, I apologized to Brother Pha. We women are holding you up.

Don't apologize, Sister, he said. I know what it is like to retrace your past. It is better to go slow, that way you are certain you won't miss a step, you won't get lost.

In a clearing high in the mountains, a small area seemingly untouched by the war, after six hours of walking, animal cries all around us now, my skin warm and wet through my shirt, I slipped off my pack. The bottoms of my feet stung with blisters. Beside a small stream that ran from a place higher in the mountains, I took out the things I had carried. Hnuhlee helped me build a small altar out of river stones. I stuck incense sticks into the spaces between the stones and lit them. I took out two bowls, filled one with rice and eggs. In the other, I placed the chicken. I poured a small cup of liquor and placed it between the bowls. On the ground before the altar, I laid the arrow and bow, knife, and umbrella.

I looked at Brother Pha, said, We do it here. His eyes narrowed, underneath stirring with doubt, held still to see if I might change my mind. His name is Yee Pha, I said. He was born in Phou Keum. He is the son of Hue and Maitong Pha, who live in America now. He is a dead of war. He has no son to send him home. I am a poor woman with only a daughter. This is all I have money for. You, as his brother, help him, please, to get where your ancestors are.

Brother Pha nodded his head. Do not worry, Sister. I will do what the spirits allow. He soaked the ground with a cup of liquor, then asked our ancestors' spirits to please hear him. Yee Pha, today we call your name to help you rise. He held his *qeej* between his hands. With the drum, I moved closer to the stream, striking it as Brother Pha had instructed. As he chanted and played the *qeej*, its sound the language of the dead, to lead my husband home, I told Hnuhlee to burn the money boats and let the ashes drift down the stream, into the Mekong, into the sea, into the ocean. Wherever the ashes washed up on, whether back on this shore or that other, and whatever they touched, whether five feet from us or five million, I wished my husband would find them and know they were from his wife and daughter.

Rise, I said, hitting the drum to let him know. Hear the call from Brother Pha's *qeej*. It is playing to lead you home from where the war has laid you down.

Rise, I said. Follow it through the jungle on trails you cut those nights you were by yourself after you left us in search of your parents.

Rise, I said. Leave your gun.

Rise and follow the trail back to the refugee camp, where your daughter was born. Rise and tread again the path we took when I decided to become your wife, after you came back from war the first time. Rise and let go of the hatred and courage you clung to during the long fighting that turned you into a man and me into a woman. Rise and regain your youth, the right to fear without shame, and know again only a body whole. Rise, go back to Fi Kha, where you first saw me, where I gave you a cucumber as a gift. Rise and go on. Return to Phou Keum on that trail now covered with weeds because the falls of our people's feet no longer land there to keep it clear. Rise, do not tire. I walk behind you, and if the fortunes are good and the spirits of our people see to it, our daughter will be long before she follows us on this road. Rise and walk between your neighbors' houses. You are almost there. Walk. Push open the door of your parents' house. Hear the blow of the *qeej*. Pick up your shirt. This is your first home, the place where you were born.

Insects stopped chirping and trilling, animals silenced their calls, and all held quiet for my husband's trip home—that is what I want to tell happened. But the *qeej* and drum had no effect on the world like a sack and engine block hitting water. No ringing silence even, like the ones in my husband's stories, those I convinced him to share on nights he could not sleep, of how every jungle skirmish, every bomb drop, every grenade explosion, always, was followed by a fleeting moment of truce to let the earth re-form full, to see where things stand, a moment to allow you to walk away, or stay—a time that many men, if by themselves, would dive headfirst into, he said—before death, again, leveled the living. In truth, the noise seemed to get louder now that I was listening. No pauses of hesitation. No silence from fright. Their cries, all bemoaning the heavy burden of living, were only confirmation for me—a language, finally, I learned to understand—that our debts to the dead must always be paid through our living.

Rise, I said, waiting, the drum beating in time with that of my heart, waiting for that silence, for my breath to catch, for the drum to stop.

Within a month, Mr. Cha made enough money to pay off the bride price of Say's wife. Within two months, he made enough to buy a three-bedroom stucco house, with a stone-floor courtyard, lights, and glass windows. They shared a hand-pumped well with ten other houses. The house was in a different section of Vientiane, and I needed to walk from Phondachet to the river where I fished, then pay a fisherman to take me across the river, then walk another ten minutes before getting there.

I knew Mr. Cha had started using opium, but had said nothing to him. Bee came and got me the day Mr. Cha awoke from a high that made him cough blood. I found him on the floor of his bedroom, dried blood at the corners of his smile. Settled into the lines of his face and cracks of his hands were dirt and opium tar.

Maiker, he said, lifting his head, stuck there in his own waste. How I've let my mother down! It is my destiny to see you, so you can scold me with a mother's tongue about cutting my hair. A Dutch orchid collector had shaved his head, $250 alone for that gold. The black veins there were like snakes around his skull.

How long has he been like this? I said, turning to Bee, to Say, to their wives.

Four days, Say said. We stopped bringing him food. He won't let me or Bee help him to use the toilet, to clean. Kept shouting, Only a woman! Only a woman! Lay there, smoked, and fell asleep. Woke up only to do it again. He won't let our wives help either.

Heat some water, I said to the wives, wondering if they had actually tried to get him cleaned, if their love or sense of duty as daughters-in-law could overcome their disgust. I pushed past the brothers and placed the big plastic tub they used for rinsing vegetables in the courtyard. Stand him up, I said. When I pulled Mr. Cha's shirt over his head, I saw his chest bones, the thin ridges along his stomach. His pants were heavy with piss and shit. Despite the smell being more awful than a dead man, I did not flinch—he could no more hurt me.

It is too much, Auntie, said Say. He backed away and slid out of the room.

You remember how your wife is in this house, I yelled after him.

Bee stood by the door, wanting to follow his younger brother. I need something to cover my nose and mouth, he said.

Mr. Cha pointed at his son walking away. My luck, he said.

Bee returned with his younger brother, both masked with T-shirts up to their eyes. I told the brothers to hold their father while I stripped off his pants. The two halves of his buttocks were caked brown as though he had sat on muddy ground, a ground already claiming his body. I rolled up the soiled pants, then the shirt over it, and used the bundle to wipe what I could from the back of Mr. Cha's thighs. I took an empty rice sack from the pile hanging from a hook screwed into the pillar of the house, and tossed in the dirty bundle.

Father, Say said. This is too disgusting.

Too disgusting? I said. Would you give up your wife? The wives were watching us from the door to the bedroom. Say's wife looked at him, and when he remained quiet, she told me the water was ready. Would you? I said to Say. You talk, but I want you to think if you can be the man your father is. Think if you can do what he did. My words made me wonder if they knew how their father had earned his money, paid off their wives. Did they even care?

The water flooded over the rim when Mr. Cha was placed into the tub, darkening the hard ground. I left them there to wash him. In Mr. Cha's bedroom, the wives and I took off the sheets, covers, and pillowcases; Say's wife took these outside to soak. I set Mr. Cha's opium kit on a high ledge, where he kept pictures of his dead wife next to three canisters of coffee. I opened the window in his room and put his fan on a chair near the doorway.

Mr. Cha sat shivering on a stool by the woodstove when I was finished with his room. His skin was rippled and starting to blue. I could not tell if he needed his opium or if he was cold. I added firewood to the stove and took a stool across the fire from him. A towel covered his shoulders, but his legs were closed.

I have observed and come to a conclusion, he said. You want to know? It is about the world. Bee's wife poured him a cup of tea.

I had my own thoughts about the world, but I wanted him to talk. If he could keep his head clear and talk, maybe he would not need his pipe. What? I said. The fire grew larger and started to pop.

He shifted, crossing his legs at the ankles, and the towel slipped from his shoulder, and I looked up. The sight struck me. Earlier, because of the smell, it did not cross my mind that I had not seen a man's private since before my husband left to find his parents. The sight disgusted me. I felt a tightening in my stomach, some muscle pushing back, rejecting, the motions of throwing up. This world has changed, he said. This isn't what we fought for.

No, I said, knowing the country we fought for was just the grounds that held our dead. But we are the brave ones. We're the ones left behind. Thinking about days long ago when, once, we were moved to fight for a ground to live on made me feel like an old woman meeting an old man after many years.

This world has made it so that just because you have life does not mean you have a right to live. He took a sip of his tea and shook his head. We were stupid not to leave. Stealing and begging—and just for food? Mr. Cha's shivers calmed as he spoke, and I started rocking on my stool. Every day a chance to sell our souls. If there is such a thing. He was staring at the open door of the woodstove. And with its many forked tongues, the fire lapped at the air, feeding on it, warming the space between us. You still think that is true, no? I wondered if he still was speaking to me—what was true? That life was only time to bargain with our souls? You still think I am a man? he said, looking up. Without his hair, he looked childish, though his face was dark and wrinkled, even powerless, no resemblance to the man who had stared down a tiger.

Yes, I said. That was not a lie: by providing for his sons, their brides, he had fulfilled his duty as a father; he had seen to it they had families of their own, that whatever happened going forward they would not go alone.

I don't feel like it, he said. Across the fire, his eyes glistened. My own sons don't see me as a man in my own house.

When they become fathers, they'll see, I said.

I wish I were a woman. It would have been so much easier, least I could do it and still show my face. Only a woman, he said, shaking his head.

No, I said. It is not so easy, not even for a woman.

He looked up at me. Hnuhlee, is she about to graduate?

I told him yes. I told him I had no idea how I would find the money to send her to vocational school to complete the training needed to become an interpreter. Still, we were sending cassettes to America, but no more was there much hope in it. The yell-to-teach voices had gone silent. Soon, Hnuhlee was to be eighteen, and people believed too old she was already for marriage. Mr. Cha nodded as I talked, but I was not sure if he agreed or understood. Say brought Mr. Cha a T-shirt and shorts, but he waved him away, sipping his tea without looking at his son. Say dropped the clothes by his father's feet.

The air inside the house felt less heavy, some steam let through the opened windows. From where the sons and daughters-in-law were huddled came muffled talking. Finally, Mr. Cha said, I want to show you something. He stood, his private hanging from the bottom of his stomach like the purple tongue of a goat. He made no move to cover himself. Here, I thought, was a person who no longer felt shame: he was naked, but there was no more the sense of a man there, and without that, a sense of something to take pride in, to remain modest about, there was nothing to protect, to cover, to clothe. He went into his room and returned with cash. He handed the money to Bee and told the sons to take their wives to buy something for dinner and a Western suit. Tie and pocket square, he said. Find one that will look nice on me. Make sure it's pressed nice, sharp lines. I am beginning to feel like a new man.

After they left, he brought from his room two coffee canisters. He removed three tins of opium from the top, then deeper into the canisters he reached. All I have left, he said, showing me six rolls of cash held with blue rubber bands. Is half enough?

Enough for what? I said.

He told me for Hnuhlee's schooling. Ten thousand here, he said.

Half would buy us a new life, I said. I thought to tell him Hnuhlee's complete schooling would cost only $750, but he had started to count the money. He rolled up five thousand dollars and bound it with two rubber bands.

Can you—, he said, allow me to feel like a man? Once more. He grabbed my hand and placed in it the money rolled tight like a cylinder of metal, and it was heavy, a grenade.

I latched the front door shut. I walked Mr. Cha away from his bedroom. I was afraid I would throw up from the smell that lingered there, and he would see I was disgusted with him, with what we were about to do. I untied my sarong and laid it on the ground before the fire. My skin became gooseflesh; I watched myself shivering. My thighs were white and thin. Still my nipples were tiny nubs, having fed only one baby. The wrinkles on my stomach from carrying Hnuhlee had smoothed away years before. You still have the figure of a young girl, Maiker. Mr. Cha grinned, perhaps to disarm me, to reassure me. I was shy but determined to go through with it, same as the first time with my husband. I told him to put on a rubber. Then I lay down on my sarong, gritted my teeth, and tried not to recoil from his touch, forcing my body to accommodate his, forgiving, as only flesh and skin can be.

All was over by the time Mr. Cha's sons returned home with a new black suit, and a roast duck and sticky rice for dinner. I excused myself, told them I needed to get home, because it was late, because still I needed to cross the river before getting there, because I knew, when Mr. Cha had finished and pulled himself from inside my body, he was a man again, and I was, again, only a woman.

Mr. Cha's death, it was not a surprise, a few days later. He, dressed in the new suit, then smoked opium until he passed out, his head hanging a foot off the ground next to the pillar in the center of the house. On the floor of his house that day, when we were done, Mr. Cha had made me promise I would make sure his sons gave him a proper burial. So I dressed in a new sarong and saw to my duties: instructed his sons on what to do, the proper way to do it; watched over his body during the funeral so no one would deface it out of envy or hatred, out of long-held grudges or the feeling that he, as a man, had betrayed us all by becoming the whites' woman. Your hair, I could have told Mr. Cha that day after we were done on the floor, will grow back, this hard heart of mine, though I do not know what my words would have meant to him.

You say widows and widowers are lucky, that only with a dead spouse are we able to justify the things we do to stay alive, and as such, it is easier to live in a broken country because we have no one to answer to. But that is not true. Every war happens half at home, and the battles there are the longest lasting. War is not a luck-giving thing. Like some big animal, all it does is decide for the world who lives on and who dies. And it is those who live on that are left with the questions of how to live, what to live for, how long to live. Questions that take a lifetime to get over. And maybe that is why I did it, because as a living-on person, finally, I settled on some answers, as I had before I led my daughter into the jungle to say good-bye to her father. I did it so only I would hear the voices, so, still, I could hope, if not know for certain, my daughter will never know how it feels to be an orchid farmer and stand on the corner and sell her flowers for America.

And you? Does it matter if your baby is a boy or a girl? Always, Hnuhlee and I appeal our disagreements to my son-in-law, and he, knowing I, in my own modern way, had let him marry Hnuhlee without asking for a bride price, as always, agrees with me.

I did see my old friend Houa again, four months since the last, on Rue Lab. When our eyes met, she turned away from me. *Yellow Squash. Green Squash.* But I have learned, when people turn their backs to you, sometimes it is an invitation for you to follow, so I hurried to catch up to her, to close the space, to share with her my luck, my hand reaching to grab her arm, this friend of my youth, the words forming on my lips—*Squash Blossom Orchid, for you the flower Asian!*—for her to wait.

Alexander MacLeod
Lagomorph

SOME NIGHTS, when the rabbit and I are both down on the floor playing tug-of-war with his toy carrot, he will suddenly freeze in one position and stop everything, as if a great breakthrough has finally arrived. He'll look over at me and there will be a shift, his quick glance steadying into a hard stare. I can't escape when he does this and I have to look back. He has these albino eyes that go from a washed-out bloody pink ring on the outside through a middle layer of slushy gray before they dump you down into this dark, dark red center. I don't know, but sometimes when he closes in on me like that and I'm gazing down into those circles inside of circles inside of circles, I lose my way, and I feel like I am falling through an alien solar system of lost orbits rotating around a collapsing, burning sun.

Our rabbit—my rabbit now, I guess—he and I are wrapped up in something I don't completely understand. Even when I imagine that I am reading him correctly, I know that he is reading me at the same time—and doing a better job of it—picking up on all my subconscious cues and even the faintest signals I do not realize I am sending out. It's complicated, this back-and-forth. Maybe we have been spending a little too much time together lately. Maybe I have been spending a little too much time thinking about rabbits.

As a species, let me tell you, they are fickle, stubborn creatures, obsessive and moody, quick to anger, utterly unpredictable and mysterious. Unnervingly silent, too. But they make interesting company. You just have to be patient and pay close attention and try hard to find the significance in what very well could be their most insignificant movements. Sometimes it's obvious. If a rabbit loves you or if they think you are the scum of the Earth, you will catch that right away, but there is a lot between those extremes—everything else is in between—and you can never be sure where you stand relative to a rabbit. You could be down there looking at an animal in grave distress, a fellow being in pain, or, almost as easily, you might be sharing your life with just another bored thing in the universe, a completely comfortable bunny who would simply prefer if you left the room.

Most of the time, none of this matters. We carry on our separate days and our only regular conversations are little grooming sessions during which I give him a good scratch between the ears, deep into that spot he cannot reach by himself, and in return, he licks my fingers or the back of my hand or the salt from my face.

But today is different. Today we have crossed over into new, more perilous territory and, for maybe just the next five minutes, we need a better, more reliable connection. For that to happen, he will have to do something he has never done before, move against his own nature and produce at least one clear sound with one clear purpose behind it. I need this rabbit to find words, or whatever might stand in for words. I need him to speak, right now, and tell me exactly what the hell is happening.

It is important to establish, before this begins, that I never thought of myself as an animal person. And since I do not come from a pet family, I never thought the family we were raising needed any more life running through it. Especially not a scurrying kind of life, with its claws tap-tap-tapping on the hardwood floors.

The thing you need to understand—I guess it was the deciding factor in the end—is that my wife, Sarah, is dramatically allergic to cats. Or at least she used to be. By this I mean only that she used to be my wife and then, later on, my partner. Like everybody else, we changed with the times and when the new word came in—probably a decade after we'd been married in a real church wedding—we were glad to have it. We felt like a "partnership" described our situation better, more accurately, and, to be honest, we'd never really known how anybody was supposed to go around being a wife or a husband all the time.

But I'm not sure what terminology you could use to describe what we are now. "Amicably separated" maybe, or "taking a break," but not divorced, not there yet. The legal system has not been called in. Sarah and I are not ex-partners. We still talk on the phone almost every day and we try to keep up with the news of everybody else, but it has already been more than a year, and I have never been to her new place in Toronto, the condo on the thirty-fourth floor.

I can imagine her there though, going through the regular Saturday morning. It is probably pretty much the same as it used to be. I see her walking from one room to the next and she has a magazine or her phone in one hand and a cup of tea in the other. She looks out a high window, maybe she contemplates traffic. I don't know. Really, she could be doing anything with anybody. Every possibility is available to her, just as it is for me, and only a few things are nonnegotiable anymore. Like the allergy. Unless there has been a medical procedure I don't know about, then wherever she is and whatever she's doing, Sarah remains, almost certainly, allergic to cats.

Her condition is medically significant, EpiPen serious, so the cat option was never there for us. And even the thought of a dog, a dog with its everyday outside demands—the walks and the ball-throwing and the fur and the drool and the poop bags in the park—that was always going to be too much, too public, for me.

If we had stayed like we were at the start, if it had been just the two of us all the way through, I think we might have been able to carry on forever and nothing would have happened. The problem was our children, three of them, all clustered in there between the ages of seven and thirteen. They were still kids at this time. It was the moment just before they made the turn into what they are now.

When I look back, I see this was the peak of our intensity together, a wilder period than even the sleepless newborn nights or the toilet training. I don't know how we survived for years on nothing but rude endurance. It was probably something automatic, the natural outcome of great forces working through us. We were like a complicated rain forest ecosystem, full of winding tendrils, lush, surging life and steaming wet rot. The balance was intricate and precise and we were completely mixed up in each other's lives, more fully integrated than we would ever be again.

The kids had been pushing and pushing us and eventually we just gave in. All the friends had animals, all the neighbors and the cousins. There were designer wiener dogs and husky pups with two different-colored eyes and hairless purebred cats. It felt like there was no way to escape the coming of this creature.

We started with the standard bargain aquarium setup and a cheap tank bubbled in our living room for about a month and we drowned a dozen fish in there. After that, there was brief talk about other possibilities, but in the end, the rabbit felt like our best option, a gateway to the mammal kingdom. Better than a bird or a lizard, we agreed, more personality, more interaction.

"Maybe a rabbit is kind of like a cat." I remember saying those words.

We got him from a Kijiji ad—"Rabbit available to a good

home"—and the Acadian man who once owned him ended up giving him to us for free.

I went to his house and visited his carpeted basement. I learned all about the food and the poop and the shedding.

"Is there anything special we need to do?" I asked. "We don't have any experience."

"You just don't eat the guy," the man said. "Rabbits are right there, you know, right on that line."

He made a kind of karate-chopping motion, his hand slicing down through the air.

"You either want to be friends with them or you want to kill them and eat them for your supper. We had two other people come here already today. And I was going to take the ad down if you were the same as those bastards. I could see it in their eyes, both them guys. I could just tell. They'd have taken him home and probably thrown him in a stew, a *fricot*, like my *grand-mère* used to make, you know? Hard to look at, I tell you, when somebody's lying to your face like that."

I asked him what he saw when he looked in my eyes.

He laughed and bonked his temple with his finger.

"I got no clue," he said. "All we can ever do is guess, right? No way to ever be sure about what's going on up there. But me, thinking about you right now? Me, I'm guessing that you are not the guy who is going to kill our Gunther."

"Gunther?" I said.

He crouched down and said the word three times very quickly and he made a clicking noise with his tongue.

The rabbit came flying out from beneath the sofa and went over to the man and stretched up to get his scratch between the ears.

"He knows his name?"

"Of course he does. Doesn't everybody know their own name?"

"And do we have to keep that one?"

"You do whatever you want, my friend. After you leave here, he's going to be your rabbit. But if you want him to know when you're talking to him, I think you better call him what he's always been called."

I stretched out my hand and Gunther sniffed at my fingers, then gave me a quick lick. His tongue seemed so strange to me then. So long and dry. The tongue of a rabbit is very long and very dry.

The man smiled.

"That there is a very good sign," he said. "Doesn't usually happen like that. Gunther, he is usually shy around new people. Normally takes him a little while to make up his mind."

The rabbit pushed his skull against my shin, scratching an itchy part of his head on the hard bone running down the front of my leg. I felt the change coming.

"So we have a deal, then?" the man said.

"I think so," I said. And we shook hands.

"And you're promising me you will not kill him?" He kind of laughed that part at me.

"Yep," I said, and I shook my head. It was all ridiculous.

"Maybe you can say the real words to me, right now, out loud?"

There was no joke the second time. He looked at me hard and I stared back. He had not yet let go of my hand and as we were standing there I felt the little extra compression he put around my knuckles, the way he pushed my bones together.

"I promise I will not kill Gunther."

"That is very good," the man said, and he smiled and then he shrugged. "Or at least, I guess that is good enough for me."

It took maybe three weeks before Sarah and I started talking about putting him down.

"This isn't working," she said. "Right? We can both see that. Whatever happens—we try to sell him or we take him back or to a shelter or whatever, I don't care—but it cannot go on like this. It's okay to admit we made a mistake."

The kids had already lost interest and the litter box was disgusting. We were using a cheaper kind of bedding and Gunther hated it. In the first couple of days he'd already shredded up two library books and chewed through half a dozen cords without ever electrocuting himself. There was an infection too, something he'd picked up in the move. Maybe we gave it to him, but it was horrible to look at. He had this thick yellow mucus matting down the fur beneath his eyes and both his tear ducts were swollen green and red. He hardly ate anything and instead of the dry, easy-to-clean pellets of poop we'd been promised, he was incontinent. For about a week, our white couch, the couch we still have, the couch where Gunther and I still sit while we watch TV, was smeared with rabbit diarrhea.

It was getting bad for me too. Something in my breathing had started to change and a case of borderline asthma was settling deep into the membranes of my chest. I felt this strange tenderness blooming in my lungs—like a big bruise in the middle of me—and I was starting to have trouble walking up or even down the stairs in the mornings. We weren't sure of the cause, yet, and it couldn't be pinned directly on Gunther. The doctors said there were other possible explanations—adult-onset conditions—that could stay dormant in your body for decades before springing up fresh in your later life. I had my own wheezing theories, though, and I felt pretty certain that this rabbit and I were not meant to be together.

We took him to a veterinarian who couldn't help us at all.

The guy plunked Gunther down on the stainless-steel examination table and he shone that light into his eyes and his ears and felt around, up and down Gunther's whole body. It took less than ten minutes. Then he snapped off his purple gloves and threw them into a sterile wastebasket.

"Look," he said, "I've got to be honest here."

He cocked his head toward the door. On the other side, in the waiting room, there were at least ten other people, all sitting there with their leashes and their treats and their loved ones.

"I think you can see, we're pretty much running a cat and dog shop here. You know what I mean? That's ninety-five percent of what we do. And I'm afraid we don't have a lot of experience with the exotics."

"Exotics?" I said. "What, is a rabbit exotic now?"

"It is for me. I'm just telling you: I've given you the standard examination that comes with our basic billing package. The next step is going to be X-rays and advanced diagnostics and I don't think you really want to go there. Not for a rabbit anyway. Not for a rabbit that hasn't even been fixed."

In that moment, it was almost over. Gunther was nearly part of our past. The way to a different version of the future, a new opening, was right there.

"Listen," he said. "How about I give you the room for a little while and maybe you can have some time to think about how you'd like to say good-bye. When I come back, if you're good with it, I can give him a little sedative that will calm everything down. Then we set up the IV and whenever you want to release the drug, that will be it; it'll all be over in a painless, quiet, peaceful way. If he can't eat and he isn't drinking and he can't see, what kind of a life is that?"

As he left the room, I watched him shifting his facial features, moving from the serious life-and-death mode he'd been using on us to the cheerful semiannual-checkup face he used for his regular clients.

I turned back to Sarah, but she was already packing Gunther up to bring him home.

"Fuck that guy," she said to me.

I smiled and nodded my head. My wife does not like to be bossed around by anyone.

We took Gunther home and she got to work on the computer.

Online she found a woman in the country who was kind to us, but no-nonsense. She was a real farm vet—herds of cattle, giant pigs, even racehorses—and she rarely worked with pets, but she sold us the antibiotics we needed for twenty-five dollars flat and she told us exactly what to do. There were teeth problems, she said. Severely overgrown teeth, looping inside Gunther's head, cutting him every time he tried to chew. The infection had started in his mouth. The other guy had never even looked in there.

"It's not pretty right now," the vet said. "And I'm not going to touch anything, but once it's cleared a little, after the medicine has worked, you're going to have to cut them back."

All of this really happened to us, to Sarah and to me. For an entire week, we fed Gunther with a plastic syringe. In our food processor, we blended up this disgusting kale smoothie with the medication mixed into it. Then I wrapped the rabbit's squirming body in a towel and held him against my chest, squeezing all four of his legs into me. His hair came out, sometimes in thick clumps, sometimes in a kind of fine translucent fuzz that floated through the room and, for sure, penetrated deep into my own body. Sarah forced open his mouth and she drove tube after tube of that green sludge into him. He tried to spit it back up, but most of it went down and the rest dribbled over his chin, where it later hardened into this thick green grit in his fur.

But the drugs worked and a week later, when he had his strength back, Sarah and I switched places and did as we'd been told. She held him in the towel and I took a brand-new pair of wire cutters—purchased and sterilized just for this task—and I peeled back Gunther's gums.

You could see it right away. It's easy to tell when things are almost perfectly wrong. Each of his two front teeth was a brownish-yellow tusk, like a miniature ram's horn, curved backward almost to a full circle with a black streak of what seemed like a blood vessel flowing inside of it. I tried to imagine how things should look if they did not look like this and I tried to summon up a picture for how a rabbit's teeth are supposed to be, although I had never seen a rabbit's tooth before.

Then I just did it. I picked a spot and I aimed the scissor point of the pliers and tried to hit it. Gunther was furious, snorting hard through his nose. Sarah could barely hold him, but even in that moment of crisis he could not generate anything more than a cough.

"Go!" she said. "Do it right now. Now. Come on."

I brought the cutters down on the surface of the bone and I squeezed hard and quick, but the tooth was much, much softer than I expected. There was a snap and a section an inch and a half long flew across the girls' room. The second piece, snipped from the second tooth, was a little longer, and it nearly went down his throat before I flipped it free with the tip of my own finger. I dipped my hand in and out of Gunther's mouth. But then it was done and Sarah let him go and he fled beneath the bed.

We were standing there together, Sarah with the soiled towel—Gunther had let go of everything—and me with the pliers in my hand and the chunks of rabbit teeth on the floor. I turned and plucked a piece of fur out of her eyebrow and I remember that she put the towel down and wiped her palms down the front of her shirt, then mine.

"That was not what I expected," she said.

"Me neither," I said.

Beneath the bed, Gunther remained perfectly silent. A stranger, entering the room, would not have known he was even there, and neither of us could tell if he was in agony under the mattress or if he felt any kind of relief.

"What do we do now?" I asked.

"I don't know," she said. "I guess we wait."

. . .

Somehow it worked the way it was supposed to. With the medicine kicking in and his teeth fixed, Gunther returned to his regular diet of raw Timothy hay. Eventually his poop hardened up and his eyes cleared. Even the kids came back to him. They played games together now, flinging his carrot across the room for fetch, and they worked up a pretty funny matador routine. If you shook a dish towel at him and shouted "Toro! Toro! Toro!," Gunther would come charging across the room and blast under the fabric. This also worked great with a pyramid of plastic cups. As soon as you built it up, he'd come barreling through, with real strength and purpose.

When a rabbit is truly happy, they do these insane joyful leaps where they launch their whole bodies way up into the air, so much higher than you think they can go. They twist in odd ways and kick all four of their legs at the same time. It's like one of those ecstatic convulsions you see in born-again churches when people are so moved by the Spirit they can't control their limbs. Gunther used to do that all the time after the bullfight game or the plastic pyramid. That kind of jumping is called a binky. That is the real, technical term for it: binky.

You can never be sure, but I think that somewhere in the blur between our decision at the vet's office and the thing with the teeth and the end of everything else, Gunther's life fit into ours and we all almost made sense. He receded into the deep background of our existence, and took up his place in the daily sequence. Taking care of him became a set of regular tasks. Each week it was a different person's job to change the bedding and blast the room with the Dustbuster and make sure his water and food were topped up. Allowances were paid for this labor and Gunther became a formal responsibility of the household, like emptying the dishwasher or taking out the garbage. When other things, new emergencies, claimed us—the year Sarah's father got sick and eventually died, or the time I was laid off for eight months, or the spring when we had to take out another loan to fix the roof and repoint the chimney and replace all the gutters—I could almost forget that Gunther lived with us. Though we shared the same space, and his presence eventually put me on regular inhalers, puffers that became automatic, I still might go an entire week without actually seeing him. We were all just barely touching and it seemed like the minivan was always running in our driveway, its rolling side door gaping for the quickest possible turnaround, like an army helicopter. Sarah or I would take one step across the threshold of the front door, before we'd be clapping our hands and yelling: "Let's go! Let's go! Let's go!"

Back and forth through the van door, into and out of traffic. Every day and every night of the week there was some other activity. Making lunches for picky, ungrateful people: whenever I cut the crusts off a sandwich or allowed someone to return a perfectly untouched, but perfectly prepared, Tupperware container of sliced cucumbers and ranch dip, I wondered if I was loving a child or wrecking her for the future. Every morning we just barely made it to the corner for the first school bus at seven thirty and the second at seven forty-five. Then showering and getting your hair okay and putting on real clothes and going to work and dealing with all the stupid people at work. The stupid things that every stupid person said and did.

Piano and swimming and soccer and music and school assemblies. In an effort to spend quality time with the kids, Sarah signed up to be a Girl Guide leader. She learned all the promises and she got the uniform and we sold cases and cases of cookies. I coached a boys' soccer team for five years, though I knew nothing about soccer in the beginning. Every morning, the morning arrived just five or six hours after we'd gone down. And every morning, when Sarah and I opened our eyes again, we were already late, already behind.

"What is today?" I'd ask, and she'd look at me and blink and stare at me like a stranger. Then she'd turn away or look up to the ceiling as if she were reading a screen, like this was the dentist's office and they had a news crawl running up there.

"Wednesday," she'd say. "Wednesday is Pizza Day. No lunches. But then violin, and the after-school thing—some meeting we're supposed to go to about cleaning up the playground—somebody has to be seen to be there. Then, if there's time after that, please, God, haircuts. Please. Everybody in this whole house needs a god-damn haircut."

"Yes."

"I'm serious," she said. "You need a haircut. You look like a homeless person."

I remember once, maybe five years ago—it was at a retirement party for a lady from Sarah's work—we snuck out during the speeches and fucked in the minivan, right there, doggie-style, on the third-row Stow 'n' Go bench. It was ridiculous but also, absolutely, the right thing to do. There were stained Popsicle sticks and food wrappers back there, headphones and Legos, even a long-lost running shoe that we were so glad to find. Sarah held it up triumphantly with one hand, even as she was unbuttoning her pants with the other. "At last!" she said. "Remind me not to forget about this when we get home."

The other cars just sat there by the curb under the streetlights and no pedestrians ever walked by to peer through our slightly tinted windows. Inside the van, we were rushed and awkward, but we got what we came for and still made it back in time for the cake, all rezipped and smoothed out.

I don't know what happened to us after that. There was no single event. No dramatic explosion, no other character that wandered into our lives. I think we just wore down gradually, inevitably, and eventually, we both decided we'd had enough and it was time to move on. There must have been something else—a pull from the inside or a signal from the outside—that compelled us in some way, but I'm not sure. Maybe we really did just outlive the possibilities of each other's bodies.

But Sarah and I: we had a good, solid run and I think we came through pretty well. Three kids is not nothing and we carried those people—we carried them from their delivery rooms to their day cares to their schools and through all their summer vacations, all the way down to the fancy dinners we hosted on the nights of their high school graduations. Then, one by one, they left our house for good and, all of us, we never lived together again. Two went to universities in different cities and one moved in with her boyfriend across town and started working at a call center.

After they left, we were by ourselves again. Together, but by ourselves now, and only Gunther stayed. The change was harder than we expected. There was too much space now and we filled it up with everything that had always been missing. Though there was no one else around, we kept getting in each other's way. I felt like the air inside the house was thickening again, but worse now, like a clear sludge was being slowly poured into every gap in our lives. We had to slog through it every day and every exchange was more difficult than it needed to be. Neither of us would ever watch the other person's shows and there were arguments, real arguments, about who should have the power to decide if an overhead light should be turned off or turned on. I did not like how she chewed her food, the way she incessantly talked about other people behind their backs, her selfishness. And she did not like the way I clicked my pens, the way I was always intruding on her plans, the way I started things, but never finished them. No single can of soup could serve us both.

The conditions were right when the transfer opportunity came. This was a real promotion, national-level stuff—much more money and the right kind of work, at last—the type of thing Sarah had wanted for years. She could not afford to let it pass. "A chance like this," she said, and we both knew.

After that, we started talking, quietly at first, about "making a change" or implementing "the new plan." We worked it all out, calm and serious and sad, and then it was decided. The job led the way, but we both knew it was more than that and we were clear about what this meant when we explained it to the kids. We needed to move on and there was no pretending anymore, no fudging the truth.

"We just want you to be happy," our oldest daughter said, and the line stuck in my ear because I'd always thought it was the kind of thing parents were supposed to tell their kids.

We kept the show running for four more months—one last school-less September through to one last all-together Christmas—and then we made the calls in the third week of January. Like everybody else, we wanted to get through Christmas before the chatter started. It was civil and transparent and even kind.

I drove her to the airport and we really did kiss and cry in a parking spot that is reserved for kissing and for crying.

"We just have to do what we have to do," she told me.

I look at Gunther sometimes and I wonder if he is typical—if he is like or unlike all the others of his kind—the rest of the lagomorphs that populate this world. I wonder if he has even ever seen another rabbit or if he thinks maybe I am a rabbit, too. They are an altricial species—another word I have learned—born blind and deaf and defenseless, so he would have no memory of his siblings or his mother, no sight or sound to carry forward from that first phase of his life. If there is a moment in your existence when you cannot survive without another's timely intervention—if you are like a hatchling bird fresh out of the shell—then you are altricial. When Gunther was born, he would have been a hairless three inches of flesh, a pink wriggling tube in the world, barely more than a mouth and a fragile circulatory system visible through his skin. There might have been eight or nine others with him in the litter. Maybe he still holds some faint feeling of them, the touch of other rabbits, all those teeming bodies pressed up against each other, huddling for heat. That's another word I like: the verb, to teem. You hardly ever get to use it.

There is so much out there. I have scrolled the images on the Internet and read the articles and followed the diagrams, the maps that show us what really happens if we follow them down the hole, through the warren and into the complex society they build down there, three feet beneath the place where we live. The largest and most complicated colonies can twist through hundreds of meters of tunnels and switchbacks, a path no predator could ever follow. Guided only by instinct, they dig dark mazes out of the ground, building their real working routes so that they run right beside a series of faked dead ends and false starts. Then they put in dozens of different entrances and escapes, some of them real, some of them decoys. The strategy is amazing, the fact that this level of deception, such advanced trickery, is built right into the great natural plan.

Despite all of this, in the wild, a rabbit gets to live for a year, maybe two. Less than 10 percent of them ever see that second summer or winter. I guess they are born for dying, a new generation every thirty-one days. But that's not how it is for Gunther. He is fifteen years old now, at least, and I suppose this makes him a nearly unique organism in the history of the world. From here on in, every one of his experiences will be unprecedented.

Today I decided I would try to show him something new. He has always been an indoor pet—a house rabbit—but this morning I brought him outside. There was work I'd been neglecting in the yard and it had to be done. I did not think he would run away— our fences go straight to the ground—but there are gaps that are large enough and I wanted to at least give him a choice.

I put him down on the lawn and gave him a good scratch between his ears.

"There you go," I said, and I spread my arms wide as if I was granting the yard to him. "All yours."

He looked up at me, less enthused than I expected, and then he just lowered his head and pulled up a mouthful of fresh clover and started munching away. He casually turned and hopped a few feet over to sniff at the base of the back porch, near the spot where we keep our compost bin and the garden hose. He did not seem to be in a rush to go anywhere.

I turned away from him and walked toward the shed. I spun the combination on the padlock, opened the door and wheeled out our dusty push lawn mower. I grabbed the snips and the hedge clippers and the sturdy old garden rake with its rectangular grin of sharp tines. I took out the wheelbarrow. For half an hour I purposefully did not look back in the direction where I had left Gunther. I wanted to leave him alone and give him a chance to sort things out for himself.

There had been so many spring Saturdays like this in our past, so many days full of lists, with things that needed to be done and put in order. I raked the dead winter leaves into a pile and I uncovered the beds and I took an initial stab at trimming back the rosebush and the other perennials that Sarah had always kept up. I tried to remember everything she had told me about how to get the angle right on your snips so that everything you cut away grows back and then grows out in the right way. Fullness was what we were always aiming for. We wanted the plants in our backyard to be full, to bloom thick and heavy. I touched each fork where the branches or the stems parted and I paused and thought about what to do. Then I eenie-meenie-miney-moed my way through the decisions before cutting one side back and letting the other side live.

I turned around just in time. There was a sound, I guess, more of a vibration in the air, but it should not have been enough. I don't know what made me look. It was just a sigh really, a gurgling exhale, like the wheezing my own lungs made at their worst, only more shallow and quicker.

The thing I saw—the thing my eyes landed on—was a completely normal occurrence in the natural world, I guess. But at the same time, it was something shocking—something completely new and troubling—to me. A snake, much thicker and much longer than the kind of animal I believed could live beneath our porch, was spiraled around Gunther's body. The drama was almost over and everything had already shifted to stillness. Gunther was stretched out to his full length and the sound coming from him, the vibration, was the last of his air being squeezed out of his body. The snake had wound round him four or five times and their heads, Gunther's and the snake's, were touching. It seemed almost like they were looking into each other's eyes. Their tails, too, were almost even, but in between—beneath and inside the symmetry of the snake—there was this wretched contortion in Gunther's body, a twisting that seemed to spin his neck in the opposite direction from his front paws. I felt, for sure, that all his bones had already been broken.

I have looked it up—I went immediately to the search engine when I came back to the house—and I know now that this other creature, the thing that once lived beneath our porch, was a rat snake, a nonvenomous constrictor, as local to this part of the world, perhaps even more local, than my New Zealand rabbit. I have learned that rat snakes, or corn snakes, make great pets, that they are wonderful with kids, that they are the gentle hit of the reptile show that comes to visit all the schools. Children love to feel them spiraling around their limbs, the dry, wet sensation of it. The rat snake in my backyard was not at fault, not doing anything wrong. Only taking up its assigned place and following an instinctive pattern it could not choose or change. Gunther too was where he was supposed to be, I guess. When all of this happened, I was the only thing moving out of order. But I could not stop myself from moving.

"No," I said, and I took four or five purposeful strides toward them. Then I reached out and I picked up this strange and seething combination of whatever it was and I held it in my hand. I do not think I will ever touch something like this again and I do not know what I felt. It wasn't heavy. The two of them together did not weigh as much as a bag of groceries. They were in my left hand and, with my right, I grabbed the snake just behind its head and tried to twist it away, to pry it off of Gunther, to separate them. It turned on me almost instantly, unspooling from Gunther and swiveling onto my arm. I flung both of them back on the ground. Gunther fell and did not move, but the snake immediately began to head toward the pile of leaves, sideways and forward at the same time.

But we were not done yet. I grabbed the rake and followed behind, and when my chance came, I swung the tool hard. It arched over my shoulder and cut down quickly through the air and I felt the resistance as the point of one, maybe two of the teeth penetrated the snake's body almost in the middle. The rake descended all the way through and dug into the ground on the other side. Both ends of the snake, the top and the bottom, kept going, zigzagging furiously, but the middle was pinned down and stationary. I walked to the head, and I waited and watched the swaying. Then I timed it right and I brought my heel down as precisely as I could. I was only wearing running shoes, but I pressed hard and I felt the bones crushing, and the liquid giving way, like stepping on an orange, maybe. But after fifteen seconds, the swaying stopped, the top half of the snake first and then the bottom. I looked back to where I had been just a few seconds before and I was prepared for what I expected to see—the crumpled white pile, unbreathing—but it was not there. Instead, over to the side, maybe two feet away from where he had fallen, Gunther was up and at least partially reinflated back to his regular rounded shape. He was perfectly stationary now, still in the way that only a rabbit can be still, and he was staring at me, staring hard at this scene.

I looked at him and then down at the snake, the length of it, the stretch of its body. The things it had done and the things I had done. I did not know what any of them meant. I did not know what could or could not be justified. I only knew what had happened and that, eventually, I would have to come back here, to this spot, and clean up the mess.

I went over to Gunther and I picked him up as gently as I could, but he gave me no reaction. He was only a soft object in my hands, almost like a stuffed animal, like a kid's toy that is supposed to stand in for a real rabbit, or for whatever a rabbit is supposed to mean. I brought him back inside, back to our house, where we are now, and I put him on the couch and knelt in front of him. I ran my fingers all along his body, like the uncaring veterinarian from years ago, but like him, I couldn't feel anything out of place, and couldn't tell if there was something else wrong, something broken deeper inside of him.

The phone rings and it is Sarah. She lives in a city where it is an hour earlier than it is here, and, for a second, I get confused about time zones and I imagine that none of this has happened to her yet.

"How you doing today?" she says.

The tone is light and easy and intimate. When conditions are right, we can fall right back into who we were. She just wants to chat about nothing, to fill in the time on an empty Saturday morning. It is quiet on both ends and I feel certain that we are both alone, at least for now.

"Well," I say. It is hard to find the right words. "Something bad happened with Gunther just now."

"No," she says, and the turn comes right away, a panicked edge sharpening her voice. "What happened?" she asks. "Is it bad? I was just thinking about him and wondering about the two of you. Is he going to be okay? Are you okay?"

"It was a snake," I say, trying to make all of this as basic as I can.

"Can you believe that? Like a real snake, a pretty big one, in our yard, and it almost had him, but then he got away. I'm just not sure what's going on with him right now. Maybe he's in shock."

I make the clicking noise with my tongue and I say the name, the word that once seemed so strange to me. I say "Gunther" and I wait for him to come but nothing happens.

The phone is pushed against my ear and Sarah's breathing is there.

"Tell me exactly what happened," she instructs. "And tell me what he looks like right now. Try to explain it to me. I need details. Maybe we need to call someone."

"He seems alert," I say, "but he's not moving."

I reach out and stroke the bridge of his nose with my index finger and I feel him nudging back a little bit, trying to meet my skin with his body.

I watch this happening—almost like an extreme close-up running in slow motion, a picture that I am in and observing at the same time—my finger on his nose and his nose against my finger. There is a pause during which nothing happens. Nothing happens and nothing happens, but it goes on for too long and the gap gets too wide. I lose track.

Sarah breaks the silence.

"David!" she shouts. "David, are you there?"

My name surprises me, like an odd noise coming from another room, something crashing, and at first I don't know how to respond, but before I can do anything, Gunther twists his head, hard and quick, pivoting both ears toward me and the telephone. He recognizes Sarah's voice—the sounds that only she can make—a cry coming out of this plastic receiver, cutting through. He turns and his expression, the shape of his face, the tilt of his head, rearranges into something I have never seen before, flaccid and seized in all the wrong places. But his breathing is strong and steady. I feel like he needs me, like I am the only one who can pull him through.

"I'm here," I say into the phone, "but I can't talk right now. I have to let you go."

I hang up and stare at Gunther and I see myself reflected again at the red center of his eye. The surface seems cloudier than normal, and I don't think he can process what is happening anymore, this hazy mixture of light and frequency that surrounds us—the familiar and the strange. I know he still knows me—he still knows us—and I try to look past my reflection. I imagine moving directly through the membranes and lenses of his eyes, down the nerves and all the way up into his brain. I think our shared past, our lives, are still there, held in his memory. Inside the mind of the oldest rabbit that has ever lived, we are a single thought—vivid and urgent and distinct—but then it passes and the rest is everything else.

John Edgar Wideman
Maps and Ledgers

MY FIRST YEAR TEACHING at the university my father killed a man. I'm ashamed to say I don't remember the man's name, though I recall the man a good buddy of my father's and they worked for the city of Pittsburgh on a garbage truck and the man's family knew ours and we knew some of them, my sister said. Knew them in that way black people who lived in the same neighborhood knew one another and everybody else black in a city that divided itself by keeping all people of color in the same place back then, no matter where in the city you lived.

I did not slip up, say or do the wrong thing when the call that came in to the English department, through the secretary's phone to the chairman's phone, finally reached me, after the secretary had knocked and escorted me down the hall to the chair's office, where I heard my mother crying because my father in jail for killing a man and she didn't know what to do except she had to let me know. She knew I needed to know and knew no matter how much a call would upset me I would be more upset if she didn't call, even though calling meant, since I didn't have a home phone yet or a direct line in my office and no cell phones, she would have to use the only number I'd given her and said to use only for emergencies, and wasn't this an emergency, hers, mine, we had to deal with, she and I, her trying not to weep into the phone she was holding in Pittsburgh while she spoke to strangers in Philadelphia, white people strangers to make it worse, a woman's voice then a man's, before she reached me with the news I needed to know and none of it anybody's business, terrible business breaking her heart to say to me even though I needed to know and would want to know despite where I was and who I was attempting to be, far away from home, surrounded by strangers, probably all of them white, which made everything worse, she didn't need to say, because I heard it in her voice by the fifth or sixth word, her voice that didn't belong in the chair's office, a story not for a chairperson's ears, but he was Southern gentleman enough as well as enough of a world-renowned Chaucer scholar to hand me the phone and excuse himself and shut the office door behind him so I could listen in peace to my mother crying softly and trying to make sense of a dead man and my father in jail for killing him, his cut-buddy I can say to myself now and almost smile at misunderstandings, bad jokes, ill will, superiority, inferiority stirred up when I switch between two languages, languages never quite mutually intelligible, one kind I talked at home when nearly always only colored folks listening, another kind spoken and written by white folks talking to no one or to one another or at us if they wanted something from us, two related-by-blood languages that throttled or erased or laughed at or disrespected each other more often than engaging in useful exchange, but I didn't slip once in my conversation with the chair, didn't say my goddamn daddy cut his goddamn cut-buddy, no colored talk or nigger jokes from either of us in the office when a phone call from my mom busted in and blew away my cover that second or third day of my first or second week of my first college teaching job.

. . .

My aunt C got my father a lawyer. Aunt C lived five doors away on our street, Copeland, when I was growing up. My family of mom, dad, five kids had moved into an upstairs three-room apartment in a row house at the end of a block where a few colored families permitted because the housing stock badly deteriorated and nobody white who could afford not to wanted to live on the busted block, after coloreds had been sneaked into a few of Copeland's row houses or modest two-story dwellings squeezed in between, like the one Aunt C and her husband could afford to buy and fix up because he was a numbers banker, but most of us coloreds, including my mother and father, had to scrimp and scuffle just to occupy month by month, poaching till the rent man put us out in the street again, but residents long enough for their kids to benefit for a while from better schools of a neighborhood all white except for a handful of us scattered here and there down at the bottom of a couple of streets like Copeland.

Aunt C a rarity, a pioneer you might say, because she worked in the planning office of the city, a good job she finessed, she explained to me once, by routing her application through the Veterans Administration since she'd served as a WAC officer during World War II and guessed that by the time the city paper pushers noticed her color disqualified her, the military service record that made her eligible for a position and elevated her to the top of the list would have already gotten her hired, the only woman, only colored, decades before anybody colored not a janitor or a cleaning woman got hired by the city to work in downtown office buildings. Aunt C, who I could always count on to find some trifling job around her house for me to earn a couple of quarters when I needed pocket change or bigger jobs car washing, neatening up, and cutting the grass in her tiny backyard when I needed new sneakers or a new shirt my parents couldn't buy, and then counted on her again years later because she was the one who knew everybody and everybody's dirt downtown, and got my father—her older brother—an attorney, a colored one who also knew everybody and everybody's dirt downtown, the man as much of a rarity or more, an exception in his way as my aunt, since he not only practiced law but served in the state legislature as majority Speaker, an honor, achievement, irony, and incongruity I haven't been able to account for to this day, but he wound up representing my father and saving him from prison, thanks to Aunt C. That same colored lawyer one day would say to me, shaking his head and reaching out and placing his hand on my shoulder, family of poor old Aeschylus got nothing on yours, son, as if to inform me, though he understood both of us already knew, that once my mother's phone call had caught up with me, Aunt C doing her best or no Aunt C, things would only get worse.

No, my father didn't serve time for murder. Lawyer plea-bargained self-defense, and victim colored like my father anyway, so they chose to let my father go. But things did get worse. My father's son, my youngest brother, convicted of felony murder. And years later my son received a life sentence at sixteen. My brother, my son still doing time. And my father's imprisoned son's son a murder victim. And a son of my brother's dead son just released from prison a week ago. And I'm more than half-ashamed I don't know if the son, whose name I can't recall, of my brother's dead son has fathered son or daughter. My guess is the rumor of a child true, since if my grandnephew was old enough for adult prison, he would be way past the age many young colored men father babies back home.

Gets confusing doesn't it. Precedents from Greek mythology or not. Knowing or not knowing what variety of worse will probably come next if you are a member of my colored family hunkering down at the end of Copeland or on whatever divided street you think of as home or whatever you may think a home is. Gets damn confusing. I lose track of names. Generations. No end in sight. Or maybe I already know the end and just don't want to think about it out loud. Whose goddamn business is it anyway. Knucklehead, fucking hardheaded young bloods and brothers. Goddamn Daddy. Goddamn cut-buddy. Words I didn't slip and say out loud that day attempting to explicate an emergency to my chairman in the departmental office.

Get away, I kept telling myself, and none of this happens.

I had always been impressed by my grandmother Martha's beautiful hand. Not her flesh-and-blood hand. Her letters. Her writing. Perfect letter after letter in church ledgers and notebooks year after year in my grandmother Martha's beautiful hand. You almost felt a firm, strong hand enfolding, guiding yours if your turn to read Sunday-school attendance or minutes of the Junior Deacons' board, each letter flowing into the next into the next word then next sentence so you didn't stumble or mumble repeating aloud what you found waiting for you so peacefully, patiently, perfectly shaped between faint blue lines on each page.

Letter after letter perfect as eggs. Perfect as print. But better. Her hand cursive. Letters flowing like alive things that grow. One growing live into or from the other, whether connections visible or not. As the Bible grows, if you are taught to read it in the fashion I was. Each verse, each psalm, parable, book, sermon connected. Truths alive and growing in the pages after you learn in church how to read Bible words. Cursive you learn in school. "Cursive" one of many strange words telling you a different language spoken in school and you will always be a stranger in that strange land. Not everybody good at cursive, not every boy or girl in class remembers new words or gives a flying fuck if they do or don't, but my grandmother's cursive flows seamlessly page after page when you leaf through one of the old Homewood AME Zion notebooks and ledgers with thick, ornate covers she filled and you are not aware until you discover one more time as you always do how shabby the world will be, how much it hurts when her hand drops yours and perfect writing stops.

My grandmother picked her husbands as carefully, perfectly as she performed her church-secretary cursive. Except every now and then she decided it was time to change scripts. After she abandoned then divorced her first husband—a dark-skinned working-man, shy emigrant from rural Promised Land, South Carolina, father of my father and my aunt C, the man I grew up calling Grandpa—my grandmother Martha chose to marry preachers. A series of three or four preachers whose names I often could not remember when they were alive, names mostly lost now they are dead, like the name of the man my father killed. Uncle this or Uncle that is what I called my grandmother's husbands and one I called Reverend because he addressed me as Professor, a darky joke we shared, minstrels puffing each other up with entitles, Yo, Mr. Bones. Wuss up, Mr. Sambo.

Same grandmother who wrote beautiful cursive, played deaf (almost but not quite her version of darky joke) when people were saying things she preferred not to hear. A highly selective deficit she displayed only when she chose. For instance, sitting on her pink couch she protected with a transparent plastic slipcover, chattering away with a roomful of other family members, if someone mentioned the name of one of ours in trouble or prison, my grandmother Martha would shut her eyes, duck her head shyly, totally absent herself as if she'd suddenly nodded off like very old folks do. If you didn't know better, you'd think she was missing the conversation. Elsewhere. Immune. But if the unpleasant topic not dropped quickly enough to suit her, she would shush the person speaking by tapping an index finger against her pursed lips. Not nice . . . shhh. Some mean somebody might be listening and spread nasty news about a son or grandson or nephew shot dead in the street three years ago or locked up in the pokey twenty years, or a slave two hundred years ago. Shhh. Whisper, she orders as she leans over, pouts, and mimics whispering. Best whisper in a family member's ear so cruel strangers can't overhear, can't mock names of our dead, our wounded, our missing ones.

I regard my empire. Map it. Set down its history in ledgers. Envy my grandmother's beautiful hand. Her cold-bloodedness. I've done what I needed to do to get by, and when I look back, the only way to make sense of my actions is to tell myself that at the time it must have seemed I had no other choice.

As far back as I can remember, I was aware the empire I was building lived within an empire ruled by and run for the benefit of a group to which I did not belong. *Mm'fukkahs, the man, honkies, whitey, boss, peckerwoods, ma'am, fools, mister, sir*—some of the names we used for this group not us, and the list of names I learned goes on and on, as many names probably as *they* learned to call *us* by. Growing up, if I found myself talking to people, small gathering or large, almost always it would be composed exclusively of members of my group or, except for me, members of the other. On the other hand, nothing unusual about contact between the two groups. Ordinary, daily mixing the rule not the exception. In public spaces we politely ignored each other or smiled or evaded or bumped, jostled, violently collided, or clashed. Passed through each other as easy as stepping through a ghost. Despised, killed each other just as easily, though since the others held the power, many, many more fatal casualties in our group resulting from those encounters than in theirs.

Majority rules, we learned. Fair enough. Except, since we spent most of our time among our own kind, talking, interacting only with each other, slippage occurred naturally. Reinforced by the presence of friends and family, we considered ourselves among ourselves the equal of others. Or considered ourselves better. Considered our status as minority, as inferior, not to be fact. Or at best a relative fact, irrelevant to us unless we assumed the point of view of the group not our group. On good days members of our group would make fun of such an assumption. Bad-mouth the other group with all the nasty names we dreamed up for them. Names and laughter like talismans—string of garlic, sign of the cross—European people in the old days would brandish to fend off a vampire. A survival strategy we practiced while the other group survived by arming themselves, by erecting walls, prisons, churches, laws. By chanting, screaming, repeating, believing their words for us.

Ain't nothing but a party, old Aunt May always said. How long, how long, sighed Reverend Felder in Homewood AME Zion's pulpit, Dr. King in Atlanta's Ebenezer Baptist's.

Aunt May's skin a lighter color than my grandmother Martha's light brown, and the difference, slight though it was, cowed my grandmother enough to look the other way or pretend to be deaf when May got loud, raunchy, or ignorant at family gatherings. May, tumbler of whiskey held down with one hand on the armrest of her wheelchair while the hand at the end of her other arm points, wiggles, summons all at once, a gesture synced with a holler, growl, and Mm-mm, boy, you better get yourself over here and gimme some sugar, boy, get over here and dance with your aunt May, boy, you think you grown now, don't you, you sweetie pie, past dancing wit some old, crippled-up lady in a wheelchair, ain't that what you thinking, boy? Well, this old girl ain't done yet. Huh-uh. You all hear me, don't you? Ain't nothin' but a party. Woo-wee. Get your narrow hips over here, you fine young man, and dance wit May.

They left something behind in Aunt May's gut they shouldn't have when they sewed her up after surgery. Staple, piece of tape, maybe a whole damn scalpel, my sister rolled her eyes telling me. You know how they do us, my sister said, specially old people can't help themselves, won't speak up—poor May in terrible pain, belly blew up and almost dead a week after they sent her home. So weak and full of drugs, poor thing, lying there in her bed could barely open her eyes. But you know Aunt May. Ain't going nowhere till she ready to go. Hospital didn't want her back, but we fussed till they sent an ambulance. Opened her up again and took out whatever festering. May got better. Didn't leave from here till she was good and ready to leave. You know May. Hospital assholes never even said they were sorry. Threw May away like a dirty old rag after they saw they hadn't quite killed her, and then got busy covering their tracks. May dead two years before anybody admitted any wrongdoing. Too late to hold the hospital accountable. Simpleminded as all those pale folks on May's side the family always been, couldn't get their act together and sue the doctors or hospital or some cotton-picking somebody while May still alive.

May's nephew Clarence, you remember him. Browner than I am, I reminded my sister as if she didn't already know. I ran into him five, six years ago, when I was in town for something. Clarence a cook now. Guess at some point May and her pale sisters decided some color might be a good idea. Two, maybe three married brothers from the same brown-skinned family, didn't they, and broke the color line, so Clarence and a bunch of our other second cousins or half cousins or whatever, after a couple more generations of marrying and mixing, got different colors and names and I've lost track, but Clarence I knew because he was my age and a Golden Gloves boxer and everybody knew him and knew his older brother, Arthur, in jail for bank robbery, put away big-time in a federal penitentiary, so when Clarence walked into Mrs. Schaefer's eleventh-grade class, which was a couple grades further than Clarence ever got, he wasn't supposed to be in that eleventh-grade classroom or any other, he just happened to be hanging out strolling the high school halls and saw me and came in and hollered, Hey, Cuz, how you doing, man. And me, I kind of hiss-whispered back, Hey, what you doing here? Him acting like nobody else in the classroom when he strutted in, walked straight to my seat in the back, loud-talking the whole way till I popped up, Hey, Cuz, and hugged him, shocking the shit out of Mrs. Schaefer because I was her nice boy, good student and good citizen and example for all the other hoodlums. You could tell how terrified the poor white lady was most the time, coming every day into a school not all colored yet but getting there and getting worse and she needed me as much as I needed her, we both understood, so who in hell was this other tall colored boy acting like he owned her classroom with nobody he had to answer to but himself and that was my cousin Clarence, he couldn't care less what anybody else thought, you could tell just looking at him once, stranger to you or not, that you better go on about your own business and hope this particular reddish brown–skinned Negro with straight, dago-black hair and crazy eyes got no business with you. You heard the stories, didn't you, Sis? You most likely told some of them to me—bouncer at a club downtown, mob enforcer maybe, got paid for doing time for the crime of some Mafia thug don and afterward Cousin Clarence a kind of honorary made man, people say, but most of the worst of that bad stuff long after we hugged and grinned and took over Mrs. Schaefer's class a minute because he didn't care and I forgot for once to care who it belonged to.

Aunt C, my father's sister, got him a fine lawyer. But things continued to get worse. Worse is what you begin to expect if worse is what you get time after time. Worse, worser, worst. Don't let the ugly take you down, my mother said. Don't let it make you bitter and ugly, she said. She had led me by the hand to a few decent places inside me where she believed and tried to convince me that little sputtering lights would always exist to guide how I should behave once I left home and started a grown-up life. Her hand not as powerful and elegant as my grandmother Martha's, but my mother wrote good letters, clear, to the point, often funny, her cursive retaining features of the young girl she'd been when she learned to write. Neat, precise, demonstrating obviously she'd been an attentive student, yearned to get right the lessons she was taught.

Earnest another way of putting it, *it* being my mom's character when she was a schoolgirl and then when she fell in love with my father, I bet, and that sort of mother too, I absolutely know, serious, conscientious without being boring, never boring because whatever she undertook she performed in the spirit partly of girls in grade school nearly junior high age, always a little scared but bold too, both idly mischievous and full of hidden purpose, full of giggles and iron courage adults could never comprehend, often dismiss, yet stand in awe of also, charmed, protective of the spark, that desire of young colored girls to grow and thrive, their hunger to connect with an unknown world, no matter how perilous that new-to-them world might turn out to be for girls determined to discover exciting uses for limbs, minds, hearts still forming, still as stunning for them to possess as those girl hearts, minds, limbs were stunning for adults to behold. In the case of my mother, from girlhood to womanhood, an infectious curiosity, a sense of not starting over but starting fresh, let's go here, let's do this, not because she had mastered a situation or a moment previously but because uncertainty attracted, motivated, formed her.

Look at this writing, I can almost hear her say, look at these letters, words, sentences, ideas, feelings that flow and connect when we attempt something in this particular, careful fashion, with this cursive we studied and repeated in a classroom, but mine now, see, see it going word by word, carefully, and I follow her words, her writing like that of a bright child who is occasionally distracted while she busily inscribes line after almost perfect line from manual to copybook. Going the way it's supposed to go. And where it's going, nobody knows exactly where but it looks the way it should and worth the trouble, the practice, because it's mine now and yours too, she tells me, if you wish, and work hard at it. Whatever. Take my hand. Hold it as I hold yours, precious boy, and let's see, let's see what we shall see.

That's the message I read in her hand, in letters my mother sent when I went away to college. Letters I receive today from home beyond these pages. Home we share with all our dead.

I thought at the time, the time when I'd just begun university teaching, that the worst consequence of my father stabbing another man to death would be my first meeting with the chair in his office after I returned from Pittsburgh. After I'd said to my mother, Don't worry, I'll be home soon, and hung up the phone and tried to explain an ugly, complicated situation in as few words as possible, and the chair had generously excused me from my teaching duties and granted me unconditional license to attend to family affairs. A terrible business, he said. Sorry it hit before you could get yourself settled in here. The worst would be wisdom, commiseration, condolences I'd have to endure one more time animating his face, in his office, in his position as departmental chair after I completed my dirty work at home and stood in his office again, forgiven again by his unrufflable righteousness.

A good man, my mother would call him. Ole peckerwood, May would say. I heard both voices, responded to neither. Too busy worrying about myself. Too confused, enraged, selfish. Not prepared yet to deal with matters far worse afflicting my father, his victim, the victim's family, all my people back home, our group that another more powerful group has treated like shit for centuries to intimidate and oppress, to prove to themselves that a country occupied by many groups belongs forever, solely, unconditionally to one group.

My sister needs a minute or so to summon up the name, but then she's certain, James . . . and I think his first name Riley . . . uh-huh . . . Riley James, she says is the name of the man our father killed. Neither of us speaks. Silence we both maintain for a while is proof she's probably correct. Silence of a search party standing at the edge of a vast lake after the guide who's led them to it points and says the missing one is out there somewhere. Silence because we've already plunged, already groping in the chill murkiness, holding our breath, dreading what we'll recover or not from the gray water.

Thought I'd recognize the name if I heard it. That jolt, you know, when you're reminded of something you will never forget. But James sounds right, anyway. And Riley James had kids, didn't he. Yes, my sister says. Three. One a girl about my age, I'm pretty sure. Used to run into her before it happened.

Coming up, did you ever think we might need to have this conversation one day?

Daddy killing someone else's daddy?

Oh, we knew. Children understand. Don't need adults to tell them certain things. Kids supposed to listen to grown-ups, better listen if you don't want a sore behind, but we watch them too. Kids always watching, wondering why big people do what they do. Understand a whole lotta mess out there adults not talking about. Scary mess kids can't handle. Or maybe nobody, kid or adult, can handle it, so you better keep your eyes wide open. Don't even know what you looking for except it's bad. Gonna get you if you not careful. But no. Thank goodness, no. Huh-uh, I'm not standing here today saying that when I was a little girl I could see my father would kill another man. But we knew, we saw with our own eyes awful stuff happening day after day and worse just around the corner waiting to happen. Grown-ups didn't need to tell us all that mess happening to them. We watched while it happened.

Wish I could disagree, Tish. Wish I could say no, but no, I think we probably did know. You're remembering right again, Sis.

Will it always be like this, then? Too late. Damage done. Another victim. Trial. Funeral. Inquest. Story in the newspaper, on TV. More tears. Hand-wringing.

It's worse now. Doesn't seem possible, but it just might be. Not only for our family. Shit no. Not just us. Everybody. Everybody jammed up here wit us in this stinking mess. Everybody just too scared or too dumb to know it, is what our brother said with his eyes when I came to town to visit and we let go of each other when time for me to leave the prison and he has to stay where he is and nothing to do but look at each other one more time, one more sad, helpless stinking time. Clang, bang, gate shuts behind me and they still got the key.

We had talked about power during that visit. Talked in the cage. Power how long, too long stolen by the ruling group to diminish and control the ruled. Power of this political system that has operated from its start as if vast gaps dividing us from the ruling group either don't exist or don't matter. Same ole shit. Ask the brothers in here, our brother says. Ask the outlaws. Ask them about law supposed to protect everybody—rulers and ruled—from one another equally. Law calling itself the will of the people. Law that got all us in here blackened up like minstrels. Color, His Honor Mr. Law says, no problem. While out the other side of his mouth he's saying color gives law power to abuse color. Look at the color around us in here. Some days I look and cry. Laugh some days. Our colors, our group. Power serves itself. Period. Exclamation point. Truth and only truth, our locked-up brother says. And he's not wrong, our brother not wrong, so how can I be right? My empire. They slam the gate shut. Blam. Time to leave my brother's cage, go back in mine. My maps. Ledgers. Theirs.

Remember when I called you couple weeks ago, Sis, and asked the man's name Daddy killed? Conversation got long, much longer than usual, nice in a way because usually conversations shortish because we skip over awful things and don't want to jinx good things by talking too much about them, but I remember I think we both got deep into the begats, both trying to recall Daddy's grandmother's name and neither could, and Owens popped into

my mind and I said Owens to you and you said, Sybil Owens—
wasn't she the slave from down south who came up here to found
Homewood? And you were right of course, and I laughed because
I was the one who wrote down the Sybela Owens story and you
knew the story from my books or from family conversations.
Same family conversations from which I'd learned, mostly from
May, about May's grandmother or great-grandmother Sybela, who
had fled slavery with a white man who stole Sybela from his slave-
plantation-owner father and settled in or near what's now called
Homewood, where one day when May was a little girl she saw,
according to her, an old, old woman on a porch in a rocking chair
smoking a pipe, woman in a long black dress, dark stockings, and
head rag who smiled at her, and she'd hear people say later the old
woman was her grandmother, maybe great-grand, and May never
forgot and passed on the memory or tale or whatever to us, a story
about Mom's side of the family, not Daddy's, and I wrote or talked
my version of it and you probably heard May herself tell it like I did
but years and years ago, and the best we usually do as we try to sort
out the family tree and put names to branches, to people, is most
likely to mix up things the way I did with "Owens" before you
corrected my memory and I reminded myself and you how family
stories were partly what one of us had heard live from the mouth
of the one who had lived the story or heard it second- or thirdhand
and passed it on but partly also stuff I had made up, written down
and it got passed around the family same as accounts of actual wit-
nesses telling stories the way May told hers about Sybela. So that
day on the phone we were begatting this one from that one and so
on, you said, Hold on a minute, and went up to the attic where you
keep those boxes and boxes of Mom's things, the papers and letters
she saved from the old people in the family, because you believed
there was an obituary in rough draft in Mom's hand on tablet paper
that might tell us Daddy's grandmother's name, the name I could
hear my father and Aunt C saying plain as day but could not raise
beyond a whispering in my ear too faint to grasp or repeat aloud to

myself. And sure enough you quickly retrieved information Mom had written down long ago for a church funeral program, maybe for the colored newspaper too, a couple sheets of blue-lined school-table paper, lines and handwriting faded, creases in the paper, the obituary notice we both had remembered but neither could repeat the exact contents of. You had the folded sheets in your hand in a minute once you got up those steep-assed attic steps I worry about my little sis climbing because she's not little sis anymore.

But sweet still. Yes. This is your eldest brother speaking to you, girl. Two of our brothers gone, just us two left and our brother in the slam and when you read me Mom's notes for her father's obituary they included Daddy's name but did not mention our father's mother's mother so of course they solved nothing, just deepened the puzzle of how and why and where and who we come from and here we are again, and whatever we discover about long ago, it never tells us enough, does it. Not what we are or what comes next after all that mess we don't even know maybe or not happened before . . . well, we try . . . and after I listened to you reading bits of information the note compiled, I thought about the meaning of long ago, and how absolutely long ago separates past and present, about the immeasurable sadness, immeasurable distance that well up in me often when I hear the words "long ago," and on another day, in another conversation, I will attempt to explain how certain words or phrases reveal more than I might choose to know, an unsettling awareness like seeing an ugly tail on an animal I know damn well has no tail or a tail negligible as the one people carry around and can't see, and I will ask you, Tish, what if I'm trying to imagine *long ago* and a shitty, terrible-looking tail appears, a tail like the one I'm sure doesn't belong on a famil-iar animal but grows longer, larger and hides the animal. Wraps round and round and takes over. Will there be nothing left then? I will ask you. Nothing. Not even wishful thinking. The life, the long ago, once upon a time I am trying to imagine—gone like the animal not supposed to own a tail and the tail I inflicted upon it.

Reading The O. Henry Prize Stories 2019

The Jurors on Their Favorites

Our jurors read the twenty O. Henry Prize stories in a blind manuscript. Each story appears in the same type and format with no attribution of the magazine that published it or the author's name. The jurors don't consult one another or the series editor about their decision. Although the jurors write their essays without knowledge of the authors' names, the names are inserted into the essays later for the sake of clarity. —LF

Lynn Freed on "Omakase" by Weike Wang

I have read any number of metaphors for the difference between novels and short stories. The one I favor concerns plum pudding. If the novel is the whole pudding, the theory goes, then the short story is the piece with the coin in it. Certainly, when I read a short story, I want to come away a bit richer.

I also like to come away surprised, as if by a truth I have known and forgotten. This is to say that a story requires, on the reader's part, some exercise of imagination. And I love a story sure-footed enough to take for granted the world in which it takes place.

We are much subject these days—especially in the academy,

but also in the literary world—to a rather cloying reverence for diversity. The broadening of horizons seems to be the point. And so one encounters a preponderance of horizon-broadening customs, exotic foods, crazy aunties, elders confounded by America, England, etc. And then, occasionally, one comes upon a story that quickly, without tricks and manipulations, takes the reader into a world both new and familiar, and does so with the divine relief of irony. "Omakase" is, for me, such a prize.

It does not start out with a bang. "The couple" is going out for sushi. "The woman," daughter of Chinese immigrants, is a rather introverted research analyst at a bank ("She was . . . the kind to create an Excel spreadsheet of everything she owned and send it to him, so that he could then highlight what he also owned and specify quantity and type"). "The man" is an extroverted American ceramic-pottery instructor, given to rolling his eyes, as if in jest, at what he wishes to distance himself from. But, in the restaurant, when the woman feels herself marooned by his eye-rolling, "a spike of anger went through [her]. Or maybe two spikes. She imagined taking two toothpicks and sticking them through the man's pretty eyes to stop them from rolling. Then she imagined making herself a very dry martini with a skewer of olives."

One of the brilliant aspects of this story lies in the matter-of-fact nature of the narration, the way it moves through the territory of the story as if from one stepping stone to the next, trusting the reader to follow. Another is the voice—deadpan, wry, sharp, relentless, and clearly, despite the fact that it is written in the third person, the woman's. It is also, clearly, Chinese, never mind that the woman herself "didn't want to be one of those women who noted every teeny tiny thing and racialized it." The fact is, race is at work throughout this story, from the start of the affair to the end of the omakase. It is endemic to the romance itself, informs her embarrassment at the man's relentless probing of the Japanese chef, is at play in his visit to her parents ("who had been taught to loathe the Japanese"), and then in the Japanese chef himself and his swipe at the Chinese.

Throughout, some of the most cogent moments take place in the woman's head, in silence. "She wanted to say to the waitress, You have no idea how hard some of us worked so that you could dye your hair purple and pierce your lip." And it is left to the reader to make (perfect) sense of it.

In the hands of a comedian, much of this material could be rendered as hilarious shtick. In the hands of a master of fiction, it delivers riches.

Lynn Freed's books include six novels, a collection of stories, and a collection of essays. Her work has appeared in *Harper's Magazine*, *The New Yorker*, *The Atlantic*, and *The New York Times*, among others. She is the recipient of the inaugural Katherine Anne Porter Award in fiction from the American Academy of Arts and Letters, two O. Henry Prizes, and fellowships from the National Endowment for the Arts and the John Simon Guggenheim Foundation, among others. Born in Durban, South Africa, she now lives in Northern California.

Elizabeth Strout on "Girl of Few Seasons" by Rachel Kondo

What a magnificent story this is! From the very beginning I knew I was in the presence of a quiet and gracious authority—that the author knew what she was doing and would deliver me with safe hands. And I was delivered; I kept thinking about this story a long time after I put it down.

I think this is because it is beautifully written—but what does that mean? It means there was one truthful sentence after another and that I felt these sentences instinctively to be true. I knew the pigeons in the coop were real, I felt Ebo's distress at having to kill the last one, I knew that the house was true, his mother, and also Daddy. Just *true*.

It also means that there were continual small—and large— surprises in the work, that as I rode the waves of the loveliness of it I was always slightly or largely shaken by one of these surprises, which never seemed gratuitous. And it means that the story unfolded without a hitch; there was a wonderful sense of its rolling forward at its own pace; the way it handled time was seamless, a peek ahead, a real glance backward, but always staying on course. The very first paragraph gives us a huge amount of information, but in a soft and tight way, each sentence flowing so naturally from the one before it. It means there was a clarity to it all, that I never felt outside of the setting and the globe it put me into.

Mostly, though, the emotional truthfulness of this story is what makes it so exquisite. One can utterly feel the experience of Ebo, and we are with him right through the unexpected and glorious ending.

Elizabeth Strout is the author of six books of fiction. Her first novel, *Amy and Isabelle*, won the *Chicago Tribune*'s Heartland Prize and was also shortlisted for the Orange Prize and the PEN/ Faulkner Award. Strout is the author of *Abide with Me*; *Olive Kitteridge*, which won the Pulitzer Prize in 2009; and *The Burgess Boys*, nominated for the Harper Lee Prize in fiction. Her latest book is a novel, *Anything Is Possible*. She was born in Portland, Maine, and lives in New York City.

Lara Vapnyar on "Funny Little Snake" by Tessa Hadley

"The child was nine years old and couldn't fasten her own buttons."

I was bothered by this first sentence, because it made me immediately dislike the child in question, and I couldn't understand why. All we're given is bare facts, the age of the child and her inability to fasten buttons at that age. Immediately after that we're told that this was a Victorian-type dress with hundreds of buttons. This information should have redeemed the child in my eyes (who among us can boast of ease with Victorian buttons!), but instead I noticed that my initial dislike was steadily growing into squeamish disgust. There was the smell of the child: "she still smelled of something furtive—musty spice from the back of a cupboard." The physical description: "a doll—with a plain, pale, wide face, her temples blue-naked where her hair was strained back, her wide-open gray eyes affronted and evasive and set too far apart." Or the creepy scene of her playing with her poorly made toys:

> One voice was coaxing and hopeful, the other one reluctant. "Put on your special gloves," one of them said. "But I don't like the blue color," said the other. "These ones have special powers," the first voice persisted. "Try them out."

But by that time it was clear to me that the disgust I felt was communicated to me through the narrator: Valerie, the young stepmother of the child, forced to be her caregiver because the child's father didn't express any interest in performing his functions. Valerie is very honest about her reluctance to spend time with the child.

> She didn't really want the child around. But Robyn was part of the price she paid for having been singled out by the professor among the girls in the faculty office at King's College London, having married him and moved with him to begin a new life in the North.

Valerie is just as clear-eyed about the feelings of her husband, the child's father. "He might have found fatherhood easier, Valerie thought, if his daughter had been pretty."

It was this line that pricked me with guilt. I realized that I felt more than simply invested in the story, I felt implicated along with the main character for disliking the child, even though nothing really warranted it, except for her lack of beauty, liveliness, or pleasant manners.

This was when I understood that I was in the presence of true greatness.

When I read about the child treating her new pajamas as her most precious possession, insisting on holding on to them during a meal at a restaurant, I felt both heartbroken and ashamed—ashamed because of my initial squeamishness. As I proceeded to read the story, getting to know more and more about the horror of the child's situation, about the true scope of the neglect, what I experienced wasn't simple compassion but true heartbreak, because I felt responsible now.

By the time the story reached its climax, I felt that the responsibility was on me in the same way as it was on Valerie. My initial guilt (as well as Valerie's) prevented me from being a neutral bystander. I needed this child to be saved for my sake, and not just the child's or Valerie's. I was so engaged with the story that I felt that it was my peace at stake here.

Most successful short stories have the power to move you emotionally or stimulate you intellectually, or even simply to entertain you. But only a few truly great ones can directly involve you like that, breaking and shaping you into something new.

Lara Vapnyar came to the United States from Russia in 1994. She is a recipient of a John Simon Guggenheim Fellowship and the Goldberg Prize for Jewish fiction. Her stories and essays have appeared in *The New Yorker*, *The New York Times*, *Harper's Magazine*, and *Vogue*.

Writing The O. Henry Prize Stories 2019

The Writers on Their Work

Alexia Arthurs, "Mermaid River"
Some stories feel closer than others. I wrote "Mermaid River" during my first year in Iowa, where I'd moved for graduate school. I was thinking about a few things: I was twenty-four, and had the terrible sense that my family, or my idea of them as individuals and as a unit, was fracturing. My brother was experiencing the United States as a black man. I was the farthest I had ever been from my mother and two siblings, which was a kind of relief. I was thinking about loving through and in spite of distance. I was also remembering Canarsie, the Caribbean neighborhood I had left behind in Brooklyn. In that place, I'd known Caribbean mothers, like Samson's mother, who left children behind in the care of loved ones, with the hopes of settling in the United States and eventually sending for them. In writing "Mermaid River," I was also thinking about tourism and how much of a place and the history of a place is done away with and reimagined for outsiders.

Alexia Arthurs was born in Jamaica in 1988 and moved with her family to Brooklyn in 2000. She has published short stories in

Granta, *Small Axe*, *Virginia Quarterly Review*, *Vice*, Shondaland, BuzzFeed, and *The Paris Review*, which awarded her the Plimpton Prize in 2017.

Sarah Shun-lien Bynum, "Julia and Sunny"

I wrote the opening of this story several years ago and then put it away for a long stretch of time as other parts of life happened. But it's always a relief to have something to return to, even if it's only a few paragraphs, and especially if you haven't written for a while and are feeling uncertain about how and where to begin again. When I returned to it, I was thinking about how much I enjoy reading stories that consider the overall shape of a thing—a career, a romantic history, the course of a friendship— and how often I reread the work of Alice Munro and Joan Silber to experience this pleasure. I wanted to try to write a story like that, and out of my attempt came this story, which I think may be just as much about the failure to discern an overall shape as it is about the shape itself—in this case, the shape of a marriage. Or the shape of two marriages. Two marriages that seem to share a single shape until it's revealed that they don't. With this story I was interested in voice, too; I wondered if a conversational, digressive, lightly offered voice could still convey the deep sense of loss that has compelled its narrator to speak.

Sarah Shun-lien Bynum is the author of two novels, *Ms. Hempel Chronicles*, a finalist for the PEN/Faulkner Award, and *Madeleine Is Sleeping*, a finalist for the National Book Award and winner of the Janet Heidinger Kafka Prize. Her short fiction has appeared in magazines and anthologies, including *Tin House*, *Glimmer Train*, *The New Yorker*, and *The Best American Short Stories*. She was born in Houston, grew up in Boston, and now lives in Los Angeles.

Patricia Engel, "Aguacero"
Every Colombian has been touched by the violence of a civil war that lasted over half a century. Though I was raised in the United States, I have known many people who were kidnapped or who've had family members kidnapped. In some cases, captives were killed, but in others, victims were eventually released and expected to just go on with their lives, often keeping silent about their imprisonment. The father of one of my best friends was held for five months; I remember the terror the family endured, how they navigated the estrangement once he came home when everything about him, from his appearance to the way he spoke, had changed. I wanted to write about intimate violence and an unlikely friendship, strangers who find comfort in each other for a time, and how, despite our fragility and impermanence, not only our traumas but the people who touch our lives in good ways can remain with us forever.

Patricia Engel was born to Colombian parents and raised in New Jersey. She is the author of *The Veins of the Ocean*, winner of the Dayton Literary Peace Prize; *It's Not Love, It's Just Paris*; and *Vida*, a finalist for the PEN/Hemingway Award and the Young Lions Fiction Award, and winner of Colombia's national book award. She is the recipient of a National Endowment for the Arts fellowship. Her books have been widely translated, and her stories have appeared in *The Best American Short Stories*, *The Best American Mystery Stories*, and elsewhere. Engel currently teaches creative writing at the University of Miami.

Tessa Hadley, "Funny Little Snake"
Some stories begin with a very decisive seed or insight, but although "Funny Little Snake" has a very particular flavor now, it actually began rather indefinitely. All the extravagant period detail

came later on: first of all, I just liked the idea of that conjunction of three females—mother, daughter, and stepmother. It felt almost like a shape I could put down anywhere, and make something interesting. Then next I had that opening, with the buttons, the helpless gesture of the child holding up her arm for fastening. I had round brown buttons like those on a dress myself, when I was a little girl in the 1960s—although nothing in my actual life apart from the buttons and that dress bore any resemblance to the material in the story. My childhood was much safer and more ordinary, thank goodness. From the buttons the whole of the rest of it unfolded. In the original three-women shape I had expected the mother and stepmother to begin in antagonism and end with a warmer mutual insight. But as the character of Marise began to elbow itself so fiercely onto the page, I realized that would be sentimental. Not that the story doesn't have its sympathy with Marise—some sympathetic insight, into her origins and history. But I knew there was no reconciliation possible between her and Valerie. And that was when I understood that the story must end in high drama—a real rescue from danger, like the one in Bergman's *Fanny and Alexander*, when the Jewish antique dealer smuggles the children out from the house of the wicked bishop. That filmic sequence was my inspiration, in writing the closing pages of the story.

Tessa Hadley was born in 1956 in Bristol, England, and grew up there. She has written seven novels—*Accidents in the Home*; *Everything Will Be All Right*; *The Master Bedroom*; *The London Train*; *Clever Girl*; *The Past*, which won the Hawthornden Prize; and *Late in the Day*—and published three collections of short stories, *Sunstroke*, *Married Love*, and *Bad Dreams*. She publishes short stories regularly in *The New Yorker*, reviews for *The Guardian* and the *London Review of Books*, and is a professor of creative writing at Bath Spa University. In 2016, she was awarded a Windham-Campbell Prize for fiction. She lives in London.

Sarah Hall, "Goodnight Nobody"

"Goodnight Nobody" was written after several life-changing events over the last few years—most especially the birth of my daughter and the death of my mother. I also became a single parent during that period. It was a time of emotional extremes and physical difficulty, but also processing the existential nature of these events was incredibly challenging. Fiction doesn't provide answers to those big questions of life and death, but it can be companionable—for readers and for the writer—in the asking of them. I was reading *Goodnight Moon* by Margaret Wise Brown to my daughter a lot, and every time I got to the blank page that says "Goodnight nobody" I would feel a kind of existential vertigo. Oddly it wasn't a wholly unpleasant sensation, more like some kind of exposure of truth. One more event triggered the writing of this particular story. There was a report in the British news about a newborn baby that had been killed by a dog in a northern town close to where I was brought up. How to explain such things? I suppose Jem, the mature questioning child in the story, is trying to simply comprehend mortality. She is, in the end, walking up to a mortuary door by herself. Don't we all, at some point?

Sarah Hall was born in 1974 and raised in the Lake District in Cumbria. She received an MLitt in creative writing from St. Andrews, Scotland. She is the author of five prizewinning novels— *Haweswater*, *The Electric Michelangelo*, *Daughters of the North*, *How to Paint a Dead Man*, and *The Wolf Border*—and two short story collections, *The Beautiful Indifference* and *Madame Zero*. Her third collection, *Sudden Traveller*, will be published in 2019. Hall is a recipient of the American Academy of Arts and Letters E. M. Forster Award. She lives in Norwich, Norfolk, England.

Isabella Hammad, "Mr. Can'aan"

While writing "Mr. Can'aan" I remember describing the experience to a friend as "sticky"—the story was coming out with excruciating slowness, at a rate of something like a sentence a day. But while the process was difficult, by the time I reached the finish line and looked back over what I had written, I did not see much I wanted to revise. This was a pleasant surprise at the end of a dark, sticky tunnel.

I did not have a logical conception of the story as I began, only a feeling. I also had a few ideas and influences floating around in my head: the work of the Lebanese artist Walid Raad, certain short stories by Alice Munro, the lives of several Palestinian historians I knew, the films of Olivier Assayas. These four things all had something to say about the life of stories: what stories can "do" in the world, the way they are passed along, how they act upon others. For me that seemed particularly relevant to Palestine. Sometimes it can feel as though Palestine has more substance in the stories people tell about it (to themselves, to others) than it has in reality.

Something else those four influences explored, or at least conjured in me, was a sense of time that wasn't straightforward or predictable. And from the beginning, "Mr. Can'aan" felt like a story that was going to leap through time.

Isabella Hammad was born in London. Her work has been published in *Conjunctions* and elsewhere, and she was the 2018 winner of *The Paris Review*'s Plimpton Prize for fiction. Her first novel was *The Parisian*. She lives in New York.

Caoilinn Hughes, "Prime"

The triggering incident or moment for "Prime" took place when I was a schoolgirl of thirteen or fourteen. Call it twenty years ago. I was a writer by then and I viscerally recall that day: the dizzy, momentous feeling that comes when inspiration (or the catalyst needed to make something decent) drops in. But I only wrote poetry at the time, and I knew that a poem was not the form for what I wanted to render. When I got around to fiction writing in my twenties, I started with the novel and wrote several of those before ever attempting a short story. "Prime" is the second short story I've written. It is the only form "Prime" could have taken. After all those years writing poetry and novels, I felt ready to try to realize it on the page. I didn't know how the story would play out or how it would be told—the span of time, point of view, setting, characters, all of that—I just had the box and the abstract role of a teacher. Everything else arrived by writing slow slowly slow and erasing every false note. *Do they really think her coat is made of carpet?* I would go back and forth on such things for hours, until I realized that the problem was in thinking of *them*. I had to enter the circle of *we*, come what may. The writing process was frightening because the story asks a lot of a reader and I believed (as I wrote it) that it *wanted* a reader—that *we* wanted the reader there as a friend—to fill the eighth chair. But readers are not always benevolent, and I was afraid for the children (and for myself) to introduce another unreliable, unpredictable presence into their/our world.

Little did I know how they would turn the tables on their teacher and on the reader both—not to be playful or coy or manipulative or to placate, but to unburden our heavy adult heads, and to demonstrate youth's wild courage and resilience.

Caoilinn Hughes was born in Ireland in 1985. Her first novel, *Orchid and the Wasp*, was shortlisted for the Butler Literary Award. Her poetry collection, *Gathering Evidence*, won the *Irish Times*'s Shine/Strong Award. Her work has appeared in *Tin House*, *Poetry*, and elsewhere. In 2018, Hughes won the Moth Short Story Prize.

John Keeble, "Synchronicity"

I don't think the buffalo were in on the start of the story. I think it started being about tractor repair, which is probably a pretty dull subject for many readers, but the buffalo came into it fairly early on. First, it occurred to me that I'd seen a neighbor canning buffalo tongues, a delicacy. It went from there. There were two young buffalo bulls that were kept in a marginal pen on a farm. As they grew older they became fearsome, and there was the place the story was set, eastern Washington, which in that summer was the site of fires. Hundreds of thousands of acres burned and so the desecration that the buffalo as a species had already endured extended incrementally. Then there was the small herd of buffalo from the Kalispel Reservation that passed into the fires. As the writing developed, there came to be people in it, who are always necessary to stories. There was a family who made connections with the two buffalo and for whom the buffalo became expressive of significant things in their natures—foolish pride, misplaced ownership, sadness, and finally despair. An unnamed narrator observes all of it.

John Keeble was born in Winnipeg, Manitoba, Canada, and raised in Saskatchewan and then in California, and so has dual citizenship. He is the author of six novels, including his most recent, *The Appointment: The Tale of Adaline Carson*. He is the author of *Out of the Channel: The Exxon Valdez Oil Spill in Prince William Sound*, which won a Washington State Governor's Writers Day Award. His collection of short stories is *Nocturnal America*. He was the recipient of a John Simon Guggenheim Fellowship. Keeble's novel *Broken Ground* was selected as one of the best books in the Oregon Cultural Heritage Commission's exhibit *Literary Oregon, One Hundred Books, 1800–2000*. He lives in eastern Washington.

Rachel Kondo, "Girl of Few Seasons"
The story drew its inspiration from my father, whose younger sister Beverly was handicapped by illness when she was very young. Beyond a black-and-white photo taken of her just prior to her illness, I don't know much about her because my father has said very little. And I don't think it's because the memory of her is lost to him, though more than fifty years have passed, but rather the opposite—his experience of Beverly before, his witnessing of his mother's grief after, all of it remains alive and vivid still. I suppose I feel drawn to those places where pain is exquisite and words are few. I'm interested in a sort of silence, not as a marker of failed communication, but as a possible measure of impossible loss.

Rachel Kondo was born and raised on Maui, Hawaii. Her most recent writing has appeared in *Electric Literature* and *Indiana Review*. A graduate of the Michener Center for Writers, she now lives in Los Angeles.

Alexander MacLeod, "Lagomorph"
In my head, "Lagomorph" is a story about time and about change and about the decisions we make when we are apportioning the little bit of care we send out into the world. I was interested in the way people love animals differently than they love people and I gave Gunther just a touch of supernatural longevity so that he and the narrator would be locked into a relationship that moved well beyond normal limitations. The unnervingly silent way that rabbits pay attention to everything around them was also important to me. I wanted Gunther to just be there with my couple for a long, long time, a quiet witness, taking it all in. Then, in the end, I wanted to imagine these two people coming together again inside his head. I wanted to see their lives as *his* memory so that, in some weird reversal, when the two of them couldn't exist

together in any other way, they would eventually end up belonging to him.

Alexander MacLeod was born in 1972 in Inverness, Nova Scotia, and grew up in Windsor, Ontario. His first book, *Light Lifting*, was a finalist for the Scotiabank Giller Prize, the Commonwealth Book Prize, and the Frank O'Connor International Short Story Award. The collection was also recognized as a book of the year by the American Library Association, *The Globe and Mail*, and Amazon.ca. MacLeod lives in Dartmouth, Nova Scotia, and teaches at Saint Mary's University.

Moira McCavana, "No Spanish"

The acquisition of language, which exists at the center of this story, is endlessly fascinating to me. The experience that I'm always hungry for, both in fiction and in my life, is the sensation of passing from a state of disorientation to orientation—that short window in which things just begin to organize themselves around you. When, in a new city, for instance, you enter an alleyway already with the vague sense of where it will deposit you. I grew up surrounded by my grandfather's paintings of his home, the Spanish Basque Country, and my father's stories of growing up in Troubles-era Northern Ireland, both of which have heavily influenced my work.

I spent the summer before writing this story living myself in Spanish, learning the way in which language can simulate that alleyway—that anticipation of arrival—over and over again. Of course, in the Basque Country, during this period, the relationship between Spanish and Basque varied from town to town, even from family to family. In "No Spanish," Basque is the new, unfamiliar language, though always at the back of my mind, and, I hope, lurking in the back of the story, is the notion that for many, many people, that painful transition happened the other way around.

· · ·

Moira McCavana was born in 1993 in Boston and raised there. As an undergraduate at Harvard University, she received the Le Baron Russell Briggs Prize Honors Thesis award and the Thomas Temple Hoopes Prize for her short fiction, which has appeared in *The London Magazine* and elsewhere. McCavana lives in Madrid, Spain.

Kenan Orhan, "Soma"
I think this story is actually about İzzet's father. He is the only one who seems to realize that his son is chasing a phantom aspiration. In fact, I too believed İzzet was right in his desire to get an electrical engineering degree to become a turbine mechanic because this was his escape from the mine, from all the terrible things the mine means to İzzet, but I was wrong.

This story is smarter than I am; it is my shortest piece, and I wrote it in a week, so there was very little opportunity for me to get in the way of it. I had to reread it before I could comment on it, and in the rereading since its publication, the ending has taken on a cold suspension, a terrible impossibility for change. İzzet has surrendered himself to the false notion that to be in the air is to be something different, but his father, thinking between bites of watermelon, is acutely aware that it is the same to go up a turbine as it is to go down a mine. Though he might not admit it to İzzet, he believes in his swimming. He is the only one who wants his son to dream bigger, to try to get far, far out of town, to escape from the village, and he tries to articulate this, but he has problems with words; he can't say it just right. And because of this, I didn't realize until I reread it that İzzet's end is a failure. He stakes his relationships in the village, his education prospects, and his future career on a race across the Hellespont only to convince himself that this short lapse from the gravity of the mine is a complete break with it when in reality he is eager to return to the village. He seems to me only alive while balancing on the surface of the water, a rare moment of transcendence that should be not a means to an end but an end in itself. İzzet should become a swimmer; his failure is in never realizing it.

İzzet's father is unable to cause a change in his son. He can't speak the spell that would magically alter his son's destiny. Neither can I; it took me this long just to see that İzzet's father, the little character at the corner of the story so full of aborted hope, is actually the center around which the fiction orbits. What can we possibly do when our heart tells us there is a right thing to do but this right thing to do is not emotionally accessible to us?

Kenan Orhan was born in 1993 in Overland Park, Kansas, where he grew up. His stories have appeared in *Prairie Schooner, The Common,* and elsewhere. He recently finished a collection of stories set in Turkey and is at work on a novel. He lives in Kansas City.

Valerie O'Riordan, "Bad Girl"
At the heart of "Bad Girl" is an exploration of the tangled mess around friendship, sex, vulnerability, and grief. I wrote it partly in response to Margaret Atwood's *Cat's Eye,* a novel that I've loved for almost twenty years; the complexities of teenage girls' friendships are an endlessly fascinating topic. I was interested, too, in exploring the aftermath of trauma: in this story, Cheryl's mother has recently died, and Cheryl is struggling to find a way to understand herself in the wake of that catastrophic loss. At the time I was working on a series of interlinked stories set in a fictional suburb of Manchester, and so the setting—a rather insalubrious pub called the Glory Hole—was already familiar to me, and in fact I went on to write further pieces about many of the more peripheral characters in this story, including one exploring the backstory of Cheryl's friend Tania. I'm still a little hung up on both characters—perhaps one day they'll make it into a novel.

· · · ·

Valerie O'Riordan was born in 1980 and grew up in Dublin, Ireland. She has an MA and a Ph.D. in creative writing from the University of Manchester, and she also studied at Trinity College Dublin. O'Riordan teaches fiction writing at the University of Bolton. Her short stories have been published in *Tin House*, *Unthology*, *The Lonely Crowd*, *The Mechanics' Institute Review*, and *Fugue*. She won the Bristol Short Story Prize, and she is a senior editor at *The Forge Literary Magazine* and coeditor of the review site Bookmunch. O'Riordan lives in Manchester, England.

Stephanie Reents, "Unstuck"

I have a good friend who has hated her house for as long as I've known her, which is going on twenty years. I happen to like her house, not because I don't see its flaws, but because it has sheltered me during some dark times. She has, too.

At some point, perhaps after my friend described yet another way the house was a bitter disappointment, I decided to memorialize it. Like her, I'm a bit of a contrarian. Of course, I couldn't make a whole story about its popcorn ceilings and poured-concrete floors. The horror! Something needed to happen, but what? I let my first pages sit for a little while—six months? a year?—until one day when I was bored or disillusioned with some other half-finished project, I reread the beginning and realized it would be really funny if Liza, the protagonist, found herself haunted by a ghost who was making the house that she loathed, and was intent on neglecting, a bit nicer. In fiction, answers always lead to more questions, but that joke kept me writing, even as I gradually learned that the story wasn't as funny as I initially thought.

Stephanie Reents was born in 1970 and grew up in Boise, Idaho. She's the author of a story collection, *The Kissing List*, and *I Meant to Kill Ye*, an account of her attempt to come to terms with the strange void at the heart of Cormac McCarthy's *Blood Meridian*.

Her awards include a Rhodes Scholarship, a Wallace Stegner Fellowship, and the Robert and Margaret MacColl Johnson Fellowship for writing from the Rhode Island Foundation. Her short fiction has appeared in *Epoch* and *Bennington Review*, among other journals. She teaches at the College of the Holy Cross and lives in Cambridge, Massachusetts.

Souvankham Thammavongsa, "Slingshot"

Whenever I encountered an old woman in a story she was always unattractive or sick or dying or a burden to those around her. It made me angry to see that. I was also annoyed with romantic stories with a young woman at the center who always gets her man. I wanted to write a love story where not getting your man can feel deep, profound, freeing. I wanted to say love isn't everything and it isn't enough. It can fail you even when it's there.

Souvankham Thammavongsa was born in 1978 in the Lao refugee camp in Nong Khai, Thailand. She is the author of three books of poetry, most recently *Light*. Her fiction has appeared in *Granta*, *Ploughshares*, *Noon*, and *The Best American Nonrequired Reading*. Her first story collection, *How to Pronounce Knife*, is forthcoming. She lives in Toronto, Ontario.

Doua Thao, "Flowers for America"

This story has as its source two anecdotes. When my maternal grandmother was dying, we were able to obtain for my aunt, the only one left from either side of my family to have stayed back in Laos, permission to visit on an emergency visa. Obtaining the visa involved a doctor's written note that said, *This patient is dying, and she would like to see her oldest daughter one last time. If at all possible, it is imperative that this daughter's visit be expedited.* While my aunt was here in the States, my mother asked her how she was surviving. My aunt, who is terrified of water, replied that for a living she woke in the dark before dawn and plied the waters of Laos in her narrow fishing boat. To do all of this without a husband, from my vantage point, was a pretty heroic deed.

The second anecdote contains a pot of flowers. When I moved to Greensboro, North Carolina, for graduate school, my mother gave me, of all the things she could think of, a pot of her coveted, special flowers. The superstition behind these flowers, as told by my mother, is that only men could coax life from their bulbs, or, to put it another way, the flowers only grew for men. My mother's belief in this superstition was underscored by the fact that, when she was first given some bulbs, they refused to grow when planted. The following year, she dug up the bulbs and gave them to my uncle. Under his care, they grew so prolifically that he returned the flowers in a bushel-sized pot to my mother. Due to its unwieldiness—I think now that pot must have been close to seventy pounds of dirt and flowers—my mother kept the flowers outside, and the pot was quickly stolen in broad daylight for the flowers' medicinal value. These flowers, my mother's gift when I moved away, were an expression of trust, I see now, that perhaps I, being a son and someone whose curiosity is such that I would even care to ask about a superstition behind a plant, would look after them. When winter arrived and the flowers dropped their petals, I stopped watering them, and the following spring, when I knew there was something I was supposed to do to help bring them back to life, I did nothing at all, and they remained dormant—some too rotted to salvage when I finally dug them up—the rest of my time in Greensboro. It was my aunt's courage, my mother's odd choice in a gift, the value of the flowers, and the superstition behind them that I kept returning to, so I wrote this story.

Doua Thao was born in the Phanat Nikhom refugee camp in Thailand. He first immigrated to Madison, Wisconsin, and then settled in Milwaukee. His writing has appeared in *Crab Orchard Review* and *Reservoir*. He lives in Milwaukee.

Weike Wang, "Omakase"

Two years ago, my now-husband and I moved to New York. Every person I met said the city takes some getting used to and I would get used to it in about two years. Now everyone says five years. Once I hit five, they will say ten. I wrote the story when I was at the height of my frustration with the city subway system. The event of getting hit in the face with a shoe happened to me on the L and while rubbing my left cheek, I consoled myself by saying that I would be able to write this someday.

In "Omakase," a couple goes out for sushi. What makes this specific sushi night different? My husband and I go out to sushi a lot. We usually have a good time. But I thought, let me change this couple and change the good time. Let me change the sushi chef. (The omakase chef we go to is so nice I sometimes have to remind him that I suffer from acute sarcasm.) When I sat down to write the story, I wrote it in four days. My best writing comes when I don't overwork it. But I did keep reminding myself that I was writing to this idea: in what ways can these three characters interact with one another so that by the end, everyone leaves a bit unsatisfied? After the story came out, I had many responses. Someone asked me if I thought women on the whole overthought. (On the whole? You mean, all four billion of us?) Someone else asked me if I thought men on the whole overexplain. (Similar response.) I didn't get it, another said, was the story about race? Naturally, questions of gender and race are never simple. And what reads "off" to one may not have any effect on another. While nuance is crucial to fiction, it is often overlooked in real life. Yet if we, as different people, are to find common ground, we need to think about the in-betweens. The question I get asked the most is if the couple stays together. My usual response is, Does that matter? But if the person is adamant, I then ask, Well, what do you think? After the person tells me, I nod, ask another question.

Weike Wang was born in Nanjing and grew up in China, Australia, Canada, and the United States. She is the author of *Chemistry*, and her work has appeared in *Glimmer Train*, *Ploughshares*, *Alaska Quarterly Review*, and *Kenyon Review*, among other publications. She is the recipient of the 2018 PEN/Hemingway Award, as well as awards from the Whiting Foundation and the National Book Foundation 5 Under 35. She lives in New York City.

Liza Ward, "The Shrew Tree"

A heavy wet snow fell one of those last nights my husband and I lived together in rural Montana. The following day was warm, glittery with sunshine, a balmy wind coming over the Swan Range. I went for a walk. I thought maybe I'd just keep walking into the mountains and never come back. I didn't want to return to the East Coast, where my husband had gotten a grant to farm oysters, but there seemed to be no choice. I made it as far as the top of the hill, where I found a bird with a missing wing flapping around in a futile circle. I wasn't the kind to look away and keep on walking. Nor was I going to gather it in a box and drive eighty miles to a wildlife sanctuary. At least I wasn't that kind *anymore*. I knew what I had to do. I picked up a stone and crushed it.

Soon after leaving the valley, I gave birth to a daughter. I wrote nothing for many years. She went to preschool on the other side of town. The land was wilder over there, tangled with brush and skunk cabbages and a barbwire fence that kept the cows from wandering out of the dilapidated dairy farm. My daughter's teacher had once lived on the farm but didn't anymore, because she was *too fond of the cows*. We met sometimes during the weekends, sitting in tiny chairs at the round tables in my daughter's classroom. The wood was a screen hiding the farm, which she spoke of with a quiet smile that glinted at the corners with a touch of animosity. Did I know riding a horse was a means of domination, and a weed was only a weed if you didn't like where it was growing? She fed the robins every season, and kept the mice as pets instead of trapping them. It was from her that I learned about the bitterness of dandelion in a cow's milk, that you should never toss to a child the empty phrase *Good job!* It was important for the child to think for herself.

I keep seeing the bird flapping in the snow as I think about the germination of this story. I think about what happens to a girl without confidence, and the preschool teacher who opened my imagination again. She told me a lilac dug up and left exposed for a whole season can still take root and bloom again. Somewhere between the tenacity of the root ball and the bird I killed came Gretel and her story.

Liza Ward was born in 1975 and raised in Brooklyn, New York. She is the author of the novel *Outside Valentine*. Her work has appeared in *The Atlantic*, *Best New American Voices 2004*, *The O. Henry Prize Stories 2005*, *Vogue*, *AGNI*, *Tin House*, and other publications. She lives in Duxbury, Massachusetts.

Bryan Washington, "610 North, 610 West"

This one happened pretty quickly. I'd been living between Houston and New Orleans at the time, working on a bunch of linked stories. Their protagonist was giving me trouble, I couldn't really figure him out, so I found myself going further and further into his past and the people who shaped him: chief among them being his mother. And the way she moved through the world. And how that conflicted with everything around her, and how that conflict reverberated in her home. I don't know if they'd actually say it, but the narrator and his mother are the two people who understand each other best in their lives—so, once I understood that, the piece unspooled in a day or two. A gift.

. . .

Bryan Washington has written for *The New York Times*, *The New York Times Magazine*, *The New Yorker*, *One Story*, *Catapult*, and elsewhere. His first collection of stories, *Lot*, was published in 2019. He lives in Houston, Texas.

John Edgar Wideman, "Maps and Ledgers"

Writing for me is one means of making my way around a world that always changes, a world different each time I look—my story is titled "Maps and Ledgers" because maps and ledgers are reconstructions that perform work similar to work that all stories I write perform for me—keeping track, locating, accounting, managing the chaos of time—maps and ledgers are imagined recordings of the form a world, if it stood still, might assume—to consult a map or ledger is to pretend it could represent a reliable approximation of something that is, itself, reliable—as if the evidence of the senses, the mind, is actually capable of arriving at that certainty expressed when a person exclaims, "Been there, done that"—maps and ledgers are games we play as if the rules and instructions invented for those games might stand outside time, somehow evade or at least circumvent change—though a changing world never ceases to be different each time I look (or don't look).

John Edgar Wideman was born in 1941 in Washington, D.C., and raised in Pittsburgh, Pennsylvania. His books include *Writing to Save a Life*, *Philadelphia Fire*, *Brothers and Keepers*, *Fatheralong*, *Hoop Roots*, and *Sent for You Yesterday*. He is a MacArthur Fellow, and has won the PEN/Faulkner Award twice and the National Book Critics Circle Award twice. He divides his time between New York and France.

Publications Submitted

Stories published in magazines distributed in North America are eligible for inclusion in *The O. Henry Prize Stories*. Stories must be written originally in the English language. No translations will be considered. Sections of novels are not considered. Editors are asked to send all stories published in each issue and not to nominate individual stories. Stories should not be submitted by writers or agents.

For fiction published online, the publication's contact information and the date of the story's publication must accompany the submissions.

Stories are considered from June 1 to June 1 the following year. Publications received after June 1 will automatically be considered for the next volume of *The O. Henry Prize Stories*.

Please submit PDF files of submissions to ohenryprize@prh.com.

The information listed below was up-to-date when *The O. Henry Prize Stories 2019* went to press. Inclusion in this listing does not constitute endorsement or recommendation by *The O. Henry Prize Stories* or Anchor Books.

Able Muse
www.ablemuse.com
submission@abluemuse.com
Editor: Alex Pepple
Two or three times a year

AGNI
www.bu.edu/agni
agni@bu.edu
Editor: Sven Birkerts
Biannual (print)

Alaska Quarterly Review
aqreview.org
uaa_aqr@uaa.alaska.edu
Editor: Ronald Spatz
Biannual

Amazon Original Stories
www.amazon.com/
    amazonoriginalstories
Submission by Invitation Only
Editor: Julia Sommerfeld
Twelve annually

American Short Fiction
americanshortfiction.org
editors@americanshortfiction.org
Editors: Rebecca Markovits and
    Adeena Reitberger
Triannual

Antipodes
www.wsupress.wayne.edu/journals/
    detail/antipodes-0
antipodesfiction@gmail.com
Editor: Brenda Machovsky
Biannual

The Arkansas International
www.arkint.org
info@arkint.org
Editor: Geoffrey Brock
Biannual

Arkansas Review
arkreview.org
mrtribbet@astate.edu
Editor: Marcus Tribbett
Triannual

ArLiJo
www.arlijo.com
givalpress@yahoo.com
Editor: Robert L. Giron
Ten issues a year

**The Asian American Literary
    Review**
aalrmag.org
editors@aalrmag.org
Editors: Lawrence-Minh Bùi Davis
    and Gerald Maa
Biannual

Baltimore Review
www.baltimorereview.org
editor@baltimorereview.org
Editor: Barbara Westwood Diehl
Quarterly (online)
Annual (print)

Bat City Review
www.batcityreview.org
editor@batcityreview.org
Editor: Leah Hampton
Annual

Bellevue Literary Review
blr.med.nyu.edu
info@BLReview.org
Editor: Danielle Ofri
Biannual

Bennington Review
www.benningtonreview.org
BenningtonReview@Bennington
.edu
Editor: Michael Dumanis
Biannual

Big Muddy
bigmuddyjournal.com
upress@semo.edu
Editor: James Brubaker
Weekly (online)
Annual (print)

Black Warrior Review
bwr.ua.edu
blackwarriorreview@gmail.com
Editor: Cat Ingrid Leeches
Biannual

BOMB
bombmagazine.org
betsy@bombsite.org
Editor: Betsy Sussler
Quarterly

Bosque
bosquepress.com
Editor: Lynn C. Miller
lynn@bosquepress.com
Annual

Boulevard
boulevardmagazine.org
editors@boulevardmagazine.org
Editor: Jessica Rogen
Triannual

The Briar Cliff Review
www.bcreview.org
tricia.currans-sheehan@briarcliff
.edu
Editor: Tricia Currans-Sheehan
Annual

CALYX
www.calyxpress.org
editor@calyxpress.org
Editors: C. Lill Ahrens, Rachel
    Barton, Marjorie Coffey, Judith
    Edelstein, Emily Elbom, Carole
    Kalk, Christine Rhea
Biannual

The Carolina Quarterly
thecarolinaquarterly.com
carolina.quarterly@gmail.com
Editor: Sarah George-Waterfield
Biannual

Carve
www.carvezine.com
Editor: Anna Zumbahlen
Quarterly

Catamaran
catamaranliteraryreader.com
editor@catamaranliteraryreader
    .com
Editor: Catherine Sergurson
Quarterly

Cherry Tree
www.washcoll.edu/centers/
    lithouse/cherry-tree
Editor: James Allen Hall
Annual

Chicago Quarterly Review
www.chicagoquarterlyreview.com
cqr@icogitate.com
Editors: S. Afzal Haider and
    Elizabeth McKenzie
Quarterly

Chicago Review
www.chicagoreview.org
editors@chicagoreview.org
Editor: Eric Powell
Quarterly

Cimarron Review
cimarronreview.com
cimarronreview@okstate.edu
Editor: Toni Graham
Quarterly

Colorado Review
coloradoreview.colostate.edu/
    colorado-review/
creview@colostate.edu
Editor: Stephanie G'Schwind
Triannual

Confrontation
confrontationmagazine.org
confrontationmag@gmail.com
Editor: Jonna G. Semeiks
Biannual

Conjunctions
www.conjunctions.com
conjunctions@bard.edu
Editor: Bradford Marrow
Biannual

Copper Nickel
copper-nickel.org
wayne.miller@ucdenver.edu
Editor: Wayne Miller
Biannual

Crab Orchard Review
craborchardreview.siu.edu
jtribble@siu.edu
Editor: Allison Joseph
Biannual

Cream City Review
uwm.edu/creamcityreview/
info@creamcityreview.org
Editor: Caleb Nelson
Biannual

CutBank
www.cutbankonline.org
editor.cutbank@gmail.com
Editor: Joe Kirk
Biannual

The Dalhousie Review
ojs.library.dal.ca/dalhousiereview
Dalhousie.Review@Dal.ca
Editor: Anthony Enns
Triannual

Dappled Things
dappledthings.org
dappledthings.carl@gmail.com
Editor: Katy Carl
Quarterly

december
decembermag.org
editor@decembermag.org
Editor: Gianna Jacobson
Biannual

Delmarva Review
delmarvareview.org
Editor: Bill Gourgey
Annual

Denver Quarterly
www.du.edu/denverquarterly
denverquarterly@gmail.com
Editor: Bin Ramke
Quarterly

Descant
descant.tcu.edu
descant@tcu.edu
Editor: Matt Pitt
Annual

Driftwood Press
www.driftwoodpress.net
driftwoodlit@gmail.com
Editors: James McNulty and Jerrod
     Schwarz
Quarterly

Ecotone
ecotonemagazine.org
info@ecotonejournal.com
Editor: David Gessner
Biannual

Eleven Eleven
elevenelevenjournal.com
Editor: Dan Keating
Biannual

Emrys Journal
www.emrys.org
emrys.info@gmail.com
Editor: Katie Burgess
Annual

Epoch
english.cornell.edu/epoch
  -magazine-0
mk64@cornell.edu
Editor: Michael Koch
Triannual

Exile: The Literary Quarterly
www.exilequarterly.com
Editor: Barry Callaghan
Quarterly

Faerie Magazine
www.faeriemagazine.com
info@faeriemag.com
Editor: Carolyn Turgeon
Quarterly

Fairy Tale Review
fairytalereview.com
ftreditorial@gmail.com
Editor: Kate Bernheimer
Annual

Fantasy & Science Fiction
www.sfsite.com/fsf/
fsfmag@fandsf.com
Editor: Gordon van Gelder
Bimonthly

Fence
www.fenceportal.org
fence.fencebooks@gmail.com
Editor: Rebecca Wolff
Biannual

Fiction
www.fictioninc.com
fictionmageditors@gmail.com
Editor: Mark Jay Mirsky
Annual

Fiction River
www.fictionriver.com
wmgpublishingmail@mail.com
Editors: Kristine Kathryn Rusch
  and Dean Wesley Smith
Six times a year

The Fiddlehead
thefiddlehead.ca
fiddlehd@unb.ca
Editor: Ross Leckie
Quarterly

Fifth Wednesday Journal
www.fifthwednesdayjournal.com
editors@fifthwednesdayjournal.org
Editors: James Ballowe, Nina
  Corwin, and Daniel S. Libman
Biannual

Five Points
www.fivepoints.gsu.edu
Editors: David Bottoms and
  Megan Sexton
Biannual

The Flexible Persona
flexiblepersona.com
Editor: Alexander Hogan
Biannual

The Florida Review
floridareview.cah.ucf.edu
flreview@ucf.edu
Editor: Lisa Roney
Biannual

Foglifter
foglifterjournal.com
foglifter.journal@gmail.com
Editor: Chad Koch
Biannual

f(r)iction
tetheredbyletters.com/friction/
Editor: Dani Hedlund
Triannual

Gemini Magazine
www.gemini-magazine.com
editor@gemini-magazine.com
Editor: David A. Bright
Four to six issues per year

The Georgia Review
thegeorgiareview.com
garev@uga.edu
Editor: Stephen Corey
Quarterly

The Gettysburg Review
www.gettysburgreview.com
gettysburg_review@gettysburg.edu
Editor: Mark Drew
Quarterly

Glimmer Train
www.glimmertrain.com
editors@glimmertrain.org
Editors: Linda Swanson-Davies
and Susan Burmeister-Brown
Triannual

Gold Man Review
www.goldmanreview.org
heather.cuthbertson@
goldmanpublishing.com
Editor: Heather Cuthbertson
Annual

Granta
granta.com
editorial@granta.com
Editor: Sigrid Rausing
Quarterly (print)

The Greensboro Review
www.tgronline.net
Editor: Terry L. Kennedy
Biannual

**Gulf Coast: A Journal of
Literature and Fine Arts**
gulfcoastmag.org
gulfcoastea@gmail.com
Editor: Justin Jannise
Semiannual

Harper's Magazine
harpers.org
letters@harpers.org
Editor: Ellen Rosenbush
Monthly

Harvard Review
www.harvardreview.org
info@harvardreview.org
Editor: Christina Thompson
Biannual

Hayden's Ferry Review
haydensferryreview.com
hfr@asu.edu
Editor: Joel Salcido
Biannual

The Hopkins Review
hopkinsreview.jhu.edu
thehopkinsreview@gmail.com
Editor: David Yezzi
Quarterly

Hotel Amerika
www.hotelamerika.net
editors.hotelamerika@gmail.com
Editor: David Lazar
Annual

The Hudson Review
hudsonreview.com
info@hudsonreview.com
Editor: Paula Dietz
Quarterly

Hunger Mountain
hungermtn.org
hungermtn@vcfa.edu
Editor: Erin Stalcup
Annual (print)

Image
imagejournal.org
image@imagejournal.org
Editor: Mary Kenagy Mitchell
Quarterly

Indiana Review
indianareview.org
inreview@indiana.edu
Editor: Essence London
Biannual

Into the Void
intothevoidmagazine.com
info@intothevoidmagazine.com
Editor: Philip Elliot
Quarterly

Iron Horse Literary Review
www.ironhorsereview.com
ihlr.mail@gmail.com
Editor: Leslie Jill Patterson
Quarterly

Jabberwock Review
www.jabberwock.org.msstate.edu
jabberwockreview@english
    .msstate.edu
Editor: Michael Kardos
Semiannual

Kenyon Review
www.kenyonreview.org
kenyonreview@kenyon.edu
Editor: David H. Lynn
Six times a year

Lady Churchill's Rosebud Wristlet
smallbeerpress.com/lcrw
info@smallbeerpress.com
Editors: Gavin J. Grant and Kelly Link
Biannual

Lake Effect
behrend.psu.edu/school-of-humanities-social-sciences/lake-effect
gol1@psu.edu
Editors: George Looney and Aimee Pogson
Annual

The Literary Review
www.theliteraryreview.org
info@theliteraryreview.org
Editor: Minna Zallman Proctor
Quarterly

LitMag
litmag.com
info@litmag.com
Editor: Marc Berley
Annual

Little Patuxent Review
littlepatuxentreview.org
editor@littlepatuxentreview.org
Editor: Steven Leyva
Biannual

Longshot Island
www.longshotisland.com
contact@longshotisland.com
Editor: Daniel White
Quarterly

MAKE: Literary Magazine
www.makemag.com
info@makemag.com
Editor: Chamandeep Bains
Annual

The Malahat Review
www.malahatreview.ca
malahat@uvic.ca
Editor: Iain Higgins
Quarterly

The Massachusetts Review
www.massreview.org
massrev@external.umass.edu
Editor: Jim Hicks
Quarterly

McSweeney's Quarterly Concern
www.mcsweeneys.net
custservice@mcsweeneys.net
Editor: Dave Eggers
Quarterly

Meridian
www.readmeridian.org
meridianuva@gmail.com
Editor: Olivia Haberman
Semiannual

Michigan Quarterly Review
sites.lsa.umich.edu/mqr
mqr@umich.edu
Editor: Khaled Mattawa
Quarterly

Mid-American Review
casit.bgsu.edu/midamericanreview/
mar@bgsu.edu
Editor: Abigail Cloud
Semiannual

Midwestern Gothic
midwestgothic.com
info@midwestgothic.com
Editors: Jeff Pfaller and Robert
   James Russell
Biannual

Mississippi Review
sites.usm.edu/mississippi-review/
msreview@usm.edu
Editor: Adam Clay
Biannual

The Missouri Review
www.missourireview.com
question@moreview.com
Editor: Speer Morgan
Quarterly

Mizna
www.mizna.org/articles/journal
mizna@mizna.org
Editor: Lisa Adwan
Biannual

Mount Hope
www.mounthopemagazine.com
mount.hope.magazine@gmail.com
Editor: Edward Delaney
Biannual

n+1
nplusonemag.com
editors@nplusonemag.com
Editors: Nikil Saval and Dayna
   Tortorici
Triannual

Narrative
www.narrativemagazine.com
info@narrativemagazine.com
Editors: Carol Edgarian and Tom
   Jenks
Weekly

Natural Bridge
blogs.umsl.edu/naturalbridge/
natural@umsl.edu
Editor: John Dalton
Biannual

NELLE
www.uab.edu/cas/
   englishpublications/nelle
editors.nelle@gmail.com
Editor: Lauren Goodwin Slaughter
Annual

New England Review
www.nereview.com
nereview@middlebury.edu
Editor: Carolyn Kuebler
Quarterly

New Letters
www.newletters.org
newletters@umkc.edu
Editor: Robert Stewart
Quarterly

New Madrid
newmadridjournal.org
msu.newmadrid@murraystate.edu
Editor: Ann Neelon
Biannual

New Ohio Review
www.ohio.edu/nor/
noreditors@ohio.edu
Editor: David Wancyk
Biannual

New Orleans Review
www.neworleansreview.org
noreview@loyno.edu
Editor: Mark Yakich
Annual

New South
newsouthjournal.com
newsoutheditors@gmail.com
Editor: Anna Sandy-Elrod
Biannual

The New Yorker
www.newyorker.com
themail@newyorker.com
Editor: David Remnick
Weekly

Nimrod International Journal
nimrod.utulsa.edu
nimrod@utelsa.edu
Editor: Eilis O'Neal
Biannual

Noon
www.noonannual.com
Editor: Diane Williams
Annual

North Dakota Quarterly
ndquarterly.org
ndq@und.edu
Editor: William Caraher
Quarterly

Northern New England Review
www.nnereview.com
douaihym@franklinpierce.edu
Editor: Margot Douaihy
Annual

Notre Dame Review
ndreview.nd.edu
notredamereview@gmail.com
Editor: Steve Tomasula
Biannual

One Story
www.one-story.com
Editor: Patrick Ryan
Monthly

One Teen Story
www.one-story.com
Editor: Patrick Ryan
Monthly

Orion
orionmagazine.org
questions@orionmagazine.org
Editor: H. Emerson Blake
Bimonthly

Overtime
www.workerswritejournal.com/
    overtime.htm
info@workerswritejournal.com
Editor: David LaBounty
Quarterly

Oxford American
www.oxfordamerican.org
editors@oxfordamerican.org
Editor: Eliza Borné
Quarterly

Pakn Treger
www.yiddishbookcenter.org/
    language-literature-culture/
    pakn-treger
pt@yiddishbookcenter.org
Editor: Aaron Lansky
Quarterly

The Paris Review
www.theparisreview.org
queries@theparisreview.org
Editor: Emily Nemens
Quarterly

Pembroke Magazine
pembrokemagazine.com
pembrokemagazine@gmail.com
Editor: Peter Grimes
Annual

PEN America
pen.org/publications/pen-america
    -a-journal-for-writers-and
    -readers/
journal@pen.org
Publication on hiatus

The Pinch
www.pinchjournal.com
editor@pinchjournal.com
Editor: Courtney Miller Santo
Biannual

Playboy
www.playboyenterprises.com
Executive Editor: James Rickman
Monthly

Ploughshares
www.pshares.org
pshares@pshares.org
Editor: Ladette Randolph
Quarterly

Post Road
www.postroadmag.com
info@postroadmag.com
Editor: Chris Boucher
Biannual

Potomac Review
mcblogs.montgomerycollege.edu/
    potomacreview/
potomacrevieweditor@
    montgomerycollege.edu
Editor: John Wei Han Wang
Quarterly

Prairie Fire
www.prairiefire.ca
prfire@prairiefire.ca
Editor: Andris Taskans
Quarterly

Prairie Schooner
www.prairieschooner.unl.edu/
   index.html
prairieschooner@unl.edu
Editor: Kwame Dawes
Quarterly

PRISM international
prismmagazine.ca
prose@prismmagazine.ca
Prose Editor: Jasmine Sealy
Quarterly

A Public Space
apublicspace.org
general@apublicspace.org
Editor: Brigid Hughes
Triannual

PULP Literature
pulpliterature.com
info@pulpliterature.com
Editor: Jennifer Landels
Quarterly

Raritan
raritanquarterly.rutgers.edu
rqr@sas.rutgers.edu
Editor: Jackson Lears
Quarterly

Redivider
www.redividerjournal.org
editor@redividerjournal.org
Editors: Jaime Zuckerman and
   Raina K. Puels
Triannual

River Styx
www.riverstyx.org
managingeditor@riverstyx.org
Editor: Jason Lee Brown
Biannual

Room
www.roommagazine.com
contactus@roommagazine.com
Editor: Chelene Knight
Quarterly

Ruminate
www.ruminatemagazine.com
info@ruminatemagazine.com
Editor: Brianna Van Dyke
Quarterly

Salamander
salamandermag.org
editors@salamandermag.org
Editor: Jennifer Barber
Biannual

Salmagundi Magazine
salmagundi.skidmore.edu
salmagun@skidmore.edu
Editor: Robert Boyers
Quarterly

Saranac Review
www.saranacreview.com
info@saranacreview.com
Editor: Aimee Baker
Annual

The Saturday Evening Post
www.saturdayeveningpost.com
editors@saturdayeveningpost.com
Editor: Steven Slon
Six times a year

The Sewanee Review
thesewaneereview.com
sewaneereview@sewanee.edu
Editor: Adam Ross
Quarterly

Slice
slicemagazine.org
editors@slicemagazine.org
Editor: Beth Blachman
Biannual

Smith's Monthly
www.smithsmonthly.com
dean@deanwesleysmith.com
Editor: Dean Wesley Smith
Monthly

The Southampton Review
www.thesouthamptonreview.com
editors@thesouthamptonreview
    .com
Editor: Emily Smith Gilbert
Biannual

The South Carolina Review
www.clemson.edu/caah/sites/
    south-carolina-review/index
    .html
screv@clemson.edu
Editor: Keith Lee Morris
Annual

South Dakota Review
southdakotareview.com
sdreview@usd.edu
Editor: Lee Ann Roripaugh
Quarterly

The Southeast Review
www.southeastreview.org
southeastreview@gmail.com
Editor: Dorothy Chan
Semiannual

Southern Humanities Review
www.southernhumanitiesreview
    .com
shr@auburn.edu
Editors: Anton DiSclafani and
    Rose McLarney
Quarterly

Southern Indiana Review
www.usi.edu/sir/
sir@usi.edu
Editor: Ron Mitchell
Biannual

The Southern Review
thesouthernreview.org
southernreview@lsu.edu
Editor: Sacha Idell
Quarterly

Southwest Review
southwestreview.com
swr@smu.edu
Editor: Greg Brownderville
Quarterly

St. Anthony Messenger
info.franciscanmedia.org/st
    -anthony-messenger
samadmin@franciscanmedia.org
Editor: Christopher Heffron
Monthly

subTerrain
www.subterrain.ca
subter@portal.ca
Editor: Brian Kaufman
Triannual

The Sun
www.thesunmagazine.org
Editor: Sy Safransky
Monthly

Sycamore Review
sycamorereview.com
sycamore@purdue.edu
Editor: Charles Nutter Peck
Biannual

Tahoma Literary Review
tahomaliteraryreview.com
fiction@tahomaliteraryreview.com
Editor: Ann Beman
Triannual

Third Coast
thirdcoastmagazine.com
editors@thirdcoastmagazine.com
Editor: Ariel Berry
Biannual

The Threepenny Review
www.threepennyreview.com
wlesser@threepennyreview.com
Editor: Wendy Lesser
Quarterly

Tin House
https://tinhouseonline.submittable
    .com/submit
Editor: Alana Csaposs
Online daily

The Tishman Review
thetishmanreview.com
thetishmanreview@gmail.com
Editor: Jennifer Porter
Biannual

upstreet
upstreet-mag.org
editor@upstreet-mag.org
Editor: Joyce A. Griffin
Annual

Virginia Quarterly Review
www.vqronline.org
editors@vqronline.org
Editor: Paul Reyes
Quarterly

Washington Square Review
www.washingtonsquarereview.com
washingtonsquarereview@gmail
.com
Editor: Joanna Yas
Biannual

Water-Stone Review
waterstonereview.com
water-stone@hamline.edu
Editor: Mary François Rockcastle
Annual

Weber
www.weber.edu/weberjournal
weberjournal@weber.edu
Editor: Michael Wutz
Biannual

West Branch
westbranch.blogs.bucknell.edu
westbranch@bucknell.edu
Editor: G. C. Waldrep
Triannual

Western Humanities Review
www.westernhumanitiesreview
.com
ManagingEditor.WHR@gmail
.com
Editor: Michael Mejia
Triannual

Willow Springs
willowspringsmagazine.org
willowspringsewu@gmail.com
Editor: Polly Buckingham
Biannual

Witness
witness.blackmountaininstitute.org
witness@unlv.edu
Editor: Maile Chapman
Annual

The Worcester Review
www.theworcesterreview.org
editor.worcreview@gmail.com
Editors: Diane Mulligan and Kate
McIntyre
Annual

Workers Write!
www.workerswritejournal.com
info@workerswritejournal.com
Editor: David LaBounty
Annual

World Literature Today
www.worldliteraturetoday.org
dsimon@ou.edu
Editor: Daniel Simon
Bimonthly

Yellow Medicine Review
www.yellowmedicinereview.com
editor@yellowmedicinereview.com
Semiannual

Yemassee
yemasseejournal.com
editor@yemaseejournal.com
Editors: Sarah Benal, Trezlen
    Drake, and Andrew Green
Biannual

Zoetrope: All-Story
www.all-story.com
info@all-story.com
Editor: Michael Ray
Quarterly

Zone 3
zone3press.com
zone3@apsu.edu
Editor: Barry Kitterman
Biannual

ZYZZYVA
www.zyzzyva.org
editor@zyzzyva.org
Editor: Laura Cogan
Triannual

Permissions